King of Swords

Miguel Antonio Ortiz

H\s
Hamilton Stone Editions

LibraryofCongressCataloging-in-Publication Data

Names: Ortiz, Miguel Antonio, author.
Title: The king of swords / Miguel Antonio Ortiz.
Description: Maplewood, New Jersey : Hamilton Stone Editions, [2022] |
Summary: "King of Swords explores the concept of free will and
illustrates the projection of Jungian archetypes. The story depicts the
lives of the author's great-grandparents, who witnessed the events of
the Spanish-American War in Puerto Rico"-- Provided by publisher.
Identifiers: LCCN 2022010533 | ISBN 9780979598609 (trade paperback)
Subjects: LCSH: Spanish American War, 1898--Puerto Rico--Fiction. | Puerto
Rico--History--1898-1952--Fiction. | LCGFT: Historical fiction. | War   fiction. |
Novels.
Classification: LCC PS3615.R825 K56 2022 | DDC 813/.6--dc23/eng/20220419
LC record available at https://lccn.loc.gov/2022010533

King
of Swords

F ROM THE TOP of the ridge Eduardo looked over his land. In places, the river caught the sunlight and became a silver ribbon lacing through the green foliage of the forest of yet uncultivated land adjacent to the coffee groves. On the far side, the tobacco fields unfolded in orderly expanses. To the east, a forest of wild citrus trees concealed the berry bushes of the underbrush. He recalled the quenepas that he had gathered as a boy, treats the land offered as a gift. The mystery of the fruits still puzzled him—why some tasted sweet like the guavas and some bitter like the wild oranges.

Perturbed, Eduardo had ascended to that spot leaving behind in the valley below whatever ailed him. The overwhelming beauty of the land was only a temporary salve for his troubles. From the heights, he looked on everything he had acquired, more than he had imagined possible when starting out. He had not counted on the dissatisfaction that constantly plagued him, the suspicion that he had paid too great a price for his achievement. No one saw his discomfort. Seeming almost as good as being, almost the same thing—by any measurement he was a successful man with all the accoutrements of happiness: wealth, family, respect, and influence; therefore it was reasonable to assume he was happy, the uneasiness that he felt ephemeral and insubstantial—an annoyance to be discounted.

All of his life, Eduardo Rincon had been the man with the touch. Whatever he undertook succeeded. He had added little by little to the plot that his father left him. It had not been much— enough for a house and a few fields to subsist on. What his father had accumulated had been divided at his death among four sons, but the other three soon tired of scratching a living from their meager lots. One by one, each moved on to try his hand at some other endeavor. Eduardo stayed. Blessed with luck, he gambled and won. He borrowed money and planted tobacco. At the end of the season, he had enough profit to buy out two of his brothers. He planted more tobacco, and the weather cooperated with plenty of sun and just enough rain. Hurricanes avoided the island that year. No one gave up smoking. His third brother sold him his plot. Eduardo had then reassembled his patrimony. Luck followed him like a puppy nipping at his heels, and Eduardo knew enough not to shoo it away. Luck is necessary, but it's not enough. It has to be encouraged to stay, nourished so that it grows. At every turn there is a temptation to kick it away, to take a respite from its insistent bid for attention.

There had been a time, long before, when he might have been happier, before the Americans came, a time when Carmen worked for him under the hot sun. Eduardo observed her from the opposite end of the field, unable to see her face under the shadow of her wide brimmed hat. He recognized her by the way she moved; the fact that from that distance he could not see her eyes suited him just as well for the day was hot enough. He didn't need to see her black hair gathered under the hat. The image of its luxury stored in his memory—a treasure that he could, like a miser, unlock at any time to enjoy in the privacy of his thoughts—eventually became insufficient. In the mind, everything can be perfect, but perfection held no fascination for him. Though he cherished the idea of his future, keeping it before him like a beacon to guide him toward his goal, the promissory note had to be cashed sooner or later. That potential, the possible trading for reality, gave it value. His imaginary enjoyment of Carmen Gutierez a note he could no longer hold—the question became whether he would regret spending it.

Eduardo Rincon believed that he always had a choice in deciding the course of his life, but fortune is like the weather, composed of many factors beyond personal control. On that sweltering day, as he considered what to do about Carmen, Eduardo followed his usual routine. After the day's pick of tobacco had been strung and hung to dry and the workers, including Carmen, had departed, he headed down the path behind his house towards the ravine. Through that gully flowed a stream that supplied fresh water to the hacienda, and the far side demarcated the southern boundary of his property at that time.

＊

In reality, although his land no longer consisted of the mere plot he had inherited, it was not the extensive holding that the word hacienda implied. But he liked to think of it that way, spurring himself on to the inevitable future—inevitable only in the mind of God, who was privy to it. To Eduardo, the growth of his holdings was still only a possibility whose realization remained fraught with uncertainties. He saw himself as the helmsman of a craft on a stormy sea, well aware that his own skill was only one factor among many affecting the successful outcome of guiding the vessel into port—the one aspect he controlled, for he could do nothing about the wind nor the waves nor even about the craft itself, which might momentarily disintegrate without any explainable cause. He had to accept on faith the thoroughness and conscientiousness of its builder, an unknown craftsman whose work—generally satisfactory, sometimes remarkable—sometimes proved disconcertingly unreliable.

He had to hold steady, but Carmen appeared as an unexpected squall. She was a respectable girl, and to openly disgrace her was not for him an option. Nothing could be kept secret in a place like Comerio. Maybe in San Geronimo or San Juan secret intrigues abounded—enough commotion in those places to let a person come and go unnoticed. In the big towns, the pretense of sophistication was bought at the price of moral indifference, but perhaps that was too harsh a judgment. After all, the necessities of human nature have to be accommodated.

He took the long ride to San Geronimo once a month to visit a certain establishment that had no counterpart in Comerio where a lack of customers made such a business unprofitable. The few like himself who could afford the time and the expense would make the trip to the nearest big town—San Geronimo even being considered a small city by the standards of the time—where a greater variety provided some enticement. Sometimes he went as far as San Juan where foreign women added to the allure of the journey.

His life, satisfactory enough at the time, might have proceeded without change, focused on his primary concerns. There would be time soon enough, if his luck held out, to consider an attachment to a respectable woman. At the moment, he had more pressing things to consider, like acquiring the land beyond the stream, good land for growing coffee, the soil just right, with large trees that would provide the needed shade. He had crawled under the barbed wire fence several times to run the soil through his fingers; no doubt about it, good for growing coffee but only an untended forest at the moment. What use could the land be to the owner, an absentee American who had scarcely set foot on it? He had only put up the barbed wire fence—a futile gesture, since it didn't keep anyone out. People still entered the forest to gather firewood, the fence only a small inconvenience to most. To others, it was an enticement because, not having an obvious practical purpose, it seemed an affront that called for defiance.

In San Geronimo, *Licenciado* Altimo Ramirez acted as the agent for the American. One afternoon, Eduardo wandered into town intending to stop by his office, but first he called at the cigar factory to chat with Alfredo Gomez, the manager. He was a rotund little man who sported a very thin moustache and whose hair shone with an overabundance of brilliantine. He fancied himself a lady's man, a description no one would dispute if he treated women half as well as he did cigars. One had to be born to it, he often said, the same as being born with the right kind of hands for rolling cigars. "Women are like tobacco," he would say. "They like to be handled gently, but firmly." Eduardo Rincon saw no reason to contradict someone with whom he did business.

Although factors other than friendship determined the price of tobacco, to be on good terms with the buyer was always an advantage. That is not to imply that Eduardo's regard for Don Alfredo had a mercenary purpose. He was naturally at ease with colleagues, and his demeanor just as readily allowed them to be at ease with him. The day he intended to visit el *licenciado*, Eduardo had Alfredo Gomez pick out a box of cigars, not necessarily the best, but ones whose quality would be noticeably above average. He asked for a box that had not yet been labeled.

Glad to oblige, Alfredo Gomez, with the wink of an eye, handed over a suitable one. His pudgy fingers lingered in a soft caress over the object, at the same time showing off on his right hand a ring worthy of a bishop. Alfredo Gomez enjoyed a good conspiracy as much as he did women and cigars. He didn't know why Eduardo Rincon wanted a box of unlabeled cigars, and he didn't ask, but he suspected that it would be used in a scheme that sooner or later would be revealed to him as a marvel of business acumen.

Don Eduardo made a gesture as if to pay for the cigars, but Don Alfredo stopped him. "No, no, my friend. You insult me." As a businessman, Alfredo felt behooved to stay on good terms with a supplier of quality tobacco; no matter how plentiful the product, another man as accommodating as Eduardo Rincon would be hard to find.

"I wouldn't want to do that. I thank you for your generosity," Eduardo said, keeping up his end of the charade.

Generosity is a quality especially prized by those to whom it does not come naturally, and its attribution to him pleased Don Alfredo. Though aware of the falsity of the praise at the moment he received it, he soon forgot that small glitch and truly believed not only in Eduardo's sincerity but also in the truth of the assertion. In fact, the dealings between the two did not involve generosity. It was a three-way symbiotic relationship among the parties, including the owners of the factory, gentlemen who no longer worked with their hands, but who left the day-to-day running of the business to Don Alfredo with the full knowledge that his compensation entailed items never to be seen on the books, an arrangement that worked well among men who understood the importance of being reasonable.

Eduardo Rincon left the factory with the box of cigars in hand, a present for Don Altimo Ramirez, who, being well acquainted with Don Eduardo and his business, did not see anything amiss in being presented with such a gift. There was nothing more natural than for a tobacco grower to exhibit the ultimate result of his product, the gift too small to arouse the suspicion of impropriety, a token from a friend who had stopped in to chat. In another place, these seemingly meaningless interactions in the middle of the workday might be considered a waste of time, but no time is wasted that contributes to the pleasantness of life and the smooth functioning of society.

They talked about the weather, an innocuous topic always of interest to a farmer, and Eduardo Rincon was, after all, just that—a simple farmer from the backwoods—*un jibaro* if you will, at least that's what he proudly claimed. *Los campesinos*, like the Cordillera Central geographically, had always been the backbone of the nation. They were one and the same, the people and the mountains. He didn't mean to disparage the learned professions. Of course not; they were absolutely necessary. He had the utmost respect for his learned compatriot. Still, the simple farmers could not be discounted. Don Altimo Ramirez agreed, exalting the intense patriotism of the humble people, none humbler than Eduardo Rincon; one would have to walk a long way and then some to find a more exemplary citizen.

"I'm thinking of going into coffee," Eduardo said, as a natural extension of a conversation about the weather, geography, and the people.

"Can't go wrong with coffee," Don Altimo said. "Everyone drinks coffee."

His posture shifted almost imperceptibly in the chair. The physical movement corresponded to a mental one, signaling his perception that the conversation had reached its true subject. This propensity to telegraph his mental states, a handicap in the profession that Altimo Ramirez practiced, would keep him from ever becoming a lawyer of the first order. But in practical terms, seldom called upon to deal with practitioners of a higher caliber than himself, the disadvantage remained merely an inconvenience. It made him, however, a truly bad card player and popular with the gamblers of San Geronimo, who always counted on enriching themselves at his expense. In dealing with Eduardo Rincon, Altimo Ramirez functioned at a disadvantage, but he continued unaware of that fact.

"True," Eduardo said, "people would rather go without rice than without coffee."

"Of course your land is mostly planted in tobacco, and land that's good for tobacco is not necessarily good for coffee."

"You are an astute man," Eduardo said, "smart enough to be a farmer. So in my place, what would you do?"

Altimo Ramirez prided himself in his ability to give advice. He believed that his counsel was the most valuable service he provided for his clients, whose prosperity, he had no doubt, increased or declined based on how closely they followed the course of action he outlined. Nothing gratified him more than a person open to his suggestions. Someone who came right out and asked for guidance, even on a subject beyond Don Altimo's practical experience, he considered a person of the soundest judgment.

"You need a piece of land that's good for coffee."

"I'm afraid you're right," Eduardo said. "The land I have now is not good for coffee. Besides, I don't want to give up on tobacco. Rather, I want to diversify."

The word "diversify" signaled to Don Altimo the arrival of a real issue. The word smacked of high finance and serious dealing. "It's not smart to depend solely on one crop," he said gravely.

Don Eduardo agreed with his advisor, allowing the *licenciado* to think that he had been the originator of the thought. "On the south side of my place there is land I believe to be good for coffee. It's only forest now. No one plants on it."

Don Altimo looked out into the distance visualizing, one would suppose, the plot of land Eduardo had described, but the look was deceptive. He had no idea what lay to the south or what bordered any side of Eduardo's land. He had never set foot on it. He imagined that it looked like any other piece of land planted with tobacco. "It's a matter, then, of getting it for the right price," he said.

"Precisely," Eduardo concurred.

"Who owns the land now?"

"An American, I believe."

Don Altimo squinted involuntarily as if a bright light had suddenly shone in his direction. Only one American he knew owned land in the vicinity. Don Altimo had tried to dissuade him from buying a piece of land that had so little potential for development. Actually, it had no potential whatsoever in Don Altimo's estimation, and so he considered it a very bad investment for an American not likely, from the looks of him, to become a farmer, and if that were his purpose he might avail himself of better land not so far inland. But the American had insisted. Young and not receptive to advice, a bad sign right from the start, no doubt he had some harebrained scheme for using the land, but he didn't share it with Don Altimo.

"Ah," Don Altimo said, but did not elaborate.

"I am afraid he doesn't want to sell the land."

"He wants to grow coffee perhaps?"

"No, he merely wants to own it."

"For any reason?"

"He's not a normal American."

"Then getting the land should be easy."

"He has an emotional attachment to it. Money is not what he wants in exchange."

That thought had not occurred to Don Altimo, and the concept disturbed as well as intrigued him. He liked problems to be clear. Ambiguity made him uneasy and elevated his emotional center of gravity, so that he feared being tipped over by the slightest force. "What then can he want?" he asked.

"He may not know," Eduardo suggested.

"That's a problem."

"Or an opportunity," the farmer said.

"Indeed," said Don Altimo letting his eyebrows relax after having acquired something to work with. He reached for the box of cigars that Eduardo had brought and taking one out and unwrapping it, he ran it under his nostrils inhaling deeply. "Don

Alfredo is a true artist," he said as if that gentleman were responsible for the aroma of the tobacco. He offered Eduardo a cigar, and the two men smoked as they discussed the likely outcome of the upcoming election of local official in San Geronimo.

*

Some men, the minute they get a little ahead of themselves, can't resist giving themselves airs and pretending that they were born gentlemen who have no need to work with their hands like peasants. Eduardo avoided that kind of pride. Even long after it had become unnecessary for him, he occasionally put in a day in the fields like a common worker just so that he would not forget the pain of straining like a beast, but that day of labor by choice had not yet arrived. Toiling in the fields still in his eyes a necessity, one less worker whom he had to pay—or maybe two—for he worked with zeal, and the others tried to keep up with him and not have their manhood shamed. Only after his holdings had become extensive enough to need his constant attention as a manager did he abandon the practice, except for the occasional symbolic day so that he would not forget. Not that the memory would ever be gone, but he wanted to prevent a different kind of forgetting, a forgetting in his body that, paradoxically, would also be a forgetting in the soul. But the practice had a more immediate and practical result, with value he had not anticipated. It earned him the reputation of being humble, a quality that in addition to his natural charm and coupled with his wealth, made him truly unique—someone for whom his neighbors were willing to forgive much.

Along the edge of what he considered the back of his land, adjacent to the uncultivated forest of the odd American, ran a stream to which the natural topography provided a sudden drop a few feet higher than a man. A bamboo grove and a slight drop in the elevation obstructed the view of the waterfall and the small pool into which it flowed, except on the downstream side, but no path approached from that direction. These natural features of the terrain, conducive to privacy, made the spot ideal for the use it had acquired. The water ran too gently to propel itself beyond the edge of the fall, so Eduardo had rigged a length of bamboo to serve as a spout that extended the reach of the falling water out into the sandy pool. For lack of indoor plumbing, a luxury unknown in the interior, the place served as a shower.

He didn't enforce his right to exclusivity, and others occasionally used the facility. When women availed themselves of the convenience, they prudently posted a lookout to prevent embarrassment to any man who unsuspectingly happened along. The use of his waterfall by neighbors mostly occurred on weekends; consequently, on the day in question, Eduardo was unprepared to run into anyone. The acquisition of the land beyond the stream uppermost on his mind—tired, sweaty, and grimy after having worked alongside the field hands—he directed his footsteps toward the river at the end of the long hot day. Had he been singing or whistling, as he did habitually when taking solitary walks, he might have given ample warning of his approach to the person in the pool. But preoccupied with the problem of acquiring the land on the other side of the stream, how he might entice the American into giving it up, he proceeded in silence. When the pool came into view, he spied Carmen standing in the water under the fall. Facing away, she didn't at first see him standing there in confusion.

Had he immediately stepped back, life would have continued as if nothing had happened. He might have ascribed the whole scene to his imagination without any incongruity. He had in fact seen her just like that, in the very spot, several nights running in the twilight of consciousness, just before being submerged into sleep. Perhaps seeing something transposed from one realm into another, and not understanding what made such a feat possible, paralyzed him. Had he walked away a mistake might have been avoided, but rooted to the spot, unable to move forward or back into the protective camouflage of the lush vegetation, he stood wholly exposed to being discovered. That was his impression at the time, but later when he reflected he became uncertain.

The meaning of Eduardo's failure to act in the prudent manner that he knew to be right may be amply discussed. Some may say that there was no failure at all, that he had a choice to stand there or not, and he chose to stand. Others might say that he had no choice but to do what he did, that every preceding event in his life led him to that spot and caused him to be rooted there and that no amount of effort exerted by his will allowed him to do otherwise. His father confessor, if he had one, would have by the nature of his calling come down on the side of choice, because without choice the concept of sin becomes meaningless. But that begs the question of what sin, if any, he committed.

Gazing upon a naked woman cannot in this case be labeled a transgression. After all, the act entailed no malice aforethought. He did not go there intending to find Carmen either clothed or unclothed. The sin must ensue from what happened on the spot, by Eduardo's state of mind as he contemplated the scene. His detractors will say that lust overcame him and prevented his acting rationally, that oblivious of common decency, he stood there lusting after the woman. If only to adhere to the teachings of the Church, the father confessor would follow that path, though reason might suggest to him some other route.

But what is lust but a mechanism of nature, enabling living organisms to fulfill their primary function. There is no sin in nature. Sin is a category created by human thought. That does not mean that it is not real or that it need not be taken seriously, only that it must be examined more closely. When a lion becomes head of a pride and kills all the cubs sired by the previous lord, we do not say that it commits a sin. Whereas if a man did the same, there would be no reluctance to say he is damned, either literally or figuratively depending on the beliefs of the speaker.

The assumption that lust commandeered Eduardo's emotions as he stood rooted to the ground gazing on Carmen as she showered is questionable, and to speculate about what he actually felt is also futile. Eduardo himself, looking back in his old age, when illness drove him to seek the comfort of the Church, identified that moment as the point of his fall, just as Adam might have looked back to the moment when he bit into the apple.

But Eduardo, too worldly a man to ascribe so much importance to so tawdry and common an emotion, didn't castigate himself for lust. He considered sinful his confusion, the momentary
lapse of focus, since by that mysterious alchemy he lost control of
subsequent events. The sin would stem ultimately from a betrayal
of himself, not so much of Carmen, though that, too, weighed on
him despite his attempts at expiation.

Carmen never reproached him. Caught in a flood of events
for which she had only partial responsibility, she did not cling
to the illusion of control. She could not say why on that day she
went to the stream to bathe by herself when she had never done
so before. She had felt an urge to proceed, and she did not resist
it, as if unaware of Eduardo's habit of going there after his workday. Some with whom she confided pointed out that deducing that
he would go there, his own property on which he had rigged the
bamboo spout just for that purpose, required no great reasoning.
When did she think he would shower, if not when sweaty at the
end of a long day in the sun?

Still, she claimed that the possibility of his appearing had not
occurred to her. She had not the benefit of formal learning to inform her that the mind contains more than consciousness. She
would have only countered that anything brought about by the
unknown merely revealed the will of God.

The father confessor, that insidious fellow, who by hook or
by crook wants to insinuate himself into these pages, would point
out that not only God works through the unconscious but also
the devil. In fact, he might say the devil primarily works through
the unconscious, because God has no reason to stay in the shadows. But we need not take that seriously, since the good father is
given to sophisms—little white lies—that he feels are necessary
to manage the members of his flock, who, unlike himself, lack the
benefit of an intellect complex enough to keep them on the difficult path to salvation.

When she turned around to see Eduardo Rincon firmly rooted
to the ground, Carmen exhibited no sign of being startled or sur-

prised. Her native modesty was not piqued to quick action, and she gracefully walked out of the water, acknowledging only that her turn was up and she would cede the facility without protest. The scene, worthy of being immortalized by an old master, by definition impossible to procure, resided only in Eduardo's imagination but with as much splendor as if hanging in the Prado or the Louvre, Venus Emerging from Her Bath. But, to this exhibit hall only one visitor was admitted, a loss to the world that only from ignorance of the deprivation did not rue the misfortune.

"So you didn't scurry out of the water to hide yourself," said Carmen's confidant, incredulous of behavior so different from what she would have done.

"Well, there was no point in doing that. He had already seen me."

"Yes, but what if he mistook your calmness for an invitation? That would have been a mistake, no?"

"Of course, but I didn't want to make him feel that he had done something wrong. He looked troubled enough."

That was an accurate reading of the expression on Eduardo's face. Whether consciously or not, he knew at that moment that his life had taken a turn that might have been avoided had he not lost power over his limbs and had turned and run, figuratively speaking; for in reality, the slowest of walks would have been sufficient. Some other force had decided what he must do about Carmen, because after gazing at her nakedness, he felt as committed as having made a verbal agreement. He never went back on his word. He sensed having been tricked, but not by Carmen—whom he never believed, as others did, had ambushed him—but by Fate, for whom she, too, was a pawn.

T HE FRIENDSHIP BETWEEN Eduardo and Rodrigo had begun long before Rodrigo considered his vocation. As boyhood companions, they believed their lives would be similar as
they grew older, a continuation into an adulthood that would resemble that of their fathers, tillers of the soil and lovers of their
country. But the tumult of adolescence overturned their childhood
ideas and confused them with longings and desires that seemed as
chimerical and as disconcerting as the ravings of madmen. Those
feelings arrived with fervor beyond what they thought possible or
desirable and propelled them in directions they had not anticipated. In childhood, destiny arrives peacefully, but later the process
becomes tempestuous.

Rodrigo had gone abroad to study after discovering his
vocation, and Eduardo, with wonderment and some resentment
disguised as pity at the leaving of so worthy a friend, watched
him go. He had no other way to look at the departure but as a
mistake on the part of his friend, giving up on life at such an early
age. He had his own path to follow, which did not include trying
to understand the allure of the Church. The memory of Rodrigo
faded along with other childhood things often recalled with pangs
of nostalgia but inevitably relegated to oblivion. At an unexpected
moment, Rodrigo made a return decked in a black cassock and
invested with the power of an institution. The two friends had lost
touch with one another: neither one of them, for different reasons,
having the necessity or impetus to write. Rodrigo's return was
unknown to Eduardo until his lost friend showed up one day at
his doorstep, in a manner of speaking, for he had not first arrived
at the house, but at the field where Eduardo toiled alongside his
farmhands.

Eduardo noticed from afar the lone figure dressed in black
approaching on horseback. The darkness of the rider, sufficiently intriguing, made Eduardo intermittently raise his eyes to the

distance where, minute by minute, the horseman proportionally grew. The *haciendero* became uneasy as he realized the costume denoted an emissary of the Church. A clergyman approaching a location ordinarily so out of the way in the middle of the day forewarned of an unusual event—the unusual often, in the experience of the farmer, unpleasant, a sight akin to seeing someone from the telegraph office missive in hand. What could that mean but one's attention being summoned to a death or an illness? He reviewed in silent apprehension the list of those who would require his presence under those circumstances.

Even when the horseman had approached close enough for his features to be distinct, Eduardo failed to recognize him, though he noted the broad grin incongruous with the supposed purpose of the visit. The horseman dismounted with élan rarely associated with members of the profession that his costume unabashedly announced. Eduardo, still fearing to be asked to perform an unpleasant duty, interpreted his deliberate strides as brazen.

"It's me," said the stranger, suddenly transformed into the long lost Rodrigo.

Eduardo's reaction surprised several of the field hands who had paused to look. Seeing a friend believed to have been irretrievably lost produced a natural joy, increased by the release of the tension that preceded recognition. At the resurrection of the buried past, the two friends leapt to hold each other with an abandon seldom seen in sober men, a state soon remedied back at the house where neither one had any qualms in trying to outdo the other in reducing the contents of a bottle of rum, the renewal of a contest they had often engaged in as youths.

In time, the renewed friendship between the two men developed to include an unspoken agreement, assiduously adhered to by both, that neither try to proselytize the other. Eduardo wondered at the acquiescence of his friend to this condition, except now and then when he suffered a bout of cynicism. Then he supposed his friend's accord to be a tactic rather than an acceptance, the taking of the long view indeed. In Eduardo's eyes this was admirable enough, requiring the patience of a saint, since he believed the wait would be futile.

Having his friend at a disadvantage sometimes troubled Eduardo. The agreement placed unequal burdens on the parties, no stricture on Eduardo to convert his friend to anything whatsoever, while Rodrigo remained bound by reason of his calling to accomplish his apostolic mission. The discomfort, however, remained occasional, its cause easily disclaimed, the pact not of his making—not his alone in any case—and could have been rejected at the beginning, and indeed cancelled at anytime.

He supplied Rodrigo with a challenge—perhaps the greatest challenge of his professional life—to do something with so unregenerate a sinner, for what else could he call himself? In return, Eduardo got something just as elusive: friendship, a continuation of the past, but beyond that, the additional dimension of Rodrigo's position in the world as a mediator with another realm. To call Eduardo's cynicism about the Church an affectation would be going too far in discrediting the expression of ambivalence. He found the idea of the Church as an institution or a business simple enough to grasp. As a producer of goods that converted into wealth that in turn provided power, he had an intuitive understanding of the process. He could reduce all systems in the world to that—the production of commodities for the ultimate attainment of power. A commodity might be material or psychological, but always it had to be real or it would fail as a dependable producer of wealth. The longevity of the Church pointed to its dependability as a producer of a commodity in high demand, and yet Eduardo remained skeptical of the reality of what the Church dispensed, but he longed to resolve the issue in some satisfactory manner. He lacked the ability to live comfortably with ambiguity, and the possibility of resolving this dilemma spurred him to maintain his friendship with the cleric.

"The larger the firm the more leverage it has," Eduardo said, "and you work for a very large one indeed."

"The largest in this part of the world," Rodrigo conceded.

"Do you ever miss the world?"

"Why? Has the world gone somewhere else?"

"No, of course. It is you who has gone elsewhere."

"I don't see it that way. I work in the world like everyone else."

"There are some limitations however."

"There are limitations in every field."

Concerned about a woman, why this woman moved him more than all others, a question on which his friend might shed some light, Eduardo's expectation lacked clear reason. He had no basis to suppose that Rodrigo had sufficient experience in that area. Rather, the opposite more likely, since a vow of celibacy created an obstacle to first-hand knowledge of such matters. Eduardo had no illusion that Rodrigo had been celibate before his vow or that he would always be in the future. Such a course seemed to Eduardo impossible, except for those who had no interest in women under any circumstances, among whom he did not number his friend. He presumed, though he didn't say so to Rodrigo, priestly celibacy to be a pose more honored in the breach than in the observance.

"Don't you miss having a woman?"

"Ah, that's what you're driving at."

"That seems a severe limitation."

"Not a limitation but rather a simplification."

Eduardo turned that over in his mind. "I can see that," he said, "but isn't that a rather drastic simplification."

"Well yes, you can say that, but the aim is rather grand."

"Ah, yes, the aim, one supposes there's a corresponding gain, a proper reward."

"Indeed there is."

They had reached the impasse—no other question could Eduardo at that point safely ask, and to this one Rodrigo had no satisfactory answer.

"You haven't answered my question."

"Of course I do," Rodrigo said, "I'm still a man."

"Precisely, and a man is subject to compulsions regardless of what he wills."

"Subject to temptations, yes."

"You propose that it's possible to always resist temptation."

"To resist, yes; to always prevail, no. God doesn't expect man to always prevail. That's why there is repentance and forgiveness."

"It's an endless cycle then. Why bother to resist the inevitable. What cannot be avoided must be natural, and is it not a sin to go against nature?"

"The devil compels sins," the priest said.

"Is he not part of nature?"

"I understand him to be supernatural."

"Well then, so is God. He's not part of nature either?"

"Nature is a manifestation of God."

"Natural disasters included?"

"Yes," Rodrigo said.

"Nature red of tooth and claw?"

"Well, yes," Rodrigo said unshaken. "We are not meant to understand everything."

"Clearly," Eduardo said. "I can't help but think that women have something to do with the soul."

Sensing that Eduardo desired to impart something that had been bothering him and to which their conversation had been leading, Rodrigo did not reply.

"Do you suppose that it is possible to be bewitched?"

It was an unexpected turn, since, if anything, Rodrigo believed Eduardo to be more contaminated with the dogma of materialism than susceptible to the allure of superstition. Rodrigo struggled to understand the question.

"Do you mean literally," he asked in turn, "as with incantations and the like?"

"I don't mean to sound so ridiculous," Eduardo said.

"I don't mean to imply that it is," said Rodrigo.

"I mean only that it would be an explanation."

"It would indeed be an explanation," the priest said, though what Eduardo wished to explain had yet to be clarified. "But all the possible avenues of reason must be exhausted before turning to that byway. Some people see no inconsistency in practicing Spiritism and simultaneously thinking themselves good Catholics, but mostly it is all superstition."

"Yes, doubtlessly," Eduardo dubiously consented. "I don't mean that, exactly. It's rather more subtle, perhaps, in a way more real in being less obvious—having no visible practice or practitioner. Commonly one might say 'I'm bewitched by that woman' or conversely 'by that man.' What I'm saying is that there is something to those words—more meaning than we ascribe in passing. The real meaning may be more significant than we allow. One may really be bewitched, if we consider that to mean that we have lost the power to act in a rational manner. There is a whole realm of existence that is, if you will, super-rational. Sometimes that gets confused with the supernatural, or are they the same thing?"

"Whether one or the other, it can all be understood within the scope of the Church," the priest said.

"There's a common belief that the spirits of the recently dead roam about before departing for the next world. They can be detected by the odor they give out—the smell of magnolias. I heard about it from Juan Ocuña who experienced it himself first hand. On his way home one day the scent of magnolias overwhelmed him. Walking up the road, he searched about to see if the flower flourished anywhere nearby and found nothing. When he got home, greeted with the news that his mother had passed away in her sleep, he believed firmly that her spirit had met him on the road to deliver the news before anyone else. What is the position of the Church on that?"

"Common folklore is just that—stories concocted by people to help them bear the shock of traumatic events."

"Then there was no scent of magnolias on the road?"

"Who is to say?"

"Who indeed? Is there not in the Church an official exorcist?"

"That's another matter altogether," Rodrigo said in the driest tone. Clearly a subject he would rather forego, and had Eduardo been less intent on some inward necessity he might have noticed that cue. "A body may be possessed of a devil."

"There are devils, then, roaming about the world intent on possessing bodies?"

"In a manner of speaking," said the priest.

"Either there are or there aren't," Eduardo insisted. "Otherwise what is an exorcist to exorcise?"

"Of course you're right, but what of it?"

"These devils must be spirits subject to incantations, and if these devil spirits are roaming about, mightn't the spirit of the recently dead do the same—that is, have a grace period before they go off to their eternal destination? Unless, of course, all these devils are but metaphorical, which they may very well be, and I have no objection to such a state of affairs."

"Well, they are and they aren't," Rodrigo said, seeing a chance to wriggle out of the uncomfortable position of supporting an irrational point of view. From the beginning, the Church had presented faith as consistent with reason. That argument had always seemed to him spurious. He had not yet been able to reconcile the two realms of thought, a weak link in the armor of his devotion. "There is a strange parallel between what happens in the mind and what is manifested in the physical world. Take unicorns for instance. You'll never see one in the physical world. Does that mean they don't exist?"

Unicorns were beside the point when Eduardo wanted to know what he should do about Carmen, or rather, what he could do about her. He had a vague premonition that he would be unable to do anything, or nothing more than he had been able to do until then, follow a path seemingly not of his own choosing. That was perhaps the crux of the matter: he needed the appearance of choice when following a path that had been predetermined but for which he would be held responsible. The odd situation seemed a trap laid for him by some malevolent being. He might shun his dilemma as something to do with Carmen, but he had a gnawing suspicion that it entailed more.

H E REFRAINED FROM taking Carmen to his own house. He might have done so, since he had no wife to prevent him, but he kept up appearances for Carmen's sake. A show of propriety was also respectful to his neighbors, though anyone close enough to notice who went in or out of his house depended on him for employment. Even on finding anything amiss, they would be reluctant to criticize him. Having a mistress was considered normal, even for married men. Only the women suffered. Each hoped that her man would be different, but when he proved to be the same as the others, she fell back to saying, "That's the way men are," and left it at that.

But Eduardo, still single, had no one to reproach him. Carmen declined to hold out for the ceremony, so she had only herself to blame for her fate. No one knew that better than Carmen, as she lay next to Eduardo in a makeshift bed in an abandoned *bohío* at the edge of one of his fields. She asked whether he loved her. The question startled him, because it presupposed the possibility of a negative answer. What more proof of his love did she need than his presence? If she had to ask the obvious, then the question might have another meaning.

"You doubt me?" he countered to keep from thinking about the possible import of her question. As she did not answer in words, he tried to read her face by the light of the kerosene lamp that flickered with tenuous persistence, creating in the small room a sense of fantasy. Perhaps, the light, becoming less potent as it receded from its source, created confusion between reality and desire. Disturbed, she turned away, making him wonder whether she wished to conceal an answer. The dimness in the room prevented reading with any certitude her usually obvious face. What he needed to see required illumination from a source other than a kerosene lamp whose physical nature, at the moment, he welcomed.

"Do you know who I am?" she asked turning again to gaze at him. Her dark eyes, in desperate intensity, efficiently gathered the scarce light.

Indeed, who was she, the object of his love? There she stood, flesh and blood that he touched in disbelief. She had materialized to his surprise by some unexplainable alchemy. From his imagination, she sprang to life full-blown to take up space in the world and ask questions like any other woman, questions to which he had no ready answers but that he could not ignore. She had the power to compel him to search for answers where there were none.

"You're the one I love," he said. The words came to him involuntarily, as if they had been dictated and he was mouthing them like an actor, with genuine emotion but from a script written by someone else.

"I see," she said.

Those words—a reproach, a complaint about the insufficiency of his answer—disturbed him, but their ambiguity prevented him from defending himself.

"What do you see?" he asked dreading to be found out, yet ignorant of what he was hiding other than his discomfort; the source of his words something else that he would have to deal with another time. Perhaps he would be spared; there were many shadows at night that suggested phantasmagoric shapes that proved quite ordinary in daylight. Anxiously, he waited for the sun to rise and dissipate the vagueness, but overcome by illusion, he feared the darkness would last forever.

"I see how you love me," she said.

He sincerely longed for that to be true, for then he would be absolved of any fault that might accrue to him for misleading her, but he did not believe himself guilty, not having promised anything but the moment. She refrained from asking for anything else, and he grew fearful of hearing something different. He listened carefully, yet, he remained unprepared to decide whether she was indeed asking for something and much less to determine what that might be. He could simply ask questions to remove his uncertainty, but that would suppose clarity of vision, a view of the path leading from where he stood to where he wanted to go. Something obstructed his sight, though that may imply more concreteness to his conception than it actually had. Rather, there was no view to obstruct; he perceived no destination. His relationship with her encompassed only a world limited by the light emitted by a kerosene lamp. Beyond that, he saw only darkness.

He accepted for the moment being caught in a moral dilemma, though the problem might not be recognized as such by anyone privy to his thoughts. His view bore little resemblance to the everyday notion of morality fashioned by society. That variety is meant to maintain order in the community—a worthy aim not to be disparaged but not in keeping with the principle of fitting the means to the end. After all, a pistol is not needed to get rid of a fly. Justice is a concept infinitely more elusive than law and order; law is used to achieve order, and in loose parlance together they are called justice. But that justice achieved by law is a crude variety in comparison to what is meant by justice in the abstract, that is, in the mind where perfect justice is possible, one by which every person receives his due. That justice may be achieved only theoretically. In practice, justice is subject to chance and is achieved only occasionally.

The morality that preoccupied Eduardo had more to do with his desire to make his actions in the world coincide with his image of himself than with any canon of morality propagated by the institutions of society. Some may think this a spurious distinction, what he thought of himself inseparable from and molded by the social environment in which he existed, but that misses the point. A personal standard may be infinitely more complex than an official one, which necessarily loses much nuance merely by being codified.

The belief that he would be truthful if she asked a direct question about their future together bolstered Eduardo, but she asked only about the present, and in the present, he belonged to her as much as he could belong to anyone. What she understood about his state of mind is another question. She may have surmised something, but that can hardly be presumed. Only her question provided an indication of concern. On the surface straightforward, she may have simply meant to inquire how he felt at the moment. But that implied a sophistication for which no evidence existed but the question itself, which may have indicated a simplicity so profound as to amount to the same thing. It may have been motivated by a desire to protect herself. In her simplicity, if it can be so labeled, she may not have noticed any danger. The fear, for himself as well as for her, may have been all his, a point that he considered only later when he had occasion to speak to Father Rodrigo.

IN THE SMALL church in Comerio, Carmen knelt before the icon of the Virgin Mary. Only the light of a single votive candle, for which she had deposited a copper coin in the offering box, flickered in the darkness. She reluctantly parted with the only coin she had, knowing that even that small amount might be necessary for more tangible needs than her tranquility. The Virgin had no need for copper coins. Nevertheless, Carmen felt compelled to offer it in evidence of the sincerity of her intentions and the seriousness of her plight. She first attempted to pray with her head bowed, but she soon abandoned that approach in favor of looking straight into Mary's face. Perhaps they could talk woman to woman.

The flame remained steady, creating the illusion of stillness. The small amount of light from the candle reached the golden halo of the Queen of Heaven, reflecting with a defiant constancy into the surrounding darkness. A local artisan had carved this representation of the Virgin in the image of his own mother. When she looked up, Carmen saw a familiar face, one that might have looked back at her from a mirror, prominent cheekbones and intense black eyes in which compassion and sensuality were equally mixed.

The possibility of speaking to Mary as one virgin to another had been lost, but what of that? As a mother, what did virginity mean to Mary? How did her tousling with the Holy Ghost differ from Carmen's own actions, except that Eduardo Rincon was a man of flesh and blood?

"Dear Mother of Christ," she said, "I came to talk to you because I know you would understand. I don't know why I love Eduardo Rincon. The reason is not that I'm wanton, as my mother says, nor that I think that I'm better than I am, as some other people think."

"Of course I understand," the Virgin answered.

The deity climbed down from her niche and flexed her limbs so long imprisoned in the wooden body. Only thanks to people like Carmen did she get the opportunity to move her stiff joints, and she appreciated the chance to relax somewhat from her formal pose, to be able to sit down and speak like a normal person, to hear once again the sound of her voice the way she had heard it back in the days in Galilee. People did not realize the essential difference between the two worlds. In the other, with no need for conversation, it had fallen into disuse, but she missed it as she missed so many other things. Without complaining, she bore the discomfort the best she could.

In any case, she had emerged to deal with Carmen's troubles, not to gripe about her own, if indeed she really had any. Sooner or later, this pining for human existence had to stop. Some things in the universe continued beyond the power, dare she say it, or even think it, of her Son, also her Father and her Lover. What a conundrum! To get used to it would take an eternity. Carmen's problem paled in comparison. It was certainly manageable. The other had been there for centuries; it would have to wait, perhaps forever.

The Virgin seemed much younger in person than in her wooden guise. She sat down on the floor of the church, perhaps because in her lifetime—that is, when she was human—church pews were unknown. But of course, she had had centuries to learn about them; no doubt, she had become familiar with all the cathedrals built in her honor. Nevertheless, she sat on the floor, her legs crossed in front of her and her tunic splayed over them. She invited Carmen to do the same. The young suppliant, at first reluctant to be so informal with so grand a personage, one before whom she usually knelt, then saw in the young Virgin's face a mischievous sincerity.

"My heart is full of confusion," Carmen said.

"You mean your head, don't you? Hearts don't allow confusion," Mary replied.

"What shall I do about Eduardo?"

"Oh my," Mary exclaimed with a little laugh. "You mean you haven't done anything yet?"

"Oh, practically nothing," Carmen said.

"Well, practically nothing's what it takes," Mary said. "In my case I hardly noticed anything. Puff and it was done. Sometimes I think I was cheated, but then, I'll never know. Of course that doesn't matter. Really, the child was what mattered, you know, becoming a mother."

"But you had more."

"Yes, a great deal more than I expected but not what you have."

"I don't know that I have anything," Carmen said.

"What do you want?"

"I want completeness," Carmen said.

"You want love."

"Yes, love."

"Does he not love you?"

"He says he does."

"But you doubt him."

"I want to be married."

"Do you?"

"You think that I don't?"

"I don't know."

"I thought you would know such things."

"How can I know about you what you don't know yourself?"

"What would you do in my place?"

"In your place I had a child."

"But you were married."

"Yes, I married but as a ruse."

"I need you to help me."

"I will always be here."

"I can talk to you anytime?"

"Whenever you wish."

"What can I do for you in return?"

"Bringing me back to this world is quite enough."

"Can I tell people of our talk?"

"Who will believe you?"

"Gregoria will."

"Yes, she'll always believe you."

"And Father Rodrigo? I must tell him when I go to confession."

"He will be skeptical."

"Then I shouldn't tell him?"

"It will make no difference."

"I see."

"I must return to my place now."

"It's dark here most of the time. Do you mind that?"

"I'm only here when you're here. The darkness is nothing."

Mary rose from her seat on the floor and climbed into the niche from which she had descended. Her gaze became fixed in the distance, and no one would suspect that she had taken a respite from her eternal vigil.

Carmen, too, rose from her seat on the floor. She was about to leave when Father Rodrigo entered through a side door that led directly to the rectory. Expecting to find no one in the church, he was startled to see Carmen. The unexpected encounter discomfited the young woman also. Only seconds had elapsed since the Virgin had been sitting on the floor, and Carmen wondered whether the priest had seen the deity climbing back to her place or whether he had heard any of the conversation that had transpired. Maybe Mary misjudged his skepticism, but Carmen concluded that the Virgin had to know the heart of the young priest.

Rodrigo's propensity to swagger, seemed to the young woman a trait inconsistent with the habit he wore, a prejudice founded on the perception that priests withdraw from an essential human activity. Perhaps his youth belied his commitment to his vow, but every priest is young once, though not everyone exuded the vitality evident and overwhelming in Rodrigo. His recent arrival a spur to rumormongers, he was already the subject of malicious gossip throughout the neighborhood of Comerio. The talk had started almost as soon as he occupied the rectory, the gossip inevitable given his demeanor and his approach to his calling, unusual for the time and place. Beyond looking after the spiritual health of his parishioners, he insisted that the material poverty of the people in his care diminished their spiritual vitality, a view directly contrary to the prevailing one in the Church that, in the eyes of the Savior, poverty aided redemption. The cult of poverty was anathema to Rodrigo, who was just as likely to be heard discussing agricultural problems with a *campesino* as to be seen performing a baptism or administering extreme unction—sacraments in about equal demand—given the poor state of health of the population which had the effect of maintaining the arrival and departure at an equal rate.

"Oh, I'm sorry to have interrupted your devotion," he said.

"No," she answered, "I was about to leave." She hesitated as if there were something else she wanted to say but couldn't find the words.

"Is there something troubling you?" he asked.

"I'm going to have a child," she stammered.

"You are blessed, then," he responded.

"But I am not married."

"Oh, I know that," he answered.

She could imagine how much else he knew, but perhaps he knew nothing at all. He might have heard gossip. He might have guessed. Eduardo might have told him, though that seemed unlikely. If Eduardo were going to confess, would he do so to a priest who was also his friend? Or perhaps there had been no confession in the formal sense; perhaps, just talk between two men.

Her blank face stared up at him, so that he could read into it whatever he wished, but he only wanted to know what she was trying to say. Surely she was trying to say something or maybe trying to let him point the way to something about which she was uncertain. Therein laid a trap that he tried to avoid. He might reveal more about himself than he would learn about her, not necessarily objectionable but in this case that might prove unhelpful, if indeed she needed a pointer in the right direction. The encounter appeared on the surface accidental, but was there in the world anything at all accidental? Might not every action be part of a vast scheme that had profound meaning when deciphered?

He pondered the meaning of details that often seemed meaningless but surely had some significance in some larger plan. The details nagged at him. If he could master them, he would be onto something, but at that moment, clarity eluded him. She might be in the same quandary, wondering what had brought about this chance encounter, a sign for her to perform one action or another. Generally disinclined to force anything, still he seemed always to be in motion. The question was whether to spur action at the moment. Constantly and inexorably, his mind flowed naturally like water in a creek. It followed the contour of the land, flowing around obstacles and always yielding to the guidance of the topography.

"Are you asking for absolution?" The question escaped him involuntarily, and he knew immediately that it might be misinterpreted. Far from his intent, it sounded like a disguised command.

Her face darkened as if a cloud momentarily passed overhead, but they were indoors and he, the only cloud having interposed inadvertently, had no excuse for obscuring the light from a radiant face. Had he been more humble and more insightful, he might have realized that the illumination came from within her and that he lacked the power to dim it. She would have been more at ease had she noticed his uncertainty. In his discomfort, he vaguely felt that he should remember something about this young woman, but the impression, spied through a haze, floated indistinctly, eluding his perception.

"Oh, no," she said, "what would be the use? I have no intention of reforming."

The clarity of her response startled him as much as her certainty fascinated him. He saw the contradiction, the sincerity with which she had come to pray while offering no repentance and asking no forgiveness. Her stance forced him to accept her innocence, and yet he could not say so. He proceeded to abandon his duty as pastor to a lost lamb and granted that she had a right to find her own way. His curiosity as to what principle she used for guidance piqued him. She stood too sure of herself to be without one.

"Then, you consider the situation satisfactory?" he asked.

"I'm glad of the child," she said.

"And the rest?"

"The rest is beyond my control."

"You mean the father is not glad."

"He will be glad when he knows of it," she said, looking away from the priest toward the Virgin.

"You're not sure," he said.

"No one can be sure of what's in another's heart."

"And you're willing to bear the burden by yourself?"

She smiled at him mischievously, intentionally misinterpreting his meaning. "This is a burden men cannot bear," she said.

"Ah, to be sure," he conceded.

"I will not be alone."

"You have faith then."

"I do," she said. "The same as you."

Her assumption of his faith also surprised him, and he looked at her more closely trying to discover in her face the secret to which she assumed he was privy. She would not reveal the identity of the father, but she took for granted that Rodrigo might make an accurate guess.

"I take it that I know the young man," he said.

She bowed her head to conceal her smile that might be interpreted either as mocking or merely an expression of embarrassment.

He remained undecided whether she was extremely self-possessed or only innocently simple. Having no need to decide the question, he let it go in hope of subduing his own feelings that churned to more turbulence than he wished to experience at the moment.

Something about the corner of her eyes reminded him of someone else, whose image caused him to lose his equanimity and transported him back to Spain. As a student there, at the home of a patron of the seminary, he met a young woman whose image caused him to lay awake at night considering whether his vocation was genuine. He remembered standing on the portico of her father's house built in the "English style," overlooking a formal garden.

"There is something very stifling about it," Isabela had said. "Nothing is left to chance. Every path and every turn is carefully laid out, not a branch, not a leaf out place. Every flower will bloom in the predicted place at the predicted time, and if it doesn't, the gardener will intervene to make it comply or at least to make it seem as if nothing is amiss." He pointed out its beauty and tranquility. "But is it real?" she wanted to know. As real as anything else, he assured her. She had then responded with a smile similar to the one now on Carmen's face.

Questions he believed to have been put to rest came back to him, mercifully with less force than when he first confronted them, but resuscitated nevertheless when he had thought them gone forever. He remembered the whiteness of her skin—free of blemishes and so smooth it reminded him of porcelain. The whiteness contrasted starkly with her hair, as black as polished ebony. As he stood on the portico contemplating the garden's artificiality that she found undesirable, he lingered conscious only of a scent that enhanced the illusion that she too was a flower in a manicured garden. His contemplation of her anything but tranquil, the very orderliness of her person agitated his emotions. The expected temptation, he decided, put in his path to test his vocation. His mentor had warned him that such an event would occur. He had not doubted the words of his teacher, but he had underestimated the subtle power launched against him.

Committing a carnal sin was his least concern; such a slip, after all, was remediable and expected, but the assault on his basic premises was another matter. He had not foreseen the two tied so neatly in one package. In retrospect, he found the dilemma, to speak metaphorically, diabolical. He safely came to that conclusion after countless hours of agonizing self-scrutiny. Eventually, he had rejected her analysis, but a residue of doubt lingered.

The labyrinthine paths of the garden were at least out in the open, but there were also enough hedges on the periphery to hide improprieties, youthful or otherwise, that might arise in moments of spontaneous indiscretion. Spontaneity suffered as the least acceptable trait in that company. The young lady objected to that restriction, the formality of the life to which she saw herself doomed and, to a greater degree, the young man from the Antilles who had piqued her imagination. She still possessed spontaneity and resisted being curtailed by social constraints. He had chosen a life she would have rejected, and she failed to understand how he could throw away what she considered an inestimable prize, his for merely being a man. But perhaps that was the answer, giving up the effortless while prizing what is lacking or difficult to obtain. She saw him entering a life of abnegation that she would advise him to avoid.

"Is not your birthplace," she asked, "covered with jungles full of wild Indians? Is that why you chose this vocation, so that you may go back there and civilize them?"

At the risk of offending her, the last thing in the world he wanted to do, he laughed at such a quaint notion. If she only knew how much he wanted to please her, she would not have been so annoyed by his mirth.

"Have I said something droll?" she inquired.

"It's been three centuries since there were any Indians in the Antilles," he said, "though some of the people there now are no less wild for being of Spanish descent."

"You must pardon my ignorance," she said. "I was told there were wild Indians in America still."

"America is a very large place," he explained, "There are none in Puerto Rico, nor on the other islands of the Antilles, or none labeled as such."

"They've been assimilated you mean?"

"I suppose one might say that," he answered.

She led the way back into the house, more of a maze than the garden whose pattern from a distance he discerned; he followed without knowing their destination. The structure so large that one might easily lose one's way among the rooms and corridors adorned with antique furniture and portraits of ancestors hanging on the walls, constant reminders to the inhabitants of the traditions to which they were heirs and prisoners. "Are you in a hurry to get somewhere?" he asked, noting her pace almost a canter for which he saw no obvious reason.

"If we hurry we might lose our shadow," she said, but he did not immediately understand. She tilted her head back slightly in the direction from which they had come and from which seemingly she was trying to escape. Indeed, on glancing back, he became aware of the figure to whom he had grown accustomed and had forgotten, the maiden aunt who made herself useful in the household by playing the role of chaperone. To achieve her purpose as a deterrent to indiscretion, she tried to remain visible as well as inconspicuous.

Rodrigo considered the precaution wasted on him, having no desire to transgress in any way. But the young lady was being watched too, and indeed she might be the one being considered a risk rather than he, a novel thought for someone rather ignorant of young ladies' emotions.

The maiden aunt, having been rambunctious herself when young, persisted fully aware of her niece's proclivity for mischief. The unhappy woman, partly blaming her present conjugal state, or lack of it, on the excesses of her youthful exuberance, and wishing to safeguard her niece from a similar fate, attempted to fulfill her role with exactitude.

On that occasion, either because she judged Rodrigo impervious to her niece's wiles or because her rheumatism was acting up, rendering quick movement inadvisable, the chaperone found herself at a crossroad of rooms without a clue as to which way the fleeing couple had turned. She availed herself of a settee, conveniently at hand, to rest and regroup, aware of her accountability for keeping an eye on the enemy cavalry that had, for the moment, given her the slip but whose trail no doubt she would pick up again with some astute reconnoitering. She wondered what kind of person required a house of such design, and for what purpose; doubtlessly, the original inhabitant was an aficionado of intrigue bent on having an abode that exemplified the ins and outs of his character. Man's vanity has no bounds, and the builder of this house, one of her ancestors, had been no exception.

"We've lost her," Isabela said, hoping that development would please him.

She had stopped her flight abruptly, and he, following, had taken one step more than he would have normally, so that for an instant, he stood so close to her that their noses might have touched had he but inclined his head by a hair's breadth. He would have immediately escaped from the awkward moment by stepping back, but she grabbed his hand distracting him from the necessary action. She brought the hand up against her cheek, warm in contrast to his hand from which the blood had drained, perhaps all going to his ears that felt on fire.

What happened next became a permanent source of agony. He managed finally to convince himself that flight had been the right course of action, but the less than graceful method of execution troubled him. Form had been the last thing on his mind. He wished he had been polite if not suave, but even good manners had eluded him in the panic of the moment. He merely turned and ran, that is to say, escaped at a faster pace than normal to exit such a house, faster than the pace at which moments before he and Isabela had fled from the austere aunt whom he startled on his way out. From the look on her face the lady feared that she had failed at her vaunted task, but she took heart in the fact that too short a time had elapsed since she had lost sight of the pair for anything of serious consequence to have transpired. It was a false conclusion, but an explanation of the occurrence would have failed to alter her opinion. Upon arriving at the side of her niece, who was still recovering from the rebuff, the aunt rhetorically inquired, "What have you done?"

"Nothing at all," the young woman ingenuously replied. "I didn't know men were so skittish."

The image of Isabela became forever imprinted in some mysterious corner of Father Rodrigo's mind. Why Carmen Gutierez had evoked the memory of Isabela, except for the obvious resemblance of the smiles, remained a question without an answer.

That encounter with Isabela seemed a long time in the past, and at the moment he had to deal with Carmen. "Is the father of your child in a position to marry you?" he inquired, compelled to ask in his role as representative of the Church, though he well knew that his compatriots often deemed a ceremony in front of a priest superfluous.

"He's not married already, if that's what you mean," she said.

"What then?"

"You'll have to ask him, won't you?"

"I should bring it up then?"

"If you wish."

"And you, what do you want?"

"Only God's will," she said.

"And whom shall I speak to?" he asked.

"To your friend," she simply answered.

He was for the moment silenced, and she walked down the aisle towards the light of the exit.

JOHN WALKER ARRIVED on the island while it was still a Spanish possession. He learned to speak Spanish, and he bought a plot of land, but he never built a house on it. His land bordered Eduardo Rincon's along the stream where Eduardo had stumbled on Carmen bathing as he ruminated how to get the American to sell him the land to plant coffee.

Although the son of a New York banker who provided him with an ample allowance, on the island John Walker worked for an exporting company. Had he stayed home, he might have worked in his father's bank or in some other firm to which his family name would have smoothed his path, or he might have engaged in some endeavor unrelated to business. As a student at Princeton, he had contemplated becoming a missionary and traveling over the world Christianizing heathens, but he soon realized that he had no special desire for missionary work, and only the romanticism of foreign places had attracted him. He ended up on a Caribbean island serendipitously. After a spree one night in New York, he and some fellow students woke on a freighter whose first port of call was Mayaguez. The days at sea sobered them up sufficiently to make them regret the trip, except John who, once on the island, decided to stay. A visit to the American resident commissioner resolved the small problem of obtaining a visa, and a telegram from his father introduced him to the Alicante Exporting Company in Mayaguez.

A lanky young man with sand-colored hair that fell limply over his forehead, John Walker stooped slightly, trying to minimize his stature, an act of diffidence to the world, as if that would make him less conspicuous. He would have done better in the Midwest where his looks would have been common. On a Caribbean island, he stood out, but the sight of him in Mayaguez soon grew to be familiar and only occasionally elicited comments from strangers.

On his excursions into the interior, he fell in love with the land, and as is often the case with men, he wished to own what he loved, even if only a small portion of it. After some inquiries as to how he might go about buying some land in the interior, he was directed to *Licenciado* Don Altimo Ramirez for assistance in bringing that plan to fruition. On that mission, having taken the day off from his duties at the Alicante Exporting Company, John Walker presented himself at the office of Don Altimo Ramirez in San Geronimo.

"I wish to buy land," he said to the *licenciado*.

Although intimately involved in the buying and selling of land, that declaration startled Don Altimo. The statement seemed odd coming from the person standing before him, a foreigner. Don Altimo had dealt with foreigners before, European *hacienderos* plentiful enough to make them commonplace. This one was not a European, but that was not the source of the enigma. He had a quality of character that made his words incongruous and made him incompatible with ownership of land in the locality. There was nothing at all tropical about John Walker. Had he wanted to buy acres in Antarctica or in the Sahara desert, Don Altimo would have thought the idea perfectly normal. Had he met John Walker under different circumstances, Don Altimo would have been hard put to associate either coldness or aridness with this mild-mannered person. That, too, seemed to be a façade, another puzzling aspect of the image projected by the young man. He seemed to have been drawn with transparent watercolors and had an overall washed-out look to him, but Don Altimo sensed that, at his core, John Walker was an iron rod.

"You have a property in mind?" Don Altimo asked in some confusion, making John Walker uncertain whether he heard a question or a declaration.

"The specifications, yes," said John Walker, "but not the particular."

"Ah," said Don Altimo, an exclamation he used to gain time to decipher his thoughts that like string once unwound from the spool had the mysterious propensity to become entangled.

"You wish to go into agriculture."

John Walker mulled that statement over for a moment and broke into a wide grin, which Altimo Ramirez interpreted as his having found the suggestion humorous, when in fact, the smile at the moment signaled distress.

"Oh, no," said the young man, "I have no inclination in that direction. I merely wish to buy land."

"To build a house on," Don Altimo suggested trying to fathom the young man's motivation. A direct question had not yet occurred to him. That would have been most efficient, but too much to expect from a practitioner of a profession predicated on making the simple complicated and the clear obscure, though he had been known to make the complex appear simple when that suited his purpose.

Thoroughly perplexed by the appearance of the young American, an unfamiliar type, Altimo relegated him to the category of land speculator and began to search his memory for something he might have missed about the current state of realty in San Geronimo. Up to that minute, there had been nothing to alert him to a possible change in land values in the vicinity. Despite his pose, he welcomed the possibility that the American, privy to some knowledge that had yet to reach San Geronimo, allowed him the good fortune to be first to get wind of it. He congratulated himself on being astute enough to recognize opportunity when it walked in his front door, even if it came in the guise of a very strange person indeed.

"No," John Walker said. "I really haven't thought that far ahead. I have an impulse to do this. It seems like a good thing."

"You might do better to invest your money somewhere else. The land around here is unlikely to appreciate significantly." Don Altimo felt duty bound to say, since, to the best of his knowledge, that was the case, although he also believed that the American, despite his youth, would have known that if he were, as Altimo suspected, a speculator. Nevertheless, punctilious in the performance of his duty, the minute that young man opened his mouth, Don Altimo assigned to him the role of client, owed the full benefit of advice even if no fiduciary arrangement had yet been reached. John Walker insisted on buying, and Altimo Ramirez took that as a harbinger of speculative activity.

John Walker bought land adjacent to Eduardo Rincon's, but that transaction had transpired at a time when Eduardo, still in the process of buying out his brothers, lacked the resources to acquire the land beyond the stream. When he approached Don Altimo with the proposal to buy it, the attorney recalled the day John Walker had entered his office for the first time.

"The land is worth more now than it was a few years ago before the American bought it. He got it for practically nothing. Had I known you were interested, I would have alerted you."

"I wasn't interested then," Eduardo said. "It's undeveloped land. Who wants it besides me?"

"The American," Don Altimo said. "He's sentimentally attached to it, as if he had been born on it. A very strange case, he lives in Mayaguez, but he comes once a month to walk on the land."

"To walk on it?"

"Yes, he rides out there to walk on his property. I asked him once why he does that, and he said he likes to be close to nature. I said that he could do that near Mayaguez, but he answered that the experience gratified him more on his own land."

"I understand," Eduardo said.

"Do you?" Don Altimo asked raising his eyebrows in surprise. Eduardo's understanding perplexed him more than John Walker's behavior. The attorney, willing to grant Eduardo a great deal of latitude in the fathoming of business matters, viewed the case of the American as falling into some other category in which Eduardo lacked experience. Nevertheless, Don Altimo decided to humor the *haciendero* on the off chance that he might be right, as often happened when dealing with matters that seemed arcane.

"I must see him," Eduardo said.

"I will arrange it then," Don Altimo responded. He sat back in his chair pleased with himself, as if introducing the two had been his idea, and the meeting would result in some historical event for which he might, albeit privately, take credit.

Eduardo decided against so formal an arrangement and opted to meet John Walker out in the open as if by chance.

"He usually comes on the last Saturday of each month," Don Altimo said. "And he takes the North Road to avoid the river."

"Why is that?" Eduardo asked.

"I don't know," Don Altimo said. "He may have a fear of bridges."

"He's cautious then. That bridge needs repair."

"He did make a formal complaint to the town council about the condition of the bridge, which as a land owner he has a right to do."

"Of course," Eduardo said. He had decided already to have the bridge repaired at his own expense. The municipality would do it eventually, but that would be a long wait indeed.

On the last Saturday of the month, Eduardo set out to waylay the unsuspecting Mr. Walker, who, true to form, trekked that day on the North Road, more a path on which two horses might pass abreast but not three. From a distance, he observed John Walker's indifferent horsemanship, but Eduardo credited him with valiant effort, understanding that not everyone melded naturally with the animals. By habit Eduardo judged a man on his strengths rather than his weaknesses. He found that advantageous, binding men to him ignorant of what attracted them.

Eduardo waited for John Walker to pass and came up behind him as if they were traveling in the same direction by chance. John Walker already knew that the manners of the country required on such an occasion more conversation than customary in his native country, and so he accepted that Eduardo, disposed to chatter, let his horse fall in step. John Walker's eyes a pale blue, their refusing to melt in the heat of the day made them seem a wonder of nature.

"You're a long way from home," Eduardo said after they had exchanged customary pleasantries.

"Mayaguez is not so far," the American said.

"I meant the United States," Eduardo said.

"Ah, that home," said John Walker. "I suppose that's far, but not as far as it might be had I gone somewhere else, China for example."

"Do you want to go there?"

"No, I'm just saying there are more distant places."

"Is your aim to be far from home?"

"No," said John Walker, "just to be comfortable."

"I take it then that home is not a comfortable place," Eduardo said.

"I can't really say that," John Walker replied. "I came here by accident, but once here, the place seemed to fit me like a worn-in set of clothes. The feeling surprised me, as if I had been born here, though it is nothing at all like the place where I was born. I wonder whether the Hindus are right about reincarnation, and I lived here in a previous life."

"I know nothing about Hindus," Eduardo said, "All my life I've been a Catholic, although I can't say that I've been a exemplary one."

"I can say the same about being a Methodist," said John Walker, "but that's neither here nor there regarding reincarnation. I have a definite feeling that if I ever lived before, this was the very place."

"We must consider you a native then, though you hardly look it, but one can't go by appearances. You're like the prodigal son returned home or the one lost sheep out of the hundred. We must all rejoice that you're finally home."

"For an indifferent Catholic you have a remarkably biblical turn of phrase," said John Walker with a grin.

"It's inevitable," Eduardo said. "Here one picks it up merely by breathing."

"Yes, the public character of religion is very striking here."

"Tell me something," said Eduardo Rincon. "In your previous life, you weren't a horse trainer, were you?"

This time John Walker had to laugh out loud before he answered. "No, I don't suppose so, but how can you tell?"

"I have an eye for those things," Eduardo responded.

"I think we might get on very well indeed," John Walker said.

"It's a wonder that we never met before, seeing that we're neighbors," Eduardo remarked.

"The fault is mine," said John Walker, "I don't suppose that I've been very neighborly, though I haven't meant to be unfriendly."

Eduardo Rincon hesitated for a moment to reflect on that statement and to consider whether John Walker was asking for an enumeration of the ways in which friendliness is gauged. Indeed, one could begin by considering the barbed wire fence which John Walker had erected around his property, which would have been understandable had he any cattle to contain, in which case, the fence would have been a boon to his neighbors who would have appreciated the consideration of having their crops protected from scavenging livestock. Conversely, had he any crops to protect from other people's cattle, the fence would have seem reasonable enough, but the absence of that condition added to the mystery of his motivation and gave rise to hostile speculation. The fence, an inconvenience to the *campesinos* who scavenged for firewood and wild fruit, pre-disposed them to attribute sinister motives to its owner.

Ignorant of the negative reaction his fence provoked, John Walker continued under the impression that he provided a necessary and desirable service, something for which, had he been in the habit of thinking in those terms, he deserved praise rather than condemnation. Actually, he gave no thought at all to what public response to his actions might be. He acted out of an inner sense of responsibility, and he felt responsible for delineating the boundaries of his property to alleviate any anxiety that an ambiguity about the matter might cause to the world in general. He had no one specifically in mind and did not imagine that any one in the vicinity thought about him. He persisted extremely conscious of the land and its beauty but oblivious of the people who lived on it. To call this callousness or selfishness on John Walker's part would be an error. The people on the land remained invisible to him, as long as he continued invisible to himself, thinking that he made no more impression on the world than the world made on him.

"We can easily remedy that," Eduardo said, meaning the state of their acquaintance, too soon to call it a friendship. He had an inkling that he had stumbled on a more complex person than he had anticipated. John Walker appeared to be more than an opportunity to acquire desirable land. What more remained vague, but the sense verged on the overwhelming, a force of nature with no remedy, like the edge of an approaching hurricane. In this case, however, the sense of impending disaster was absent, and only the awe of enormity loomed obvious. The benign quality of the premonition became an enigma to Eduardo, running counter to his natural inclination to be suspicious of foreigners, especially one whose manner seemed incongruous to the setting, but he had long before resolved to trust his intuitions, a habit to which he owed much of his success.

"I'll depend on you then to show me the way," John Walker said in good humor.

Pleasantly surprised to find Altimo's description of John Walker, if not erroneous, at least woefully inadequate, the door on which Eduardo had resolved to knock swung open more easily than he had expected. The young American possessed a subtle charm that had escaped the lawyer or that had been beyond his verbal ability to convey. The former was more likely, Don Altimo being an exemplary member of his profession in his ability to churn out words, if not immediately to the point, bound sooner or later to hit the mark by consequence of volume.

The encounter between Eduardo and John Walker took place in December just before the Christmas holidays, providing an opportunity for Eduardo to invite the American to partake in an island custom bound to be of interest to him, as well as serve the purpose of introducing him to his neighbors in a jovial setting. The invitation also conformed to the general chessboard principle of making each move bear against more than one square.

John Walker accepted the invitation without hesitation, having heard about the extravagant celebration of the season in the hinterland. He didn't suspect his host of a motive other than conviviality, a feature that Eduardo possessed in an abundance bordering on the prodigious. This quality in the natives fascinated the American. To him, it seemed to differ in some essential way from what might be considered in his compatriots the equivalent attribute. He had yet to discover its mercurial nature or, rather, its ability to coexist with darker traits. That condition to a native failed to constitute a contradiction, but to an American from a Puritan tradition, it seemed at least an oddity.

"It's not the same in the country as it is in the city," Eduardo said to his new friend, referring to the celebration that started on Christmas Eve and continued until the day of the Kings, twelve days and nights of partying more or less, punctuated by occasional breaks for sleep, because not even the most inveterate reveler could go twelve days without sleep. Eduardo became a lavish host, his *batey* the scene of spectacular fireworks on Christmas Eve or *Noche Buena*, followed by eating, drinking, and dancing until midnight mass. On New Year's Eve there were fireworks again and on the eve of Three Kings Day, *paranda*. The band of revelers from the immediate vicinity gathered at Eduardo's *batey*. Thirty to forty men and women, mostly young people, congregated on horseback. Some carried musical instruments; the *paranderos* providing the entertainment while the host provided the food and drink.

"And now what?" John Walker asked once he had mounted a horse that Eduardo had lent him because his own had gone lame that same day.

"Now we sing for our supper," Eduardo replied. "At each stop we ask for *aguinaldo*. That is to say, we demand in good humor to be treated to a lavish feast, which the host is more than honored to supply."

Sitting on his horse, Eduardo led another fully-saddled animal by the bridle.

"And is it customary to have an extra horse?" John Walker inquired.

Eduardo laughed and explained that they would pick up a

friend on the way, and John Walker understood everything when they stopped by the house of Juaquin Gutierez and Carmen emerged. She swung into the saddle expertly without any help from anyone. Despite the already darkening sky, John Walker judged her by far the most beautiful woman in the cavalcade and perhaps the most beautiful woman he had ever seen.

Doña Andrea also came out of the house to wish Eduardo and his friends a good Kings Day. Doña Andrea exhorted Carmen to moderation, though she knew such words were wasted on the young.

"A good Kings Day to you," said Eduardo to the good lady, "and don't you worry about Carmen. She'll be home safe and sound before the sun comes up."

Doña Andrea took that for its worth, but restrained from expressing her opinion. Don Juaquin stayed in the house for fear of being uncharitable, an unforgivable transgression during the festive season. Better to pretend to be away from home, even if Eduardo knew otherwise. The fox getting into the hen house sometimes inevitable, still Juaquin remained reluctant to acquiesce.

The events of the night fascinated John Walker, the whole experience for him novel. Although, in his country, the custom of caroling involved going from house to house, the resemblance ended there. *Paranda* was a raucous traveling party, each host more extravagant than the previous in providing all manner of festive food while the guests repaid with exuberant music both traditional and improvisational to which everyone danced. Enhanced by the holiday spirit, good manners were sincerely expressed, and John Walker was treated at every stop like an old and close friend.

Eduardo had made expecting the unexpected a tenet of his life, but liking John Walker more than he had anticipated surprised him nevertheless. John's sincerity, and the young man's ability to poke fun at himself fascinated Eduardo, who first took the absence of bravura in the American as a lack of will, but he soon realized his error. The American wanted to be unobtrusive, but he failed. His genuine love for the land made scheming to wrest it from him difficult for Eduardo.

"Your land is good for growing coffee," Eduardo told John.

"You think I should become a farmer?"

"Not at all," Eduardo said, "but you do not use the land, and it goes to waste. I'll buy it from you to plant coffee."

"You do not understand my use of the land," John Walker said. "I like the wildness of it."

"Coffee grows in the shade. The land does not have to be cleared. It will look just as wild as it does now, only it will produce a crop. A cash crop is a good thing, and you will always be welcomed to enjoy the wildness of it."

"But it will not be mine."

"There is another alternative," Eduardo said. "You can lease me land with an option for me to buy if ever you decide to sell. That way I can plant the coffee, and the land will still be yours."

"I don't know," John Walker said, "I'll have to think about it."

The Three Kings had provided Eduardo with the opportunity to present his need to John Walker, as much of a gift as Eduardo had expected. After presenting his idea, he returned to the festive mood, his attention fixed on Carmen who provided the illusion of a world without schemes. In John Walker, a seed was planted, and though on that night of the Three Kings he ignored it, or rather had not yet become aware of it, later it grew in him, and the result of a night he had spent in festivity perplexed him. Owning a piece of land in a country he could not call his own became uncomfortable. Yet, while he lived, he would not give up the land, so the pleasure it provided became a burden he had to bear for the rest of his life.

In Manila Bay, the Spanish navy had been routed, according to the newspaper read aloud in the cantina in Comerio by Antonio Rodriguez, one of the few patrons of that establishment who could read and write. Antonio Rodriguez would write a letter for anyone for only one bit per page. At the cantina, he read the paper without charge, partly from a sense of civic duty but mostly to be the center of attention. He fancied himself an orator of some talent, a public figure akin to a theatrical star, a pose more apt to draw ridicule than praise, except that reading and writing were skills in short supply and served to maintain his status among his acquaintances.

"What else does it say?"

"It says that an American warship in San Juan harbor bombarded the city on the 12th of May, that is to say, two days ago."

"What? Are you saying San Juan is destroyed?"

A wave of patriotism surged through the listeners at the suggestion of demolished buildings in the capital, although most of them had never been there and had no true picture of the city on which to base their image of destruction.

"No, not at all," continued Antonio Rodriguez with affected impatience after a sufficient pause to add dramatic texture to the account in the newspaper. "They fired over the Ballaja garrison and only a few buildings in the city were damaged."

"And the soldiers in the garrison, what did they do?"

"They shit in their pants, that's what," someone replied to which everyone else snickered, except for Antonio Rodriguez, who wished to maintain a sense of decorum.

"There is no mention in the paper of defecation," he said.

"I can vouch for that," said Ernesto Rojas, known in Comerio for his practical jokes, a young man always jovial and ready to engage in any activity that promised to produce laughter. Although everyone feared being the butt, Ernesto's contagious good cheer inevitably resulted in his companions abandoning their discretion. He had little respect for veracity, although the more charitable said only that his imagination avoided contact with facts. The last person from whom anyone would seek testimony on a historical matter, his vouching for anything immediately seemed a preamble to a joke. His usual intent, always to entertain rather than to deceive, led his audience to anticipate a facetious anecdote, but this time he spoke seriously. "I was in San Juan two days ago," he said. "Everything in the paper is true," he continued, "except the part about the soldiers shitting in their pants."

"That wasn't in the paper," said Antonio Rodriguez exasperated at having lost the limelight, the dry facts gleaned from the newspaper no match for an eyewitness report, especially one coming from Ernesto Rojas, who even if he refrained from embellishing the account with fanciful details had the advantage of a jokester's personality. "And anyway how would you know what went on in the garrison?"

"I was there," he said.

This taxed the credulity of the listeners. Only under arrest could they imagine Ernesto in the garrison, but had that been the case, in all likelihood, he would still be there. "Why did they let you go?" someone asked. Everyone there was familiar with the Civil Guard's arbitrary manner of exercising power; no one asked the reason for the arrest.

"I wasn't arrested," Ernesto said. The story became more incredible by the minute. "I went there with the delegation."

A delegation sounded like an official body of some kind, and how or why Ernesto would be included in one remained beyond the imagination of even the most gullible. The tale seemed to be headed toward the outrageous, increasing the possibility of it being amusing. Only a delegation of liars would include Ernesto, and why one would be convened in San Juan on the day of the bombardment became a curiosity.

"And what delegation was that?" asked Antonio Rodriquez.

"A delegation of *peninsulares* went to the garrison to demand that the army defend the honor of Spain. I bumped into them only by chance. After the bombardment, I was the only person on the street and trying to get out of the city in case the Americans started firing again."

"This delegation wanted the Civil Guard to fire back at the American ships?"

"Well, I don't know," Ernesto said, "and neither did the captain who came out to meet with them. I think they wanted to be protected against those who might welcome the invasion."

*

Two days before, on the 10th of May, one of the smaller ships of the eleven vessel American flotilla had ventured closer to the city defenses. Through his spyglass, Captain Rivero could not make out the name of the ship that refused to show its colors. The captain nevertheless ordered the batteries to open fire, signaling to the Americans the intent of the Spanish to put up a vigorous defense. The intruder withdrew without returning fire, and a cheer went up from the men at the battery. They applauded prematurely. The Americans would land with a massive force against which the island defenders could muster no more than eight thousand men. Lacking information as to where the Americans would land, and not knowing whether they would take more than a one-prong approach, the eight thousand Spanish troops were not concentrated in any one spot, but the bulk of them prepared to defend the capital.

Governor Macias and his senior military officers assumed the landing would be in the north. They reasoned that the mountains would impede invasion from the south, the Americans wanting to avoid getting bogged down in the passes where a few Spanish troops could hold off a larger column. The American commander, General Nelson Miles, was a veteran of the American Civil War and had fought the Indians out West. It sounded reasonable that he would follow that simple strategy.

Captain Rivero, a native of the island, received his military education in Spain, from where his parents had immigrated to the Caribbean. Like most Creoles, he had mixed loyalty and considered the treatment of the island by the mother country as less than just. Immediately before the war, after his arrest and imprisonment for political activities, he sought a discharge from the army, but Governor Macias, aware of the strong possibility that the threatening hostilities would become actual, offered him a promotion and responsibility for all the military buildings in San Juan.

From his headquarters at San Cristobal Castle, Captain Rivero ordered the firing on the USS Yale, the first shot in the conflict in Puerto Rico. Two days later, the American flotilla bombarded the city for two hours, with the Ballaya barracks the primary target and not San Cristobal Castle, from where the island defenses had fired. The American shelling demolished a large section of the eastern wall of the barracks and poked holes in the facade. The church of St. Joseph, unfortunately situated close to the military installation, was a casualty. An errant shell penetrated the stucco facade and wreaked havoc in the nave. No. 21 San Sebastian Street, a civilian dwelling, also sustained damage; luckily, the occupants managed to escape.

To the civilian population, the two hours of bombardment seemed interminable, but the military judged it to be ineffectual, although the four soldiers killed might have had a different opinion on the matter had they been able to express it. The civilians naturally linked the naval bombardment to the attack on the Yale, so their fear and frustration focused on Captain Rivero, believing that if he had refrained from shelling the American ship, the Americans would have been content to blockade the harbor without firing. This thinking compelled them to attempt to petition the governor to relieve the captain of his command. Four citizen leaders first went to the governor's residence, la Fortaleza, where he kept them waiting for an hour before he sent word that he was too busy to see them that day, that if their business was urgent, they should return the following day, but that laboring under a state of emergency, he would prefer civilian matters be deferred for the time being.

"We are civilians, that's true," said Don Rodrigo to the governor's secretary Lieutenant Marias, who had delivered the governor's message, "but we have come on a matter concerning the military. We are troubled by the reckless behavior of a certain officer that puts the civilian population at risk."

A young man who still had Romantic notions about his military career, the present conflict his first service under fire, Lieutenant Marias, even though an adjutant to the governor rather than an officer of the line, thought of himself in heroic terms. Duty required him to take a criticism of the army personally. He visibly stiffened and became more formal as soon as he heard what business these gentlemen had come to discuss with the governor. Lieutenant Marias immediately recognized the officer in question, Captain Rivero having become an instant hero among the younger officers, mortified by the failure to challenge the American affront of blockading the harbor. Under the circumstances, none of the Spanish warships in the bay in any condition to sally out with any hope of success, and honor a concept of paramount importance, Captain Rivero's action took on symbolic dimensions.

Lieutenant Marias instinctively gestured as if to remove a glove from his hand, which supposedly he would have flung in Don Rodrigo's face. Two powerful circumstances prevented such rash course of action. First, he was not wearing gloves at the moment. Second, a credit to his discretion, he realized that being attached to the governor's staff required him to refrain from melodramatic gestures that might embarrass the governor, whose forgiving nature might be overtaxed and whose position in Spanish society made his influence on Lieutenant Marias's career inevitable, regardless of whether the young man stayed in the army.

"It seems to me," said the lieutenant, assuming an air of superciliousness, that he thought appropriate in addressing civilians, "that military matters should be left to those who are trained to perform them."

Don Rodrigo, in turn equally sure that incompetence riddled the army or matters would not be in such dire straits, noted the lieutenant's tone. Was the governor aware of the threat from within, an issue more serious than having American warships at the mouth of the harbor, a threat being fueled by the irresponsible actions of Captain Rivero?

Don Rodrigo, was a Spaniard whose loyalty was not in doubt, but the same could not be said of some of his neighbors, who considered themselves *Borinqueños* rather than Spaniards and who saw no reason to put their lives in jeopardy for the sake of an empire that, even in the best of times, had failed to protect their interests. Though in the capital overt violence against *peninsulares* had yet to erupt, unmistakable hostility made reasonable the supposition that as soon as certain elements took heart from the presence of the Americans, the violence breaking out in the countryside against Spanish and foreign *hacienderos* might, with little provocation, erupt in the cities as well.

Don Rodrigo tried to explain all of this to the lieutenant, who listened with growing sympathy toward his fellow countryman. But at that point, Don Rodrigo lost all the ground he had gained by saying, "And wasn't Captain Rivero recently in prison for subversive activities?"

To question the honor and loyalty of a fellow officer, one who had shown no hesitation in confronting the enemy, incensed Lieutenant Marias. "You're fortunate, sir," he replied, "that you're speaking to me and not to the governor. He would have you in irons. If you have an accusation to make against the captain, I suggest that you be man enough to make it to his face."

Don Rodrigo who likewise lacked a glove also lacked a fiery temper, but his manhood had been called into question in front of his delegation, and although none of the other men there would have been able to stand up to the lieutenant, Don Rodrigo felt compelled to respond in some face-saving manner. "If you think that I am afraid to confront the captain, you are sadly mistaken," he said, knowing that the weakness of the reply had to be compensated with action. "And in fact, I will take my appeal directly to the captain."

The lieutenant noted that the accusation had become an "appeal." He gave Don Rodrigo a contemptuous look, unceremoniously turned his back on the civilians and proceeded to leave the room.

Upon leaving la Fortaleza, the other members of the delegation naturally assumed that their business for the day had concluded. None of them seriously considered that Don Rodrigo meant what he said about confronting Captain Rivero that same day or any other day. At the end of the Nineteenth Century, dueling still persisted in the officer corps of the Spanish army, an indication of the state of mind in which they entered the war and the shock at realizing that gallantry insufficiently compensated for the lack of modern weaponry.

In 1898 Alexander Dumas was still the most popular author in the Spanish speaking world. Every officer in the Spanish army looking in the mirror saw, more or less, the image of d'Artangnan or of Edmond Dumont, Count of Monte Cristo. Dumas may have had more influence on military history than is commonly supposed. Even sixteen years later, the prevailing ethos among his compatriots in the French army pushed élan as the paramount component of a fighting force, a quality they believed they possessed sufficiently to contain the Germans, a belief that led them to the brink of disaster.

Aware of the propensity of officers to settle disputes by dueling, but his judgement clouded by rage at having been insulted by a mere boy in uniform, Don Rodrigo insisted that the delegation walk across the city to San Cristobal Castle, Captain Rivero's command post. Don Rodrigo's companions tried to dissuade him by pointing out that the captain had no power to remove himself from his post. "He's only a captain. What can he do for us? Better to speak to the governor," emerged as the consensus.

Don Rodrigo would not listen. If he thought himself a coward, he would be unable to emerge from his house the next day. He had to make some gesture on which to pin his self-respect. On the trek across the city, they ran into Ernesto Rojas walking in the opposite direction, toward the bay, hoping to catch a ferry to the mainland. He was unaware that ferry service had been discontinued for the day after one of the boats crossing from Cataño had come under fire from the Americans.

Ernesto effusively greeted the four gentlemen, although they were obviously men of a different social class and people with whom generally he would have little contact. But these were extraordinary times. Artillery shells flying overhead and landing randomly throughout the city distorted social perspectives in ways barely imaginable in normal times. So felt the four gentlemen, or rather three of them, for the fourth seemed to be preoccupied with other matters and anxious to get moving again. His companions considered running into Ernesto a piece of good luck, the reason a mystery to Ernesto, who nevertheless assented to their proposal that he accompany them to San Cristobal Castle.

Ernesto failed to grasp the reason for the visit. To him, his new friends seemed to believe that the commander of that fortification bombarded the city. This was a puzzle to Ernesto who was certain that the Americans were the culprits. The idea crossed his mind that despite their attire these four might be escapees from the insane asylum near El Morro. The bombardment might have damaged that building allowing inmates to escape. However, his curiosity to see the inside of the fort, along with the thrill of arriving there as a member of an important delegation, outweighed his fears. He judged that if the four were indeed sane, they must be important to believe that they would gain access to the fort during the crisis.

In view of their reason for attaching him to their party, even someone of sounder judgment might have entertained Ernesto's suspicions about the sanity of his new acquaintances. They believed that they would elicit a more sympathetic response from Captain Rivero if the delegation included someone from that segment of society they thought he championed. Most certainly a Creole, and despite the fact that they had found him roaming about San Juan, Ernesto seemed a *jibaro*. If they could get him to support their point of view, whatever ire their visit might draw from the captain might be mitigated sufficiently to avoid a disastrous confrontation between him and Don Rodrigo. Ernesto seemed simple minded enough to be malleable, and he did nothing to dissuade them from that view.

At San Cristobal, soldiers toiled to clear the debris from shells that found their targets and damaged a cannon, at the moment being dismantled from its carriage, presumably to be repaired and reinstalled as soon as possible. The wounded had been removed from the yard into an interior room of the fort that served as an impromptu infirmary, but blood was still visible on the paving stones. "There's the blood of patriots," said Ernesto Rojas to his new friends, who merely stared at the stains on the stones and said nothing. They had no way of knowing whether the blood indicated more than a wound.

Even Don Rodrigo realized that this was the wrong time to be there. He had not expected to be admitted into the fort when he had proposed the visit. When he embarked on the trek across town from the governor's residence, Don Rodrigo's plan was vague. At the moment, he realized that he had wanted to create a scene at the gate for the benefit of his fellow delegates, and then retire in indignation, after showing his willingness to confront the captain but denied the opportunity.

To their surprise, the gate of the fort flew open without delay, as if their arrival had been expected. In consternation, the original four wondered whether Captain Rivero, having received word from Lieutenant Marias, had decided to lure them into a trap. The official military couriers traveled about town on bicycles. One of them would have had sufficient time to get to San Cristobal long before the delegates who, besides traveling on foot, had stopped to recruit Ernesto. The fact that they had committed no crime failed to allay their fear, since even in peacetime the island's military lightly regarded civil liberties. In time of war they vanished altogether.

Ernesto Rojas, ignorant of the intentions that brought his companions to the spot, remained the only lighthearted one among them. He had detached himself from the party to talk with some of the men from the volunteer brigade, a considerable number manning the batteries as auxiliaries for the duration of the conflict. They were mostly shipyard workers who maintained the ships of the Spanish navy that put into the port of San Juan. They were working people like himself, and he did not hesitate to ask them about what happened in the fort during the bombardment, especially about the bloody stones that had yet to be washed. The captain had already instructed that water be fetched for that purpose, but the order had yet to be carried out.

"Ave Maria, it was hell here, shells bursting all over the place," said one of the volunteers, barely old enough to shave. He believed that the battle would be fun, but once the bombardment began, he reconsidered.

Ernesto began to gather as much information as possible, already envisioning the notoriety that would accrue to him back in Comerio when he retold the tale as if he had been an eyewitness. If necessary, he would supply details of his own to enhance the account, but he understood the advantage of having a basis of truth so that credibility might be bolstered by some agreement with competing reports.

"How many were killed?" he asked.

"Here no one was killed outright," the young gunner said, "but Martin Cepena's arm was blown clear off. That's his blood right there."

"A devil of a sight that must have been," Ernesto said.

"I never saw anything like it in my life," the boy said, "It made me throw up."

"Get on," said another man, "you were throwing up the whole time the bombs were flying."

"Martin's arm coming off made me barf," the boy insisted.

"Sure," said the man winking at Ernesto.

The boy ignored the ribbing, assured of the good opinion of his comrades just for having stayed at his post. The teasing normal, his youth made him vulnerable, and they would have found something else to tease him about even if his stomach had been made of iron.

"Martin got knocked over by the force of the blast, but he got right up, and he turned to the captain, standing near him, and said

'Do not fear Captain, I still have one arm.' That's what he said, and he would have kept loading the cannon with one hand if the captain hadn't had him taken away to the infirmary."

"*Eso son cojones*," Ernesto said.

"That's the truth," said the other man. "He'll go down in history, no doubt about it."

"He deserves to," Ernesto said, and he meant it, especially having acquired a story he could tell to good advantage. The arrival of Captain Rivero interrupted Ernesto's conversation with the volunteers, and the gentlemen with whom Ernesto had entered made sure that he joined them to face the officer.

Captain Rivero's demeanor defied expectations. At first glance, only his uniform betrayed that he was a soldier. He had the puffy look of indolence and indulgence that belied the discipline of barrack life. Under the military kepi lurked the incongruity of a moustache on the face of a cherub. His mouth always seemed on the verge of a smile, so how he kept discipline with sternness so alien to his features defied the imagination. It was easier to think of him as a bon vivant flirting with the ladies at a ball than as a commander directing men on a battlefield.

Don Rodrigo and his companions would have immediately abandoned their apprehension, but the captain's well-established military reputation had preceded him. Under the circumstances, the bombardment having ceased, but no telling whether or when it would resume, the captain's affability surprised them even more.

"Ah, gentlemen," he said, "we're all in this together. God willing, we'll get through it with success. Civilians as well as soldiers must do their part." He beamed at them like a schoolboy assured that his team would dominate all the field day competitions.

The members of the delegation began to emerge from their stupor as each realized that the captain had mistaken their party for some other expected committee. The question became whether he should be disabused of his error. They left the decision up to Don Rodrigo, the acknowledged leader, and the one after all who had insisted on facing the captain.

"Yes, God willing," Don Rodrigo agreed. Having the necessity of finding something to do with his hands to relieve his anxiety, he had removed his hat. With both hands, he held the brim of the tightly woven straw object, and his fingers, like going from bead to bead on a rosary, worked their way along the edge. He, too, realized the captain was proceeding under a misapprehension, making withdrawal still possible without running the risk of giving offense, but that option would leave him in a worse predicament than the one that had compelled his visit. "The bombardment was terrible," he said by way of inching up to the subject he had to address.

"It was," the captain agreed, "but it might have been worse. Luckily many of the American shells did not explode. They were badly made or badly prepared for firing. They are not as mighty as they think, these Americans."

"It might have been avoided all together, don't you think, captain, if we had not fired on their ship first?" Don Rodrigo chose his words gingerly, spreading the responsibility all around to avoid singling out the captain. That way, he would mitigate any offense against the officer while still making his point.

"No, they meant to shell us sooner or later. You have to understand the mentality of a soldier. We're at war, and they brought all those ships out here. Why waste an opportunity to fire all those magnificent guns at a real target. One gets tired of shooting at make believe enemies. True, we need not have fired on their ship when we did. It was useless, the ship out of range by then, but it took General Macias more than an hour to decide whether or not to fire."

"It wasn't your decision then?"

"I wanted to fire right away, when the ship was close enough, but I sent to the governor for authorization. The ship didn't show its colors, and the governor was uncertain whether it was an American ship or a British one. It wouldn't do to fire on the British and have them also attack us."

"Why did you fire then, when it was too late?"

"It was the governor's decision. He thought they might show their colors if we fired, and since there was no possibility of hitting them at that point, any international incident would have been minimal."

"It wasn't minimal for us who reaped the consequences."

"The bombardment was inevitable. It had nothing to do with the firing on their ship."

"So you say," commented Don Rodrigo emboldened by the captain's friendly demeanor.

Though he wanted to be cordial to his guests, the captain tired of the subject. A change came over his features that indicated the exhaustion of his good humor. "It's good of you gentlemen to show your support for the fighting men," he said by way of bringing the conversation to where he thought it should be.

Ernesto had remained silent, content to observe the interchange between the captain and Don Rodrigo in the hope of clarifying for himself the still mysterious intent of his new acquaintances. At last he saw his chance to chime in to some advantage. "Of course, we support you 100 percent, captain," he said. "It's a pity that we can't do even more to share with you the ordeal and the glory of the front line."

The sound of his voice discomfited the delegates, who feared that he might say something to give them away, but a violent explosion at the other end of the yard distracted them. A shell that had failed to detonate on impact had chosen that moment to do so. Observing a great deal of smoke and commotion at the site of the blast, the captain rushed off to investigate how much damage had been done.

Don Rodrigo and his cohorts took that opportunity to extricate themselves from their precarious position and made as much haste toward the gate as consistent with dignity. Ernesto Rojas, oblivious of dignity but with an unerring sense of opportunity, saw no reason for delaying his own exit. Too busy to demand a proper farewell, Captain Rivero caught their departure out of the corner of an eye, and recognizing the natural inclination of men to flee from unfamiliar danger, he subdued an instinctive reaction to wish all civilians to hell.

F ROM HIS HOUSE Don Emiliano Gonzago, the mayor of San Geronimo, heard the rumbling of the artillery miles away. Thunder, he first thought, and he went out to the porch to look up at the sky. Odd, not even a hint of a rain cloud on the horizon. Then he recognized the sound of cannon fire, the noise of the battle wafting over the hills.

The Spanish column had arrived the day before and had camped south of town to await the Americans, who had landed at Guanica and were advancing. Colonel Soto, the commander of the detachment, had paid a courtesy call to Don Emiliano to reassure him that the Spanish army stood ready to repel the invaders and that citizens of San Geronimo had nothing to fear, since he and his men would make a further American advance unlikely.

As mayor of San Geronimo, Don Emiliano considered politeness to the colonel a duty, and although it required considerable effort, he punctiliously exhibited all signs of respect. Don Emiliano, a man who had arrived at his position through the exercise of his natural abilities, had enriched himself in the tobacco trade, and he felt an obligation to repay his country for its bounty by becoming a public servant. Known and respected well beyond the jurisdiction of San Geronimo, he received ample information about the movement of the American column as well as its strength. Intelligence from other towns as well as from the countryside flowed to him through his private network of informants. He had taken stock also of the Spanish detachment as it had marched through town to its encampment on the outskirts of San Geronimo, and though the men exhibited high morale, especially the junior officers, he concluded that the colonel's optimism was misplaced. Don Emiliano could have easily accepted the optimism had it been based on self confidence, but he judged the colonel to be a blusterer who had little grasp of the realities of the situation and who attempted to hide that fact, even from himself, by presenting false courage, a game that he had played well enough so far but at that moment for the first time facing the enemy.

"Tomorrow morning I will send a company out to scout," Colonel Soto said to Don Emiliano and to his second in command, Colonel Suau, who had already been designated commander of the rear guard.

Don Emiliano pondered the situation but refrained from voicing an opinion about the wisdom of waiting until the next day to gather information that the colonel should have already obtained—information that Don Emiliano had at his disposal but which he judged useless to share with the colonel. Why the rear guard detachment required the command of a colonel also baffled Don Emiliano, who wondered whether prudent standard procedure called for such a designation, or whether Colonel Soto had already, before gauging the strength of the opposing force, determined the likelihood of a retreat.

Colonel Suau, silent and sullen, stood apart in an ambiguous pose that might have been construed as contempt for the ranking officer. In Don Emiliano's estimation, this configuration contained one colonel too many.

"And what do you think, Colonel Suau?" Don Emiliano queried trying to get a measure of the man.

"We will do our duty, sir," the colonel answered. "That's all that we can promise. The outcome is in God's hands."

A safe answer, Don Emiliano concluded, but he also knew that men seldom invoked God when confident of carrying the day by their own effort.

That conversation had transpired the day before the battle, or rather the skirmish, for the action, in terms of the number of men involved and the casualties that resulted, was minimal, a battle only in the context of the other actions of the war on the island. Colonel Soto, following the plan he had explained to Don Emiliano, sent Captain Jose Torecillas's detachment to feel out the advancing American column. One hundred and twenty regulars from the Sixth Company of the Alfonso VIII battalion and twenty-five irregular volunteers under Captain Juancho Bascaran comprised Torecillas's unit.

About nine o'clock in the morning, Torecillas deployed on Hormiguero Heights, from where he had a view of San Geronimo Road running through the valley formed by the hills of Hormiguero and the Alta Ridge directly opposite on the southwest. Close to midday, the American column, showing no appreciable haste to arrive at San Geronimo, took a two-hour break for lunch. Captain Bascaran's irregulars, deployed closer to the road near a wooden bridge across the Guanajibo River, confronted the vanguard of the American infantry at one thirty in the afternoon.

The twenty-five irregulars had orders only to test the strength of the enemy, so after a brief exchange of fire across the bridge, Bascaran, being confronted with a force much larger than his own, ordered his men to retire. Torecillas, hearing the gunfire, moved his troops to Silva Hill, closer to the road. He instructed his men to take cover and to use white powder to prevent smoke from revealing their exact position, but they had a limited amount of white powder, making that stratagem possible only during the first hour of the battle.

The American cavalry, having been informed of Bascaran's retreat toward Hormiguero Heights, took a detour from the road to investigate what forces the Spanish had in that direction. General Schwan, the American commander, finished his lunch at two o'clock, and hearing the gunfire at the front, he ordered the column, stretched out for some distance along the road, to close ranks. A detachment of American artillery managed to get across the Juanajibo Bridge and deployed to the northeast of Silva Hill. Don Emiliano heard the sound of those cannons eleven miles away in San Geronimo.

*

In Comerio, Eduardo Rincon also heard the guns, and he paused to wonder about the likely outcome of the conflict. He tried to go back to his work, but his thoughts kept returning to scenes of combat. He had never seen a battle between armies, and the thought of it made his heart beat faster. Still a young man, military action had a Romantic aura for him. This might be his only chance to ever see a battle. When would there be another war on this island that he never contemplated leaving? He walked back to the house and ordered his horse brought around.

"Will you be back for supper?" Gregoria asked.

"I may ride all the way to San Geronimo," he answered, "in which case I will spend the night there."

"That's the prudent thing to do," she said. Her age gave her license to speak to him in a motherly tone. She had known his mother, and she saw him come into the world. Gregoria would have kept him from riding in the direction of harm if she could, but she accepted the futility of trying to prevent nature from taking its course. Men naturally did foolish things. Eduardo was more reasonable than most. That much she had to admit, though she would rather on this day that he stayed home. From the kitchen, she brought a small bundle of food, *morcillas* and *yautias* and a mango for dessert, in case he should find himself on the road at suppertime.

When Carmen Gutierez spied him as he rode out of the *batey*, she surmised that he was headed toward San Geronimo Road, toward the cannon fire. If she cut across the copse on the north side, she could intercept him and have a word with him out of sight of anyone else. He might be angry with her, but she would chance that. Anger would be little enough to bear if she could prevent him from riding into danger. She walked quickly to the edge of the field. No one would think anything amiss in her taking a break from work.

Once she reached the trees and was out of sight, she broke into a run. Flushed and breathless when she reached the road, she intercepted him just in time. Had he not been in love with her already, that moment would have ignited that emotion. Again, she appeared to him as something beyond human. She might have been a forest sprite, her black eyes blazing through an aura of energy generated by her exertion to reach him in time. Her hair disheveled, her bosom heaved to guzzle in the air that maintained the inner blaze.

He reined in the horse and gazed in wonderment as he waited for her to speak.

"Don't go," she stammered, attempting to deliver her message and catch her breath at the same time.

"I won't be gone long," he said.

"You're not needed there," she said.

"God knows," he answered.

"Why do you go then?"

"I must."

"And me? What will I do if you don't return?"

"I will return," he said.

Filled with expectation, like a child's balloon with air, that her desire would be sufficient to squash his need to expose himself to danger, passion suddenly drained out of her. The effect of his words, pinpricks to her exuberance, confused him. The reaction sufficiently indicated the gravity of the act. Had some other man done that to her in his presence, he would have drawn his dagger to avenge the insult, even if the cause was ambiguous. But as he had committed the fault; fleeing from the scene followed as the only remedy. He spurred the horse, and luckily for the beast, it remained insensitive to the weight his master suddenly had acquired. The man, less fortunate, rode away not quite knowing why he felt ashamed. He sat straight on his horse, but his spirit bowed under the unexpected burden.

*

The American cavalry returned from Hormiguero Heights, after finding that the Spanish were no longer there. The irregular contour of Silva Hill, rocky and overgrown, was inhospitable to cavalry. An attempt to execute a flanking maneuver, with a coordinated charge uphill, though clearly impossible was being attempted anyway. Torecillas's men as well as Bascaran's detachment dominated the heights and fought from under cover. However, by then, they had exhausted their white powder and were forced to use the black, giving away their positions.

American artillery pounded the hill, but for the most part, the bombardment proved ineffective against the entrenched men. Torecillas worried that powder and shot would give out before reinforcements arrived. Wondering why the main column had not advanced to support him, he assumed that it had met with American forces arriving from a different direction. He had no orders to withdraw, and even if he had, he would have been reluctant to obey them except for strategic reasons. Anything else would compromise his and his unit's honor. He planned to descend the hill with fixed bayonets once the ammunition ran out. God only knew the chances of success of so desperate a maneuver, but Torecillas was willing to leave the matter in the Lord's hands. His duty was clear, and that was all that concerned him.

Arriving at the vicinity of the conflict, Eduardo rode up a hill neglected by both sides, and fancying himself a one-man detachment, he occupied the site, intending to hold it until that became impractical. He tied his horse to a sapling and climbed to a convenient perch on a tree to get a panoramic view of the valley. Through his binoculars, he observed the state of affairs on both sides. He had picked up the gadget in San Juan for as much as he would have paid for a cow, to any rational mind a silly deal. They had been an object of little use, except to amuse himself exploring his domain, but the novelty of that pastime soon wore off and subsequently the toy had little to recommend it. At last, he had found a practical use for it, and on his way up the tree, he congratulated himself.

From his perch, he observed American forces still arriving and only the vanguard of the column already engaged. Concentrated on the hill, the Spanish fire became more intermittent, and from the smoke, Eduardo deduced that there was a much smaller number of defenders than attackers. The Americans had to take the hill if they wanted to continue on the road to San Geronimo, but they had yet to make the commitment. Unable to observe the other side of Silva Hill from his post, Eduardo could not determine whether more Spanish troops were arriving from that direction to support those already engaged. Without reinforcements, the troops on the hill would have to withdraw or be overrun.

Being a civilian, Eduardo failed to imagine Torecillas's plan. An offensive against a force so numerically superior was inconceivable to him. Had he been aware of the captain's idea, he would have thought him mad. Eduardo still clung to the illusion that men were rational, a belief that might have been shaken had he considered his own position: a grown man perched in a tree spying on the actions of other men engaged in the equally bizarre behavior of trying to kill one another. If two civilians engage in a fight where the victor appropriates the possessions of the vanquished, the event is considered anarchy and thievery. But when the action is performed by masses of men in uniform, both sides believed it to be an honorable undertaking.

Captain Torecillas's explanation to himself of why the main body of the Spanish force had yet to appear was partially true. Colonel Soto believed that American forces were approaching from more than one direction. A rider had arrived from Mayaguez with the news that Americans troops and equipment had disembarked in large numbers. The messenger, a stranger for whom no one in San Geronimo vouched, left with the same alacrity with which he had arrived, presumably to carry the news further into the interior. Ordinarily, this information was easily verifiable by telegraph, but the telegraph line to Mayaguez went dead a few hours before the arrival of the messenger, giving credence to his story. The news of the supposed American landing in Mayaguez soon spread throughout San Geronimo, and against his natural inclination to refrain from interfering in a military matter, a sense of duty compelled Don Emiliano to get word to Colonel Soto.

After conferring with senior officers, the colonel decided to send two companies towards Silva Hill prepared to support Torecillas but not to engage until they received further orders. The rest of his force readied to march to Mayaguez if necessary. In the meantime, he sent scouts to verify the presence of enemy forces in that direction, and he went back to San Geronimo to wire Governor Macias for more instructions.

The telegraph line to San Juan, still in operation, turned out to be of little help to the colonel. General Macias pointed out that being further from the scene put him in less of a position to instruct. The general had no way to affirm or contradict the report of a landing in Mayaguez. If true, the Spanish forces were caught in the jaws of a slowly closing vice. In that case, General Macias instructed Colonel Soto to retreat northward to Arecibo and from there withdraw by rail to facilitate the moving of the artillery.

In fact, no American landing had taken place in Mayaguez, and there would not be one until they secured the city by land, part of General Schwan's objective. But the rumor had widespread credence even in Mayaguez, where a walk to the waterfront, an easy distance from any point in the city, would have disproved it. The story may have resulted from spontaneous mass hysteria or from an organized effort by those partisans who wished it to be true and who saw the fabrication as a way of terrorizing the Spanish military, a small payback for the years of colonial abuse. In either case, the effect compounded the ineptness of the Spanish defense.

After ascertaining the falsity of the rumor, Colonel Soto rode back to his camp to find that the companies he had ordered forward to support Torecillas had returned and that indeed his whole camp was preparing to move in the opposite direction. Finding the situation to be other than what he expected, the colonel flew into a rage that he made no effort to disguise. He brusquely summoned Captain Jaspe and Captain Huertas, commanders of the companies that he had ordered forward. Not waiting for their explanation, he berated them for their insubordination.

The accusations of incompetence dismayed both officers who knew very well that they had been punctilious in the performance of their duty.

"We followed our orders, Colonel," said Jaspe, the more senior of the two and by nature the more prone to take offense at criticism, whether justified or not.

"What orders were those?" the colonel shouted. "I never gave orders to withdraw."

"But, Colonel," Huertas stammered, "we received orders."

Colonel Soto then believed that he had further reason to be indignant. Not only were these men guilty of abandoning their post, but they refused to take responsibility for their actions. Colonel Suau was also summoned to the commander's tent, and on his arrival, Colonel Soto ordered him to place the two captains under arrest.

That proved too much for Captain Jaspe to bear with grace. "This is ludicrous," he asserted, placing his hand automatically on the handle of his saber. "Colonel Suau conveyed the orders to us."

Colonel Soto looked to Colonel Suau for recrimination at being so vilely accused to his face by the two miscreant subordinates, but Suau stood placidly by as if he had merely been summoned for afternoon coffee with his fellow officers. For an instant, Colonel Soto experienced the vertiginous delusion of losing his mind. Perhaps he had been whisked into the pages of Alice in Wonderland, and he might expect a white rabbit, holding a pocket watch in one paw and dressed in a frock coat, any minute to walk into the tent. "Colonel Suau, what have you to say?"

"I conveyed the orders as you instructed," Suau responded. A sense of urgency absent from his demeanor, he delivered his words with superciliousness more appropriate to a courtier than to a soldier. He might have been in a Madrid salon rather than in a tent only a few miles from a battle in progress.

"Sir, I never gave such an order," Soto declared, beginning to sense the intended malevolence. He turned to Colonel Osè, the third ranking officer present, for some sign of support, but Colonel Osè looked away to avoid eye contact.

Emboldened by Osè's withdrawal, Suau continued. "If you cannot remember your orders, sir, we are in a sorrier state than I had imagined." To this he appended a sarcastic laugh that he delivered in the direction of the junior officers as if to invite them to join in the disparagement of their commander. The two captains, who had at first been relieved to be exonerated, were then horrified by the turn of events. Open dissension among the senior command was tantamount to disaster.

Captain Jaspe, never one to hold his tongue, proceeded to scourge his superiors. "This is a shame, gentlemen, a shame! This day is a disgrace to the honor of the Spanish army."

The arrival of a messenger from Torecillas caused the commotion to subside for a moment. He sent word that with ammunition quickly depleting, he intended to lead a bayonet charge. This news had a sobering effect on the bickering officers, who, to their credit, saw that Torecillas's resolve made their behavior all the more reprehensible. To let him die so uselessly would blot the conscience of each of them, something they would rather avoid if possible.

"He must withdraw," Colonel Soto said to the messenger.

Confused as to whether the colonel wanted that order delivered verbally or whether he intended to issue written instructions, the messenger stood rooted on the spot. The colonel, still smarting from the skirmish with Suau, smoldered uncertain whether his authority was again being questioned, this time by a sergeant.

"Torecillas will not willingly withdraw," Jaspe said. "He will not give that order to his men."

"We must make him withdraw," Colonel Soto said. "I will write the order."

"Yes," Osè concurred. "He cannot disobey a written order."

"He won't read the order," the sergeant said.

"The sergeant is right," Jaspe said. "I know him. He would rather die."

"You must persuade him then," Colonel Soto said. "You and Huertas go and speak to him directly."

"It will be too late unless we stop talking," said the sergeant.

Colonel Soto flicked his wrist indicating that the two captains should leave immediately.

*

By six o'clock, Eduardo on his perch was getting bored.

The battle had settled into a routine without much variety. The American forces were pinned down on the road and unable to continue their progress towards San Geronimo. Either they considered a massive assault on the hill too costly or they expected some other event to make it unnecessary. Several times the cavalry tried to maneuver to the east side of the hill, but it failed to have any decisive effect. The best bet, to dismount and act as infantry, was to a horseman tantamount to slumming. They preferred to rattle their sabers and tire the horses. The action might all have been a game but for the occasional bullet that drew blood. The Americans had set up two machine gun posts that now and again spewed intensive fire but only served to damage low-lying vegetation. The same could be said about the artillery that had first laid an intensive barrage on the hill but had soon been reduced to intermittent shots, mostly to show that they were still there with little hope of making an impact on the defenders.

Eduardo, his muscles cramping from maintaining the same position for so long, debated how much longer to hold his post. Afraid to miss decisive action, he had been down from the tree only once to urinate and stretch his legs. Suddenly, the American troops on the road rushed up the hill. Eduardo, not having observed any change in the defense, at that moment noticed a lack of fire from the Spanish line. The defenders had either run out of ammunition or had withdrawn.

Eduardo was observing the effect of the machinations of Jaspe and Huertas. On the way to Silva Hill, the two officers concocted a plan to achieve the withdrawal of Torecillas's company. Jaspe believed an attempt to persuade Torecillas to withdraw would be futile, and Huertas agreed. They would have to achieve their aim by stratagem, even though that might earn for them Torecillas's enmity at least for a while. They had to take that chance to save his life and those of the other men. The plan was for Jaspe to take Torecillas aside under the pretext of discussing the situation, while unbeknownst to him, Huertas would order the troops to withdraw. Once the retreat was in progress, they hoped Torecillas would see its wisdom.

Jaspe and Huertas rode up the northeast side of Silva Hill and dismounted before they reached the crest. The rest of the way they traversed on foot to avoid needlessly exposing themselves as they approached the line of fire. Certain of reinforcements when he saw them, Torecillas readily assented to Jaspe's suggestion that the two of them withdraw behind the line to discuss a plan of action. To Torecillas, this meant a plan to move forward. With his few men, he had halted the American advance. Once the whole of Colonel Soto's command moved up, the Americans would be driven back towards Guanica.

"You got here just in time," Torecillas said. "What kept you?"

"A slight confusion as to what the orders were," Jaspe answered.

"Ah," Torecillas said, filling in what he thought as a likely scenario of confused orders, a situation common enough in battle. "Everything sorted out now?" he asked.

"Sure," Jaspe replied.

"And the main column is ready to move?"

"Yes, of course," Jaspe said, this time telling the literal truth while failing to mention the direction of the move.

"The Americans haven't occupied Alta Ridge," Torecillas said. "That's a mistake on their part. If you place your men up there we'll have them in a crossfire. That is, if you brought enough ammunition for my men. We're almost out."

"How do you know they're not up there?" Jaspe asked trying to keep the conversation going.

"There's no activity at all that I can see," Torecillas said. "Their whole operation seems haphazard. Once Colonel Soto gets here, we'll drive them back."

Huertas had informed Captain Bascaran of the situation and of the plan to withdraw, and with the help of that officer, the withdrawal began. The troops were halfway down the hill before Torecillas became aware of their altered position. American riflemen, firing down on the retreating Spaniards, occupied the crest of the hill. For Torecillas, taking the offensive was now out of the question. He looked at Jaspe in consternation. All Jaspe could say was, "Colonel's orders," which he recognized as an insufficient explanation for Torecillas, who contemplated a charge up the hill all by himself.

Jaspe grabbed him by the arm. "Don't be insane," he said. "It's useless. We'll regroup in Arecibo. We'll need you then." Recognizing some sense in that, a dispirited Torecillas followed his men down from Silva Hill.

The Americans, content with the summit as their prize, halted their advance.

SEEING FROM HIS perch that firing had ceased and that the Americans were setting up camp for the night, Eduardo decided to ride on to San Geronimo. Although the distance to town was shorter than the route back to his own place, the trip to San Geronimo might take just as long, since he was reluctant to use the main road and chose instead to pick his way through lesser byways that were often little more than foot trails. The Americans might prevent him from going through their lines, thinking him a spy for the Spanish. He could ride around them and regain the road west of their camp, but then he ran the risk of being intercepted by retreating forces. It was no secret that many *Borinqueños* saw the war as an opportunity to get rid of the Spanish, and even some were ready to push for annexation to the United States. He might be mistaken for an *independista* working as a scout for the Americans and be arrested before he reached San Geronimo.

Night overtook him on the trail. In the darkness, mercifully mitigated by the light of a three-quarter moon, the foolishness of his action began to weigh on him. The environs were full of armed men who even in plain daylight had no reason to recognize him, tired and edgy men who, after a day of avoiding death, might shoot first and ask questions after. Aside from riding through a battle zone, an excursion in the night in these unsettled times was an indiscretion he would have castigated anyone else for undertaking. The anti-Spanish everywhere, in the dark they would fail to recognize him as a *criollo*, even if in fact they made such a distinction. It was more likely that, like common brigands, they concerned themselves less with the identity of their victims than with satisfying their own rapaciousness. To die in the night at the hands of outlaws would be an ignoble death, and not to see Carmen Gutierez again would be too great a punishment for a rare lapse of judgment. Ironically, in his haste to see the battle, he had left the house without a weapon, and at the moment, he rued that oversight.

Courage in the presence of others was simple, but maintaining it without an audience to appreciate the posture was a great feat. Though sometimes Eduardo might fool himself, he wanted to avoid making it a habit. So he admitted that he feared death, and at that moment the sight of flickering lights from the Spanish camp in the distance buoyed his spirit. He would arrive at San Geronimo soon enough. In the dark, Eduardo's horse found his way to Don Emiliano's house with hardly any prompting from its master.

With warmth and surprise, Don Emiliano and his wife greeted the young man arriving so late from the direction of the battle. They restrained themselves from chiding him, although they clearly thought him foolish for risking his life merely to satisfy a curiosity. Nevertheless, Don Emiliano eagerly listened to Eduardo's description of the action. His account confirmed what Don Emiliano had already learned from his informants.

"The main force failed to engage," Don Emiliano said.

"It seems that way."

"No doubt they will retreat further tomorrow morning. We must prepare for the arrival of the Americans."

"Oh my!" Doña Esmeralda exclaimed, suddenly realizing that this would be a novel social situation for which she had not planned. "I have nothing to wear."

The perspective assumed by Doña Esmeralda momentarily arrested both men as they realized that the social ramifications of the event had to be recognized along with the political. "Oh my dear, you do exaggerate," Don Emiliano said to his spouse with genuine kindness, believing she would admit the wealth of her wardrobe as soon as she gave the matter a little more thought.

"If I had only known," she said, "I would have ordered a new dress."

"A new dress would be lost on the Americans, my dear," he responded, "since they haven't seen any of your old ones."

"I was thinking of Clara," Doña Esmeralda said. "No doubt, she will have a new one."

"You think she had advance notice of the American invasion?"

"I think she gets new dresses regularly, and she must have one no one has yet seen."

"I do sympathize with your dilemma," said Don Emiliano.

"And what shall I serve? I have no idea what Americans eat."

"You needn't worry about that. Armies travel with their own kitchens. We can't afford to feed the whole American army."

"We must have the officers to dinner or at very least to lunch," she said.

"Ah, yes," Don Emiliano agreed.

Eduardo stood there befuddled as he witnessed the transformation of the war into a social event.

"The first order of business is to organize a welcoming committee," Don Emiliano continued. "We'll raise the American flag as soon as Colonel Soto withdraws his men."

"Where will we get an American flag?" Doña Esmeralda inquired. Her mind easily glided to things that were lacking.

"There must be an American flag somewhere in this town," Don Emiliano said, though for the moment its whereabouts eluded him. "In the morning, we'll send out a call for whomever has an American flag to produce it for the welcoming ceremony."

Right after breakfast the next day, Don Emiliano made that the first order of business but no flag turned up.

"How can we not have a flag?" he inquired aloud.

"We can borrow a flag from the Americans," Doña Esmeralda suggested. "I'm sure they have an extra flag they can lend us. If we send a messenger right now, he can be back with it before they arrive."

"That won't do," Don Emiliano said. "We have to come up with a flag on our own."

"Yes, of course," Eduardo agreed.

"Then we'll have to have one made," Doña Esmeralda said. She knew better than to argue with men on a point germane to their pride. She had Fiola Escobar, the seamstress, on her mind since the issue of a new dress had come up. An overnight request was too short a notice for a new dress but a flag was another matter. Certainly Fiola could whip up a flag in no time at all.

"Yes of course," Don Emiliano exclaimed and he grabbed his Borsolino straw hat and personally rushed off to see Doña Fiola so that he might explain to her exactly what he wanted.

*

A height of less than five feet made Fiola Escobar the shortest person in San Geronimo. This curious fact would have been irrelevant in her profession but at first, she had trouble reaching the pedal of her Singer sewing machine, an object she had acquired through the Sears Roebuck catalogue. Before that, she had sewn everything by hand, and she still sewed many things without the aid of that machine—whatever needed extra care and an artisan's touch. As the premier seamstress of San Geronimo, Fiola was widely acclaimed by her townspeople as not only the best on the island but perhaps the best in the world. San Geronimians believed that their town contained the best practitioner of every craft.

The development of her extraordinary skill to some degree compensated for her diminutive physical stature, a handicap that was insignificant when working with her hands but which sometimes presented a challenge when fitting or measuring a client. To overcome that obstacle, she had, in her fitting room, a circular platform with a hollow center. The customer would remain on the floor while Fiola stood on the device. This gave her the necessary elevation to reach the shoulders of even the tallest woman in town. Conversely, when working on a hem, the client and the seamstress changed places, eliminating the necessity of having to stoop. This device of her own design proved the fecundity of her mind. Likewise, she solved her problem with the sewing machine. If she could not get her foot to the pedal, she had to get the pedal to her foot. She had the blacksmith alter the machine, and he raised the mechanical pedal to make it sufficiently comfortable for her.

Fiola's lack of height failed to detract from her womanly charm. However, although still a fine seamstress, she seemed unaware that her best years as a coquettish charmer had passed. On the morning of August 11, although she suspected that the mayor's visit was not a social one, she had difficulty repressing her flirtatiousness, since Don Emiliano represented, as close as possible on this earth, her ideal man.

"An American flag will be no trouble whatsoever," she said once he explained what he wanted. "Draw a picture for me of what it looks like," she said fetching paper and pencil for him to produce the diagram.

He complied with the request, though he believed it a ruse on her part to keep him there longer than necessary. He had already declined the obligatory offer of freshly brewed coffee, citing the necessity to return home to oversee the preparations for the official welcome. The night before, he stayed up late drafting a proclamation, which that day would be printed and distributed in San Geronimo. The document praised the American forces for their liberation of the island from the clutches of imperialist Spain. It read in part: "Citizens! Today the Puerto Rican People celebrate a glorious day. An American sun shines over our valleys and hills. By the miraculous intervention of God, we are returned to the bosom of America in whose waters nature has placed us...Long live the government of the United States of America! Long live its valiant troops! Long live an American Puerto Rico!"

Eduardo delivered the handwritten document to the printer and publisher of the San Geronimo Chronicle, Don Valentin Flores, who immediately commenced setting type. Don Valentin also offered to oversee the distribution.

"I should have sent you to deal with Fiola," Don Emiliano said to his wife as soon as he had returned. "The woman wanted to keep me there forever."

"I dare say," Doña Esmeralda replied with a knowing tilt

of her head. "Fortunately, you aren't partial to small packages. Others are not so particular."

"I dare say," Don Emiliano answered.

"On the other hand, if you were, I might have as many dresses as Clara."

"You might at that," he replied with a frown to indicate a desire to change the subject. This was not the time to get into malicious gossip about Clara's husband and Fiola, if ever there was such a time.

"There must be music," Doña Esmeralda said, revealing more of her anticipation.

"Of course, music," Emiliano exclaimed, "Pachin's band must play."

"But they don't play American music," Esmeralda fretted. "What will they play?"

"The American national anthem."

"Do you know what it is?" she asked.

Emiliano ransacked his mind to find the answer to the question, but the answer had never been there. "Well they're musicians; they must know it."

"Do you really think so?"

"Any military music will do," Don Emiliano said to calm his nerves.

"Altimo Ramirez might know," Esmeralda suggested.

Altimo Ramirez, the lawyer, perhaps the most educated man in San Geronimo, had the dubious repute of knowing as much Latin as any priest, granted that some priests knew more Latin than others. Still he compared favorably with the bishop, who, whatever his faults, was an impeccable Latinist. Doña Esmeralda did not consider how knowledge of Latin related to whether the barrister knew the words to the American national anthem, a song presumably in English. But Altimo Ramirez had once been to New York, and he might have acquired that knowledge. Esmeralda's restless mind also neglected to consider how that would help the musicians. She saw her task as generating suggestions; Don Emiliano would have to sift out their usefulness. They had collaborated in this manner for many years, and from her point of view, with mostly happy results. Whether Don Emiliano felt the same about the arrangement remained questionable. He may have considered Esmeralda's suggestions obstacles rather than rungs on the ladder to solutions.

"He might at that," Don Emiliano said. "I will ask him as soon as I see him, which will be soon enough. If I know him, he's probably at the town hall right now waiting for me."

"There's so much to do," Doña Esmeralda said. "I wonder if Clara would lend me her cook?"

The idea of entertaining the American officers had firmly lodged in Esmeralda's mind, and Don Emiliano saw that it would be beyond his power to dissuade her. A dinner for the liberators would eclipse any other social event in the recent history of San Geronimo and would give Doña Esmeralda, as the hostess, an edge over Doña Clara Castillo, her most bitter rival in such matters. The two had been friends since childhood, but that didn't lessen the intensity of their rivalry for social standing.

"It's not fair that she has the best cook as well as the most extensive wardrobe," Doña Esmeralda said to no one in particular but certainly aware of her husband's presence. She subscribed to the belief that God intended fairness to reign in the world or at least in the social class to which she belonged. She never considered the existence of the poor an obvious refutation of her worldwide. The advantages enjoyed by Doña Clara had to be redressed by divine will, and the approach of the Americans presented the perfect opportunity for Esmeralda to achieve a long overdue social triumph.

"She might lend you her cook, if it were a joint venture," Don Emiliano said, to which Doña Esmeralda turned a deaf ear, wondering how men could be so obtuse about social matters.

He had planted the seed, as much as he could do in that area. Now, he had more pressing matters to attend to. He left Esmeralda to her devices, and he removed himself to the town hall from where he could better orchestrate the local features of the American entrance into the town.

Pachin's band agreed to play despite being completely ignorant of the American national anthem. Altimo Ramirez recalled the title, "Star Spangled Banner," but he had forgotten the words and the tune was only a vague memory. It was a very appropriate song for the occasion, he thought, with "bombs bursting in air" and "rockets red glare," but that was as much as he recalled. Don Emiliano had the leaders of all the civic organizations summoned to his office in the town hall, and together they orchestrated a significant turnout for the welcome. The flyer setting the tone for the celebration had been distributed. The Americans would be viewed as liberators.

✳

In the early morning, the Spanish troops retreated along Lares Road, despite orders from San Juan stipulating they withdraw to Mayaguez and from there with all the heavy equipment by railway to Arecibo. To the contrary, Colonel Soto, still fearing that American ships easily able to shell the railway lurked along the Mayaguez coast, chose to take his chances on the mountain road, forcing him to abandon most of his artillery.

By three o'clock, the advance contingents of the American column arrived at the outskirts of San Geronimo. Don Emiliano deemed the moment appropriate to raise the American flag that had been personally delivered to the town hall by Doña Fiola. She had wrapped the flag in brown paper and tied the package with cord as if to post it. To do otherwise would have seemed frivolous given the momentous nature of the event. The packaging also kept the object from public view on its transport through the streets of San Geronimo. After all, a degree of uncertainty existed about the propriety of being in possession of an American flag soon to be displayed in a public ceremony while the Spanish were still nominally masters of the island.

Affecting an air of indifference to disguise her purpose, brown paper package under her arm, her heart beating with illicit excitement, she might have been a secret agent involved in a conspiracy of international scope. Samuel Turbano, the town clerk, greeted her when she entered the door of the *alcaldia*, but she refused to relinquish the package. She wished to hand it personally to Don Emiliano. In his office, she found him rehearsing, in front of Eduardo Rincon and Altimo Ramirez, his speech welcoming the American commander, General Schwan.

"Ah, Fiola!" Don Emiliano exclaimed seeing the diminutive lady, carrying the package, that, as it passed into the mayor's hands, revealed what had seemed its disproportionately large size as a trompe d'oeil.

Don Emiliano gazed for a moment at the daunting series of knots that adorned the wrapping, and being a methodical man, automatically launched his attempt to undo them as the others waited to see how long his patience would last. Had he been alone in his office, he would have continued the task. A challenge, the pleasure of seeing the knots come undone under his fingers would have been well worth the time, but being watched, he felt foolish. The knots devised by Fiola took on a Gordian aspect, and the same feeling that prompted Alexander to draw his sword moved Don Emiliano to pull from his pocket a penknife and make short shrift of Fiola's handiwork.

The cord disposed of, the brown paper opened at the instigation of Don Emiliano's hand like a blooming flower, and the brilliant colors of the fabric leaped into the sunlight. Don Emiliano held it up for all to see. Fiola had outdone herself with magnificent work. Only Altimo Ramirez reserved his praise, which prompted Don Emiliano to wonder whether he had misjudged the political leanings of the attorney.

"Doesn't the American flag have forty-five stars?"

"Of course it does."

"This one has only forty-four," said Altimo Ramirez.

Don Emiliano took several seconds to process that information, his jaw remaining locked in the open position so that flies might have flown into his mouth without his being able to prevent them. Everyone else in the room silently verified the accuracy of Don Altimo's observation.

"This is a total disaster," said Don Emiliano without looking at Fiola. Even in his consternation, sensitive to the lady's feelings, he avoided hurting her further by casting blame.

"I followed your instructions to the letter," Fiola said intending to brazen her way out of the dilemma.

Don Emiliano was certain that he had written down "forty-five stars" in the instructions he left for her, but he kept silent on that point.

"What are we to do? A flag would have been impressive."

"You can still fly the flag," Don Altimo said. "No one will notice the number of stars."

"You noticed right away," Don Emiliano said.

"I have a gift," said Don Altimo pulling himself up tall as befits a man with a gift. "It's very rare."

"The Americans might take it as an affront."

"Believe me, they will not stop to count stars on their own flag. You can always claim that it's an old flag from when there were only forty-four states."

"Was there such a flag?"

"There must have been. They started with only thirteen."

"I don't know," Don Emiliano said.

"Your intentions are good. There's no malice in it. I say fly the flag."

Don Emiliano, inclined to take Don Altimo's advice as a legal opinion, let the flag be raised. Fiola stayed to view the American troops from the balcony of the town hall with the other dignitaries and guests of the mayor who, along with Eduardo Rincon and Altimo Ramirez, included Aurelio and Clara Castillo. The major remained uneasy, awaiting the arrival of the Americans who, true to Don Altimo's prediction, enjoyed seeing their flag already swaying in the wind when they arrived. With no effort to make the march into town a formal parade, some of the soldiers broke rank and cheered when they saw the flag. Don Emiliano realized that counting the stars on a flag hanging from a flagpole was practically impossible.

Doña Esmeralda's dinner for General Schwan and his staff

was a great success. The general insisted on contributing to the festivities by bringing the military band to play for the guests, and Don Emiliano not to be outdone, invited Pachin's band to play also. The party took on the guise of a friendly musical duel between the two groups of musicians, a cultural exchange of sorts. A banjo that one of the Americans had brought, even though not a standard instrument for a military band, fascinated Pachin. Sergeant Henry O'Higgins, leader of the regimental band, was himself taken with the *cuatro* and the style of picking used by Pachin to get so varied a sound from so small an instrument, neither a guitar nor a ukulele.

The Americans remained reluctant to dance to Pachin's music until they realized that the *danza* sounded very much like a waltz, and that to pass up the opportunity to take a turn with the five Castillo girls would be a shame, although the two younger ones were still children. The general wanted his men to make a good showing. After all, the dance instruction they received at West Point had its practical application.

They would follow the retreating Spanish up Lares Road through the mountains the next day. On such difficult and unfamiliar terrain, there would be hell to pay if they encountered a hostile general population, a situation they'd not yet encountered. The cultural ties that bound the people of the island to Spain submerged in a tide of resentment against political and economic burdens placed on them by the colonial power. The would-be new master was a closer neighbor than the old one, and that promoted the illusion of familiarity, mitigating the effect of the maxim that the devil you know is preferable to the one you don't.

The general himself set a good example by dancing with Doña Esmeralda, with Don Emiliano's permission of course. The lady was thrilled to be whirled around the room by a general no less. To have so many beribboned officers in her parlor was a dream come true and as close as she would ever get to a palace reception. This proved even better than the governor's ball in San Juan, where inevitably, the transient Spaniards, on the island only to plunder, looked down on her as a Creole. The plunderers came from all over Europe. She remembered the Krögers, whom she had known in her childhood. She remembered when young Tonio Kröger had left to be educated in Munich. "I will come back," he said to her. His eyes the color of the water of the southern beaches, not quite blue and not quite green but somewhere in between, calm like the Caribbean in the spring, their coldness made them impossible to read. He had not returned, and his family had eventually sold their land and moved back to Germany. "They come to get rich and then they leave," her father had said bitterly. "We are still plagued by pirates." She had only a vague idea of what he meant. Although she felt robbed of something by Tonio Kröger, she sensed that he also might have been a victim.

The festivities broke up earlier than would have been normally the case, but the general pointed out that technically he was in the middle of a campaign. In the morning, he would have to pursue the Spanish, and for that purpose he and his officers should get a few hours of sleep. The wisdom of that plan readily obvious to Don Emiliano, he nevertheless expressed his disappointment at cutting short so convivial a gathering.

"I hope," he said, "that when the hostilities are over we may have the opportunity to offer you a more extended hospitality."

"That is most gracious of you," General Schwan replied.

With the general about to turn, his adjutant stood his ground and cleared his throat to remind the general that he had a gift to dispense. As if by slight of hand, the adjutant produced a package that reminded Don Emiliano of one he had received earlier that day from Fiola.

"It's a flag," the general said. "This one has forty-five stars. After the war we may have to make it forty-six, who knows?"

For the second time that day Don Emiliano's jaw became immobile. He responded to the general with only a slight nod, and the soldier turned and contentedly walked into the night.

CARMEN CARRIED A bundle of clothes to be washed. After many years, the basket she used to carry them down to the creek had finally fallen apart beyond repair, and she had not yet found the time to make another one. She could buy one in town, but that would be a needless expense for something that could be made at home. She had asked her brother, Tito, to get the straw, but he neglected the task. The production of a basket did not much concern him. Her father would have fetched the straw for her right away had she asked, but she refrained from adding to his burdens. She would get the straw herself when she got a chance, gather the reeds, and hang them to dry so in a few weeks they would be ready to be woven into a basket.

In the meantime she would make do by tying the clothes in a bundle. She put the bundle up against her hip the same as she would a child, something she would soon have to do. Then she would have the child on one hip and the basket on the other when she walked down to the river, but not yet. She had just the clothes that day—and not even the basket, only the bundle pressed against her hip with one hand. In the other, she carried the wooden paddle to beat the dirt out of the clothes.

From the top of the ravine, she looked down to the creek that gurgled on and disappeared into the lush greenness of the mountain. She picked her way along the path that descended to the washing place. Several women, already at their task, soaked the clothes in the running water and beat them with paddles against flat stones, all while maintaining a steady stream of talk.

"*Hola*, there! Make room for me," Carmen shouted to be heard above the noise of rippling water, the sound of the paddles on the wet fabric, and the ongoing conversation.

She spotted Gregoria who still went down to the river to wash clothes. All her daughters married, had moved away, and she had no one to do that chore for her, but she didn't mind. As a social event, going to the river was its own reward. Gregoria, feet in the water, felt the gentle lapping, a soothing massage against her ankles, a simple pleasure for an old woman.

"Here's a good stone, right by me," she said turning her head to Carmen. The glance a reflex, a quick look to acknowledge the presence of the new arrival, but Gregoria did not quickly look back to her task as usual.

"What? Why are you staring at me?"

"Nothing, child, nothing," the old woman said, and she continued her work.

"Oh, we're just surprised to see you here, that's all," said the woman next to Gregoria, Inez Santamaria, who had not turned to look at Carmen.

"Why shouldn't I be here? Every Tuesday I wash clothes as always."

"We thought your condition in life might have changed," said a third woman, Ana Maria Santiago, Carmen's cousin.

"What condition is that?" Carmen asked alarmed that her pregnancy might already be a topic of gossip. But that couldn't be. She had told only the Virgin and Father Rodrigo, neither likely to have told anyone else.

"We thought you might be a fine lady by now with servants to do your washing."

"And how do you suppose that might have happened," Carmen asked, piqued by the effrontery of her neighbors.

"They say that a certain *haciendero* is very rich, even if he works in the fields like a common man," Anamaria said.

"And what is that to me?" Carmen asked, though she had no illusion that her trysts with Eduardo Rincon had gone unnoticed.

"'What is it to her,' she says. It would be great deal to me, if I were spending my nights with Eduardo Rincon."

"And the days, too."

"I work in the fields along with a lot of other people."

"What kind of tobacco do you tend at night?"

"The kind you can put in your pipe and smoke," Carmen said. She put down her bundle of clothes and squatted by Gregoria who pretended to be intent on the washing even as she gave Carmen an occasional sideways glance to confirm her original assessment.

"Tobacco fields have to be watched carefully," Gregoria said. "You don't want to be growing anything else unintentionally."

"Perhaps you wish to give Eduardo Rincon lessons on how to grow tobacco," Carmen said, a little annoyed by everyone's interest in her private life. But she had expected nothing less. Nothing was really private in Comerio where there was little to occupy a person's interest other than the lives of neighbors.

"I'm sure he knows how to grow tobacco without any help from me. I'm more concerned with you."

"What about me?"

"Some things are easy to plant but difficult to cultivate," Gregoria said.

"Farming is on everyone's mind today," Carmen retorted.

"Everything grows easily here," Gregoria said.

Everyone was familiar only with the tropical climate, and only vaguely aware of the cold winters in the north; they had no experience to render that abstraction real. For them, climate remained synonymous with tropical, where nature appeared everywhere fecund as well as inexorable.

Carmen had no answer to Gregoria's observation. The young woman laid down the bundle and began to apply the paddle to a piece of clothing, gently at first but with increasing vehemence as she lost herself in thought.

"You will wear out the fabric hitting it so hard," Gregoria said soothingly.

"You're right," Carmen retorted, "I get carried away."

"Apparently," Gregoria answered. "Are you angry at him or only at yourself?"

"It makes no sense to be angry at him," she answered.

"Are we talking sense?"

"I suppose not."

"Have you told him?" the old woman asked in a low voice so that her words were audible only to Carmen.

To dissemble useless, the young woman looked at the older one inquiringly as if to demand the source of her information.

"No," Carmen answered.

"You must tell him."

"It will be obvious soon enough."

"That's true," Gregoria said, "but there's more to it than that."

"Is there?"

"He will feel better having the opportunity to be honorable."

"Ah," she said, "men have that need?"

"They do," Gregoria said.

"I got myself into this," Carmen said.

"All by yourself?"

"You know what I mean."

"I do," she said. "Nevertheless, he deserves to know."

"I told Father Rodrigo."

"Ah," Gregoria said, dipping a garment in the water and wringing it out as if she were squeezing the life out of a living thing. "What good would that do?"

"None I suppose, but he surprised me in the church and the words came out."

"Perhaps it's all for the best," Gregoria said.

"But you're not sure."

"Even in a cassock, a man is still a man."

"I suppose so."

"I spoke to the Virgin."

"And did she respond."

"She did," Carmen said.

Gregoria took a deep breath but without another word continued applying the paddle. Carmen also decided to drop the subject. After a pause, Gregoria resumed with a seemingly unrelated inquiry.

"And have you heard from your brother?"

"No," she said, "nothing at all. We didn't expect him to be gone so long."

"It's only been a few weeks."

"Two months. I thought he would be back in two days, as

soon as he realized he would have to do everything for himself. Who cooks his meals? Who washes his clothes? I have no idea how he manages. At home he never did any of that."

"There's nothing like necessity to make a man self-reliant," Gregoria said.

"But he's only a boy," Carmen replied.

"And your mother—how is she taking it?"

"By day she's resigned. You know how she is, like a saint. But sometimes I catch her; when she thinks no one is looking, she cries. But most of the time she just says, 'What has to be, has to be.'"

Aᴼᴛᴇʀ ʜɪs ᴇɴᴄᴏᴜɴᴛᴇʀ with Carmen in the church, Father
Rodrigo returned to the rectory in a state of anxiety. The
memory of Isabela had descended on him with unexpected force
akin to the bursting of a dam that had, until that moment, exhibited no outward sign of strain. For a man whose profession
involved looking after the souls of others, he had neglected to
keep a close eye on his own. Back in his room, he paced back and
forth in an attempt to calm himself or at least clearly determine
the reason for the agitation. He could do nothing at that point
about Isabela's escape from the vault into which he had crammed
her years ago. He could not, with a clear conscience, imprison her
again. On the other hand, to let her roam about his consciousness
at will was also untenable. He had to find out whether he was sufficiently strong.

He knelt to pray before the crucifix that hung on the wall.
The simplicity of his present surroundings contrasted with the
opulence he had observed in Spain. Had those material comforts
been what he longed for, the problem would have been manageable. Content with a life of poverty, he didn't characterize his life
as poor for the lack of material comforts; the simple house that
served as the rectory, one that Isabela might have called a shack,
was ample enough for him. He would not trade his shack for the
mansion where he had met her, and yet he could not rid himself
of her. She had followed him home, mansion and all, to camp in
his psyche.

With no need to appear, she had remained hidden for a long
time, begging the question, "What need was there now?" Certain
that she had resurfaced for a more significant reason than causing
anxiety, but having no evidence to support that, the idea remained
purely speculative. Lacking evidence for so many of his most
cherished beliefs, its absence no longer prevented conviction as
it once had. In this case, as in many others, he willingly relied on

intuition—or translating into the parlance of his trade—faith. If faith came down to only this, then he was safe enough, but was faith all that was necessary? It was another question to which he had no answer, but maybe he had no need to answer right away. One answer at a time might be sufficient, indeed necessary, one leading to another.

A more practical question hovered before him at the moment. What did Carmen have to do with all of this? She triggered Isabela's reappearance, something beyond coincidence. Carmen being abandoned by her lover would constitute a crime that involved a child. What constituted the crime, the abandonment of Carmen or of the child? Could that be separated? No, of course not, mother and child comprised one unit. Why did crime come to mind rather than sin? Were they synonymous? Was a crime always a sin? A sin certainly did not always point to a crime: a crime was only a transgression against the state; a sin was a transgression against Nature.

He had fled from Isabela to avoid sinning. He had committed no crime. There had been no child to abandon, at least not a flesh-and-blood one. The abandonment of something more than the woman, that they together had created another entity, for which he bore some responsibility, arose at that moment as a novel and excruciating thought. They had but touched hands once, yet he sensed that may have been enough. Carmen's plight offered him a means to make amends, to redeem himself through some appropriate action, saving her and the child from abandonment. Details of the necessary action eluded him for the moment, but he was convinced that he had an essential role to play, even as he continued ignorant of who else was involved in Carmen's predicament.

"Speak to your friend," she had said. That left him in the dark, for which of his friends did she mean? He befriended everyone as well as no one. "Lord, enlighten me," he prayed. Looking up at the crucifix, he saw a tobacco field shrouded in the protective gauze that kept the sun from burning the leaves.

From tobacco to Eduardo was a short leap. He had been obtuse in failing to see the answer immediately.

He considered whether to wait for the next opportune moment to broach the subject with Eduardo. On a regular basis, Rodrigo rode out to the mountain to look in on parishioners who neglected to make the trek to the church on Sundays, a journey that invariably led him to the Rincon hacienda, where he would stop for refreshment both physical and spiritual, nothing being more soothing than conversation with a friend. He might act immediately while his resolve was still intact and unimpaired by considerations of decorum, or he might wait for Eduardo to come to town to smoke a cigar and play cards with his old friend, a meeting that invariably led to serious conversation.

Uncertain whether he confronted a moral dilemma or a procedural one, he struggled to decide whether to apply the rules of propriety to the circumstances; whether he had the right to meddle in the personal life of his friend without being expressly asked to do so; whether Carmen's invitation sufficed; or whether his role in the community as shepherd of the flock granted him authority to act. The opportunity did not often present itself in a case like this one. He refrained from the impulse to saddle his horse and head for the country. The matter could be taken up when Eduardo came by in a few days. That had the practical advantage of allowing him enough time to formulate a tactful approach. In the end, he suspected that whatever he did would seem clumsy and inappropriate, or at the very least presumptuous, a risk he had to take and ultimately the price he had to pay. He would be acting as a representative of the Church rather than personally, but the complications of their friendship blurred that distinction.

Eduardo always brought produce from the hacienda for Rodrigo's kitchen, and Rodrigo accepted it as Eduardo's donation to the maintenance of the Church. The *haciendero* also provided a bottle of rum every time he visited, and they drank some together. When he left, Rodrigo would put away what remained. The cupboard eventually contained multiple unfinished bottles of rum for which the priest had little use. He tried to get rid of them by furtively giving them away to parishioners on festive occasions such as baptisms and weddings. Nevertheless he always had more on hand than necessary.

The simplicity of Rodrigo's dwelling at first bothered his friend who saw no reason for so close a reading of scripture as to raise poverty to a virtue.

"The parish should build you a new house," Eduardo said.

"This one is good enough," the priest replied. "Most of the parishioners have no better than this. To ask them to house me better than themselves would be unfair."

"There are enough *haciendéros* to collect from," Eduardo said.

But Rodrigo would not hear of it. "My needs are sufficiently met," he insisted.

"And has this anything to do with needles and camels?" his friend asked.

The priest laughed and shrugged his shoulders. Eduardo dropped the matter, knowing that his friend would refuse to move into a new house if one were built for him. In time, Eduardo adjusted to the simplicity of Rodrigo's place, which reminded him of his own youth. He recalled that he had worn the cloak of his prosperity self-consciously before he got used to it.

"I ran into a young lady at church the other day as she prayed to the Virgin," Rodrigo said to his friend who waited to hear how this ordinary and usual occurrence became worthy of recalling. But the priest faltered, as if he had forgotten in mid-thought why he had brought up the subject. He visualized the Holy Spirit taking flight from the crown of his head, an inverse Pentecostal event. As if he were a human candle, the tongue of flame had fluttered above him but was suddenly extinguished.

Believing that Eduardo had noticed the flame flicker, the priest was embarrassed by the desertion, but at the same time, another part of him considered the idea absurd. The flame's presence had to be intermittent, for constancy would have indicated a perpetual state of grace or something akin to it, something beyond his power to achieve. The irregular nature of the flame's visitation, consistent with the character of the phenomenon, seemed natural to him, but being publicly abandoned disconcerted him. His concern was needless. His assessment of the situation proved flawed. Eduardo's perception of the matter was simpler than his friend supposed.

"She was in the right place then," Eduardo said.

"Yes," the priest answered regaining his composure or rather feigning that it had all along been intact. "Certainly in the right place."

"But there was a problem," Eduardo took a guess.

"Yes," the priest said once again and stopped, as if too tired to search for words of more than one syllable. Eduardo's inquisitive look compelled his friend to continue. "It seemed she was having a conversation with the image."

"You mean she pretended to talk to the Virgin."

"She wasn't pretending."

"I mean she pretended that the statue spoke back to her."

"There were two voices."

"You heard the Virgin talk?"

"I heard two voices but saw only one person."

"It's always dark in the church."

"Not as dark as all that."

"What then, a miracle?"

"God knows."

"To be sure. And what did they talk about?"

"Motherhood. The young woman is pregnant. She sought advice."

"She would have done better to consult her mother," Eduardo said, "for practical advice."

"Practical advice isn't always what one wants, and she will have no lack, I'm sure, of the practical."

"What then did she want?"

"Moral support, I should think. She's not married."

"An occurrence common enough to be a tradition."

"This case may be more complicated."

Father Rodrigo's tone contained a tinge of alarm, or so it

seemed to his friend, across whose mind flashed the desire to escape. Perhaps the priest had signaled the availability of an option, leaving the decision up to his friend. The offer potentially freed the priest of a dilemma. However, Eduardo's awareness of being offered a means of escape but not knowing from what, and curious to know what he should fear, made the offer difficult to accept.

"Of course, otherwise it wouldn't be worth the mention."

"It's not that," said the priest.

"Would it be a breach of confidence then for you to reveal the identity of the young woman?"

"It wasn't in the confessional that I spoke to her, and in any case, she gave me leave to do so."

This added another wrinkle. The conversation had been foreseen. Though he yet had time to withdraw, he remained at a disadvantage. Rodrigo would refrain from pressing the matter at the slightest objection or even at any apparent one. But at the moment, Eduardo needed more clarity. Momentum thwarted him; the ability to suddenly change course required more skill than he possessed.

"You have another reason then for the suspense."

"You judge for yourself," said the priest. "It was Carmen Gutierez."

Claiming surprise at this revelation would have been fatuous of Eduardo, though a degree of that element mixed in the concoction that at the moment represented his feelings of disorder. He dealt the cards as the priest spoke, and the ace of swords had turned up as the name emerged. The coincidence seemed an ominous omen despite his propensity to discount that class of events, being by inclination, if not by education, a rationalist. At the moment, retaining control of his consciousness required such effort that focusing on external matters became impossible. For an instant, sensory impressions ceased to be processed, his mind a locomotive suddenly entering a tunnel from which it would momentarily emerge after having experienced an artificial but total eclipse.

"Ah," he said, "so you know."

Father Rodrigo silently contemplated the meanings of the word know, reluctant to make such a claim. He knew very little in comparison to what he suspected. He realized the unfairness of reading more into the word than Eduardo had meant. He would attempt to be fair, but doubted whether he would succeed. Nevertheless, he had to attempt to take on the challenge. He became vaguely aware of having, at that juncture, hit upon something of more significance than he had the opportunity to immediately explore. "I wouldn't claim that," he finally said.

"You would like to know more," Eduardo said stalling for time to formulate what he might truthfully say without appearing evasive. He wanted to be honest, but that seemed a formidable task, his mind as clouded as the vicinity of a frightened squid with tentacles flaying about unable to grasp anything substantial.

"What I would like is not relevant," said the priest.

"Yes," Eduardo agreed, "it's more in the nature of what's required."

"If you will," Rodrigo said.

"I must do what's right," Eduardo said, finally grasping something more than inky water. "It's as simple as that," he concluded turning up another card.

"Is it so simple?" the priest inquired.

"It has to be," his friend replied.

For a moment, they gazed at the card that had been turned up, neither one of them venturing an interpretation of the happenstance. The queen of hearts, a personage for whom time did not exist, lay passively on the table.

THE RAIN FELL steadily all day, but maybe it would stop during the night and not rain the next day. Hitting the thatch roof of the *bohio*, the raindrops made a dull sound. Zinc roofs, coming into use in the towns, amplified the sound of the rain within the house, but a thatch roof muffled the rain enough so that you would not know that it was raining unless you looked outside. You could, if you wanted, stay inside and pretend that the sun was shining. But the rain that day was different. Even from the thatch roof, the large raindrops were audible.

Juaquin Gutierez marveled at the size of the raindrops. He figured that only a few would be enough to fill a cup if he indulged in such a pastime. One, two, three raindrops and the cup would be full. He had an urge to place a cup outside just to see how fast it would overflow, a silly idea, and anyway the rain fell too fast for him to be able to discriminate between raindrops. He would only know how fast the cup filled, but not how many drops had converged to fill it. He would not even know exactly how long the cup took to fill because he did not have a watch to time the process, an interesting but silly idea. Silly ideas came to him often and he had to discard them as useless. When younger, he thought that silly ideas were left over from his childhood, and they would stop as he grew older. But the ideas kept coming. He had just to ignore them and get on with practical things.

Juaquin Gutierez hoped that the rain would stop soon, but it would probably pour all day. With the sky dark as far as the eye could see, no wind blew away the clouds that came by and decided to stay for a while. Sometimes an acquaintance walks up the road and stops to chat, and his arrival is a welcome break in the routine, but sometimes he stays and stays and becomes a disruption in the necessary flow of the day. Juaquin called them the talking people. The talking people start moving their mouths and don't know when to stop. They must relate every detail of every event that has occurred in their lives since they saw you last, as if you had been waiting anxiously to hear, and you would be insulted if deprived of a single detail. There was no polite way to make them stop. The talking people remained impervious to hints that they had said enough.

The family would take turns, some listening to the unending story, while others went to the kitchen to perform a magic ritual in hope of getting rid of the guest. Carmen, the most proficient in its performance, always made Juaquin laugh as she solemnly draped a shirt around a broomstick and swept with a flourish in the direction of the talking person in the next room.

These clouds reminded Juaquin of a talking person, but the broomstick ceremony was ineffective against rain. It may not have been any good against the talking people either, but at least it provided humor. The bad timing for so much rain took away all the humor. Along with the river rising and washing away everything in its path, came the danger of mudslides on the sloping fields. Nothing could be done about the rain except hope that prayer would prove more effective than the broom ceremony. Juaquin had lit a lamp in front of the icon of Saint Sebastian and made a request for intercession in stopping the rain. The lamp burned olive oil, which Juaquin could ill afford, but he judged it a worthy investment if the offering worked. In normal times, the amount of oil would have seemed negligible, but at that moment burning the oil without any guarantee of success worried him. Perhaps his sacrilegious doubt would interfere with the efficacy of the request. Nothing in life was simple.

What could a man do but take life one moment at a time and try to stave off despair? Too much thought got in the way of happiness. Best to stop thinking and focus on actions that would engross his full attention. Really no point in worrying about the rain, it would stop when it would stop. He needed to be practical and make good use of the time. He sat down on a bench by the door to sharpen and mend the tools that needed care. The handle of the hoe needed adjusting and tightening into the socket of the blade.

He did that first. Next, he took the whetstone to his machete. He stroked it with even methodical movements along the cutting edge. When he had done that sufficiently on both sides, he picked up a smaller stone, and with the point of the blade anchored on the bench, he applied the finishing stone with circular motion.

Despite his reluctance, occasionally Juaquin looked out into the yard spread out in front of the open door. A thick sheet of water covered the *batey*. The rain fell faster than the clay ground could absorb it and faster than it could run off in the shallow ditches that flanked the yard. The clay ground made the water red as if the ground itself were bleeding. Maybe the blood of the mountain drains away like the blood of a slaughtered pig hung over a tub to catch the ebbing life. The image startled him. Rain often turned the ground as red, but never before had such a dire image overwhelmed him. Perhaps Satan accomplishes his work that way, letting loose in the world a host of dreadful ideas that float about until they lodge in people's minds, seeds of despair that must be yanked out before they take root and become an endless jungle.

Better to listen to Carmen's singing. From the other room, the melody floated to his ears. She sang as naturally as she breathed. There was no way to repress that urge in her, and who would want to? Whether the words of a song were humorous or sad, the song always gladdened the heart. How she came by that gift still a mystery to him, neither he nor his wife, Andrea, particularly musical, but their daughter was blessed with the desire and the ability to sing.

She sang while ironing clothes. On rainy days, the moisture in the air made the fabric less resistant to the iron. A wrinkle would have to be tough indeed to withstand the hot instrument. The hollow body of the iron filled with charcoal was stoked until it glowed with fierce intensity. Each article of clothing, sprinkled with water and rolled into a ball to retain the moisture, waited in a pile on the table. Carmen retrieved each item one by one, shook it and laid it out on the ironing board. Occasionally, she set down the iron on a metal trivet and carefully swung open a small flap to check whether the coals inside still glowed. If not, she blew into the contraption to resuscitate it.

Ironing was tedious, but the singing kept her from boredom. She sang the story of a young girl whose lover went away in search of fortune. He planned to become a wealthy man and make her a queen. Many years passed but he failed to return. She waited faithfully for him until she heard that he married someone else across the sea.

Juaquin Gutierez listened to the song his daughter sang, and recognized in it a truth about life in general. In youth, life promised a great deal. What had he expected from life as a young man before he married and had children? He could not remember the details. Perhaps there never were any details, only the expansive feeling of grandness. No grandness remained—only the details of everyday life, the fixing of a hoe or the sharpening of a machete and going into the field to plow, nothing grand at all.

There had been moments of triumph: the moment Andrea had agreed to marry him although he had barely expected her to do so; the day his son was born was a triumphant day, and the day Carmen arrived, that too was a good day. Were they grand? Difficult to remember when troubles overwhelmed him. He had been forced to sell the ox. What would he plow with when the next planting season came around? It was a while away yet. He would figure out a solution. Not everyone had an ox. He would have to borrow one or rent one if he had something to exchange for it. That problem lay down the road.

One could walk a stretch down the road and disappear like Tito had done. Juaquin did everything he could to keep him from leaving into the uncertainty of a strange place, but the future seemed just as precarious at home.

"There's nothing for me here," the boy said.

"At least you have a roof over your head," his father replied.

That answer made sense to Juaquin but not to the boy. It would not have satisfied Juaquin either when he was a boy. He had a vague awareness of that. The world had a different feel to it then. When still a boy, almost a man but not quite yet, a roof over his head was not enough.

"Where will you go?"

"Down to Ponce. They say there's work at the central."

"There are many people there already."

"There's more work than there are people. That's why they pay high wages."

Juaquin said no more, no argument against a dream. A dream will always look better than reality, even when reality is good enough, a claim unsustainable at the moment, simple as it was.

"Don't go," his mother pleaded. "At least here you have enough to eat."

The boy looked away without a word, because it needed no uttering.

"All right," she said. "Come back soon."

"I will," he said.

"God and the Virgin go with you," the mother said.

She watched him walk down the road until he disappeared around a bend. He looked so small, though almost a man. He seemed to her the same as he had been at eight, when he went down to the school next to the church in Comerio. Then he walked down the road with his lunch of *yautias* and *bacalao* in a lunch pail, like a little man going off to work, but this time he carried a small bundle of clothes, all that he owned in the world. This parting is unavoidable, Juaquin thought in an attempt to comfort himself. He fought the impulse to say the same to Andrea. She would not be comforted. Something was being yanked from her, and the pain was greater than when the boy was pulled from her womb. He could say nothing to diminish her anguish.

The rain kept falling while Juaquin sat by the door mending his tools and thinking about his family. Tito went down to the plain to find work, tilling the soil not enough for him. Perhaps he had a dream of being a *haciendero* like Eduardo Rincon, who had become the largest landowner in the neighborhood. Eduardo started with very little, but he had luck and everything always went his way. That's what people said, and Juaquin Gutierez reckoned that the truth. He never knew anyone in his family to be that lucky. Eduardo Rincon was the kind of man who would walk out in this rain and not get wet. That kind of luck was rare.

Eduardo Rincon was a lucky man, but even so, Juaquin preferred that he stay away from Carmen. She was poor enough. What need had Eduardo to take from her the only thing of value she possessed?

"You have to be careful," Juaquin said to his daughter. "I hear talk about you and Don Eduardo."

"It's just talk," she said. "I can't help what people say."

"He won't marry you," Juaquin said.

"I only work in the fields," Carmen answered.

"He'll marry a town girl from San Geronimo, even if he wants you. That's his destiny, and there's nothing anyone can do about it. Not even he can change it." As he spoke, he realized that his words were useless, that Carmen would not heed them even if she understood them and agreed.

Tito Gutierez walked in the shade of the forest that covered the side of the mountain. Along the trail, he passed isolated dwellings whose inhabitants invariably came out to chat with him. He gave them news of Comerio, and they in turn related whatever they thought might be of interest to anyone down the road. On his way back, they expected him to bring news of where he had been. That was the custom. No one went by without stopping to chat to keep current with events up and down the mountain. If he happened by at mealtime, he was fed, the food well worth the time he lost getting to his destination.

Most of the people of the mountain were poor. Coffee was their cash crop, because it could grow in small plots under the shade of the mountain trees, but *haciendelos* with large holdings of land, like Eduardo Rincon, favored tobacco.

At the foot of the mountain, the landscape changed dramatically. Even the texture of the soil differed. Tito found himself walking through fields of sugar cane, the flat terrain alien and unfriendly with no shelter from the unrelenting sun. The cane grew taller than a man but not so tall as to throw a protective shadow over the road. It grew close together, and one could not stray from the road without running the risk of being cut by the edge of the leaves. Nothing pretty about the fields, but they offered the hope of employment. On the flat land, the journey more desolate but less solitary, he met another young man going in the same direction with the same purpose.

"How far have you walked?"

"I came from Comerio."

"That's far," the boy said.

"I walk slowly," Tito said.

"It's still far."

"What about you?"

"Not so far," Agusto answered. He appeared to be about the same age as Tito. His eyes were set wide apart, and his chin came to a point like a rodent's. He shifted his gaze quickly from one thing to another with a jerky movement of his shoulders consistent with the habits of one who scavenged for survival.

"They say there's work at the central," Tito said. His confidence in that assumption had been shaken by comments he heard as he progressed down the mountain. He hoped that Agusto would say something more encouraging.

"Maybe there is," Agusto said.

"You're not sure?"

"Nothing's for sure in life," he said, affecting the tone of an older person.

"It's a long walk then for nothing."

"The walk is something," Agusto said.

"There's no pay for walking."

"Maybe there is and maybe there isn't," Agusto said.

Tito mulled that over, but he remained perplexed. He looked to the horizon, as if there he might find an explanation. He saw the brilliant blue of the sky and a few luminescent clouds, but as bright as the sun shone, it cast no light on his confusion. Absorbing some of the brilliance of that sun would be wondrous. To that, at least, he was entitled along with a little mental clarity.

"I don't know what I'll do if there's no work," Tito said. For the first time since he left home, he let himself dwell on that possibility. How could he go home empty-handed, sorrier looking than when had he left? He had never walked so much in a single stretch before, and the soles of his feet hurt. His shoes, which pinched in several places when he started out, were now more uncomfortable, sure to create calluses the farther he walked.

The peddler who sold them swore that they were almost new and that they would fit perfectly once they molded to his feet. "It's just a matter of breaking them in," the peddler had said. "I'm practically giving them away." Juaquin, willing to pay, agreed on a fair price for a pair of shoes in such good condition, because his son was practically a man and should have shoes. The idea of leaving for the city had taken shape already, and Tito figured that shoes would be good for the long journey. The road to the city stony, after walking for a distance, the shoes felt uncomfortable, so he took them off and walked barefoot for a while. When he came to another stretch of stony road he put the shoes on again to prevent more damage to his feet.

"There'll be work," Agusto said, as if he forgot what he said before about uncertainty.

"I hope so," Tito responded.

"And anyway, in the city something is bound to turn up. There's always something happening there," he said with the air of someone who knew a thing or two.

"That's true," Tito said though he felt far from certain. He wanted to seem just as sanguine as his companion, but he could not escape his anxiety. "Have you been there before?"

"To Ponce? Yeah, I've been there lots of times with my uncle to sell produce. That's when we had a couple of burros. We'd load them up with vegetables and head down to the market. After we sold everything, we'd have a good time in the *cantinas* before heading back. Those were the good old days," he said as if he were an old man looking back on his youth.

"So why are you walking there now?"

"The burros died," he said.

"Both of them?"

"That's the strange part," Agusto said. "My uncle Toño is convinced they were killed through witchcraft, but he can't figure out who would do such a thing to him. Sometimes, you know, it's the person you least suspect who has it in for you. It's a mystery, if you believe in witchcraft, that is."

"And do you?"

"Believe in witchcraft? Well sure," he said. "As plain as daylight, there's witchcraft in the world. Sometimes you can hear witches flying over the house at night. If there are witches, there has to be witchcraft. It's plain as daylight."

"I don't know," said Tito. "I've never seen one."

"Sure you have," Agusto insisted. "You just don't know it.

It's not as if they reveal themselves. They go about in disguise. You have to know what to look for."

"I suppose so."

"No question about it. How else are you going to protect yourself? Don't be such a chump. You got to learn these things. If we see any on our way, I'll point them out to you. I can do that for a pal."

"That's very kind of you," Tito said. "I have a Saint Christopher medal." To show Agusto that he wasn't totally unprotected, he took out the brass medal that hung on a chain around his neck.

"That's practically useless," Agusto said. "Against strong witches you need at least a pair of scapulars." He took his out to show Tito.

Somewhat armed against the unseen evils of the world, they continued their journey, avoiding any thought of the more pressing problem of having enough to eat if they found no work. Toward evening, they left behind the cane fields and arrived at a stretch of undulating countryside. Thinking of finding a place to spend the night, they reached the crest of a hill, and gazing down, saw a river winding through the valley. The road continued down the hill. A bamboo grove extended to the right. They guessed a bridge, not visible from the spot, spanned the water, its actuality of little importance, the river looking narrow enough to easily swim across. The current seemed tame; a conclusion influenced more by their state of mind, set on minimizing obstacles, than by what they saw, the distance too far to yet gauge the actual speed of the current.

They noticed signs of human activity. Slowly dissipated by the breeze, wisps of white smoke rose above the foliage. A figure emerged several times from the cover of the bamboo and disappeared again. From the top of the hill, the boys were unable to tell whether the same person repeatedly appeared or if it was a different person each time. They took the roadside camp as good fortune, for they dreaded the prospect of spending the night in the open with only the protection of a Saint Christopher medal and a pair of scapulars. Even against the supernatural, they figured there was safety in numbers.

At night the darkness of the outside world merges with the darkness within, and in that union, there is a terror still surviving from a primordial time when the ego had just awakened, its supremacy still in doubt. Night brings out the fear of being overwhelmed by the darkness to which our demons and monsters have been banished, and we seek other humans with whom to huddle around a fire to keep at bay those forces that would drag us back into the chaos against which our reason continues to struggle.

The men in the bamboo grove saw no need to increase their number, but neither had they anything to fear from two boys. So before Tito and Agusto arrived, being observed as they descended from the crest of the hill, a wordless decision was reached to accept them if they sought refuge for the night. When the two boys entered the bamboo grove, they were greeted as if they were expected all along, and the camp had been established to await their arrival.

"Shouldn't you boys be home with your mothers at this time of day?" They expected the ribbing; meant in fun and taken that way, they ignored it. Sometimes men forgot themselves either by pushing teasing too far or, at the other end, forgetting to be forbearing or mistaking the intention of the jokester, situations more likely to occur when everyone involved had been drinking at a feast or a dance, though at a dance the cause of an altercation was more likely to be a woman.

"The way things are, I think our mothers are glad to be rid of us," Agusto said.

"Is that so?" commented one of the five men who constituted the band occupying the copse. The oldest of the five, actually younger than he looked, with a couple of days growth on his face, tan and drawn from time in the sun, would have been taken for an unsavory character but for the light that danced in his dark eyes. "Where are you coming from?" he asked.

"From the mountains," Tito said making a vague gesture in the direction from which he had come.

"Everyone comes from the mountains," the man said.

"Comerio," Tito elaborated.

"A true *jibaro*," Agusto said.

"And you, you're not a *jibaro*?"

"It's a matter of degree, isn't it?" Agusto responded sensing that he had misspoken.

"Either you are or you're not," the man said, "no degrees about it. Are you from Comerio?"

"No, from Dos Piedras."

"Not so far," the man said.

"We met on the road," Agusto explained, "but we're pals."

"Same as if you had suckled on the same tit," the man said.

"The very same," Augusto agreed refusing to take offense. "That would make us more than pals; brothers, that's what we are."

"No shit," said the man.

"Truly," Agusto said refusing to be intimidated.

"I see how it is," said the man.

"You're welcome to share our stew," said another, fussing with the fire and the cauldron propped over it on three stones. "The *haciendero* who lives down the road generously donated two chickens for the comfort of us traveling journeymen."

The cook's right leg, shorter than his left, caused his torso to sway from side to side when he walked. His upper teeth protruded over his bottom ones giving the impression that he had been assembled from spare parts that didn't fit together. A large knife on his belt, more than the accoutrement expected of a cook, gave pause to anyone contemplating the idea of mocking nature's handiwork.

At the mention of the chickens, the first man gave the cook a glance that caused the misshapen one to look away. The interchange, meaningless to Tito, caused the more experienced Agusto to conclude that the generosity of the *haciendero* might still be unknown to that gentleman and that the man who had first spoken, obviously the leader of the group, would prefer to keep the good repute of the *haciendero* from spreading.

"And where are you boys headed?" asked the cook to draw attention away from his gaffe.

"We're going to work in the central," Tito said.

"You can save yourselves a trip then," said a third man. "There's no work there. I was there myself, and they turned me away."

"That's because they knew what kind of a worker you'd be," said the cook.

The other men laughed and so did Agusto, but Tito looked dismayed. Tired, dusk approaching, he saw his dream dissipating. The crickets began to orchestrate their nightly opus. From the river, the frogs answered in counterpoint. A melancholy dissonance mirrored the gloom rising to submerge Tito's youthful optimism.

"You never know what tomorrow will bring," said the first man who noticed Tito's gloom at hearing about the lack of work. "A whole new set of possibilities comes up with the sun. The evening is no time to ponder the future. Rest and renew your strength for tomorrow. My name is Gaspar," he said, "and this cripple here is Ausencio."

Tito extended his hand to shake the one offered to him by the kindly stranger, and he shook the cook's hand too. The other three men gave their names but didn't offer their hands. Agusto made one of his quirky sudden moves with his head when he heard the name "Gaspar." His lips moved to form a question that died in his throat. For once, his mind was quicker than his tongue. At the first opportunity, under the pretext of wanting to wash the dust and sweat of the road off his face, he drew Tito down to edge of the water, away from the rest.

"I think we've fallen in with a band of desperados," he said.

"What are you talking about?"

"That's Gaspar Cienfuegos, the bandit."

"Bandits wouldn't be camping by the side of the road, inviting the Civil Guard to come by and arrest them, would they?"

"That's just it. He's known for those kind of action. I'll bet they were in Ponce right under the noses of the Civil Guard who are none the wiser."

"Well, so what?"

"What if they cut our throats while we're sleeping? We have to find an excuse to get away from here."

"Even if you're right, they have no reason to do us any harm. We have nothing for them to steal."

"You're such an innocent," Agusto said. "They don't need a reason. Desperados kill just for the hell of it."

"They would have done it already. Why would they wait until we're asleep? I should think they would do it before supper, so as not to waste good food on us. You can go if you want to. I'm staying."

"All right—it's your funeral. I'm cutting out as soon as I can."

The appearance of one of the supposed outlaws interrupted the conversation. The two boys had been too engrossed in their talk to notice his approach, or the man had purposely sneaked up. The boys wondered which of those two possibilities was the actual one and how much of their conversation had been overheard.

"If you boys want to eat," said the man, "you better help yourselves before it's all gone. This bunch isn't modest about eating."

Tito scrambled up the riverbank, closely followed by Agusto who wanted to avoid being alone with any of the strangers. After supper, the men sat around the fire reminiscing about their homes and their families, ordinary stories just like any ordinary men might tell. Hearing them convinced Tito that Agusto's fears were unfounded. When the time came to turn in for the night, Agusto was calmed by the conversation and lay down near Tito without a word about leaving.

The boys gave up trying to count the stars, a futile attempt by nature to fill the void. The sound of the crickets also evinced a gargantuan number, perhaps one for every star. The mountains forever sprouted a lush cover to clothe themselves in luxury. All of this abundance made incongruous the desperateness that Tito tried to keep at bay. "Fertility is effortless," the forest seemed to say, but in the hollows and the hamlets of the sierra, poverty abounded, the night a velvet case filled with diamonds, none redeemable for a single morsel of bread. Was this God's sense of humor? With no answer, only bitterness resulted from dwelling on it. Many times in the little church in Comerio, the priest proclaimed the ways of God as unfathomable. With that in mind Tito fell asleep.

He stirred, awakened by a sound muffled by his state of somnolence but nevertheless sufficient to bring him back with a jolt from a dream where a ferocious dog was pursuing him while his legs progressively lost their power. He ran in place while the dog, perhaps also afflicted by the handicap, still nipped at his heels. A great commotion had ensued in the camp, and there were a great many more men at the moment than when he went to sleep. These new arrivals, all dressed in gray uniforms, held carbines. In a few minutes, after rubbing his eyes clear, he recognized the newcomers, the Civil Guard, one of them pointing a carbine at his face.

"Leave the boys alone," Gaspar said to the policeman. "They're only here by chance."

"Shut up," said the captain shoving Gaspar back behind an imaginary boundary that, in the captain's mind, Gaspar had crossed.

Gaspar Cienfuegos exhibited no fear. He stood proudly, as if he, not the captain, had the upper hand. The captain took that as an affront. He clearly perceived insolence, and had he been a totally stupid man, that would have sufficed to incense his rage against Cienfuegos, but the captain thought of himself as a man of sensibility and he tried to refrain from excessive emotion. A man standing straight when he should be cowering in fear might be considered courageous, and to brutalize him would add to his stature. On the other hand, to attribute the sublime quality of courage to such a desperate character, a thief and a murderer, seemed to the captain an affront to Divine order. He found the dilemma difficult to reconcile at the moment.

"It's true captain, it's true. We only ran into these men last night. We're on our way to Guanica to work, and we had no idea who they were."

"And who pray are they?" asked the captain.

"You know well enough," said Agusto, "Gaspar Cienfuegos and his gang."

"If you didn't know that last night, how do you know it now?" asked the captain with a triumphant sneer. "No one has identified them but you."

For a moment, Agusto appeared crestfallen, but he had the uncanny ability, a blessing really, to quickly forget his mistakes. His intelligence having no hope of improvement, at least he was spared the chagrin of prolonged mortification.

"Enough talking," said the captain. "Tie them up."

One of the guards produced a rope, and the prisoners were tied in tandem, the rope going from one neck to the next creating a human chain.

"I should shoot you right here," said the captain to Gaspar, who still showed no sign of consternation at the turn of events. "But I'll do my duty and take you back. Let the magistrate pronounce your sentence. It'll be a spectacle to see you hang."

Cienfuegos, perhaps not human, perhaps the devil in disguise and having no fear of death, only smiled amused by the captain's fantasy. No human could be so indifferent to whether he lived or died. If he had committed all the crimes attributed to him, how could there be any doubt as to his evil nature? At the very least, he had the devil's own luck. At the moment when Cienfuegos was about to be tied by the neck, the horses of the Civil Guard that were tethered together at the edge of the grove, bolted through the camp creating confusion among the soldiers. The captain turned for an instant, giving Cienfuegos the opportunity to grab him in a chokehold while simultaneously appropriating his sidearm. The face of the unfortunate captain, his supply of oxygen seriously curtailed, turned a light shade of purple. Of course, the embarrassment of having his own pistol pointed at his head may have been just as responsible for his coloring as the lack of oxygen. Some of the other soldiers also had their weapons snatched from their hands at the moment of surprise, but one of them had grabbed the mane of a horse and vaulted into the saddle to make his escape. The few remaining soldiers who still had their weapons clustered together and pointed them at the bandits, who had increased in number.

Their captain in a precarious position, the soldiers with raised weapons hesitated. If they fired, the captain might be killed outright, and they might not escape either, their opponents at present also armed. The Captain, though absolutely convinced of Cienfuego's villainy, found that insufficient reason to forfeit his own life prematurely. He might be heroic and insist on resistance by those still able, but that would be suicidal for them as well as for him. Being an optimist and hoping that the tables might yet turn once again, he chose a more reasonable course. "Put down your arms, you fools," the captain shouted once the hold had been relaxed sufficiently for air to pass through his trachea.

The soldiers, relieved to have the decision taken from them, put down their carbines, while another worry supplanted the first. They, too, were convinced of the bandits' fatal intentions.

"So, captain, the shoe is on the other foot," Gaspar said.

"You have gained nothing," said the captain.

"I wouldn't say that exactly," Gaspar answered, clearly enjoying the captain's discomfiture. "We gained some arms, a few horses, not a bad haul for a night's work."

"You're digging yourself a deeper grave," said the captain, beginning to see the desperateness of the situation, and slipping into a melodramatic mode he thought appropriate for someone who might soon be dead. Unable to read Gaspar's intentions in his demeanor, the captain took the bandit's eyes, pools of blackness, for a reflection of the man's soul.

"A grave's depth is of little consequence," Gaspar responded philosophically. "The sentence is the same, I'm told, for one murder as for two."

"You laugh now," said the captain mistaking the bandit's equanimity for indifference, "but when you're facing the noose, it will be a different matter."

"I dare say that you're right, captain," Cienfuegos said, "but that's yet to come. Right now, we must deal with the issue at hand." He turned his head to survey the scene, and in doing so, he caught sight of the boys. "The two of you better scurry along. This is no place for you now," he said to them.

"Without breakfast?" Agusto complained.

"Don't be an ass," Tito said. "Let's go."

They gathered their belongings and headed for the bridge. Once across, Agusto stopped to look back, but Tito urged him on. In a few seconds, both spontaneously broke into a trot, trying to quickly put as much distance as they could between themselves and the bamboo grove.

IN THE DISTANCE, Tito and Agusto observed the stacks of the sugar mill belching gray smoke. Along the road, they followed a caravan of oxcarts that slowly made its way toward the structure. A team of oxen guided by a drover pulled each two-wheel cart, brimming with cane, to be unloaded and stacked in sheds that surrounded the belching building. After losing several men in an accident, one having his arm torn off by the machine, and several others deciding to take their chances elsewhere, the foreman reluctantly agreed to hire the two boys.

The grinders, two large rollers propelled by a steam engine, were fed a steady supply of cane to extract the syrup. Below the rollers, the juice gushed into large vats to be treated with slaked lime that settled out the dirt. The syrup was then boiled until it crystallized, resulting in a mixture of sugar and mother liquor that was spun to separate the two. The brown granules went to refineries to be transformed into white sugar. The leftover juice became molasses and was sold to rum distilleries. The chewed pulp was recycled as fuel for the steam engines. The dirt that was removed with the lime was carted back to the fields. Continuously in operation, the furnaces produced steam for the engine and for the cooker that reduced the cane juice.

At first, the job of feeding the machines seemed simple. The boys assumed the foreman's concern about their ability to last the day was a joke, but soon the repetitive task of fetching enough cane to satisfy the voracious grinders began to take its toll. At midday, the sun directly overhead, the ambient temperature in the mill became unbearably high. The energy exerted by the boys to fetch enough cane, combined with the mounting heat, drenched them in perspiration. By noon, their thoroughly wet clothes added to the discomfort of muscular exhaustion.

They stopped to eat the lunch they brought with them, having contracted with their landlady to provide it for them every day along with their other meals. They had, in effect, already spent a good portion of their first week's wages before receiving them.

"This is bitching work," Agusto said. "I don't know if I can take much more of it."

"The day is half done," Tito said. "We'll make it."

"The second half is harder," Agusto said.

"You've got to set your mind on it," Tito urged.

"My mind evaporated in the heat."

"Well, then you're all set," Tito said. "I guess it's true what people say."

"What's that?"

"*Jibaros* are like donkeys. They can work till they drop. It's a virtue," Tito said.

"Then I'm glad to be degenerate."

"You have your good points too," Tito said.

"You're a pal," Agusto grimaced.

When they got to their room that night, they scarcely had enough energy to wash their faces before dropping onto their cots, where their aching bodies took a while to relax into sleep.

*

On Saturday they got paid. When they arrived home from work, the landlady met them at the door and demanded the following week's rent in advance, which left them with only half of their wages. After supper, they went out to explore the big town on a Saturday night. Agusto heard of places where they might try their luck at cards along with a drink.

"We might lose all our money, and we'll be back where we started," Tito said.

"We'll have a good time," Agusto answered, "so that's not exactly where we started."

Tito saw some sense in that, but the words made him uneasy. Having a few coins in his pocket made him feel more comfortable than having none. Putting a jingling pocket on a scale against having a good time, the scale would tip in favor of the coins. That was good enough for him.

"If you use all your prudence now," Agusto argued. "What will you have when you're an old man?"

Using up all of anything did not appeal to Tito. They were on their way before he realized that prudence increases rather than diminishes with use. Down an alley, not too far from the rooming house, an open door spilled light, laughter, and music into the night. They hesitated at the door before walking in. A haze of tobacco smoke distorted the view of the room. Leaning languidly against the wall and looking over the shoulders of the card players, a woman in a green dress glanced toward the new arrivals. A quick look was sufficient for her to know how much attention they required. She remained in place, pretending not to have noticed them.

The bartender and proprietor, a rotund little man with oily skin, also gave them the once-over as he did all strangers who passed through his door. There were more strangers lately, *jibaros* who came to work at the mill. Not yet used to the ways of the town, they arrived at his small establishment with knives and machetes. After a few drinks, they were disposed to pull them out in support of the slightest argument. For that reason, he posted a sign on the wall informing his patrons that all weapons were to be left at the counter. Of course, only one *jibaro* in ten could read, and the chances of that one walking into his establishment were slim, so he read the notice to new patrons as they walked in.

Some of the regulars, after observing the procedure several times, inquired why he bothered to put up the sign. He beckoned them to lean closer, and he whispered a fact he had discovered through experience. "People are more likely to comply," he said, "with something that is written than with something I merely say." An incontrovertible truth, everyone knew that the proprietor created the rule, but once posted, it acquired an official aura, like a government decree enforceable by the Civil Guard.

"Are you coming in or are you going to stand by the door all night?" the proprietor asked to the laughter of several men standing at the bar.

"We're coming in all right," Agusto said.

"You must be the hare," said one of the men who had laughed. "And your friend must be the tortoise." That generated more guffaws.

"We're in luck," Agusto said. "We get the comedy for free."

"Well, that's about all you're going to get for free," said another man.

The proprietor pointed to the sign on the wall.

"Sure we can pay cash," Agusto said mistaking the meaning, all writing gibberish to him.

"We have no weapons," Tito said.

"An intellectual," one of the men said. "This place is definitely getting high-brow."

"A *jibaro* who can read! Will wonders ever cease?"

"That's not all we can do," Agusto said.

"So show us what you can do."

The proprietor waited for them to put money on the counter. Then he poured two shots of rum. Agusto downed his in one gulp. He wanted to be accepted by the men at the bar, and he looked around defiantly. The burning taste of the rum less than pleasant, Tito sipped his drink slowly. He wandered toward the card table, but his ignorance of the rules made the action meaningless to him. He furtively eyed the clearly delineated body of the woman in the green dress. Ignorant of the impossibility of being uncouth in that setting, he pretended not to notice her. Agusto walked to the card table and asked to be dealt in.

"Put your money on the table," the dealer said.

Agusto emptied his pocket.

"That's not enough," the dealer said.

"It's all I've got," Agusto said.

"You've got to have at least four bits," the man said.

"My friend here will vouch for me," Agusto said.

"You've got four bits?" the man asked Tito.

"Sure I do," Tito said.

"Put it on the table."

"I don't want to bet."

"You can't play," the man said to Agusto.

"We'll come out ahead. I never lose," Agusto said to Tito.

Tito looked skeptical.

"Ah, go on," the woman said. "It's your lucky night."

The scent of her hair was like a flower, both familiar and exotic as she moved closer to Tito. His fears fled along with his sense of time. Only the present existed. He took the money from his pocket and passed it to Agusto.

By the end of the night, all the money gone, Agusto discovered his singing voice. On the way back to the boarding house, as he staggered from one side of the street to the other, he sang about amorous exploits, while Tito brooded that the scent of a woman's hair had caused him to lose his resolve.

*

Several weeks later, they still weren't accustomed to their daily routine.

"Now I know how the donkeys felt," Agusto said. "Except we treated the donkeys nice. We fed them and gave 'em water and we rubbed them down when they got sweaty. Nobody's rubbing me down when I'm sweaty."

"You want the foreman to rub you?"

"I just want him to stay off my back, the son of a bitch."

"Don't work yourself up. You'll make it worse for yourself."

"How much worse can it be?"

"We can get fired. Then we'll be out on the street with no money."

"We never have any money anyway."

"And why do you suppose that is?"

"Tell me."

"Because we gamble it away?"

"You have a screwed up view of the world. Men must have

recreation; otherwise what's the use of working? If you work all the time without play then you're no more than a donkey."

The foreman didn't much like anybody who worked under him in the mill, but he had developed a special animosity toward Agusto.

"I'm going to get even with that son of a bitch," Agusto said. He had a load of cane on his back, far more than he could comfortably carry, but his vanity had been wounded, spurring him to prove his manhood to everyone around. "He's going to be sorry he ever started in with me," he muttered.

"Ah, forget it," Tito said, "You're going to drop dead before the day is out."

"I don't take insults from anybody," Agusto said.

"Do yourself a favor and ignore him," Tito said.

"He didn't insult you," Agusto whined. "It's me he has it in for and for no reason. I work as hard as anybody."

"Don't take it personally," Tito said. "He's rude to everybody."

"No one says that I'm not a man and gets away with it."

"He didn't say that."

"He implied it. It comes to the same thing. Everybody understood his meaning."

"He didn't mean you in particular," Tito said.

"He was looking straight at me all right. He is going to pay for that insult."

Hannibal Bienvenudo, the foreman, had a face that may have well resembled that of his ancient namesake, dark complexion and jaw muscles habitually flexed into a tight expression. Above his right eye, he sported a scar, evidence of carelessness in a brawl in which an opponent's knife had found its mark. Hannibal started at the mill as a laborer when only fourteen years old. He persevered and survived the grueling regimen of back-breaking work, while others around him succumbed, leaving for other work, if they could find it, or dying of diseases aggravated by exhaustion and malnutrition. His success failed to make him sympathetic to those unable to maintain his pace, and he grew to have a low opinion of his fellow workers. He considered failure the result of either weakness, for which he had no compassion, or indolence, which he also could not abide.

A native cunning led him to fawn on those for whom he worked, while he disdained those who worked for him. To see him in the presence of Don Ernesto Continutino, the owner of the mill, afforded some amusement to those who marveled at the transformation of the tiger into a mouse, although some considered a mouse too high in the hierarchy to describe him. They thought him more akin to those creatures that buzzed about piles of dung. Had he been ignorant of his transformation in the proximity of higher rank, the foreman might have been a happier man. He had as much contempt for his metamorphosis as those who observed it. He was no more able to prevent it than to prevent the self-loathing that followed, dissipated only after lashing out at the first subordinate who might cross his path.

The mill workers noticed the pattern and tried to avoid him whenever they suspected the onset of his dark mood. Agusto, being new at the place and still ignorant of the circumstances that made the foreman irascible, categorized the boss' bad temper as unpredictable. In retaliation for all the insults, Agusto planned to ambush the man and thrash him. In vain did Tito try to dissuade him.

"You have to help me," Agusto said.

"You're insane. We'll end up in prison or worse. He might kill us both."

"We are more than a match for him, if we catch him by surprise."

"Two against one is not very sporting."

"Just to scare him a little. That's all."

"We'll get fired."

"He won't recognize us in the dark."

"It's a crazy idea," Tito said.

"I was counting on you," Agusto said. "What kind of a friend are you?" With only a vague sense of what constituted a crime, he put forth an aggrieved air as if asking a friend to commit one were a perfectly normal.

"An insult isn't righted unless the challenge is in the open," Tito argued.

"I'll feel better," Agusto said.

"That's doubtful. If you're dead you won't feel anything, and if you survive you might wish that you were dead."

"I'm doing it with or without you," Agusto said.

Without making a commitment, Tito followed Agusto, vaguely hoping to prevent the matter from getting out of hand.

Hannibal lived in a barrio in the outskirts of town, and the road to his place wound through several neighborhoods, adding distance and time to the journey. He usually preferred the path through the woods, the shortest route home. Three times a week, he played dominoes in the back room of the cantina, and often he drank too much. On one of those nights, Agusto and Tito waited for him.

"We'll knock him to the ground and pummel him till he's good and sore," Agusto said. "He'll go down easy if we catch him by surprise, and we'll disappear before he recovers sufficiently to know what happened."

"Sounds too easy," Tito said.

"You're scared," Agusto countered.

"And you?"

"I'm not scared because there's nothing to it."

In the darkness, even if they had stayed in the open, only a nocturnal animal would have been able to see them as they waited for Hannibal behind a tree wide enough to hide them both. Time seemed to cease its march in the dark. Crickets and frogs conspired to produce an unnerving cacophony. Occasionally, the call of an unknown bird shrieked through the darkness.

"We've been here a long time," Tito said. "I don't think he's going to show up. We don't have to do anything. We can't stay here all night."

"Maybe you're right," Agusto said, his resolve beginning to dissipate with the long wait. "We can get him another time."

Reluctantly, he got up from the ground where he had been sitting propped against the trunk of the tree, but hearing a different sound from the natural ones of the night, he pulled back. "Someone's coming," he whispered.

The sound of someone stumbling along the path got closer. Agusto tied a handkerchief over the lower part of his face as an extra precaution against being recognized, and he urged Tito to do the same. The hesitant, Tito complied though he had no intention of participating in the assault.

"How do you know it's the foreman?" Tito asked. "You don't want to get the wrong person."

"It's him all right," Agusto said, "I can smell him."

The noise got closer, but the complete absence of moonlight kept the boys from identifying the figure.

"He's so drunk he can hardly walk," Agusto said.

The shape advanced closer to the hiding place, they might have reached out and touched it. Still neither boy moved as the form stumbled on. Glad that Agusto had a change of heart, Tito was about to relax his stance when Agusto sprang forward and delivered a blow. The staggering form wobbled but remained standing—contrary to Agusto's expectations. With surprising re-silience, the man wheeled about so quickly weapon in hand that Agusto failed to avoid the knife. Too soon to feel the pain and in the dark failing to see the blood, only bringing his hand to the wound let Agusto know that he was bleeding. "Run," he yelled, his first responsible act of the night. Tito needed no urging, and they both ran as fast as they could, trying in the darkness to avoid a collision.

"I'm hurt," Agusto said when, feeling free of pursuit, they stopped to catch their breath.

"How bad is it?" Tito asked unable to see the blood.

"I don't know," Agusto said. "Seems like a lot of blood." The wound began to sting, and he felt the moisture.

"Can you make it back to the house?"

"I think so."

"But maybe we oughtn't to go there," Tito said trying to sort things out. They had to get help, but how would they explain the wound? The landlady at the boarding house would know of a doctor, but she might also, if suspicious, report them to the Civil Guard.

"We got to do something," Agusto said. His bravura had left him.

The lateness of the hour reduced the likelihood of running into anybody. They decided to return to their lodging to examine the wound. In the room, the light of the lamp revealed a trail of blood.

"Take off your shirt."

Agusto took off the garment and Tito, after bringing the lamp up close, wiped the wound with the part of the shirt that was still dry.

"It's a lot of blood, but it's not deep," Tito said. "Maybe we can bind you up to stop bleeding."

"I'm going to die," Agusto said.

"You're not going to die," Tito assured him, rationalizing that a potential lie was permissible under the circumstances. He took the sheet off the bed and ripped off a strip.

"What are you doing?"

"We'll bind you up with this."

"The landlady is going to make us pay for the sheet."

"That should be the least of it," Tito said.

"What's going on in there," the voice of the landlady came from the other side of the door.

"Speaking of the devil," Agusto whispered.

Tito opened the door to see Doña Estremadura. The light from a kerosene lamp lifted to the level of her nose gave her face the strange and luminous appearance of a disembodied form.

"We've had a little accident," Tito said.

Doña Estremadura peered into the room and saw Agusto curled on the bed. She held the lamp forward, but she didn't enter.

"What's the matter with him?"

"He's wounded."

"He needs a doctor."

"Maybe not," Agusto said.

"What's that?" she asked, indicating the spots on the floor.

Tito didn't answer.

"Maybe he needs a priest," Doña Estremadura said impassively.

"It's not that bad," Tito said.

Doña Estremadura looked at him skeptically. She walked in and placed the lamp down. The light in the room seemed to increase exponentially. "Get some water from the well," she said to Tito, who went out to fetch it. She went back to her quarters and returned with some jars and a bowl. She cleaned Agusto's wound, then she rolled some of the strips of sheet that Tito had cut and put the pad over the wound. "Hold this here," she said to Agusto. She gave Tito the task of cutting more strips from the sheet. She poured into the bowl the contents of two of the jars, mixing them with water until she had a pasty substance that she then applied to the wound. Agusto groaned.

"It stings a little," she said as she wrapped the strips of cloth around Agusto, putting pressure on the wound. She muttered some words unintelligible to either one of the boys. "You're going to be all right," she said when she had finished. "The Civil Guard is another matter. I don't want to know what the two of you were up to, but the sooner you leave the better."

"How can we ever repay you?" Tito asked.

"You can repay me by staying away from my house."

"We'll be gone before dawn," Tito said.

"That will be smart," she said, and without another word she picked up her lamp and left the room.

*W*ELL, WHAT WAS she to do? She was with child and unmarried just when many coffee and tobacco haciendas were falling into ruin. Many blame the Americans for that, but I don't know about such things. Then there was San Siprian. You remember that storm, the worst we ever had. It destroyed the whole crop that year and so many people died. Even Don Eduardo suffered great losses from the storm, but he had the devil's own luck and recovered faster than most. He had connections in America, they say, an unlimited line of credit secured for him by his friend John Walker, who owned the land adjacent to his across the stream. Don Eduardo had a knack for befriending people. Men liked him, whether his own people or Americans or Spaniards, it made no difference. He had them eating out of his hand in no time. It's a rare person—man or woman—who can resist Don Eduardo's charm. He never took advantage of it with women the way other men did. It was unusual to be faithful in his own way to two women; he always loved Carmen even after he married Antonia. But his love for Carmen had only one outlet, and that was their daughter Juana.

Not many understand why Carmen gave her up to Eduardo, but maybe it's not right of me to put it that way. It wasn't as if it was a battle between the two for the child. There was no resorting to the law or anything like that. Eduardo would have accepted whatever Carmen decided. He was reasonable. He offered to take the child. Well, he offered to take them both, but she wouldn't marry him. She couldn't do it after the accident.

As I said, it was a bad time, and the ruin of coffee and tobacco made it difficult to feed another mouth, but Eduardo had no such problem. Times would eventually improve. The Americans promised an economic recovery, and there was no reason to doubt that. Why wouldn't the wealth of the mainland spill over to our little *island? It was inevitable, but even before that, Carmen reasoned Eduardo had a lot more to offer the child. It wasn't just wealth. There was social position to consider. Carmen would never have that, and why should she deprive the child of a better life? Well, what she thought would be a better life. We all have our dreams, but life doesn't always turn out the way we expect.*

At first, she wouldn't see him, but he persisted. Father Rodrigo got involved. He was Eduardo's friend, so he knew the whole story. He was very concerned with the lives of his parishioners, in their worldly lives, not just the so-called spiritual ones. It wasn't religion that motivated him to be close to people, but the other way around. That was unusual for a priest. God forgive me for saying so, but the clergy seem to be made entirely of self-righteous people, self-absorbed in a peculiar way. Pride is a sin. They know that, so they go around pretending to be selfless. Rodrigo was the exception to the rule. He took a special interest in this case. He and Eduardo were boyhood friends, and to some it seemed more than that. There's nothing to stop tongues from wagging especially where a priest is concerned.

He was worried about his friend, naturally, and he was concerned for Carmen, too. She was part of his flock, his responsibility, and he took that very seriously. Even if it had been concern only for Eduardo, that would have been enough. Eduardo was on the verge of madness when Carmen refused to see him. That's what people say, and perhaps it's a bit of an exaggeration, but perhaps not. I ran into him one day during that time, right after the sugar harvest. He was wandering about the empty field on foot as if he were looking for something. It was the middle of the afternoon, and he was unshaven.

"Have you lost something, Don Eduardo?" I asked him. He looked up puzzled to see another person.

"No," he said, but after a pause he added, "The cane is gone."

Well, of course the cane was gone. It was harvest time. But he knew that well enough, and he didn't need me to tell him. More than the cane was gone, but at least he was paid for the cane.

He persisted, and Carmen finally relented and spoke to him. He had kept an eye on her from afar, especially when she grew big. Sometimes she would catch sight of him observing her from a distance, perched on his horse on a hill.

He told her he would take care of her and the child even if she didn't want him, but she said she wouldn't take anything from him.

"It's for the child," he said.

But stubbornly, she refused until the child was three years old, and then she partially relented. She wouldn't go back to him, though he still wanted her. He wanted her more than ever. His desire for her grew the more she resisted.

"Can you say that you don't love me?" he asked her.

She kept silent. She couldn't say it, but neither could she say the opposite.

"Take the child," she said. "I know she'll be better off with you."

He had not expected that, and she was afraid for a moment that the shock on his face was a refusal, but it was only surprise. Immediately, his mind was at work on the details of what that would mean. He was a single man; what would he do with a three-year-old child? He had to make some domestic arrangement, a temporary one, because if the child came, wouldn't the mother follow soon after, or eventually at any rate? Juana was his connection to Carmen. He would always be Juana's father; nothing in the world could change that. If Juana lived with him, the connection would be all the safer.

"Who will take care of her?" he asked himself out loud.

"Gregoria can do it," Carmen replied thinking that the question was directed at her. Why she thought of me immediately, I don't know. We hadn't discussed it, and I was an old woman already, too old to be chasing after a three-year-old. Still, I must say it turned out to be a good idea. It worked out for all, I suppose, for a while.

Don Eduardo had a hard time of it when Carmen married Lucas Sotomajor. It was the only time I ever saw Eduardo drunk.

I mean so drunk he couldn't walk straight. It's a wonder that he got home in one piece. I don't know how he stayed in the saddle. I suppose the horse knew its way home. His master was in no condition to guide it. Eduardo staggered into the house to fetch his gun. I suppose he had gotten it into his head to shoot the new-lyweds. Of course, he couldn't get back on his horse, and thinking the poor beast was part of the conspiracy against him, he tried to shoot it, but he missed. He discharged the gun into the air several times, and Juana woke up crying. The poor child had no idea what was going on.

"It's only thunder in the sky," I said to her. "The storm will pass soon enough." And I held her until she fell asleep again.

In the meantime, Eduardo passed out in the batey. I had Manolo carry him into the house and lay him on the bed. The next day Eduardo didn't remember any of that, and if it weren't for the hangover, he would have denied that he had been drunk at all.

Still, he knew perfectly well that Carmen was married, and he had to give up all hope of getting her back. Then he only had Juana to remind him of what he had lost. I don't know what was going through his mind. Sometimes he was intensely involved with the child, in every detail of her education. Other times, he would forget about her completely, as if she didn't exist. What Juana made of that, I don't know. She never said. Of course, when she was a child, there was no way for her to tell whether that was normal. Pretty quickly, she got used to not having her mother about. I suppose she was content enough to have me instead. I was always there. Children are very adaptable, but you don't really know what's going on inside. They themselves don't know.

SAN GERONIMO WAS not New York or London or Paris. It was smaller than San Juan, Mayaguez or Ponce, but the eyes of its inhabitants reflected a city nevertheless. San Juan and San German could boast of continuous settlement for centuries—San Geronimo, a parvenu in comparison. The growth of the town resulted from the explosion in coffee production that caused a population shift to areas that were previously the preserve of fugitive Indians, runaway slaves, and deserters from the Spanish army. The European craze for coffee fueled a migration from the coastal areas to the mountains as ambitious entrepreneurs searched for land on which to grow coffee. For a while, money did indeed grow on trees.

A city is known for its institutions, and though calling San Geronimo a city might be an exaggeration, that would only be so in comparison to the great metropolitan areas of the world. In 1830, nothing graced the spot where San Geronimo presently stands. Bartolomeo Cintrón first built a house on the actual site of the present city. He had been an itinerant peddler for a few years, traveling from town to town and settlement to settlement with a bundle of wares mostly of interest to women. He sold needles and thread and all sorts of colored ribbons with which garments might be adorned. Sometimes he carried with him bolts of cloth, but they were a bulky item and he only went to that trouble with fabric of exceptional quality that was sure to sell quickly. When he first embarked on that occupation, he traveled on foot, and sometimes by chance he hitched a ride on an ox cart going his way. Not obliged to go in any particular direction other than one in which he might find customers, he sometimes for the sake of convenience let the destination of the drover be his own.

His business prospered enabling him to buy a mule that facilitated his travels into the mountainous regions where the narrowness of the trails added to the difficulty of the generally poor condition of the roads. The influx into the coffee region made it possible for Bartolomeo to establish a base of customers and prompted him to consider setting up a permanent store. That way, his customers might come to him instead of him going to them. To tell the truth, he rather liked traipsing about the countryside hauling his wares, and his decision to stay in one place stemmed more from meeting a young woman with whom he wanted to be permanently allied. He missed her when he was away, and when he was home, she constantly campaigned to make him see the wisdom of giving up his travels. Refusing her wishes became for him impossible.

Known in those parts as Inez the Beautiful, her looks counterbalanced a bad temper that manifested itself despite all attempts by her feminine modesty to keep it in check. Her family feared that the trait would keep Inez from ever finding a husband, and they considered Bartolomeo's interest in her an instance of good luck but his occupation a drawback, an itinerant peddler being akin to a gypsy, and only a rung above a horse thief. Still, a slightly objectionable husband would prove better than no husband at all, and the volatility of Inez's temperament seemed to attract rather than repel him.

He set up shop with Inez to help him. Smugglers provided some of the most prized items that Bartolomeo sold in his store, products manufactured in Europe or in the United States but unavailable legally, because the tariffs imposed by the Spanish government made them prohibitively expensive or altogether unavailable. American and European ships facilitated a brisk trade with Jamaica, a British possession, from where goods flowed illegally to Puerto Rico. Inez proved a sharp businesswoman, more vigilant of every *bit* than her husband, so when striking deals, customers preferred to do so with Bartolomeo rather than Inez who drove a harder bargain. Aware of that, Bartolomeo sometimes wished that she went down to the coast to deal with the smugglers, who pulled into the numerous hidden inlets of the island to deliver contraband goods. But sending a woman by herself was too risky, and they could not both go, as someone had to mind the store.

The trips to the coast involved some risks, including the ever-present possibility of encountering the Civil Guard, whose zeal varied depending on whether the officer of the day was a native or a transplanted Spaniard. How the existing governor happened to interpret his responsibility was also a factor. Some governors, more apt than others to recognize that the interests of the island-ers differed from those of the people who created the laws back in the home country, tended to sympathize with the Creoles. The leanings of the governor, by some subtle chemistry, were trans-mitted to the Civil Guard without any explicit official order.

In the Nineteenth Century, all Spanish colonies in America chafed under the oppressive attitude of the mother country, and one by one they all attempted to throw off the yoke. Puerto Rico no exception, in September of 1868 a group of *independistas* based in the mountain town of Lares, in the middle of the coffee region, launched an armed revolt. The small Lares contingent of only 400 men established a network throughout the island, and they counted on those supporters, after the initial push by the Lares brigade, to join the revolt and propel it to victory. But the Spanish having advance word of the uprising brutally suppressed it. Few managed to escape.

One of those was Enrique Rincon, Eduardo's father, a young man caught in the excitement of political intrigue and patriotic fervor. He dreamed of glory and noble causes. Nothing was no-bler than to fight for the political freedom of one's homeland, something that would benefit the people, an entity both concrete and vague, endowed with mystical powers. The reality that con-fronted him on that day, on the road from Lares, shocked him. He had considered only a triumphal conclusion to the adventure. There would be a battle, but in his imagination that meant only the firing of his musket at some faceless enemy. Instead, he faced a wall of fire from trained soldiers who refused to be intimidated by an armed rabble. He saw comrades fall beside him in bloody spasms. Then, his stomach churned and gave up the unrecogniz-able remnants of his previous meal. When he looked up again, he saw fixed bayonets advancing. With few *independistas* left standing, some older men volunteered to cover the retreat as the rest scattered, each to find his own path through the forest. The Spanish army made short work of those who remained, and most of the retreating rebels were captured. Luckily, Enrique escaped arrest that first day of intensive pursuit. No one identified him as a conspirator, and his name didn't appeared on any documents seized by the authorities. Afraid to return to Lares or to his hometown, he fled southeast until he arrived at Bartolomeo's general store.

Whether Bartolomeo took pity on the young man, or had some other motive, was never clear to either of them. In subsequent years, even after the danger had passed and Enrique Rincon became established in Comerio, they never spoke of that first meeting when Enrique, desperate and hungry, risked coming out of the forest.

"I don't have any money to pay you," Enrique had said, after a meal.

"I didn't think you did," Bartolomeo responded. "You can work it off."

The meeting turned out to be fortuitous for both of them. Bartolomeo had been considering a cock-fighting establishment in conjunction with his store as a sure way to increase business.

"I want to build a *gallera* near the store," Bartolomeo said. "I need a strong man to help me clear the plot and put up the corner posts and the roof."

"I can do that all right," Enrique said. "I'm good with the birds too."

"Are you?" Bartolomeo rhetorically asked.

"I've trained a few," Enrique answered, "before I got involved in other things."

"Well, then if we stick to business, we should be all right," Bartolomeo said.

Enrique got the gist and kept silent about what else he had been involved in.

"This is a quiet mountain. Nothing much ever happens here, and the coffee grows peacefully. We need a *gallera* to add a little excitement. It's legal and profitable."

The two men cleared the land near the store and built a *gallera,* the second structure to be erected in San Geronimo. The first was Bartolomeo's house, which also served as the store. On Sundays, men from all over the mountain brought their fighting birds to the *gallera,* and all day the cockfights and betting went on. The store did a brisk business in ale and rum in addition to the usual weekend business when the *campesinos* stocked up on the necessary supplies for the week. Inez cooked and sold food all day on Sunday, her fried *platanos* the best from anywhere in the vicinity. What she did to make them taste so distinctly delicious remained a mystery; after all, frying was frying. Some people speculated that she didn't use lard from pigs, but no one ventured to name another source.

Aided by the geography of the mountain, the store and the *gallera* made the spot a natural gathering place. Bartolomeo, by instinctive cunning, built his house in a place that naturally developed into a crossroads. Inhabitants of surrounding lands frequently passed by in their regular travels, although no road yet existed, only several paths that led to the various sections of the mountain. A river cascaded over the rocky terrain and provided a convenient watering place for cattle and horses.

Enrique proved true to his word and trained some champion fighting cocks for which Bartolomeo provided the initial capital. Soon, Enrique accumulated money of his own and bought land, but instead of planting coffee like everyone else, he planted tobacco, a faster crop. Had he started planting coffee from scratch, five years would have elapsed before he had a marketable product.

Whether the ecclesiastical authorities noticed on their own that a congregation of souls had sprouted or the community felt the lack of spiritual leadership and applied to the bishopric for assistance is clouded in the mist of history. No doubt the Church is always on the lookout for lost sheep, though lost sheep are often unaware of their disorientation and would be content to go on their merry way in total ignorance of their perilous state. Probably no resident of the area requested a priest to be dispatched, but, with ritual activity a deep-seated human need, everyone welcomed his arrival. Although the Church provides for impromptu delivery of sacraments in emergencies, the presence of an ordained priest to perform baptisms, weddings, and extreme unction relieved many, especially the women, most often the guardians of those customs. A small church became the third structure to rise on the site where the city of San Geronimo stands, and that church in time, propelled by the power of coffee, transformed into the cathedral of San Geronimo.

The school founded by Father Domingo Tierrapiedra was another institution that boosted the renown of San Geronimo. At the time of our story, Sister Sylvester, who might herself be considered a singular institution, ran the school. Sister Sylvester's non-Spanish name sometimes confused strangers, and led them to think she was a foreigner or at least of foreign origin, but that was not the case. Her family had lived on the island for two hundred years, but she had concrete knowledge of her antecedents only back to her great grandparents. Beyond that, her family history was a mystery that she saw no need to resolve. She came from humble people, tillers of the soil for the most part. As the first person in her family to distinguish herself in any way, she rendered reasonable the supposition that opportunity had been previously lacking, a more reasonable idea than the alternative, that her talents were anomalies previously absent in the family.

The establishment in San Geronimo of an elementary school brought about the circumstance that led to the discovery of Sister Sylvester's talent for learning, that is to say Nilda Sylvester's talent, as she had yet to become Sister Sylvester. The school was unusual at a time when schools on the island were few, especially outside the larger coastal cities. What's more, the opening of its doors to girls as well as boys distinguished it as unusual, and provided Nilda Sylvester her chance to be discovered.

Father Domingo Tierrapiedra, the founder and only teacher at the school, noticed Nilda right away—tall for a girl, thin as broomstick, and covered on top with a copious quantity of red hair. When he saw her for the first time, Father Domingo assumed, perhaps due to the intensity of the hair color, that she would be a problem, but by reason of her sex, he also expected her to be pliant and demure. On all counts, he was mistaken. She had an aptitude for book learning, and she applied herself diligently to her lessons. Curiously, she had a disconcerting propensity to interpret what she learned in the oddest way and to ask disturbing questions for which Father Domingo had no ready answers and that sometimes shook the complacency of his faith. He occasionally wondered whether the devil put her there to ensnare him, or God to test his resolve.

But those were fleeting thoughts, and he brought himself back to reality with the admonition that she was only a child, and children are prone to see things from the strangest angles. Of course, that's why they needed to be educated. Father Domingo, like educators the world over, had a vision of uniformity as the product of his efforts, which led him to view his greatest successes as his most resounding failures. Nilda, the most brilliant of his pupils, aroused in him the most qualms. He feared for her salvation, because he didn't know where her questioning attitude would lead her. He strongly suspected that it would lead to her perdition, but she confounded him again by expressing the desire to become a nun.

She went away from San Geronimo for her religious training, but eventually she returned to become a teacher in the school where she had started her journey. Father Domingo, glad to have her back and get some assistance in the running of the school, still failed to understand why Sister Sylvester's mind bolted in certain directions with what seemed to him frivolous impetuosity. She developed an academic interest in etiquette and social comportment. She made a study of the subject, exploring it from historical and cross-cultural perspectives, and she wished to add training in social etiquette to the curriculum of the school. She believed that the exercise of good manners had value far beyond what was normally claimed. Father Domingo, although somewhat mystified by her reasoning, saw no harm in letting her do as she wished, so he shrugged and assented. San Geronimo soon came to be known throughout the island as the center of good manners, and even the well-off in the capital were envious of the results achieved in San Geronimo. The eternal charge that the younger generation was not as well mannered as the previous applied everywhere except in San Geronimo.

16

Days before, the sky still clear, Doña Echevaria began to prepare for the storm. Round faced, flat nosed, with a pudginess that made her look like a doll whose plump cheeks, like a rising tide, attempted to overwhelm her eyes as they made a valiant effort to keep from being submerged, she moved about with great deliberateness as if the weight of her body was a greater burden than she could bear. She read signs invisible to others. She observed the birds. She listened to the cricket and to the frog, *el coqui*, that spoke of the storm to all who would listen. Doña Echevaria took note, and the message frightened her. She noticed a slight change in the consistency of the air. The signs of her alarm also remained cryptic and invisible to most people—slight changes, a quickening of her pace, an angularity introduced to motions that normally flowed.

The necessity to alter daily rituals that kept the uncontrollable forces of the universe in check bothered her. Every day, she waged a quiet battle against the chaos that threatened to overwhelm the world, and by the grace of her effort, her neighbors and compatriots, perhaps the whole human race, continued their existence in relative tranquility. Scattered over the world, others like her also engaged in the task of keeping chaos at bay, an unnoticed and unappreciated service often misunderstood.

The approaching danger differed from the everyday. Chaos took on a physical form. It emerged from where it normally dwelled, in the dreams of human beings, perhaps in those of animals also; she still uncertain whether they, too, had remnants of that state that existed before the Creator wrested the world from the formless void; very likely their dreams revealed it to them also. The force escaped from dreams and congealed over the ocean, churned up the wind and the water, then traveled blindly seeking victims on whom to wreak destruction.

To Doña Echevaria, the approaching calamity indicated a psychic failure to keep the forces of chaos within their proper bounds, but recrimination was, at that point, too late. As she began to prepare for the onslaught, she hesitated, but searching her memory for an alternative, she found none. She stood in front of her cupboard full of jars of herbs and concoctions she mixed from odd ingredients, organic and mineral, for cures of physical and emotional ailments. She treated her clientele often after medical doctors at the municipal clinic had failed, perhaps through no fault of theirs, but because their patients lacked faith in science.

She took down the bottles and jars and placed them in a basket to carry them to the storage space she constructed in the backyard, a hole in the ground lined with wooden slats, to place the valuable and perishable items. She would then cover the lid of the box with earth and stones to keep her store safe from the storm. Gregoria arrived while Doña Echevaria fussed with those tasks.

"You can help me," Doña Echevaria said.

"What are we doing?"

"There's a hurricane on the way."

"The sun is shinning," Gregoria said.

"Not for long," said Doña Echevaria.

They each carried a basket out to the storage place in the yard.

"Have you enough room for all of your bottles?"

"Plenty of room," Doña Echevaria said.

"But not for yourself," Gregoria observed.

"How will you stay safe?"

Doña Echevaria ignored the question.

The next day, the wind picked up. From the ocean, dark masses of clouds moved toward the land. The storm was still far away, but the tops of the trees swayed in the wind. The large leaves of the banana trees spread out like sails. The tops of palms arched like slender gymnasts trying to touch their toes. Every hacienda had a *baraca*, a small windowless structure built close to the ground, with a ditch around it to conduct the water away from the building and well anchored to withstand the fury of the god Huracan.

Huracan was a noisy god—heard but not seen in the shelter that had no windows and a barricaded door against the wind and the water. The wind whistled through the trees and howled across the land; demons had escaped from the underworld to rampage above, knowing that they would soon be forced back to their prison and wanting to make the most of their time on the surface.

Huracan, drunk with power, picked up trees by their tops and exposed their inadequate roots. He tossed them about with no regard to where they might fall. Houses, too, he picked up, and the ones that resisted, he dismembered, the zinc roofs torn from the joists and hurled helter-skelter about the land. Dogs, chickens, and cows, and every other sort of animal caught unprotected, were flung against trees and walls. Geese and goats floated along impromptu streams that formed at the insistence of Huracan.

He disgorged an abundance of water to drown the land. Having sucked it from the inexhaustible ocean, he failed to hold it as he traveled. The proud mountains retaliated incessantly gashing him, their peaks scratching against his belly. Rushing through the wounds, trying blindly to find its way home, the homesick water poured, overwhelming the normal paths—the rivers and streams that flowed to the ocean. Sheets of water cascaded down, sweeping debris with them. The remnants of houses floated in the current along with carcasses of animals that had failed to scurry to safety. Peals of thunder echoed over the *baraca*.

"Will we have to live here forever?" Juanita asked.

"Of course not, child," Gregoria assured her. "The storm will pass soon enough."

"Maybe our house will be gone," Juanita said.

"Hush, child. The house is strong. We only came here as a precaution. Your father's house will still be there tomorrow."

Tomorrow seemed far away to Juanita, and the storm would have much time to work on uprooting the house where she had lived for so long but not always. She had a vague memory of living with her mother somewhere else, a much smaller house, like Gregoria's. She wondered whether she had invented that memory, and the house in her mind was really Gregoria's house. There had been an older woman there too who resembled Gregoria.

By the kerosene lamp Doña Echevaria sat on a crate dealing out an old deck of cards. The card with gold coins appeared and then the queen of hearts. Eduardo watched her from a dark corner of the *baraca*. The storm was sure to destroy the season's crop, so the gold card was out of place, and the queen of hearts was not a card for him; Doña Echevaria turned up the king of swords.

"I remember a someone who had cards like that in a house where I lived a long time ago," Juanita said.

"So you do," Gregoria said. "She was your grandmother."

"She was a talented fortune teller," Doña Echevaria said.

"Is she dead?"

"She's dead," Eduardo answered before Gregoria could decide what to say.

Gregoria expected the question to come up sooner or later, but she didn't expect it that day. What a child remembers is very peculiar. Who would have guessed that the cards would trigger the memory? She was barely three years old the last time she saw her grandmother, Andrea Gutierez. How strange that she remembered the cards. Which card in particular did she remember? That would be interesting to know—a message in itself. Gregoria dared not ask, fearing that the question or the answer might upset Eduardo. Leave well enough alone, but well enough receded as too vague a term on which to decide the matter. The question of responsibility hovered over Gregoria, but she often found herself making decisions with unpredictable results. How could she be responsible for something beyond her power to control?

"Mama is in the storm," Juanita said.

"Your mother is all right, Juanita. She's in a *baraca* also. She's safe from the storm," Gregoria said.

"She should be with us," Eduardo said, from his dark corner. "The fault is not mine."

The attribution of fault at the moment perplexed Juanita. "Are you telling fortune?" she asked Doña Echevaria.

"I don't tell fortune," Doña Echevaria answered. "I just turn up the cards. Fortune reveals itself."

"What do the cards say about me?"

Doña Echevaria gathered up all the cards and shuffled them seven times. Then she began to lay out the cards in a row, her face impassive.

"This is only a game," Gregoria said to Juanita.

"Just to pass the time while we wait out the storm," Doña Echevaria concurred. She had laid out seven cards, and three of them had swords.

"We should play a different game," Gregoria said.

"I think you're right," Doña Echevaria said sweeping up the cards face up on the crate.

"What's my fortune?" Juanita insisted.

"You'll have a long and happy life," Doña Echevaria said.

"Of course she will," Gregoria said.

"It's only a game," Doña Echevaria said.

"What about love?" Juanita asked.

"Love is up to you," Doña Echevaria said.

"Stop this nonsensical talk," Eduardo said. "There's enough ignorance in the world without you spreading more."

The two women remained silent for a moment. "There'll be plenty of work tomorrow," Gregoria then said to dispel the tension.

"There's always work after a storm," Doña Echevaria added. "It took weeks to clean up after the last one."

The wind kept howling throughout the night, but eventually all the occupants of the *baraca* fell asleep on the straw and blankets, all except Eduardo who propped himself up in his corner and stayed awake thinking of the work that would have to be done to get the hacienda back in operation with minimal financial loss. Also, he thought about Carmen. He would send someone to get news of her as soon as the storm abated. Toward morning, he dozed off for a bit. When he awoke, silence pervaded outside except for the solitary crowing of a cock that had survived the night. He pushed open the door of the *baraca* and let daylight stream in to wake the women.

Eduardo's house sustained minimal damage. Some of the roof loosened and was slightly displaced. A tree was blown against the rear, creating a diagonal crack in the exterior wall of the kitchen. The stable also survived, but two of the horses had panicked and kicked holes in the doors of their stalls. Only two stakes remained where the chicken coop had been, and the sugar mill that produced for the neighborhood caved in on one side, impairing the machinery. Gregoria's house suffered the most damage. The roof was completely gone and the walls collapsed inward. Running across the muddy yard, Juanita tripped over the carcass of a goose that, having escaped from the barn, fell victim to the wind.

17

J UANITA NEVER REPROACHED her mother for leaving her. She had no sense of being left, and not until she was an adult did she realize her life might have been different if she had spent her childhood with her mother instead of her father. She had not been abandoned nor put up for adoption. She lived, after all, in her father's house, and her mother was more than a shadowy figure in her imagination, though not there every day to console and pamper her. She saw her mother occasionally as circumstances permitted, and a long time elapsed before she realized that children usually live with two parents.

She also considered her father beyond reproach; or rather, Juana didn't know of anything with which to reproach him, except that look of fear she sometimes caught in his eyes, the fear of being blamed for something never mentioned. That look made her uncomfortable, and more so when she realized that she was the only one who called it forth from a man reputed to be fearless, the very model of *macho completo*. Proud to be the daughter of Eduardo Rincon, she didn't want to be the cause of anything that detracted from his stature in her eyes or in anyone else's. She failed to see what caused his fear to surface when he looked at her, so she tried to ignore what she saw, but sometimes guilt overcame her for a fault she could not identify.

"You're the mistress of this house," he said to her when she, still a child, had only a limited notion of what that meant. She interpreted his words as permission to go wherever she pleased in the house or the barns or the fields. Wherever the daughter of the patron went, the workers made way for her with a smile. In the orchards, young men cut grapefruit for her, and she sat on the ground and ate the fruit. They gave her oranges to take home to eat whenever she pleased. And why not? They were her father's oranges and grapefruits. Sometimes she would go to the barn, where the tobacco hung to dry, and she stood there just breathing in the aroma of the leaves.

"You like the smell of it, eh, little one?" said the man who hoisted the tobacco leaves up into the air on lines raised and lowered on pulleys.

"I sure do," she answered.

"It's a good smell," he said. "It's the smell of money."

Why did he say that? she wondered. Grown-ups said the most peculiar things. Tobacco did not smell at all like money. But maybe she didn't know enough about money to know how it smelled. She hardly ever had any, and no place to spend the little she had except at the country store, and there they didn't care whether she had any money. Sometimes she would forget to take the coins her father gave her to spend on candy, and the shopkeeper would give her whatever she wanted anyway. "But I forgot my money," she would say. He thought her concern amusing. "What's a few centavos between friends," he said with a chuckle, "I will put it on your father's account."

Perhaps paper money smelled like tobacco. She never had any paper money, only coins. She had more bits than she could spend, so she kept them in a hollowed-out gourd that served as an *alcancia*, except once the coins were in, she had no way to get them out without breaking the gourd, and she didn't want to do that. She kept putting in coins until the gourd filled completely, so full that the coins would no longer rattle in it. Then she had to get another gourd to fill. Surely Gregoria would get her another one from wherever she got the first one, from someone in her family who hollowed out gourds and decorated them to sell in San Geronimo. Townspeople bought such gourds, beautifully decorated with strange stick-like figures and angular designs.

"You see these pictures," Gregoria said. "They're just like the ones the Tainos used to make hundreds of years ago."

"What are Tainos?"

"They are the people who were here before the Spaniards came."

"So where are they now?"

"They're hiding," Gregoria said. "From Spaniards who wanted to enslave them."

"Why don't they come out, now that the Spaniards are gone?"

"*Hay querida,* Spaniards are never gone. They just disguise themselves as something else. Tainos know that. They're better off hiding."

Gregoria, too, said the strangest things. Where would Tainos hide from the Spaniards? And how would Spaniards disguise themselves? The minute they opened their mouths, they gave themselves away. They spoke with such strange accents, like the man who lived up the road, the one called *el Gallego.* Because he spoke funny, as soon as he opened his mouth, everyone knew exactly where in Spain he came from. Disguised Spaniards, trying to get Tainos to come out, would have to walk about silently in their disguises, or else the Tainos would be alerted to the presence of their enemy. Juanita had two ways of recognizing a Spaniard: if he spoke she could tell by his accent, and someone who refused to speak had to be a Spaniard in disguise trying to entice Tainos from their hiding place.

"Gregoria, if I wanted to find a Taino, where would I look?"

"Right under your own nose would be the best place," Gregoria said.

Gregoria knew a great many things, but she must be wrong about where to look for Tainos, because if any Tainos lived in Comerio, Juanita surely would have found one already, unless of course they too donned disguises.

Gregoria was the oldest person with whom Juanita was personally acquainted, as old as Juanita's grandparents would have been were they still alive. She was certain her paternal grandparents were dead. She and her father visited the cemetery to lay flowers on their graves. She presumed that her maternal grandparents, too, were dead since she never met them, but neither had she verified that assumption. When she visited her mother, too many other concerns arose, and she never thought to ask her father, having noticed his discomfort with anything to do with her mother. Juanita had tried to broach the subject with Gregoria, who when she took Juanita to visit her mother, hovered in the background like a hen expecting at any moment a hawk to swoop down, but the old woman had been more evasive about grandparents than she had been about where to find Tainos.

Although Gregoria spent most of her time in Don Eduardo's house, cleaning and cooking and doing all the other things that women do around a house and seeing that Juanita was fed and clothed like a proper young lady, she had a house of her own not too far from the big house on the other side of the *batey*. Gregoria had insisted on the house as a condition of employment when she came to work for Don Eduardo. He agreed and had the small house built within shouting distance of his, although the little house could not be seen from the big one because of an intervening stance of banana trees. In Gregoria's house, sparsely furnished with wooden furniture made right on the hacienda by Enrique the carpenter, there were no sofas or chairs with caning and pillows to lean on. Guests sat on wooden benches, but Juanita didn't mind that. She felt quite comfortable in Gregoria's small house, a much more manageable home than her own. Gregoria's house contained no imported mahogany furniture, although Gregoria herself and not Don Eduardo cared about the fancy furniture in the big house.

"Hay, don't be wild. You'll put a dent in your father's chair. Then what will he say?"

"He never says anything," Juanita responded. "I think he would rather sit on a bench."

"Hay, *Dios mio*, ten *misericordia!*" Gregoria exclaimed. "He's too good. All the more reason why you should behave like a lady."

Behaving like a lady was not fun, but Juanita had no choice. Sooner or later, she had to make concessions. She was forbidden to climb on the mahogany chairs with her shoes on. She would rather not wear shoes anyway. All the other children who roamed about her father's property did so barefoot. Why did she have to be the only one who wore shoes?

"Outside you must wear shoes," Gregoria insisted.

"Why must I? No one else wears shoes."

"Ladies wear shoes," Gregoria was adamant.

"I'm just a girl."

"You're the lady of this house," Gregoria said, "for now anyway."

"What do you mean for now?"

"*Hay*, you ask too many questions. It's not for me to talk about such things," Gregoria said, turning to walk to the kitchen.

"Gregoria, you must not keep secrets from me."

"I do not keep secrets," Gregoria said.

"Tell me this then: sometimes when I pass by and people think I can't hear them, they say, 'Poor little thing,' behind my back. Why do they say that Gregoria? I'm not poor at all. If I were poor, people wouldn't talk behind my back."

"That's a small price to pay for your blessings, child, be happy," an insufficient answer, but the only one Gregoria would give.

THE GRANDEST BUILDING in downtown San Geronimo housed the coffee growers club, *El Club Nacional de Cafeteros*. In deference to God, the cathedral reigned as the larger structure, but directly across the square, *El Club Nacional* made its claim to importance with its garish green roof and mosaic tile-studded columns. *El Club Nacional* made the cathedral possible. In fact, all the civic wonders of San Geronimo depended on the club, because the institution represented the wealth that made ornamentation possible. The organization hired the architect who designed the church and the town square along with the surrounding buildings. The club's two stories with smooth arches of yellow stucco proclaimed the Moorish influence that not even time and Catholicism could remove from all things Spanish.

In the sun, the green tiles of the roof glistened so that, from a distance, the structure might be mistaken for an enormous emerald, an apt enough appearance for a building patronized principally by gentlemen likely to be partial to that gem. That preference had no obvious explanation other than a possible reaction against diamonds, the stone of choice of the rest of the world. Part of the Spanish character consisted of arbitrarily latching on to tastes and mannerisms for no other reason than to exhibit a marked eccentricity. Some say that, cut off from the rest of Europe by the Pyrenees, the Spanish developed a madness peculiar to themselves, like an inbred family, nursing a strain of insanity that blooms now and again, the Spanish Inquisition having been one of its most virulent outbreaks and fascism in the Twentieth Century a close second.

Whether the penchant for eccentricity is Spanish or Catholic is moot, because just as the Moorish strain cannot be extracted from Spanish art, neither can Catholicism be separated from anything Latin. The question is, to what degree did the Spanish character survive transplantation to the New World? Certainly it did not remain intact for long. The influence of the native people is unmistakable. The pre-Columbian natives of the island preferred death to slavery. Historians claim that they disappeared by the end of the Eighteenth Century, but, in fact, you can see them still if you look closely at the faces and note the characteristic gentleness of those who still prefer to be known as *Borinqueños*.

Don Aurelio Castillo hung out at the *Club Nacional*, fondly referring to it as his home away from home. All his friends understood that he went there to get away from the women of his household, more in number than he wished. The father of five legitimate daughters and supposedly several others who conveniently were attributed to the husbands of their mothers, he suffered from the unfortunate circumstance of having no sons. His wife, Doña Clara, passed childbearing age, offering no hope that a legitimate male heir to Don Aurelio's fortune would be forthcoming. He even gave up on the possibility that he might have a son with some other woman, having come firmly to believe, after several experiments, that he was cursed with the inability to sire a male offspring. The thought that he might be to blame, and not Doña Clara, had at first thrown him into a panic, but after some reflection and a stoic acceptance of his fate, the silver lining of this darkest of clouds manifested itself in enhanced relations between husband and wife.

Though the improved domestic condition abated the urgency to be constantly away from home, it did not completely remove the need to get away from a house full of women, if only to get a respite from the reminder that he missed what he had looked forward to as a major gratification in his life, the sharing with a son what had taken him a lifetime to accumulate. His friends, in a misguided effort to comfort him, occasionally suggested that a son-in-law might be a good alternative and might lessen his disappointment. This suggestion more often than not had the opposite effect on *Don* Aurelio. In this area also, he seemed to be unfortunate. He could not tell whether the younger generation was in general inferior to the one that preceded—that is to say, his own, replete with men of the most excellent character, like himself. Perhaps something about his daughters continually attracted young men whom he found to be wanting in the most essential qualities.

Perhaps he was responsible for this too, for living in a house in town instead of in the country, on the land that had provided his wealth. He had tried to be fair to Doña Clara, who grew up in town and who never adjusted to life in the country, although the family holdings were not all that far from town.

Doña Clara valued attending Mass every Sunday in a big church with real stained-glass windows. *Don* Aurelio did not understand that preference, since, as far he knew, God was just as present in the country church as in the cathedral, or so he had been told. He couldn't say for sure, God's way of thinking still unclear to him. Christ had been, after all, a poor carpenter, or rather an impoverished carpenter, for surely he had been a good carpenter, more likely to have felt at home in a modest country church than in an ostentatious cathedral. Well, ostentatious was perhaps an exaggeration. The cathedrals in Madrid—those were ostentatious. In San Geronimo, the ostentation arose only relative to the country church. Who's to say what God's church-going habits are? Perhaps He only makes brief appearances at the country church out of obligation, and He spends the bulk of His time in the cathedral. That wouldn't be difficult to understand. That made sense. Doña Clara surely was onto that; the priests don't fool all of the people all of the time. They carry on about humility and vows of poverty, but there is no reluctance to pass the plate every Sunday and build cathedrals for which large donations are required.

And what of the nonsense about the eye of a needle? He imagined Saint Peter standing by the heavenly gate needle in hand, the eye a hoop through which every soul had to jump, and of course one's soul was bound to be just as plump as one's body. Wide body, lean soul just didn't make sense. He could see himself stuck in the eye of the needle and all because he was a rich man. He could see through the ruse. The more he gave to the Church, the better his chances of passing through that needle. Those priests weren't born yesterday, no sir, but they didn't count on Aurelio Castillo. The meek shall inherit the earth—that was another piece of nonsense. The saying didn't seem to apply to those infernal Americans gobbling up all the good land despite the five hundred acre law. Well, they could break their own law if they wanted to. To tell the truth, they weren't any worse than the Spaniards, a bit more civilized in *Don* Aurelio's opinion. At the very least, they didn't torture their prisoners, not in public anyway.

Old as he was, he wasn't old enough to remember Rafael de Aristegui, Count of Marisol, nor Juan Primm, Count of Reus, names once used by mothers on the island to scare little children into good behavior, but he heard about them from his father, who assured Aurelio that the terror they inspired was not exaggerated. The Count of Reus, an especially dreadful man, was deathly frightened of black people. Perhaps the color reminded him of his own soul. Blackness, after all, isn't a matter of skin color. Aurelio called his youngest one *la negrita*, because he loved her best.

She rode a horse like a man and her skin as white as could be expected of one who refused to carry a parasol. With those traits, she would never find a husband, but maybe he could do something about that, sweeten the pot a little. The right man had to be found. Who would want to marry a woman who acted like that? She was the most beautiful of his daughters, as if the best had been saved for last. She was the sweetest too, if only one made the effort to understand her. She just wouldn't be ruled by a man. But what of that? Was there really any woman ruled by a man? All a sham, and some men believed it. Poor fools! Didn't Voltaire say, "History is a myth agreed upon?" The same can be said about the subservience of women. Antonia was just one of those who didn't want to pretend. Only a special kind of man puts up with that. Precious few, those men, and none of them called at his house. Aurelio got to see the ninnies and dandies, waiting to inherit their father's money. In the meantime, they pranced about in imported clothes meant for the totally different European climate. If only they knew how ridiculous they looked! Well, at least they dressed well when they went to Madrid, in pursuit of an education, they all claimed. The men Aurelio would have preferred were busy making their way in the world, too busy to call on his daughters.

"Mark my words. When the small land owner can't hold on to his land, no one's safe." The words came floating across the room to make *Don* Aurelio turn from the bar to see who continued the perpetual and futile political discussion. Talking politics was the national pastime, more popular and less expensive than horse racing and cock fighting. Shooting off one's mouth didn't cost anything, especially at the moment with the Americans in charge. They had made freedom of speech a fetish. You could say anything as long as you didn't stand in the way of their taking all the land.

The speaker, *Don* Fao Araguay, was about the same age as *Don* Aurelio, but all his hair had already turned white. He was as partial to the left wing of the Liberal party as *Don* Aurelio, and his loquacity sprang, no doubt, from a high rate of metabolism that supplied his mouth with more energy than necessary for the conduct of ordinary business. This chemical peculiarity also kept his physique from expanding; consequently he cast a shadow considerably thinner than *Don* Aurelio's, a feature that *Don* Aurelio did not begrudge him, having elevated his own girth to a symbol of status.

"Inviting the Americans was a mistake. I was against it all along," continued *Don* Fao.

"So you're saying we invited one guest too many to the *fiesta*, my friend," said Altimo Ramirez, also a member of the party. Pleased with himself for having come close to what he considered a witticism, he grinned as he pulled on a cigar.

"I wasn't aware of invitations having been sent out," said Alfredo Gomez. "It was not the conservatives who sent them. I'm sure of that. You can't follow a course of action and then complain about it when it doesn't pan out." He had been partial to Spain throughout, but without deep-seated convictions, he could be swayed by whatever side presented the most heated argument. The group having no other true conservative, and the conversation likely to be one-sided, spurred *Don* Alfredo to make a token presentation of the conservative view to keep the discussion interesting.

In truth, his appearance concerned him more than who pulled the strings of government. Business would go on as usual. Whether he had to ease his way through customs with pesetas or with dollars made no difference to him. He had experienced, as had they all, a financial setback with the currency change when the Americans took over, but that had been temporary for most people in his circle. However, there had been many less fortunate, smaller landowners and subsistence farmers who failed to recover and lost their holdings. There was nothing to do about that, except wait for the economic turn around that the Americans promised.

The situation was not completely bleak. Opportunities were there for those who, like Eduardo Rincon, recognized them. His being better off at the moment than five years before may have resulted from his dealings with Americans. He represented the kind of man who made his way despite external circumstances, though he would have disclaimed that. In that respect a modest man, he always attributed a large measure of his success to luck. Aurelio Castillo noticed Eduardo and pondered his views on luck. To *Don* Castillo, capable men seemed always to be luckier than the rest, so he hesitated to agree with Eduardo's attribution of success to mere chance. Eduardo stood out as one of the young men Aurelio wished to entice to call upon his daughters, but he had so far been unsuccessful. *Don* Aurelio rightfully concluded that Eduardo had some romantic interest tucked away in the country, but to *Don* Aurelio's knowledge, Eduardo was not officially engaged, so whatever attachment he had was less than permanent.

For Aurelio to expect a young man like Eduardo to refrain from romantic entanglements in the course of his daily business would have been unrealistic. Country girls had a charm of their own to which he had succumbed when he was young. But marriage existed in a different realm, having very little to do with charm or romantic love, though with luck, that, too, could be part of it.

"Whether we invited them is of little consequence now,"

Eduardo said. "In any case, they would have invited themselves sooner or later."

"Perhaps not," said Altimo Ramirez. "They would have been content with Cuba."

"The Cubans are too belligerent to hold by occupation, and it's too close to Florida to make much of a strategic difference. They needed this island in the middle of the chain. From here they can dominate the whole Caribbean militarily."

"You mean they didn't come to help?"

"They came to help all right, to help themselves to every-thing."

"We got out from under the thumb of Spain, and that's what we wanted."

"The question is whether it is better to be under a thumb than under a heel?"

"It's not as bad as all that. Enlightenment counts for some-thing."

"You think the Americans are enlightened?"

"They have democracy. They abolished slavery twenty years before Spain did. They are in favor of education while the Spaniards were not. 'Education breeds revolution' was the Spanish motto."

"The Americans don't care how educated we are. They know we're powerless."

"Education is fine, but it won't save us. The thing is to hold on to the land. Don't sell to the Americans."

"That's easy for you to say. Your land is not mortgaged. What about the poor bastard who is up to his neck in debt and his wife doesn't stop giving birth?"

"In that case selling the land doesn't help much."

"But he has no choice. The price of coffee will never be as good as it was when we were selling to Spain, and tobacco also has taken a plunge."

"Sugar is what the Americans want. They're buying the land to plant cane."

"So how much of your land is in sugar cane, Eduardo?"

"Not much," he answered.

"Aurelio was the only one of us who foresaw the sugar craze."

"I didn't foresee anything," Aurelio said. "I planted cane because my father did. I'm a traditionalist."

Don Aurelio abhorred political discussions, and he didn't want to be reminded of the tumultuous events of the American invasion. True, the Americans tried to make the military takeover as smooth and as bloodless as possible. That worked out even though their troops, for the most part, consisted of men with minimal military training who volunteered for an adventure away from home.

After the Spanish military left the island, the Americans took months to establish civil control, and the *Borinqueños,* having been armed by the Spaniards to defend the island, saw their chance to take revenge on those who had oppressed them for centuries. Bands of raiders arose overnight primarily in the mountainous coffee-growing regions. Their faces stained black with charcoal, they acquired the name of *tiznados.* They attacked the haciendas owned by Spaniards, but occasionally class distinction overwhelmed nationality and a Creole's hacienda fell victim.

In contrast to *Don Fao, Don* Aurelio was a man of few words. Politicians invariably gave him a headache with the exception of Jose de Diego whom he considered not really a politician but a poet gone astray. One couldn't help but fall under his spell when listening to Jose de Diego, but afterward when you thought about what he said, only a dream remained. Aurelio would not go as far as to discard that dream, but certainly it was not enough, no substitute for hardheaded action. Muñoz Rivera, a more practical politician, kept the autonomists in line, well, as far as a bunch of hotheads could be kept in line. He understood the chimera of independence. To go at it alone would be suicide. Having the Americans around wasn't exactly ideal, but the relationship would get better or perhaps that was a dream too. Who could tell?

Everyone guessed about the future, and those whose predictions coincided with events were thought to be wise. A toss of a coin would have been just as reliable, just like his fields of sugar cane. He had not calculated what would be the most profitable use of the land. He simply, with plenty of qualms when everyone else planted tobacco, continued what his father had started. When the price of sugar went up and tobacco went down, his repute as a man of foresight spread among his neighbors. Knowing the truth, he didn't take his celebrity seriously. If the situation were reversed, everyone would have been talking about the stubborn old fool he had been. In fact, he expected conditions to turn sooner or later. In a world replete with fools, some amiable enough but fools nevertheless, nothing could be done but ignore their foolishness and enjoy their amiability. That emerged as Aurelio's formula for enduring life's inevitable disappointments.

As the father of five daughters, resigned to the prospect of having fools for son-in-laws, he hoped for at least one on whom he could look with favor and not have to pretend approval. He was prepared to do his duty and smile at whomever fate, or as Doña Clara would prefer to say, God, sent along. While at the *Club Nacional de Cafeteros* an idea came to him that, if successful, would yield his wish. The problem became one of presentation. Aware of the potential for misunderstanding, he feared his plan might fail for lack of proper execution. The scheme might appear crass to one who didn't understand it, seeming as if he were trying to buy a husband for one of his daughters, for Antonia, of course. He would rather make the effort for her than for any of the others, although she would be the least appreciative. She would never understand, so she must never know that he had anything at all to do with putting a man in her path. The gentleman need not know either. How could he? A gentleman would never accept such a proposition, especially a gentleman like Eduardo Rincon, or would he?

This wasn't a novel idea. Men married for money. Women did it almost exclusively. Though doing it openly had gone out of fashion. These days, everyone put up a pretense of falling in love, as if that were a reliable basis for marriage.

One could see in Eduardo Rincon an ambitious young man, if one knew what to look for and looked closely. The signs, lines on his face, became more apparent with a smile, hardly perceptible around his lips and on his forehead. They could be read just like Gypsies read the lines on the palm of the hand. His amiability did not hide Eduardo's ambition, not from *Don* Aurelio who saw it clearly. Not a vicious ambition, *Don* Aurelio would not tolerate viciousness around Antonia. Eduardo's healthy ambition seemed a natural desire to exercise his faculties. Not content to stand still or tread water, he always moved toward a destination, and once there he started out for somewhere else. Such men sometimes wore themselves out while still young, never enjoyed their achievements, unaware of them, blindly caught in the momentum of the journey, but not Eduardo.

At neither of the extremes, both to be deplored, at peace with himself, Eduardo would smoke a cigar. Those who lived for pleasure without thought of how to pay for it were more common than those who worked blindly without respite, more common and more reviled, because others would end up paying. Joylessness, too, was a vice but the victims were less obvious. Often said of the joyless person, "He's a good man. He has no vices." But Aurelio knew better. He had been observing Eduardo for a while, just as pleased to see him at the horse races as to deal with him at the tobacco exchange. A man who enjoyed horses had to be taken seriously, especially if the horses attracted him to riding and not to gambling. Eduardo liked horses. He and Antonia would have that in common—a good sign, a head start on the way to love.

Aurelio thought of the future in that manner, a concession surely, but he was used to concessions, everything in life a compromise. Antonia would have love. She would demand it. One could not explain to a young person that romantic love equaled a trick played on the mind by desire, an instrument of nature to keep the species going. Well, maybe that wasn't quite right. Mere lust would keep the species going, but also needing an orderly society, lust had to be kept in check. But who would give it up without something of equal value in exchange? Love had to be that something, a very clever invention indeed. Women, asked to give up the most, with good reason, held on to the illusion more desperately, and men lagged not far behind. *Don* Aurelio, not a psychologist and much less a philosopher, did not spend much time sorting out these thoughts into a coherent thesis. No one asked him to deliver a lecture on the topic. In conversation he had to be circumspect. The men at the *Club Nacional* would think him odd if he spouted pronouncements on love. At home, too, he kept quiet on the subject, since his daughters, by reason of their sex, all considered themselves greater experts than he.

Doña might listen and agree with him from a sense of duty, but as soon as he left the room, she sided with her daughters. No matter. He knew what he knew. This love business resembled starting a fire: only some tinder needed and a spark to set it off. The tinder always there, he wouldn't even have to strike two stones together, having acres and acres of matches. *Don* Aurelio's invitation only mildly surprised Eduardo. "Stop by the house next Sunday after mass. Doña Clara will feed you a lunch you will remember for a long time."

Don Aurelio was right about that. Eduardo would remember that day for the rest of his life, just like he would remember the day that he first saw Carmen bathing under the waterfall. He recognized something unusual in an invitation that assumed he would be at Mass in the cathedral on an ordinary Sunday, neither Easter nor Christmas, not even the feast of Saint Geronimo, the patron saint of the town. Even on those holidays, he rarely attended the cathedral or any other church. Not since his mother died of typhoid fever had he been a regular attendee at church services. Since churchgoing was an activity for women, they dragged their men behind them. After his mother's death, there had been no woman to compel his attendance at Mass. Then, he had no fear of hell, his own death being an abstraction. The death of his mother had been vivid enough, but it did not translate to the possibility of his own. Still, he complied with the requirement of attendance at least once a year, not because he feared being outside the Church but because, even from beyond the grave, his mother compelled him to do the minimum.

Around the anniversary of her death, each year he attended

Mass in remembrance of her, because he knew that would have pleased her. The Sunday in question fell close enough to the anniversary of his mother's death to qualify as an appropriate time to fulfill his yearly obligation. *Don* Aurelio, unaware of Eduardo's church-going habits, fortuitously assumed that he would be at Mass in the cathedral that Sunday.

"For some reason, at my house Sunday lunch is the most sumptuous meal of the week. You will not regret it."

"No meal at your house can possibly be regrettable," Eduardo said.

"Ah, that's another matter all together," said *Don* Aurelio lightly patting his paunch. "There is some business matter I want to discuss with you."

"Well, Sunday is your day of rest. Business we can discuss right now."

"No, no, it will be clearer if we discuss it in a, shall we say, domestic setting." He paused to consider what he had just said, and judging it to be appropriate he repeated, "Yes, a domestic setting is what's required for this talk."

THE INHABITANTS OF San Geronimo considered their church a cathedral, but in reality it was no such thing. That is, it lacked official designation as such, though in size and splendor no less grand than the cathedral in San Juan, the official seat of the bishop. At most, the church of San Geronimo might be called a semi-cathedral, a status not recognized by the official protocol of the Roman Church. The history of this odd status, neither fish nor fowl, elucidates a political trait of the islanders, a willingness to tolerate ambiguity in order to avoid all-out conflict. If you are straddling a fence, you need not give-up one side or the other, so you may pick fruit on the north side when the harvest is good in the north or from the south when you prefer the pickings there. If someone asked you whether you were a southerner or a northerner, you would answer depending on which way you faced at the moment; or preferably, you would consider the question impolite and ignore it altogether.

In dealing with Spain, the Puerto Ricans had not struggled for independence the way the Cubans had, nor wanted to be a protectorate of the United States, as did the Dominicans. Puerto Rico sought accommodation within the Spanish empire, but no great sense of loss resulted from being ceded to the United States. In 1898, American troops met little resistance from the native population. The peace was maintained even in subsequent years when political and economic adjustment proved difficult. All in all, Puerto Ricans considered one master to be as good, or as bad, as another. Eventually the status of the island vis-à-vis the conqueror came to reflect this penchant for ambiguity. Not absorbed into the American nation as a state, the island hibernated without the prerogatives of an independent nation. Though the inhabitants clung to a distinct and separate national identity, the majority considered complete independence undesirable. Accommodation within an empire felt safer, so the pattern begun with Spain continued with the United States.

The status of Saint Geronimo Church arose from the same conflict that prevented the embracing of an independence movement against Spain. Despite inextricably entwined interests, the merchants and the growers failed to agree on a common approach. The planters depended on the merchants to sell their commodities on the world market, and without the planters, merchants had nothing to sell. Nevertheless, they looked on each other with suspicion because their short-term goals differed. The merchants controlled the flow of capital and didn't look with favor at competition from foreign financial institutions. The planters, whose wealth was tied up in the land, needed capital and favored the establishment of more banks to create competition and bring down interest rates. All of this had little to do with religion, but a great deal to do with economic divisions manifested in the trappings of society, among which ornate churches may be numbered. The influence of the merchants dominated urban centers, San Juan being the most prominent. Having been instrumental in the original construction of the cathedral in that town, and having continued to be major contributors to its upkeep, they associated the church with that segment of society.

Not to be outdone, planters, tobacco growers in particular, lobbied Rome for a bishopric, but their request failed. Refusing to be thwarted, they proceeded to raise the necessary funds to rebuild the church in San Geronimo on a grander scale. Whether officially a cathedral or not, it became a cathedral to them, but a cathedral without a bishop was a contradiction. A thorny problem to solve, for having already been turned down by the Vatican, no earthly power remained to which an appeal might be made. Hardly anyone in the world would consider humility a Latin trait, much less the suppliants in this case. They would have no compunction to supersede the Pope had they a practical mechanism for doing so, but short of death, gaining an audience with someone of higher authority seemed impossible. The efficacy of prayer being unaffected by wealth, a condition considered unfair by those involved, a more pragmatic route had to be found.

Those trying to legitimize the cathedral in San Geronimo directed their efforts to the bishop himself. A clergyman is only a man whose virtues and foibles are likely to be no different from that of any other man, except that in the case of Catholics there is a pretense of celibacy. The word *pretense* made the idea more manageable for the members of the *Club Nacional*, who found celibacy a difficult concept to accept. Within the confines of the club and in the exclusive company of men, the opinion was often expressed that the bishop, indeed any priest, had to put on his pants one leg at a time the same as any other man. The members of the *Club Nacional* accepted the need for pretense if only for the sake of tradition. Anything good enough for Saint Augustine was good enough for them, the fact notwithstanding that the conditions that drove Augustine to his conclusions had long ceased to exist. In the natural history of religious practices, segments become mired in the morphology of their origin.

Prevalent and easier to disguise, greed and vanity are more acceptable foibles than concupiscence, so the club deemed approaching the bishop by that common avenue more appropriate and more likely to succeed. As businessmen, the members of the *Club Nacional* perceived that the bishop needed them as much as they needed him. Mutual need, a simple relationship, is the basis of all successful business transactions. The bishop saw his way clear to dividing his time between the cathedral in San Juan and the one in San Geronimo. So on the Sunday that Eduardo Rincon was to lunch at the home of *Don* Aurelio Castillo, the same Sunday that Eduardo made his obligatory annual penance of sitting through a complete service, the bishop officiated at High Mass in San Geronimo.

Only later did Eduardo Rincon consider the physical aspects of that day. The air felt unusually cool for July, though the temperature fell within the normal range for the month, but more than a memory of the temperature remained with him. The brightness of the day impressed him, as if he perceived normal days through a filter, but for this one, the filter had been removed. The tropical sunlight imparted to all colors a luminescence usually muted for those who experienced it every day, but on this occasion that insouciance brought on by familiarity lifted from Eduardo. He could not be sure whether he noted the difference at the moment of perception or whether a mechanism of memory provided the enhancement of clarity—a puzzle without a solution, for a perception once acquired can only be reviewed through recall, and unless an evaluation of the observation is stored at the same time, in retrospective judgment there is no choice but to factor in the quirks of memory.

If someone attempted to convince Eduardo that special preparations had been made for that day in San Geronimo, he would have easily believed it, for the exterior of every structure that he passed on his way to the plaza seemed, if not newly painted in the most brilliant colors, at least newly scrubbed into a festive look. He might have taken a hint, had he been suspicious, that what he perceived surpassed the work of the citizens of San Geronimo, for even the vegetation had taken on a more vigorous hue. A little thought would have soon revealed the qualities that rendered such a feat beyond the power, if not the desire, of his fellow citizens, even had they been contemplating a royal or papal visit, an event inconceivable even in the most exuberant of their imaginations.

Seldom in San Geronimo on Sundays, the gaiety he perceived that day startled him. Even the children seemed irrepressibly joyful at the prospect of going to church, a state of mind he could not understand, ignorant of the fact that children live for the moment, and only after they are well into it do they fret about sitting through the long dull service. At that point, not understanding it, they find various ways to distract themselves. The fact that God loves children perhaps explains why churches have stained glass windows, for losing themselves in the intricacies of the brilliant color images is one of their preferred ways of enduring the service. High mass has the advantage of having more variety, the music going a long way to alleviate the boredom but at the price of making the service longer.

The ladies, too, provided an unintentional distraction for the children by the use of folding fans. Not only were these fans painted with scenes of exotic places and fantastical mythological beasts but their wielding also produced an aesthetic experience. The act of fanning herself is a less casual activity for a lady than it may first seem. The skillful use of the fan has a great deal in common with a choreographed dance despite the limited range of movement, but what is art without limitations? Constriction constitutes a challenge, and what is aesthetic pleasure but the recognition of a challenge met? The ladies of San Geronimo competed second to none in the skillful use of their wrists, in the snapping open of a fan, the beating of the stubbornly sultry air, and again the closing of the fan to round off the compulsory sequence of movements. An aficionado of the art observed more than the movement of the hand that held the fan. The almost imperceptible movement of the upper torso and the distinctive tilt of the head, allowed each practitioner, within the strict confines of the art, a degree of individuality.

Children doubtlessly benefited from this virtuosity, one of the spectacles to which they turned to relieve the boredom of the service, but they were not alone. The young men of the town, whose courting invariably included a show of piety, if not to impress the object of their desire at least to reassure the prospective in-laws, enjoyed the display. Mothers always preferred pious young men for their daughters, counting on the Church to aid the young women in keeping their future husbands reasonably within the bounds of marital propriety. The hope persisted that the daughters would prove more successful than their mothers. The fathers, too, enjoyed having their prospective sons-in-law in church, seeing no reason why the younger generation should escape an ordeal its senior had to endure. The young men, no less bored with the service than they had been when children, kept their eyes furtively on the young ladies, but as they had been indoctrinated in catechism class about the danger of giving free reign to their imaginations, at least while in church, they tried to focus their thoughts on the fans and not on the anatomy of their wielders.

The ladies themselves benefited from the distraction their performance provided. The young ones were fully aware of who watched them and what effect their slightest movements produced. Those not yet committed engaged in an unspoken rivalry with their fellow performers in the same position, an undeclared contest of flirtation. The more mature ladies saw no reason why they, too, might not show off their skill, if only to engage in nostalgic flashbacks to their youth. Some were fully aware that they still had the power to agitate hearts no less than they did their fans, those hearts belonging not necessarily to their husbands. So, the exercise of the fans persisted as a popular art that fulfilled the needs of significant and various segments of the community. Surprisingly, little note of it has been taken in folk literature nor by popular novelists who are apt to scavenge for such tidbits of local color to enliven their pages.

Eduardo Rincon would have liked to think himself as beyond the reach of such obvious quirks of popular culture. But finding himself in Saint Geronimo Church, seated close to the Castillo family, all six of whose female members expertly wielded fans, and having but the vaguest idea of the literal meaning of the bishop's Latin drone, he naturally fell under the spell of the fans, a condition from which he might have been saved had his education been more expansive. He rose from a class for whom education remained a luxury of unproven value, and book learning requiring a degree of immobility difficult for him to master, the ethos prevalent in that social milieu reinforced his natural disinclination. He managed to escape even his mother's desire for him to become an altar boy, which possibly might have provided him with enough Latin to understand the bishop's verbiage. But that knowledge, too, may have proved useless, since familiarity is often detrimental to attention.

Eduardo himself would be the last to lament the state of ignorance that rendered him susceptible to the influence of the fans, and there is no conclusive proof that even were he a doctor of *belle lettres*, were he Aristotle himself reincarnated, he would have been immune to the spell of those seemingly innocuous contraptions of bamboo and silk. All evidence pointed to the contrary. The congregation included educated persons, some who knew Latin quite well. Altimo Ramirez reputedly, though Eduardo could not vouch for it, had the ability to recite in the original, from beginning to end, Caesar's *Commentaries on the Gaelic Wars*. The liturgy engrossed these educated people no more, least of all Altimo Ramirez, than it did Eduardo Rincon. The fault may not be imputed to the language but to the bishop himself, whose promotion to the post clearly had not depended on the fervor with which he performed the Mass. The reaction to the sermon delivered in Spanish, the mother tongue of everyone there, no foreigners being in attendance that Sunday, not even Americans, reinforced the view that to bask in the grandeur of the office, the congregation willingly overlooked the bishop's lack of oratory skill.

Before laying too much blame at the feet of that anointed personage, note that in all probability, no amount of oratory prowess would have kept Eduardo's attention from straying to the Castillo ladies, almost directly in front of him. He had the most unobstructed view of Antonia, by chance the one closest, assuring him an opportunity to better judge her facility with the fan. Initially, he thought that she had not achieved the proficiency of the others. Her style had none of the flourish and flamboyance exhibited by her sisters who considered themselves second to none in the art of the fan. Indeed, they considered themselves second to none in virtually any pursuit in which young ladies competed, all still single only due to the lack of young men good enough to deserve them, a view held by each about herself but not about the other four.

Eduardo's attention stayed on Antonia, although he had difficulty at first naming the quality that fascinated him, something usually expressed in a more active manner. He could call it nothing but defiance. He observed that she occasionally broke into the most brilliant use of her fan, but becoming aware of her action, abruptly stopped. Only a lapse of her will, brought on by the heat and the babbling of the priest, caused her to forget her purpose, the thwarting of a habit imposed by the arbitrary mores of femininity. Amused, Eduardo mistakenly attributed her effort to youth.

This little incident of the fan, in itself trivial, serves to illustrate one of the ironies of life: actions often have unexpected consequences, indeed, results often contrary to the intended. Antonia attempted to avoid falling into the same mold as her sisters. On this particular occasion, she sought to avoid using her time in church for general flirting. A resolve not motivated by piety, though hers no less than anyone else's, she merely wanted to be different, wanted to be herself, even if she was uncertain of what that meant. She sought that self, and she realized that to find it required more than the acquiescing to predefined behavior. While in church that Sunday, she remained unaware of her effect on Eduardo Rincon, an effect due in large part to an accidental cause impossible to feign—her innocence. It captivated Eduardo.

More than simplicity dominated the scene. *Don* Aurelio's estimation of his daughter's beauty came close to the mark, but her appearance did not comfortably fit into the canon of the place and time, her looks more compact than the common standard allowed, due more to her style of dress than to anything else. She avoided the frills and enhancements that were then the staple of feminine fashion. Eduardo, more accustomed to the usage of the country and foreign to urbanity, accepted her relatively Spartan appearance. In fact, although he noted her look to be different, he could not have articulated what constituted the difference.

Anyone privy to *Don* Aurelio's plan would have been apt to wonder whether that august gentleman had foreknowledge of what would transpire in the church that Sunday, whether he proceeded at least aware of the possibilities or whether the actual happenings fortuitously coincided with his desires—luck, like planting cane before the price of sugar began to rise. When the number of details he would have had to arrange is considered, the possibility of orchestration seems improbable, the confluence of factors too great, beginning with the decision by Eduardo to attend high mass at the cathedral. He might have accepted Aurelio's invitation to lunch without attending mass at all, more in keeping with his usual practice, or he might have attended mass at the village nearest to his home, also more within the usual. Once in the church, he sat in a place that provided an advantageous view of Antonia. That fact lacked design. Eduardo having had no foreknowledge of where the Castillos would sit, much less where Antonia would be in relation to her sisters and her mother, knowledge whose value he could not have predicted, since before that Sunday he had no interest in Antonia. Adding Eduardo's frame of mind to the brew of all these coincidences, the result fell just short of a miracle; that is, a miracle from Aurelio's point of view, because a miracle is just something that happens against all odds from the perspective of someone to whom the event matters. If the sea always parted on command, the event would not be a miracle. Neither would the incident be a miracle to someone with no interest in getting dry shod to the other side. Imagine a shepherd casually walking by a parted Red Sea, Pharaoh and his chariots nowhere to be seen. The occurrence would be a mere curiosity; it would not be an event at all; ah, there goes the Red Sea parting again.

Eduardo's frame of mind was a key factor in bringing to fruition *Don* Aurelio's scheme. And what control could that anxious gentleman have on the mood of his friend? None whatsoever. The possessor of it himself had no control. Eduardo did not will himself into a receptive mood. Unaware of any oddity in himself, he attributed to external factors everything happening at that moment, beginning with the heightened intensity with which physical objects assailed him since his arrival in San Geronimo that morning. The fact that the choir sang more exquisitely that day impressed him, and he credited the effort of the choirmaster in training those under his charge and in assiduously seeking talent among the parishioners of Saint Geronimo. The quality of the performance made him aware of how much time had elapsed since he had last been in the church, ample time for the improvements to occur.

The church disgorged the worshippers into the square to the sound of the bells announcing the end of the service. On a normal day, Eduardo would have been voluble enough. He had never been accused of reticence, but on that Sunday he felt like a shaken soda bottle, no way to repress the bubbles and no one wishing to do so. The Castillo ladies knew him only in passing, so they had no reason to judge his behavior unusual. Only *Don* Aurelio noticed Eduardo's effervescence and took it to be the result of Antonia's proximity. On emerging from the church, the two gravitated to each other, but whether Antonia or Eduardo had engineered the confluence had escaped Aurelio's notice.

On Sunday mornings, though after high mass the sun had just crossed the meridian and time had to be reckoned as afternoon, another ritual took place of equal importance if not solemnity: the weekly renewal of social ties by those who had not seen each other for a week, or perhaps longer, for not everyone attended mass at the same time every Sunday. Among the men especially, few attended regularly. Some, like Eduardo, attended so infrequently that their presence caused people to wonder whether some calamity, for which they deemed divine intervention necessary, had befallen the family. Direct inquiry the height of rudeness, everyone looked for indirect references from which a story might be pieced together, the ladies of San Geronimo so adept at the process that publishing their results would have propelled them to the forefront of fiction writing in the genre known as *bochinche,* an advanced form of gossip.

The Castillo family dispersed in the square, the ladies branching out in search of material. Every tidbit gleaned would serve as a basis for hours of speculation during the week. As industrious as Ruth picking over the field of Boaz, they did it with more delight, toiling for amusement rather than livelihood. The Knights of the Holy Name sequestered *Don* Aurelio, importuning him to become more active in the organization. In a moment of weakness he allowed them to inscribe his name in the membership roll, thinking that they only wanted the status that the name would confer on the organization, but then they wanted him to become president, an honor he wished to avoid. At the *Club Nacional* the title would be outwardly respected, but the quality of his machismo would be silently cast into question. Already he had no sons. He could not afford another burden on his name. As he looked beyond the men speaking to him, he observed with some relief Antonia and Eduardo sit down on a bench to wait for the re-gathering of the family for the walk home for the midday meal.

Antonia took it upon herself to look after the guest, thinking her mother's and her sisters' flagrant neglect of their duties as hostesses reprehensible, but in all probability they had only relaxed after they saw Antonia take on the task. They may have decided to wait until he arrived at their home before considering him their guest—in church, he was a guest of God or at the very least of the bishop. The square of dubious jurisdiction, as the church dominated it, God and the bishop might still be responsible, especially on Sundays, but as the town technically owned the square, the mayor, as the civic representative of the community, would have to be the host of record. If push came to shove, *Don* Aurelio might be held the most responsible. The rest of the family considered Eduardo a business acquaintance and not a social one. They only knew him in connection with the Tobacco Exchange and the *Club Nacional*, institutions closely related and intimately connected to *Don* Aurelio's business. A few times they had seen Eduardo at the racetrack; that is, Antonia had seen him there more than once. Her mother and sisters, not partial to horses, considered a lady's attendance at the track somewhat disreputable. Modernity, playing havoc with propriety, let otherwise respectable ladies act like women of pleasure, appearing in places that would have been unthinkable a few years before.

Antonia judged Eduardo Rincon an unusual sort of man. Amiable and charming, he lacked, and did not pretend to have, the polish of the men she was used to. Doña Clara would think him not quite suitable for any of her daughters; certainly, the danger of that had not yet entered her mind. She remained as ignorant as Antonia of *Don* Aurelio's design; otherwise, she would not so easily have left the young man in Antonia's charge in favor of scavenging for gossip. Aurelio, in order to survive with some degree of independence, had become adept at anticipating what motivated the various members of his family. Doña Clara's possible objections to Eduardo would further Aurelio's cause with Antonia, but any chance discovery by the young lady of his favoring Eduardo would counterbalance the gain. To deceive them both became a necessity, a passive enough deceit, consisting chiefly of keeping his mouth shut, a task well within his ability.

Getting Eduardo's participation seemed the more difficult part of the scheme. This, too, required a degree of subterfuge. Possibly, Antonia's charm would be sufficient to snare the young man. Uncertain, Aurelio suspected that Eduardo had some other attachment yet to be formalized, the delay suggesting an imperfection that he might exploit. Perhaps a married woman lurked in the background, the rift inevitable. Regardless, Aurelio counted on the pragmatic streak he had observed in Eduardo. Some would think *Don* Aurelio willing to take a chance with the happiness of his favorite daughter in seeking an alliance for her with a man perhaps already committed, but he didn't see that as taking a chance. On the contrary, he considered his method more likely to yield a satisfactory result than any alternative. Nothing in life was guaranteed. Of that he was sure. A man had to take prudent precautions and pray for the best. In this case, he had something somewhat more reliable than prayer. He trusted Eduardo's sense of honor. Eduardo would not commit to a course of action he could not sustain, and once committed he would not shirk his responsibility. He would be honor-bound to it as much as can be expected of a man. As for love, that was another matter. Aurelio would leave that for the couple to work out. They would surely come to a satisfactory arrangement—preferably sooner, but later would be good enough.

To the delight of Doña Clara, the bishop, too, agreed to come for lunch. The lady felt that Aurelio's having a business acquaintance to lunch entitled her to have someone for herself and the girls, and who better than the bishop? Her neighbors would die of envy, the very best ailment to inflict a neighbor. It didn't require any sanitary precautions. Having the bishop to lunch would make up for having Eduardo Rincon, a charming enough fellow as it turned out, but how was she supposed to have known that ahead of time? Despite Eduardo's charm, he was still a country bumpkin and Aurelio such a bad judge of social necessities. Why couldn't Aurelio conduct his business at the *Club Nacional*? He spent enough time there.

"It must be awful living all the way out in the country the way you do," Doña Clara said to Eduardo, just as the fried catfish was brought to the table.

"It has its drawbacks," the young man said.

"Is it true that you have no running water?" asked Yolanda the eldest of the Castillo girls.

"Of course it's not true," said Antonia. "How can you ask such an absurd question?" The color had risen to her face, as if an insult had been hurled directly at her.

"No, of course it's not true. There's a stream right near the house," Eduardo said.

Everyone at the table laughed except for Yolanda and Antonia: Yolanda embarrassed at being mocked and Antonia because she took it upon herself to be annoyed for Eduardo.

"It wasn't too long ago that there was no running water in town either," *Don* Aurelio interjected.

"I don't remember that," said one of the other girls.

"Your father has no sense of time," Doña Clara said. "We've had indoor plumbing for so long that even I don't remember exactly when it was installed."

"It must be awful to live so far away from town," said Iris, next to the youngest, and who had the distinction of being the only blonde among the five. When they were children, her sisters were apt to tease her by saying that she was adopted. When they got older they claimed she must be the postman's daughter, despite the fact that the postman was only a shade lighter than midnight.

"You're not being kind to your mother," *Don* Aurelio would say when he overheard the comment. "Oh, but we didn't say who her mother is," they replied. *Don* Aurelio would only shake his head at their impudence.

"Why don't you move to town?" Iris continued addressing Eduardo.

"Who would look after my land?" was Eduardo's excuse.

"You can do like Papa and have a *capataz*."

"Your Papa has much more land that I do. That makes sense for him, but for me it would only be an unnecessary expense."

"That situation won't last long at the rate you're going," said *Don* Aurelio.

"It's in God's hands," Eduardo replied in all sincerity. He had an unerring sense of what words were appropriate for the company. A cynic might consider him cunning, but his unconscious choice of words lacked the intention to deceive anyone or misrepresent his true opinion.

On hearing God mentioned, the bishop, who had been intent on the catfish, looked up to ascertain whether his offices as a clergyman were being summoned. He had only a vague notion of the topic being discussed, having been so enraptured by the succulence of the fish, even a second helping of which had yet to trigger diminishing returns. The word "land" floated aimlessly in his head like a goldfish in a tank, but the aspect of land being discussed remained a mystery. No one looked to him for an opinion, so he retreated to stating the obvious on a subject on which he had indisputable expertise. "God is bountiful," he said with as much flourish as he could muster between bites, and as he had ample proof before him of the truth of his assertion, he didn't anticipate having to defend it. Another challenge interested him more. A mountain of sweet potatoes smothered in onions sautéed in olive oil sat on a platter before him, and he considered diminishing it his duty. His conversational skills not in high demand at the moment, he set about the gastronomical task with the zeal of a missionary.

"I have a plan that I wish to discuss with you," *Don* Aurelio said to his young guest.

"Aurelio, really I must insist on the rule," said Clara.

"Yes, of course, I meant after lunch. I've been forbidden to discuss business at Sunday lunch," *Don* Aurelio explained.

"A very sensible rule," Eduardo said to Doña Clara, who had made her request with a considerable amount of anxiety. She didn't want to seem, in front of the company, to have curtailed her husband's right to do whatever he wished in his own house. To let the rumor get about that she was that kind of a wife, which she wasn't, wouldn't do at all. This prohibition of business as a topic, just a little rule that she insisted on, otherwise Sunday would become intolerable with talk about tobacco and sugar cane and, at the moment, about Americans. That at least provided a new subject, sometimes interesting. What more could be said? They were here, and there was no way to get rid of them. Still, details about Americans went over better than the price of commodities, a topic men seemed to relish. The bishop, at least, displayed no interest in prices, though she could not be sure of that, since he had disappointed her by not talking much.

At least, his appreciation of the food pleased Doña Clara, although she did not cook the food herself. Still, as the hostess, she had the right to feel gratified by the sumptuousness of her table; after all, she took credit for finding and hiring the cook. Ana Santiago was no ordinary cook but the very best cook in San Geronimo, a place renowned for its cooks. Ana's reputation reached San Juan, from where unscrupulous people tried to lure her away with offers of more money, a breach of etiquette that had incensed Doña Clara.

"But Mama, there is no rule that says a cook can't be offered more money by someone else," Yolanda the oldest daughter said. "What book is it written in?"

But Doña Clara, for whom law did not need to be codified in writing, did not accept that argument. Common knowledge indicated such a thing was forbidden, and that was good enough, even if the knowledge was *common* only to her.

After the meal, Doña Clara led the placid bishop into the garden where aperitif was served. *Don* Aurelio took the opportunity to invite Eduardo into the study on the pretext of showing him some rare maps supposedly used by pirates who in the

Seventeenth and Eighteenth Centuries plied the Caribbean, and many of them, in their old age, retired to Puerto Rico.

"I know your tricks, Papa," Antonia said, "and it won't be fair to keep *Don* Eduardo in your study for too long, since it's Sunday and a day of rest." Antonia saw no inconsistency in taking her mother's tack when that suited her.

"Looking at old maps is very recreational," *Don* Aurelio said. "It's the most relaxing thing in the world."

"Don't let him bully you, *Don* Eduardo," she said to the young man. "The garden is much more relaxing."

"I'm sure you're right," he said, "but I do wish to see the maps."

"I expect you to be out soon," she said.

"I shall not disappoint you," he assured her.

After letting her wishes be known, in full expectation that Eduardo would be true to his word, she departed with a pert little walk to join the others in the garden. She relied on the effect of her charm on him, and she accurately discerned that his word might more literally be counted on than her father's, but in truth she could not complain about the treatment she received from him. She loathed crediting the charge made by her sisters that their father favored and pampered her, and in moments of lucid and brutal truth, she glimpsed the reality of the situation, but she didn't dwell on it. Mostly she ignored it, there was not much else she could do, having no idea why her father favored her over the others and being too smart to suppose that the reason stemmed from anything intrinsic to her. To fathom the motivation of the old man seemed pointless. While aware of the absurdity of the stance, at melodramatic moments the problem became her cross to bear.

In the study, *Don* Aurelio quickly dispensed with the maps, using them only as an introduction to talking about land.

"I want your opinion on an idea of mine," Aurelio said. "You know the Americans have imposed a law limiting the amount of land any one person can own."

"True, but it has little effect on most of us. Very few people are in your situation of being over the limit. The Americans are worried about each other and not about us."

"But they circumvent their own law by creating subsidiary corporations to own the land. It makes no sense."

"The law can be dormant for a long while and be awakened when necessary. A sleeping watchdog can always be aroused. We can circumvent the law just as well as they."

"My thought precisely," said Aurelio. "I was thinking that if I gave my daughters land, that, as a family, we could have another five hundred acres for each to add to my own."

"If your daughters owned the land wouldn't they take it with them when they marry?"

"True, that could be a drawback, but not if they marry reasonable men, and anyway all I want is to provide for them."

"In that case, the plan is good but not if you want to control the land."

"I'm considering trying it out with Antonia first and see how it works out."

"Will she be the first to marry?"

"I have no idea, but it seems to me she'll make the most sensible choice. Don't you think so?"

"I am sure they will all do well."

"Then you think my plan is good?"

"Yes, if what you want is to provide for your daughters. It will also serve to keep some land out of the hands of the Americans, except of course, if your daughters marry Americans."

Don Aurelio laughed. "Very little danger of that," he said. "Very little danger indeed," he repeated slapping Eduardo on the back as they walked towards the door of the study. "Ah, I almost forgot," *Don* Aurelio said stopping abruptly, "Alfredo sent these over the other day." He walked to the mahogany humidor on a table between the bookcases, and opening it revealed to Eduardo the contents, banded with the ostentatious crest reserved for the highest-quality cigars produced at the local factory managed by Alfredo Gomez. "We'll have to sneak up here later to smoke them," Aurelio said. "If we don't get down to the garden soon,

Antonia's forgiveness will cost me dearly. She has taken a liking to you, and no doubt she thinks it very unfair of me to monopolize your time today, when I can see you any other day of the week."

"Smoking can wait," Eduardo said. "It's never a good idea to keep ladies waiting, even when the bishop is providing ample entertainment."

Don Aurelio could not repress a laugh that rolled up from his solar plexus. "If you really think so, your magnanimity is greater than I imagined," he said.

Sᴀɴ Gᴇʀᴏɴɪᴍᴏ ꜰᴇᴀꜱᴛ day began with a church service in
the morning followed by an outdoor procession led by The
Knights of the Holy Name. Eight of them, two at each corner of
the pallet, bore on their shoulders the statue of San Geronimo
taken from its niche in the cathedral. Once a year, the saint
got to enjoy the outdoor sunlight, and from his perch up above
everyone's head he might have had an unobstructed view of the
whole pageant but as a plaster figure, he could not turn his head.

"If they carried him backward, he would see everything,"
Juanita said to Gregoria, who spontaneously crossed herself.

"*Hay Dios mio*, to carry the saint backward, what a thought,"
she crossed herself again to exorcise the image that involuntarily
appeared. "I don't know how these thoughts get into your head."
The image of the saint riding backward made her want to chuckle,
but still being the solemn part of the day, she refrained.

The eyes of the saint fixed on a point in the distance. Against
the blue sky floated bank after bank of luminous clouds that slowly metamorphosed into various spectacular shapes. On an ordinary day, they would demand and receive the children's gleeful
attention. On feast day, the saint may have been the only one to
notice them as they emerged over the horizon, but he could not
turn his gaze upward to follow them as they filed overhead in a
competing procession.

The Knights of the Holy Name marched stiffly beneath the
ostentatious sky, and behind them came the Daughters of Mary in
their white dresses and blue sashes, followed by an explosion of
color and imagination as the people of San Geronimo vied with
one another to present the most outrageous interpretations of
Renaissance-style costumes. Potbellied mendicant friars cavorted
with Venetian ladies who, depending on the outlook or the age of
the onlooker, might be taken for princesses or ladies of the night.

Not to be outdone by the peasants who danced along, cavaliers twirled their oversize moustaches and kicked up their heels, tankards in hand filled for the moment with make-believe ale. More than a few shepherds and shepherdesses pranced along, among whom might also be spied scholars, supposedly from Salamanca, recognizable to all by their wan and starved appearance, a neat trick achieved by youths used to feeding on rice and beans. Children, too, romped in the parade, likewise dressed in outlandish costumes, ostensibly representing characters who might have associated with the saint. They exhibited an outrageous sense of color and a penchant for excess ribbon with no purpose but to gratify the taste for spectacle of the onlookers, as if the saint in his life had consorted only with carnival performers.

Everyone ignored historical accuracy, aiming instead for mythic reality. Clergy and lay people with unbridled enthusiasm undertook the task, despite the fact that none could have explained, had they been asked to do so, the significance of what they were doing. Those of a religious disposition needed no explanation other than the obvious one of honoring the saint, to them a self-explanatory activity. Those who didn't care a wit about saints could not deny the value of festivities no matter what the excuse for them might be. So everyone proceeded to have a good time for his own reason.

The opening procession dominated the morning, but the horse race reigned in the afternoon. The sport had an allure for the vast majority of town people and for the *campesinos* from the surrounding area. In the not-too-distant past, the race took place right in the town, certain streets marked off for the course, but as the town grew and the renown of the festival spread, which attracted a sizeable number of spectators from other municipalities, riding through town streets became too raucous an activity for the responsible officials of San Geronimo to tolerate. A racetrack was built at the outskirts of town and promulgated in the name of progress. At the track, the races took on a character different from the one they had in the more informal setting. Not all patrons liked the change, but eventually, a more controlled and sedate atmosphere being preferable to no race at all, everyone accommodated to the new location.

Despite the track, the races at San Geronimo were not yet a professional affair governed by a racing commission and involving professional trainers and jockeys. The gentlemen of San Geronimo often rode their own entries in the race, as would be the case on this occasion when Eduardo Rincon would ride his horse, *Relanpago Derecho*. The informality of the track did not preclude large amounts of money being gambled at the event. The members of the *Club Nacional* affected an indifference to gaining or losing money in such an activity. Without pretense, Eduardo wagered only token amounts. For profit, he relied on the buying and selling of the horses and not on betting, but he seldom lost a bet and sometimes he won considerable amounts despite his indifference.

Taking Juanita to the racetrack burdened Gregoria, who disapproved of young ladies going to the track, though she didn't object to being there herself. Her curiosity overwhelmed her scruples as to the propriety of her own attendance, but in the case of her charge, she remained more obstinate. In relation to Juanita, Gregoria soon ceased to consider herself a mere employee of *Don* Eduardo, and saw herself as the instrument of a higher power and charged with the welfare of the child in place of her natural mother. To do right by this child seemed possibly her last chance to finally make up for her mistakes, an opportunity provided by God, who decided to make the difficulty of the task commensurate with the transgressions.

Traipsing through a racetrack the least of it, Gregoria had to deal with what might possibly become a crisis for Juanita, a crisis that might last a lifetime. Gregoria castigated herself for not having prepared herself or the girl for the inevitable eventuality, one at the moment upon them. She had been lulled into complacency by the details of everyday life and had been oblivious to Eduardo's move to alter his domestic arrangement. The signs were there. She was aware of them, but she ignored them. She promised Carmen Gutierez to look after her child, and Carmen's function as an instrument of the Lord's scheme for Gregoria's own salvation rendered the promise to Carmen tantamount to a promise to God. She believed that He would not give her a task beyond her abilities, so she attributed her confusion to a lack of effort.

Those thoughts plagued her as she made her way with Juanita to their seats in the owners' box where Gregoria did not feel comfortable among people who might look askance to her being there. Eduardo had insisted that she accompany Juanita and stay with her, so whatever discomfort Gregoria felt, she added to her penance. She tried to be as inconspicuous as possible and made no pretense to being there in any capacity other than as caretaker of the child. Most of the other spectators in the box were indifferent to the presence of them both. *Don* Aurelio Castillo, the one exception, greeted Juanita with affability, a quality he possessed in such abundance that he lavished it effortlessly on Gregoria as well. His daughter Antonia, accompanying him, also proved friendly although more reserved. She perceived better than her father the nuances of the situation, not only concerning Gregoria, but more importantly, Juanita.

"So, have you bet on your father's horse to win?" *Don* Aurelio asked Juanita.

"I am too young to place a bet," she responded in all seriousness.

"Well, I have placed a bet, and I will share my ticket with you," he said.

"That is very kind of you sir, but it's not necessary," Juanita responded in a manner she thought would be pleasing to Gregoria.

"Don't you know that I am a man well known for doing the unnecessary?" *Don* Aurelio answered amused by his own wit as well as Juanita's propriety.

"If you wish to share, you can share with Gregoria," Juanita said.

"We will split the ticket three ways," *Don* Aurelio said.

Before Gregoria could object to *Don* Aurelio's proposal

Antonia offered another solution, "I will share my ticket with Gregoria."

"Oh no, *Señorita,* you cannot do that," Gregoria exclaimed.

"Oh, yes, I can. It is done," asserted Antonia who would brook no contradiction. The minute she uttered the words, she knew the tone had been wrong, and she tried to rectify the situation by smiling, but she suspected that her response might be perceived as insincere. The battle had been joined, with both women seemingly having the same objective. "Let us not argue about nothing," Antonia said when she regained her composure, "The tickets are worthless unless Eduardo wins."

"Of course he will win," *Don* Aurelio said. "He has the best horse."

"It would be a perfect world indeed where the best horse always won," Antonia said.

"Amen to that," said Gregoria.

The flag went down before the conversation had a chance to continue. The field of horses, bunched at first, began to stretch out soon after the first quarter, a few in the lead, most taking up the middle and some bringing up the rear, *Relanpago Derecho* with those in the middle. It was Juanita's first time at the races. The noise the horses generated, their hooves shattering the turf, sending dirt flying behind them, projecting a sense of power, their muscles rippling under their skin in rapid succession—it all startled her and took her breath away. She wasn't quite sure if she liked the sensation.

Checking the reactions of the women beside her, from Gregoria she got nothing but impassive observation, as if the action produced in her no emotion. Antonia, in contrast, offered a spectacle almost as dramatic as that of the horses. The excitement palpable, her face transfixed in an attitude reminiscent of some images Juanita had seen in *The Lives of the Saints*, a book given to her by Sister Sylvester, except that watching Antonia had more impact than the illustrations of the book, mere shadows of emotion. A possible connection between saintliness and horse racing moved Juanita, the images in the book failing to depict the difference between holy and profane ecstasy. Antonia's transfiguration raised her beauty into the realm of the extraordinary, so that even the child was struck by it. The transformation would have been disruptive, but the men in Antonia's proximity, intent on the race, failed to notice it.

The horses then on the far side of the track, *Relanpago Derecho* had advanced, but he was still in third place. Antonia could not sit still. Her hands clenched, she moved her fists up and down to the rhythm of the beating hooves. Under her breath she chanted the name *Relanpago* over and over as an incantation essential to the task of winning the race. Looking around at other spectators, Juanita saw that they were all equally excited and some quite more demonstrative than Antonia. In fact, even if her intensity could not be matched, her behavior under the circumstances might have been considered subdued. Some people shouted at the top of their voices and waved their arms over their heads.

In this setting, Antonia's fervor in her litany to the horse didn't seem out of place, but just as *Relanpago Derecho* advanced to be neck in neck with the third horse, the name of the horse vanished from her lips to be replaced by the jockey's. Juanita had never heard her father's name pronounced with such fervor before, and that made her uncomfortable. She looked to Gregoria for consolation, but the old woman had either not caught the transition from one name to the other, or she had yet to decide what the proper response should be. She seemed as impassive as she had been at the beginning of the race even though *Relanpago Derecho* had advanced to third place. If she had been, like Juanita, observing Antonia, she gave no hint of doing so.

Suddenly in a change of mood, the crowd in the stands, as in one body, rose to its feet letting out a cry of consternation, whose cause Juanita had missed having had her eyes on her two companions rather than on the horses. The second place horse stumbled throwing the jockey and causing *Relanpago Derecho* and the horses behind it to suddenly veer to avoid the fallen horse and rider. *Relanpago Derecho,* the closest behind the stricken horse and its jockey, was in the most in danger of colliding with them and increasing the scope of the accident. Blood drained from Antonia's face, a phenomenon not lost on Juanita, who immediately connected the dramatic change in color in her companion to her father's peril. The uncertainty lasted but an instant as the riders quickly adjusted to the circumstances, the momentum of the race only slightly altered.

"He's all right," Antonia said turning to the child but not lingering on her. The words had escaped rather as an involuntary assurance to herself than to Juanita.

Gregoria put her arm around the child and squeezed her shoulder, "Your father is all right," she said.

Juanita had not for an instant thought otherwise, but more intent on Antonia's behavior and its possible meaning, she accepted the comforting without protest.

"Magnificent riding," *Don* Aurelio exclaimed. "Your father is a true horseman," he said to Juanita to further reassure her.

Indeed, Eduardo made a remarkable recovery, and *Relanpago Derecho* was about to overtake the leader with almost a quarter of the course remaining.

"What about the man who fell?"

"We'll find out about him soon enough," *Don* Aurelio responded.

The man didn't get up, but he moved enough to indicate he was conscious. The first-aid crew, on the course with a stretcher, ministered to him on the ground. The horse on its feet, right foreleg limped, as a groom led it off to the stable.

"What about the horse?" Juanita inquired.

"I'm afraid it doesn't look good for the horse," said *Don* Aurelio. He picked up the anxiety in Juanita's voice, and the child's sensitivity impressed him. He attributed her unease only to concern about the victim of the accident.

Relanpago Derecho, neck and neck with the horse that had the lead from the outset, in the last twenty-five yards made an extraordinary effort and crossed the finish line a nose ahead of his rival.

"He won! He won!" Antonia shouted leaping from her seat and jumping up and down as if her shoes were on springs. In a few seconds she realized that the activity was causing her to look disheveled, an inappropriate appearance for a lady.

"Of course he won," said *Don* Aurelio, "No other outcome was possible." He had his thumbs in the pockets of his linen vest and with his other fingers he patted his ample tummy, a habitual gesture when extremely satisfied with himself.

THE PREPARATIONS FOR the evening activities still under-
way in the plaza, the Rincons and the Castillos returned from
the races to rest and refresh themselves before returning to enjoy
the festivities. Doña Clara and those of her daughters who had not
attended the races had gone to an afternoon party where those of
a sensibility too refined to enjoy the exertion of horses consoled
themselves with less plebeian activities. They, too, returned to the
house and at that moment, in their respective rooms, napped to
shake off the sluggishness that resulted from drinking, inadvertently they claimed, too much punch from the bowl intended for
the young men. The boys, apparently were more adept at discern-
ing which bowl was meant for them, also avoided the pink crystal
one that contained the "virgin" punch, a sobriquet of ambiguous
meaning, either referring to the lack of alcoholic content or to the
intended consumers, or perhaps to both.

Those Castillo women who by acclimatization or good luck,
for prudence can be safely ruled out in this case, had escaped the
state of somnolent semi-inebriation at the moment obsessed about
what they should wear that evening. They were to stroll out in the
plaza and return to dine and dance, the Castillos having a tradition
of winding up the saint day celebration by hosting a ball to which
they invited all their friends and neighbors. Juanita and Gregoria
were assigned a room of their own, and they waited there not
knowing what to do with themselves, neither sleepy nor in need
of making wardrobe decisions. Neither of them was comfortable
in a strange house where they had equivocal status, but at the
moment most of their discomfort stemmed from what they had
observed at the racetrack.

The rider who was thrown suffered only a broken leg, as had
the horse, but for the horse the consequences proved more drastic.
The gunshot startled Juanita. No one had seen any need to shield
her from that experience. Although a country girl used to ani-

mals and their inevitable deaths, the mortality of large animals, especially those not raised for consumption, remained less apparent than that of small ones. She had no personal connection to the horse that stumbled, nor did she see it die, but she imagined the scene. Her presence at the execution may have been more advisable, since under the circumstances imagination became an enhancer of terror.

Juanita did not ordinarily dwell on the morbid, but the image of the dying horse lingered.

"She didn't care at all about the dead horse," she said to Gregoria.

"Who?"

"Antonia, of course."

"It wasn't her horse," Gregoria said.

"Still, she's very callous, isn't she?"

"Not more than anyone else," Gregoria responded. "No doubt she has plenty of faults. We need not invent additional ones."

Her first time at an official race, Juanita had no experience to compare to the action in the winner's circle, where the mayor, also the president of the racing association of San Geronimo, hung around her father's neck the first-prize gold medallion. The slim and straight figure of her father in his riding outfit projected the adept look of an adventurer, rather like the dashing hero of a novel, but she knew him to be nothing of the kind, being more used to seeing him in his sweaty work clothes when he rode home from the fields. At the racetrack, he displayed a vague smile that spread across his face just under his thin moustache. Everyone offered congratulations, which he took with a diffidence she knew to be exaggerated. Proud of his horses, he boasted of them in private, not to her directly, because at her he projected a different image, one she had difficulty integrating with his other guises, one very guarded, as if afraid to let her see who he really was. He put on a face for her alone, presumably the way of a father with a daughter, a portion of him so meager as to always leave her confused and wondering if she was to blame for his reticence.

She knew him to be so much more. Left to roam at will, she

had ample opportunity to observe him in everyday interactions with other people, both those who worked for him on the land and those who came to the house on business. She noted that, in public, he deprecated his skill as a rider and as a judge of fine horses, but at home he showed no such modesty with Ernesto the stable keeper or with any of the other workers. He guarded more against her, with whom he ate dinner every night, than against strangers, and that perplexed her.

At the officiating stand, everyone moved aside to make way for Antonia, as if they all recognized that she had a right to be close to the winner. Juanita watched unprepared for the emergence of Antonia at the center, obliterating everything else, including her father, ostensibly the man of the hour or at least of the moment. Juanita normally held the spot closest to him, although only ceremonially, for she never escaped the feeling of being a substitute. She didn't know for whom or for what, only that something or someone else should have been there but was absent. Who or what was missing she had yet to ask either her father or Gregoria.

Juanita, unconcerned about her displacement, focused rather on the dimming of Eduardo by Antonia's overwhelming presence. Instinctively taking on a protective role, she feared for her father rather than for herself. Her urge to warn him was stymied by the fear of doing something silly that would embarrass him. A false step would also draw displeasure from Gregoria, at the moment in a cheerless mood.

Don Aurelio, the only one unabashedly himself, projected exuberance of increasing emotional complexity rearranged by the emergence of Antonia on Eduardo's arm. A mass of jolly corpulence, *Don* Aurelio seemed the only one to have been prepared for the event, as if he had engineered it. Even Antonia, the protagonist of the drama, her performance nearly perfect, exhibited some hesitancy that betrayed surprise at the ease of her success. Having only to be himself, *Don* Aurelio played his part very well, the situation requiring precisely what he had to offer. He gave Juanita his arm, and she graciously accepted, acting the part of a lady who would not make a fuss, even as someone stole her father from right under her nose. *Don* Aurelio, far from a fair exchange but still better than nothing, had the distinct advantage of being all there, his apparent emotional simplicity a welcome comfort, an easily accessible grandfather perhaps a good thing to have.

In the house, matters remained as complicated as they had been in public.

"I promised your mother that I would look after you, and I have failed. I am so sorry," Gregoria said in an outburst that surprised the child.

A *pipetre* sitting on a branch of a tree in the garden cheerfully articulated his distinctive song for the enjoyment of his mate and as a warning to other birds to keep out of his territory, but Gregoria remained oblivious. The old woman, sitting on a stool by the window of the room through which a slight breeze ruffled the lace curtains, stared at a spot on the wall above the dresser opposite from her and directed her words in that direction rather than at Juanita, who for that reason was uncertain whether the apology was meant for her. Deciding that Gregoria was not talking to herself, she earnestly responded, "Why do you say that? You take care of me very well."

"I saw this coming, but I didn't prepare you for it."

For a moment Juanita thought that Gregoria had forgotten to pack the clothes they were to wear to the party that evening, but the door of the wardrobe ajar, she had a clear view of them.

"I am prepared," Juanita said.

"Then I'm the only one who's not."

"No, your dress is there, too," Juanita said.

"Ah, dresses," Gregoria exclaimed. "You will need a new dress."

"There is no time between now and this evening to get a new dress," Juanita said suspecting that at the track Gregoria had been too long in the sun. She had heard of people who lost their reason and hallucinated from being in the sun without a hat. Knowing the effect to be temporary eased her concern for Gregoria. "Perhaps you should lie down for a bit," the child said.

"I am not at all tired," Gregoria responded. "I'm only upset that your father has not told you and that I haven't either."

"Told me what?"

"About Antonia."

"I've decided she's not so bad."

"Have you?"

"Yes, it's not her fault that she is beautiful."

"No, it's not, and perhaps it will all be for the best."

"What is it that you haven't told me about her?"

"That your father is going to marry her." Once Gregoria had unburdened herself of those words, to her surprise, the anxiety left her. She had not anticipated relief of any kind, even briefly.

"You mean she will be my stepmother."

"Yes, you might say that."

Only fairy-tale stepmothers came to mind, none a sympathetic character, not even a beautiful one like Snow White's stepmother, evil underneath, and the father no use at all in protecting the child against her.

"But I will still have you, won't I?"

"Yes, you'll still have me, no matter what."

"You're my stepmother too."

"I suppose you might say that." A solitary tear escaped Gregoria's eye and slowly journeyed down her cheek, the old woman unable to arrive at a satisfactory conclusion about the fate of a child with so many mothers.

*

The games of chance already in full swing in the early evening as the Castillos and their guests made their way back to the plaza. Soon the lanterns would be lit to illuminate the festivities and keep them going long past the setting of the sun. Gregoria kept an anxious eye on her charge to discern any effects of the afternoon's revelation. Juanita gave no sign of either being pleased or disturbed. She gave no indication of thinking about the matter at all. In the plaza, the child, fascinated by the mock horse races and everyone betting just like at the racetrack, moved from booth to booth examining the contraptions, little wooden horses with wooden jockeys, horse and man carved from a single block of wood and painted to resemble a real horse and rider. There were other games of chance and skill but horse races the most numerous and the most popular. In the simpler booths, a straight course painted green and subdivided into squares on which the horse advanced depending on the throw of a die by each bettor, the horse whose number came up moved forward. Some depended on a pinwheel rather than a die to select which horse would advance. The more elaborate racing booths contained a mechanical track where machinery underneath the table advanced the horses. How one horse advanced more than another independently of the operator's manipulation remained a mystery to Juanita, but the illusion of being closer to the real thing persisted, though the horses and the jockeys were wooden and painted with minimal skill. The gears and pulleys, visible through the slots through which the horses moved, called for a pretense of ignorance to make the gliding of the horses, with no human hand touching them, a satisfying fantasy.

At one end of the plaza, sporadic fireworks erratically illuminated the area with sudden bursts of exotic colors drawing spectators. The exuberance extracted from inanimate matter amazed the grown-ups as much as the children. Each round of pyrotechnic display encompassed a complete drama: expectation, sudden climax, and a draining denouement. Observing a few times emotionally exhausted many people, as if they had experienced the performance of a major dramatic work, difficult to decide whether comedy or tragedy. The spent shells strewn about, reminders of an inevitable demise inherent in every object, suggested a tragic outcome.

No matter how much potential existed before ignition, or once set off, how brilliant the display, the ruptured packages and the memory fated to fade in the minds of the spectators were the only remnants. But who thought of that at the moment when sound and color exploded and illuminated the expectant faces of the onlookers, a joyous moment followed by the raucous laughter of children, oblivious to everything but the wonder of it? The more sober-minded wandered away from the fireworks and the games of chance toward the steps of the church that stood looking over the whole spectacle in bemused condescendence, as if consciously representing something that had survived hundreds of years of transitory spectacles. On the steps, the various religious societies and youths groups vied to present scenes from *The Life of the Saints,* dramatic vignettes separated by the choir's performances of corresponding choral works.

After making the round of the plaza to her satisfaction and greeting the people to whom, for some arcane reason, she considered necessary making her presence known, Doña Clara felt compelled to go home to attend to the final preparations for the evening. The two older daughters went with her, but the other three remained. Doña Clara was certain that too many cooks spoil the broth and a convocation of all her daughters on a project guaranteed dissension. Doña Clara would have felt better had all five young ladies stayed behind. An expert at recognizing capable domestics at a glance, she would have appreciated Gregoria as her aide, having been automatically and surreptitiously evaluating her without having made a conscious decision to do so, not, after all, in the market for another servant.

The fact that Eduardo Rincon, through no fault of hers, was about to become her son-in-law put her in a quandary. Not having been consulted on the matter, the event presented to her as a *fait accompli,* she was powerless to prevent it. She had dreaded for a long time the possibility of just such a dilemma with Antonia, who had been since birth strong-willed, an undesirable trait in a daughter, Aurelio having made the problem worse by spoiling her. Doña Clara, when bearing Antonia, realized that Aurelio considered that his last chance to become the father of a son, and once again having been disappointed, he failed to reconcile completely. Subsequently, to Clara's chagrin, he treated Antonia to the same liberties he would have accorded a son.

More apt to forgive Antonia her willfulness than she was to

forgive Aurelio for facilitating it, finally Doña Clara saw that swimming with the tide was easier than swimming against it, even if, as a general observation in such matters, she could not say that ease was the overriding factor. Nevertheless, she saw no reason to make her life more difficult than it had to be and readily compromised when the odds turned against her. The fact that Antonia was only one of five went a long way to alleviate Doña Clara's discomfort. After all, she had four other chances to get something closer to what she considered an ideal match for a daughter, and she had, more or less, gotten used to the idea that in Antonia's case Aurelio had to be the dominant influence. Matters might have been far worse. Antonia choosing to marry someone pleasing to her father was a bonus of considerable value, which Doña Clara decided to take into account.

When evaluating Gregoria, Doña Clara got a fix on Eduardo by proxy. The presence of the child novel enough, to whom he entrusted her care became as telling as anything else about the man. To have a child out of wedlock was common enough among men, and Doña Clara supposed among women too, since the participation of a woman was a necessary condition for the event, but those women belonged to a different class and so, in Doña Clara's view, hardly counted at all. She would not have admitted to such an opinion. She considered herself a model Christian, aware of the doctrine that sinners were to be embraced rather than excluded from the fold. Had not the bishop himself preached a sermon on the good shepherd, who had abandoned the flock of ninety-nine for the sake of the one lost lamb? It was one thing to be high-minded on Sunday in the presence of the bishop, God's local representative, and another to be so the rest of the week beyond the eye of the prelate, even if presumably one remained always in God's direct line of vision, a fact easily forgotten given that He had delegated so much power to lesser beings.

Doña Clara did the best she could to keep Church doctrine and her own inclinations in proper alignment, a matter that required the mangling or at least the bending of one or the other. Of course, doctrine became difficult to recognize after passing through the prism of interpretation; what seemed red to one devotee might look blue to another. For that reason, to avoid the protestant dilemma, keeping the number of prisms at a minimum was important but not Doña Clara's concern. She had only to make peace with herself about Eduardo Rincon—that too, more easily said than done.

Seeking to make the problem more manageable, Doña Clara focused attention on the child, but she had to admit to herself that she would have objected to Eduardo Rincon even without the child. An upstart from the country! Who could say where his family came from? She could trace hers back for hundreds of years to the very village in Spain where they originated. This knowledge served as a mainstay of her fortitude, although perfectly aware that it made very little difference to most people on the island, her own husband apt to make fun of her genealogy and point to his as an example of how foolish such pretensions could turn out to be. He also could trace his ancestors back for hundreds of years—to pirates who had sailed the waters of the Caribbean; hence his interest in the maps purported to have been used by those who plied that trade. That's what he called it, just to rankle her no doubt, a *trade*, similar to being a shoemaker or a grocer.

"Of course it's different," he said. "That's the point, isn't it?"

"What's that got to do with Eduardo Rincon? What do we know about his family?"

"I know him very well," *Don* Aurelio said. "So what does his family matter? The important thing is that Antonia is happy. Eduardo is a man of character, and he is far from penniless."

"If it comes to that, there are many others just as good."

"Well it doesn't come to that."

"And what about the child?"

"He has done well by the child, which resounds to his credit. He might have behaved badly in the matter and society would have absolved him. As far as I'm concerned that raises him above the common. If anything, he's too good for us."

She well knew that he was alluding to his transgressions, of which she pretended to be ignorant, the arrangement an unspoken pact between them. She would not reproach him, if he would not humiliate her by speaking of them. She could ask only for discretion, nothing more. Men by nature roved. God had made them that way, and to ask that they be different was futile and perhaps sinful, since the ways of the world existed for a reason unintelligible to the human mind. Still, her acceptance of the situation did not prevent the surfacing of resentment at the thought that the town might be replete with young people who, if they were not legally entitled to the name Castillo, as her daughters were, had at least some moral claim to it. What was she to expect from a descendant of pirates—murderers and rapists to a man—God forgive the thought.

"Too good for us indeed," she said, the color unevenly rising to her face, so that she seemed to have suddenly contracted a disease for which she would have to be quarantined. "Perhaps his ancestors and yours cavorted on the same ship. No doubt he has a collection of skull and crossbones to match your maps."

The sharpness of her response startled him. Although as reluctant to bring up the past as she to hear of it, he sometimes forgot the boundary and she reminded him. He would have liked to point out that Eduardo was, in respect to philandering, more to be trusted than he, and that consequently, Antonia would be spared the very anguish that at the moment engulfed Doña Clara. But mentioning the subject would be a breach of the agreement, if it could be called that, for he didn't recall the occasion when he had made it, only that it resembled stumbling into an ocean and being caught in the undertow without the possibility of escape. "I meant only to say that he is different," Aurelio explained by way of appeasement, though altogether unclear why that would calm her.

She didn't immediately respond but seemed to consider whether the difference provided any advantage. To be consistent, the answer would have to be no, but consistency as a virtue was not mentioned in Scripture. Moreover, the concept was unfamiliar to Doña Clara. But difference did upset her about Eduardo Rincon, especially the most obvious one, that he embraced his mistakes. The very quality that Aurelio pointed to as a virtue disturbed her the most. What, after all, could you do with a man who rubbed in your face his indifference to the good opinion of society? On the other hand, he was honest. You got what you saw, but if that was preferable, then her life had been a mistake. A man who bowed to the conventions of society could be depended on to behave in a certain way, perhaps not the most desirable way, but at least in a predictable and manageable one.

Antonia refused to be convinced of the importance of appearance, and one could not save her from her obstinacy. She would not dissemble, so she discarded one of the most useful tools a woman possessed. She would go defenseless into her marriage. The question remained whether Eduardo Rincon could be depended on to be what he seemed. Even with the benefit of the doubt, his intentions remained unclear. After the wedding, did he intend to flaunt his independence, or would he willingly put up a front of propriety? Clearly fond of the child, perhaps too fond, he could just as well have kept her hidden in the country, where such matters were hardly noticed. Being so fond of the child, did he not necessarily have an attachment to her mother? Was Antonia willing to put up with that? Doña Clara despaired of ever understanding her daughter.

Returning to the house, Doña Clara managed to occupy the two daughters who had accompanied her by setting them to the harmless task of supervising the placement of the flower arrangements in the main parlor. She then repaired with Gregoria to the kitchen where the real work was taking place. To be sure, neither one of them needed to be there since the cook had matters well in hand, but Doña Clara cherished the illusion of being indispensable to the success of everything done in her kitchen, and though she seldom touched anything there, even the mechanics of lighting the stove vague in her mind, stepping into the kitchen before a big function for a brief moment persisted as a necessity from which she could no more escape than migratory birds their journeys.

On this occasion, she had a dual purpose for visiting the kitchen. Not only did she make her obligatory trip, but it was also the route to a private sitting area outside the house, separated from the formal garden by a tall hedge of ornamental bamboo. That area, an anomaly of design in a house such as the Castillos', was seldom used by anybody except Doña Clara. Presumably, this space right off the kitchen was intended for the servants, but if they had any time to sit, they didn't want to do so in a place where they might be observed. Being most conveniently reached from the kitchen, other members of the household had no reason to prefer that space rather than the main garden, more ample and easily accessible from other parts of the house. Doña Clara found its seclusion soothing. Its proximity to the kitchen satisfied her need to feel connected to that part the house that she deemed the sole and exclusive domain of women but which, for any practical purpose, the circumstances of her life made unnecessary for her to frequent.

"Let us sit for a bit," Doña Clara said to Gregoria. "This walking about the plaza is meant for the youngsters. My legs are ready for a rest."

As much as she welcomed the proposition for physical reasons—Gregoria's legs, being older than those of Doña Clara and despite their being accustomed to more rigorous use than those of the hostess, by that time of the day tired enough—Gregoria hesitated to comply. The confusion stemmed from Doña Clara's deviation from her previous treatment of Gregoria with a degree of disdain not only due to the difference in their social position but also because Gregoria represented Eduardo Rincon, a person to whom Doña Clara attributed the cardinal sin of complicating her life.

Gregoria had no choice but to sit, and she did so with the resolve to be wary, not too great a change of attitude from the one she assumed since her arrival at the Castillos'. She had not felt as actively under assault as she did at the moment attempting to interpret Doña Clara's apparent turnabout.

Doña Clara saw no reason to dawdle at the edge of the water, either because a quick immersion would be the least unpleasant, or because she could not wait for a gratification so much desired.

She got right to the point. "Do you have children of your own, Gregoria?" she asked.

"I had," Gregoria answered. "They're no longer children, and they're all gone."

"You mean they've all passed away?"

"No, not all," Gregoria said, "just that they're grown, and I don't often see them."

"I see," Doña Clara said, "that must be hard on you." Being cut off from her children was a possibility Doña Clara had not dwelled on, but at the moment, it tumbled on her with unexpected force. She recalled the incident when as a child on holiday in the country, playing in a stream, suddenly a torrent of water had appeared, preceded by a rumbling that she had been unable to interpret until the water swept her away. She was lucky that time to get caught in the root of a waterside mango tree that held her long enough for her father to reach her and envelop her in a more tender if not more crucial embrace. Curiously, the panic had overwhelmed her only after she was rescued, but this time, aware of the danger, panic loomed closer at hand and though she would have gladly waited to experience it after the fact, she was not so fortunate. Who would rescue her from this danger that, unlike that first one, she could see in the offing but had no greater power to avoid?

"One copes," Gregoria responded, "with God's help. He never gives us more than we can bear." She had no evidence for that conviction, but her belief could not be shaken. She saw Doña Clara in need of such assurance, the reason less than apparent at the moment. Had she been thinking of this encounter as a game, she would have been aware of scoring a point, even if the stratagem by which she had done so was not immediately obvious.

Doña Clara took in the words, and though to doubt them seemed sacrilegious, a position in which she could not see herself, they didn't comfort her sufficiently to stem her fear.

"Have you daughters?" she asked, trying to fathom the mystery of so optimistic a point of view.

"Three daughters," Gregoria answered.

"And they are married?"

"Yes, all three, one without the benefit of the Church, and I dare say she has the best marriage of the three. The ways of the Lord are often mysterious."

"Well, then you see my point, don't you?"

Gregoria didn't see any point other than Antonia's impending marriage occupied Doña Clara's thoughts. Gregoria, already aware of that, wondered whether she missed something else. Not being a fine lady, and not needing to be coy in a conversation, she inquired without ceremony, "And what point is that?"

"That a daughter's marriage can be quite a source of anguish."

"No less than a son's," Gregoria replied.

"That I will never know," said Doña Clara.

"Ah, of course."

"But I do need to know about *Don* Eduardo."

"He is a man. What more need there be said?"

"What indeed!" echoed Doña Clara.

"He's better than most," added Gregoria by way of preventing being party to any slander against her employer.

"Cold comfort indeed," said Doña Clara.

"The world is what it is," Gregoria said.

"You're fond of the child, I take it."

"As if she were my own," Gregoria answered.

"I wish that she were," Doña Clara said.

"Would that solve your problem?"

"I suppose not," said *Doña* Clara, "but it would simplify Antonia's."

"The child will not be a problem to Antonia. She is a model of good behavior."

"I am thinking more of the child's mother," said Doña Clara who, following Gregoria's example, continued to be forthright.

"She will be grateful for any kindness shown to her daughter."

"The form of the gratitude is what I'm concerned about, or rather who the recipient of it will be."

"I can assure you that *Don* Eduardo receives nothing now

206 / MIGUEL ANTONIO ORTIZ

from that quarter. What incentive would there be to change that after he is married?"

Doña Clara had no answer to a question that implied logic in human behavior, men's in particular, something that in all her years of observation failed to be apparent. "You mean there's no willingness on her part?"

"I would think rather that there is no desire on his."

"We are now in the realm of the unusual," said Doña Clara.

"Only because our understanding is limited," said Gregoria. "The matter is perfectly clear to The One Above."

"That may be," said Doña Clara, "but it is of little use to me."

"The problem is solved if you put yourself in His hands," Gregoria said, risking overstepping her bounds. Doña Clara was the mistress of the house, and Gregoria but an employee of a guest, but she would have felt derelict in her duty as a Christian if she held her tongue. She considered also that Doña Clara gave her leave to speak the truth when she had asked her to sit down as an equal.

"Is it as simple as that?" asked Doña Clara rhetorically. The words might have been scornful, deriding a simplicity that created an unbridgeable chasm between them, a gap more unbridgeable than the social differences that separated them, but they came out more as regret that she could not share in the simplicity that would have made her problems more bearable.

"Nothing is simple," Gregoria said, knowing that she had been misunderstood and that her meaning could not be conveyed in words.

"You are acquainted with the mother of this child," *Doña* Clara continued seeing another avenue of possible comfort, "and she has put the child in your care, as a trust, one might say."

"One might say that, though *Don* Eduardo is my employer."

"So then your loyalty is to him?"

"The welfare of the child is my main concern," said Gregoria who had, up to that point, not considered that a conflict might ever arise between her interests and Juanita's.

"That is why her mother trusts you," continued Doña Clara.

"That may be," said Gregoria.

"Mightn't you do the same for me?" asked Doña Clara.

"And what is that?" asked Gregoria not following what Doña Clara had in mind.

"Look after my child."

"That's something all together different," Gregoria said. "Antonia is a grown woman; she will not want to be looked after."

"She will need to be nonetheless," said Doña Clara.

"There is a more insurmountable problem," continued Gregoria. "Just as no man can serve two masters neither can a woman."

"I understand your concern," Doña Clara said, "but consider that as things will be, the two tasks will be inseparable."

"Then what need is there to talk of them?"

"The need is only to clarify the approach."

"I am bound to protect Juanita."

"I only ask this: that if there is a choice between two courses of action, neither of them detrimental to Juanita, you consider also which is good for Antonia."

"That is the Christian thing to do," said Gregoria.

"Ah yes, we are all Christians," said *Doña* Clara, betraying the failure of that thought to reassure her. "And I am prepared to be as Christian as anyone."

"Certainly," said Gregoria.

"I will do my best for Juanita."

Gregoria noted the distinctly conditional tone of the statement and wondered what brand of Christianity the lady practiced. No doubt the Christianity of the town differed from that of the country. She did not come shopping for a bargain. She had not been shopping at all, but the offer could not be refused. Townspeople were not half as clever as they thought, judging from Doña Clara's offer to pay for what she would have gotten for nothing. The coin being presented was of doubtful value, presupposing that Juanita might someday be in some need, perhaps merely longing for the absence of malice. The value of the offer could only be judged against the lady's willingness to do harm, and as she was human the potential was great. Of that, Gregoria had no illusion. She doubted the lady's ability to surmount obvious obstacles: evil no less strenuous an activity than good, Doña Clara, by all signs, seemed more inclined to indolence than to toil.

Still, maternal instinct had to be considered, and Gregoria presumed that *Doña* Clara might be aroused to extraordinary action were her offspring threatened by real or imaginary danger. The imaginary, being limitless, proved often of more consequence than the actual. For that reason Gregoria took little comfort in the fact that Antonia had nothing to fear from Juanita or her mother. Perception was all. Doña Clara needed a guide to the proper vantage point, a place from which she could see the vista that would reassure her.

"And I for Antonia," said Gregoria without the need to again stipulate the conditions that she assumed they both understood.

"We shall be friends then," said Doña Clara.

Overwhelmed by the possible meaning of that statement, the consequences of accepting it difficult to instantly perceive, Gregoria remained silent for a moment. Then she simply stated, "We are allies."

That satisfied Doña Clara well enough, and they reentered the house ready to face whatever the evening might bring.

Anticipating a good time, those fortunate enough to be invited looked forward to the saint's day dance at the Castillos'. Friends and neighbors appreciated the Castillo flair for entertaining, more a reflection of Don Aurelio's character than Doña Clara's, but she had, early in their marriage, grasped that he would value her assistance in satisfying his need to spread good cheer among his friends and neighbors by hosting lavish festivities. The events kept him happy, and she enjoyed sharing the adulation of the crowd. The inevitable wear and tear on the house, unavoidable under the circumstances, gave her an excuse to redecorate and refurbish more often than otherwise might have been considered seemly. The Castillo house, by all standards of the day and place, sumptuous and one of the largest private structures in San Geronimo, stood out among the homes in the neighborhood by having two stories. For the occasion, the parlor was transformed into a ballroom, overlooked on one side by a balcony occupied at the moment by the musicians in order to maximize the dance floor down below. As the guests began to arrive, the band struck up the national dance.

For the occasion, Doña Clara decided to use an outdoor motif by decorating the room with potted vegetation of such luxuriousness as to suggest the rain forest had been transplanted in her living room. She seemed content enough with that decor, and Don Aurelio in his good nature willingly tolerated it. He had, as Gregoria might have said, "other fish to fry." In effect, the tables had been turned, for this time he, instead of his wife, moved about on pins and needles. More than a few of the guests had an inkling that something was afoot in addition to the usual celebration of the saint's day, if only because Don Aurelio appeared to have misplaced his typically complacent composure, and Doña Clara, to compensate for her husband's discomfiture, decided to forego flitting about like a plump butterfly, her usual mode at the start of her parties.

Juanita, who had never seen so many people at an indoor event, found the large potted plants convenient props to use in her attempt to be inconspicuous. No one else her age still present, most children, having had enough to do all day long at the festivities, secretly appreciated staying home with their caretakers, who had an easy time after the initial but largely ceremonial protest by the little ones at being left behind. Juanita, even if curious to see what went on at a ball, wished that she were not there in body. She would have considered it ideal to make herself invisible to observe everyone else without having the inconvenience of being observed in turn. She sensed being a curiosity for a reason other than the obvious one of being the only child. She noticed that most people expressed no surprise to see her at the ball but rather gawked at her and would have been disappointed had she managed to disappear. Some, caught in their perusal of her, tried to disguise their ill manners by quickly looking away, but the more brazen made no attempt to hide their compulsion, as if they had a right, guaranteed by some code superior to common propriety, to make her uncomfortable.

When she sallied from behind the protecting plants, where she could not stay all night, if only because Gregoria, zealous in her duty, pushed her to overcome her timidity by urging her out of the hiding place that she had already discovered offered little protection from the predatory eyes of those who wished to find her. She learned that the crowd did not gaze in silence, but that she was also the subject of conversations that abruptly came to a halt or lapsed into non-sequiturs when she approached. This must have been the way the cat with a bell around his neck felt at a convention of mice, except that Juanita did not want to pounce on anyone. She would have preferred to have a louder bell to give ample warning of her approach and be spared the snippets of talk that made her uneasy.

Inevitably, the situation forced a comparison between the people she was used to and the town folk with whom her father

wished her to mix. Born and raised in the country, where everyone looked at her as the daughter of the *patron*, the attitude and
behavior of town people seemed novel to her. She dressed as well
as anyone else, her father never sparing any expense. Though
raised among country people, she had been taught by Gregoria
how to be a proper young lady and make sure that she had impeccable manners, privately coached by Sister Sylvester who ran the
school in Comerio. Most of the people she came in contact with
in the country depended on her father for their livelihood, and that
perhaps made them more deferential to her than anyone in town
where he had less influence. Still, Don Aurelio declared that he
had never met a more proper young lady.

It was true that, at a country festivity, she was never the only
child, only one among many with whom she ran about and danced
in imitation of the adults. In the country, almost any excuse would
do for a festivity. The musical instruments always close at hand,
the *cuatro*, the drums and the maracas all that were necessary on
most occasions, and sometimes old Javier Rodriguez joining in
with his fiddle when his arthritis wasn't acting up, but increasingly due to his gnarled fingers, he had difficulty hitting the right
place on the strings, so he only watched, remembering when he
made the bow fly across the catgut to make the instrument sing.

The children ran around barefoot except for Juanita, whom
Gregoria would not let out of the house without shoes, but
Gregoria's vigilance had its limits, and Juanita's persistence had
youth on its side. Slipping out of her shoes, she tucked them away
under the steps of whatever *bohio*, the one-room dwelling most
common in the country, hosted the festivity, often her own house
that could not be called a *bohio*, not even in jest, except by her
father, who seemed less sardonic than nostalgic for the loss of
something he once had. He often invited his neighbors to use his
batey, the customary courtyard in front of country houses, a feature borrowed from the Tainos, who long ago disappeared from
the island, though Gregoria insisted they were only hiding. The
humblest *bohio* had a *batey*, but *Don* Eduardo had the largest one
anywhere near Comerio, proportionate to the size of his house.

Don Aurelio's house had no *batey*. There was no room for that in town, the houses close together with only small ornamental gardens in front, but some like the Castillos' had large gardens in the back, away from the street.

Few in Don Aurelio's house at the moment had ever set foot in a *batey* or danced barefoot on the clay ground. But that was less than obvious to Juanita more concerned with shaking the discomfort she felt at being singled out for scrutiny. She saw no apparent reason for so much interest but that she was her father's daughter, and he was the man who had won the race earlier in the day. Unwanted attention must be the price of fame. If so, she preferred obscurity. Perhaps she would live in the country forever and not come to the city again. She would be a *jibara* all of her life. That would be good enough for her.

"Come, come look lively," said Don Aurelio, who descended on her unexpectedly, "Will you dance with an old man? This is a very happy occasion?"

She could not imagine any other kind of occasion for Don Aurelio. He always brimmed with cheerfulness. When he approached, being infected by his mood became inevitable, so Juanita accepted his offer to dance. If people wanted to look at her, she would give them something to gawk at. She could dance better than her father could ride. She only hoped that Don Aurelio's age and portliness would not prevent him from leading her in a show worthy of her talent. Of course the exhibit would be more elegant if she had a partner her own size—Don Aurelio towered over her like a dancing bear, although he was certainly more agile.

"You dance like an angel," he said.

She wondered how he knew that, since in all likelihood he had never danced with one. She pictured angels dancing and getting tangled in their long robes. The archangel Michael was the only one whose legs she had ever seen depicted, always a warrior, armor over his short tunic, sword in hand and wings splayed. Surely his wings would get in the way, not at all the dancing type. "Thank you," she answered. Compliments, like so many other things that didn't make sense when examined, had to be acknowledged nevertheless. That much she had learned already.

"You know I'm going to make a very important announcement tonight."

"Yes, I know," she said, the words disconnected from her thoughts. She could not remember what she knew, preoccupied rather with where a dance of angels would take place, among the clouds no doubt, but the consistency of clouds might not be at all suitable for a dance floor, the red clay of her father's *batey* far better.

"Of course you know," he murmured almost to himself, satisfied that she had been amply prepared, a task beyond his responsibility. Suddenly aware of its necessity, he had found himself in a quandary: approaching Eduardo with the matter, presumptuous, and speaking directly to Gregoria too conspiratorial. So finding Juanita at peace with the proceedings relieved him.

Neither one of them noticed that the other dancers had yielded the floor to them, until the end of the dance when the room burst into applause. Juanita's face flushed, embarrassed by again being the center of attention, even if this time she had been the instigator. Don Aurelio bowed and Juanita curtsied. Not wanting to prolong her agony, nor wishing to give her any more reason to be displeased with the progenitor of the one about to stake a claim on her father, he led her off the floor as rapidly as consistent with decorum.

Shortly after his dance with Juanita, Don Aurelio ascended to the balcony occupied by the band and asked for a fanfare to call for attention. Some of the guests, their gaze having followed his laborious climb, were already prepared to comply. Aurelio, waited for the moment with anticipation, and was now inclined to prolong its savoring. Doña Clara, standing when her husband began to speak, immediately realized that he intended to carry on for some time. She took the prudent precaution of sitting down, knowing that her fortitude would be taxed both by the length and the content of his speech. True to Clara's prediction, Aurelio began by enumerating the virtues of his prospective son-in-law before making the reason for doing so clear to his listeners. He described his daughter's virtues less effusively, and Doña Clara, at first annoyed by the contrast, decided to spare herself by ascribing overconfidence to her husband. No doubt, he assumed that Antonia needed less tooting since she was better known to those assembled.

Had he stopped there, his breach of the rule of brevity would have been slight, but the fact that few orators of his day subscribed to that rule is a word in his favor. Keeping with a tradition and a style of long-windedness, whether ignorant of the brevity rule or wishing to ignore it, *Don* Aurelio spoke at length about matrimony, a subject he felt owed him a great deal, having grappled with it more or less successfully for so many years. He refrained from alluding to his success partly from modesty but also from an awareness that the judgment might be deemed overblown, especially by ladies in the room apt to have differing standards and who would, if they knew the facts, wish for Antonia a better marriage than her mother's. Indeed, he wished that also, but phrasing the wish in plain words was impossible. Avoiding propriety would have redeemed his verbosity. Many in the room would have been glad to know more of the story.

From his vantage point high up on the balcony, Don Aurelio looked on his world with some satisfaction. Though all things earthly fell short of perfection, he was blind to any defect in what he saw. He focused on the pair that he had worked assiduously to bring together.

Indeed, Eduardo and Antonia fit the image of a fairy-tale couple. Eduardo stood like a ramrod. He had not had, like so many around him, the temptations of an easy life to dull the edges of his physical presence or obscure the certainty of his moral will. To the men, he was a model of *machismo*—his word to be trusted, he willing to back it with physical courage. For the women, not as acquainted with those virtues, more visible in the realm of business, he had the appearance of a heroic idol, with the added attraction of having no artifice.

Antonia, for her part, had the overwhelming advantage of

youth. In a peach-colored dress that accentuated the blush of her cheeks, she belied the inclination to be shocking and to flaunt the conventions of her class. Those who knew her well surmised that Eduardo did not know what he was getting into, and that if he expected domestic tranquility, he would be disappointed. Those willing to take her at face value, primarily the men, saw one more reason to envy the good fortune of Eduardo Rincon.

Champagne had been distributed to coincide with the end of Don Aurelio's speech, and he called for the couple, as well as Doña Clara, to join him on his perch, from where he made a toast heartily endorsed by all. No one gave a thought to the little girl who tried to inch her way back into the shadows of the potted plants, no one but Gregoria who reached out to hold her hand.

23

A NTONIA, DESPITE OFTEN looking unhappy, lost her town stiffness. Away from the eyes of society, for the first time she was free to be herself—if only she knew who that was. In the absence of that knowledge, she easily reverted to childhood conceptions. More than once, Juanita had the distinct impression of hearing Gregoria mutter something about having "two children to look after," and on one of those occasions the implication seemed more that Don Eduardo had "two daughters to bring up rather than one," which momentarily engendered the fear in Juanita that, in similar circumstances to her own, another child had surfaced for whom she would have to make room. But no such person materialized, and Juanita concluded that Gregoria must have been referring to Antonia, even if that made no sense, because after all, Antonia was a married lady even when her behavior appeared odd.

On one occasion, Juanita tiptoed to her room, her shoes in hand, not realizing the greater likelihood of her bare feet leaving tell-tale dirt for Gregoria to interpret. An all-too-common lapse in judgment by Juanita made this skulking about necessary, after she was enticed by her friends once again to abandon the ladylike ways nurtured by Gregoria. Arriving home from Sister Sylvester's etiquette class, and informed as she crossed the *batey* that a deep-water place in the stream had been discovered abundant with catfish easily caught with one's bare hands, she succumbed to temptation. Pedro Soto, a swarthy boy about Juanita's age with whom she shared the leadership of the band of children who, when not in school and not working in the fields alongside their parents, roamed freely about the Rincon hacienda, had delivered the invitation. She could see the rest of the band hanging back at the edge of the *batey* in the shadow of the banana trees that shielded Gregoria's house. They waited there in expectation of what she would do, testing her to see whether, despite her fine dress, she was truly one of them. She couldn't ignore the challenge.

There was no turning back once at the vaunted place of abundant catfish. She would not have heeded the thought of restraint, even if it had occurred to her. She knew enough to take off her shoes, before wading into the pool, the only way to fish barehanded, but her dress became a casualty, once wet, mud invaded. Fish, impossible to catch by noisy children splashing about even had they been properly equipped, became secondary spoils of the excursion.

For Juanita, the disappointment compounded when she realized that, unless lucky, she would have to explain to Gregoria why she had gone fishing in a dress good enough to wear to Sister Sylvester's class. She resolved to attempt a change of clothes before Gregoria had a chance to interrogate her.   On its own, that plan had a fair chance of success, but it also revealed shortsightedness, the common flaw in youthful transgressors. The success of Juanita's plan would only postpone the reckoning, for the dirty dress would sooner or later come to Gregoria's attention unless Juanita were planning also to wash and iron it herself, steps conspicuously absent from her plan.

Juanita had little to fear, and though she appeared to be motivated by a desire to avoid personal unpleasantness, the anxiety stemmed more from her wish to please Gregoria and from a feeling of failing to behave in the prescribed manner, rather than from any apprehension of harshness from the old woman. Juanita intended no mischief as she snuck about the house on that occasion. Only a fleeting shadow through the half-opened door forewarned her of an occupant, so she hung back to observe what in her absence transpired in her room.

Her caution may have been part of her general plan to avoid Gregoria, except that she had thought Gregoria to be in the kitchen—a belief unconfirmed by sight, as doing so would have imperiled her attempt to proceed unnoticed. On entering the house, she had heard the distinct shuffling of the old lady's footsteps in the kitchen, assurance enough. The heavy presence of her father would have been immediately recognizable, so elimination left only one other person likely to be in the room. Juanita refrained from announcing her presence. She had no reason to ascribe sinister motives to Antonia. But curiosity about the new member of the family overwhelmed all scruples against spying on her, if looking into one's own room could be labeled spying.

What she observed increased her wonder. Antonia was sitting in a child's chair, part of the furnishing in Juanita's room and a diminutive remainder of childhood on the verge of being discarded. On the matching table, Antonia set out the toy coffee set to serve refreshment to a select group of Juanita's dolls occupying the other chairs. A lively conversation was transpiring among the members of the party, whose voices all sounded suspiciously like Antonia's, but their personalities quite distinct.

Juanita wondered what made a doll party desirable to someone with the power to have a real feast with real dishes and real people. But having a more immediate and pressing concern, the solving of that puzzle had to wait. Standing outside the room increased the risk of being discovered by Gregoria, likely to come searching at any moment, surely realizing Juanita's overdue return from Sister Sylvester's class. Making noise to alert Antonia might also attract Gregoria but to walk in on Antonia seemed inadvisable. As is often the case, inaction produces results of its own, and while she debated which would be the best course, Gregoria's dreaded approach took the matter out of Juanita's hands.

"Is that you up there," Gregoria called out as she shuffled up the stairs.

The sound of Gregoria's voice accelerated Juanita's heartbeat and warned Antonia that she was on the verge of being discovered. Being more experienced than Juanita, or having a personality difference devoid of the Rincon propensity to freeze at crucial moments, she leapt into action. Whether Antonia realized that Juanita had been standing outside the door long enough to observe what she had been doing was unclear, but she immediately abandoned any attempt to dissemble. Being discovered did not discomfit her sufficiently to impair her ability to see the predicament revealed by Juanita's dress. Antonia rushed to the door and pulled her stepdaughter in.

"Quick-change," she whispered to the girl.

Immediately Juanita saw that an exchange was being made.

"We're both up here," Antonia shouted back to Gregoria. "We're having a lovely time."

The old woman uttered a grunt of acknowledgement, but her shuffling steps continued to approach. Juanita slipped out of her dress and wiped her dirty feet with the dry part of it. In seconds, she pulled another dress from the wardrobe and slipped it over her head, but the new dress had a bow to be tied in the back, and in her haste Juanita fumbled as if she had fat fingers. Once again, Antonia came to her aid, dexterously tying the bow and kicking the dirty dress under the bed at the same time. As if by prestidigitation, a comb materialized in Antonia's hand, and she was combing Juanita's hair when finally Gregoria appeared at the door.

The old woman looked in suspiciously, sensing something amiss. She had to admire the optimism of the young, always thinking that they could get away with something, always supposing that they could put one over on an old woman. Didn't they know that she herself had been young once and had tried the very same tricks with an equal lack of success? She had gained experience in detecting subterfuge, and her experienced eye caught the toy dishes on the table and the dolls on the chairs doing their best to remain inconspicuous, their deafening silence a sure sign of conspiracy. Those toys had been in storage for a while, and their reemergence had to be watched.

She remained silent at the door, shaking her head ambiguously to give notice that she saw the charade. The telltale signs of the doll party drew her attention away from the fact that Juanita was wearing a dress other than the one she had on when she had left for Sister Sylvester's class. This detail bobbed up in the minds of both Juanita and her accomplice as they awaited the outcome of their deception. Gregoria gave no sign of being the wiser as she shuffled off, satisfied that she had seen enough to make her trip upstairs worthwhile.

"Don Eduardo will be home soon, and dinner will be at the usual time," she belatedly said, as if to justify to the young ladies her trip to look in on them.

24

Dᴏ̃ᴀ Cʟᴀʀᴀ ᴅᴇᴛᴇsᴛᴇᴅ the countryside, an anomaly among her compatriots, the humblest of whom took pride in the beauty of the island, even if it was a feature insufficient to keep their bellies full. The expectation that someone in Doña Clara's position would be inclined, as an adjunct to the means, to appreciate the splendor of the landscape was thoroughly reasonable but, in this case, misguided.

Country living failed to provide the safeguards against some hazards to which she had a visceral aversion. The lack of sidewalks presented a major obstacle to her enjoyment of the setting. The close proximity to the earth that tended to turn into mud insulted her sense of propriety. Mud lacked the good sense to stay where it belonged but rather clung to her shoes and to the hems of her garments, places where it didn't belong and where it was not wanted—an affront to her sense of an orderly universe. She might have been more accepting of those ills if she had a coterie with whom to commiserate, but that too was absent in the country, its inhabitants content to befriend adversity or at least to bear the inconveniences without complaint, an attitude she considered more an affront than the physical discomfort occasioned by the lack of amenities. She continued unprepared to deal in a pond where she was the odd duck.

"You didn't warn me," Gregoria said to Doña Clara on one of that lady's rare visits to the Rincon hacienda.

Doña Clara was slow to respond to Gregoria's complaint. Using the time to figure out what particular instance of the crime Gregoria had noticed, since Doña Clara withheld so much about Antonia. In fact, she told nothing, having left everything to be discovered by direct observation. Her silence was not meant to conceal, but rather to prevent obfuscation that would surely result from her inability to describe accurately Antonia's needs. Clara only wondered how much Gregoria already knew and how much she could reveal without further incriminating herself.

"I dare say there have been many oversights on my part," Clara said. "Though there hasn't been much opportunity for discussion."

"True," Gregoria replied. "It's not as if we're neighbors."

Doña Clara stifled the impulse to cross herself against the images evoked by the word "neighbor" in relation to Gregoria. Clara first imagined herself living in the country, an unpalatable thought, but the ramifications of having Gregoria for a neighbor in town proved no more acceptable.

"Yes, everything would have been so much easier had they set up a home in town," Doña Clara said without conviction. That thought was a leftover from a previous era that to Clara seemed a long time ago, but in fact was only a few months in the past.

She had since made a complete turnaround on the subject and concluded that she preferred having the newlyweds out of her sight, or rather out of everybody else's. The couple's presence would have fueled constant gossip about the marriage, and Doña Clara foresaw that steady gossip about her daughter would be an unbearable thorn. She believed the fire of gossip needed constant stoking and that in the absence of that attention, it would quickly die. The particulars of Antonia's marriage would soon fade from people's memories to be replaced, if at all, by a fantasy only vaguely related to reality. That was the natural history of history, and grasping that fact allowed a person to create a version suitable to his own needs.

"But things are what they are," Doña Clara said in a mock attitude of resignation that she easily assumed. She had much practice in doing so, finding it a useful stance for eliciting sympathy. Using it on Gregoria seemed ironic; however, Doña Clara consoled herself by labeling it *only* a ruse.

"How is she doing?" Doña Clara asked, as much to get information as to extricate herself from the position of being interrogated, although Gregoria had not asked any direct question but had merely implied a desire for an explanation.

Gregoria would not be diverted easily. She restated the question as "How are *they* doing?"

Doña Clara, chastened but not showing it, wondered whether the "they" included only two or all three, and if only two, which two, for she had immediately grasped that Gregoria perceived a reality different from hers.

"A marriage is always difficult at the beginning," Gregoria continued, "and this one is no different in that respect."

"I see," Doña Clara said, words opposite of what she was thinking. Actually, all of her concrete images of the Rincon household became blurred—shocked, she realized that her view was rather positive, a fact she could not reconcile with her early expectations of disaster. "But there is hope, don't you think?"

"There is always that," said Gregoria. "But you know better than I what your daughter is capable of."

"I was hoping that you might be able to help her."

"The real question is, how much help does she need?"

"She's only young," Doña Clara said.

"Then time will cure that ill," Gregoria answered.

"She will have the time, do you suppose?"

"Time is more plentiful than is commonly believed, if that's your real question."

"How is Don Eduardo taking to it all, is the real question."

"He leaves early and returns late," Gregoria said.

"I know the pattern," Doña Clara said turning her head to gaze through the window at the mountainous landscape. "Aurelio was the same way."

"And you survived."

"One hopes for more than survival."

"Ah, she already has more," said Gregoria.

"I mean more than wealth."

"That hardly needs to be said."

"What does she have?"

"She has family."

"She had that before she married."

"No, I mean she has Juanita, and she has Eduardo too."

"Does she have him really?"

"He never stays out a whole night."

"For whose sake is that?"

"Does that matter?"

"It matters a great deal, I should think."

"It's a start," Gregoria said.

"Ah, yes, one must start somewhere," Doña Clara continued thinking back to where she had started. "I hoped that it would be better for her," Doña Clara said with a bewildered look on her face.

A universe that denied her so simple a wish was one ruled by perversity. As was often the case, she did not pursue the implications of her thought, afraid to arrive at a place from where she might not be able to extricate herself, like a cat up a tree with no philosophical ladder to rescue her from the predicament.

I N BUSINESS AFFAIRS, Eduardo saw his way clearly. In farming and his dealings with other men, the rules seemed simple and the consequences obvious, but family matters were more complicated. Intimate relationships defied simple rules, and the consequences of following one course of action over another refused to be predictable though many people believed the opposite. Self-deception worked well enough for some, but Eduardo Rincon expected more from himself. He did not make that decision though sometimes he believed that he had. Decision implies choice, like taking one road instead of another. In going to San Geronimo one might take the most direct route, but that road featured stretches along a precipice: a mistake there might be fatal. The safer route avoided the dangerous side of the mountain but added hours to the trip. A prudent man when traveling with his family took the safer route. That was a choice. For Eduardo Rincon self-deception was beyond choice, a matter of character, and being out of his control, he refused to take credit.

He believed his family had a right to expect him to always know the right course, but how was he always to judge in advance what the results would be? Doña Clara, after accepting the separation from her daughter for a while, again began to agitate for the move of the Rincon family into town. Doña Clara declared it unfair for Antonia to be deprived of town life. Her insistence would not have been sufficient to shake Eduardo's confidence in the appropriateness of his choice, but he had other reasons to question his judgment. Certainly, Antonia did not clamor for a return to San Geronimo, but Eduardo saw that as an attempt to please him. That, too, by itself, was a negligible burden on his conscience. Rather, he squirmed at not having recognized that she was too young to have made the choice, and he had taken advantage of her innocence.

No one had reproached him for making a mercenary move. No one but Aurelio knew that the five hundred acres were discussed in advance, and even if the whole world knew, the matter would not have been shocking, such arrangements common enough. In any case, he could not say that the acres tipped the balance. Antonia was a logical choice for a wife without them. Why, then, did he still question whether he had done right by her? He loved her enough. Who was to say that he didn't? Only he, if he chose to do so, and he did not. He acted as if he loved her, and that was in effect the same thing. He wondered whether she loved him in return. The evidence from his side conflicted. He had only a man's point of view, perhaps insufficient, from which to judge. He pondered the fact that she chose to marry him against her mother's wishes, and why would she do that if she did not love him? At times, he thought the question foolish. She was his wife, and all that was required was that she play the role she had chosen.

Still, her reticence on their wedding night had been a blow to his vanity. At first, he ascribed it to maidenly modesty and ignorance. After all, he didn't expect his bride to be experienced. That would have shocked him even more and would have put him in a dilemma; he could not have exposed her without making himself the object of ridicule. At the same time, he could not live with the knowledge that at least one other person knew that he had received less than he expected. So he didn't think her shrinking from his touch that night unusual. He saw that she tried to be valiant. With characteristic bravura, she had undone her nightgown, pulled it over her head and dropped it on the floor, but at that moment, standing there bare and vulnerable, she had lost her nerve. In bed, she turned from him with a disconcerting rigidity, so that if he wanted her, he would have to take her by force. He rejected that course of action. She turned her reluctant face towards him to reveal tears that puzzled him even more, the last thing he had expected from her. He tried to read her hazel eyes but failed. The fact that he knew so little about her disturbed him.

"Why are you crying?" he asked, hoping she might tell him

a problem within his power to address, for he would have done anything for her, if only he knew where to apply his effort.

"I don't know," she said.

The answer annoyed him, unable to imagine himself being ignorant of why he acted one way instead of another. Even if later he turned out to be wrong, at any one moment he could readily explain the reasons for his actions, all except for that one time when he had frozen on the path to the waterfall where Carmen Gutierez surprised him. How different she had been. No holding back for her; she gave him all that he wanted then, and all that he at the moment wanted from Antonia but which she was unable or unwilling to provide. On his wedding night he found himself evoking Carmen's image as consolation. He would have preferred to avoid the dangers that lurked in those thoughts, but he needed Antonia's help to keep himself on course.

For the moment, Antonia could not see beyond her own predicament, but unwilling to succumb to her fears, she forced herself to let her husband have his way, perfectly aware that this could not be the best response to the problem. Among strangers that first week, she had no one to turn to for advice and consolation. She would have wished to open her heart to Eduardo, if she could, but the words eluded her. She lacked concepts to describe what she had never experienced or spoken about before. Someone should have warned her about this possible predicament, and the fact that no one had done so led her to classify her feelings as peculiar, leading her to reticence as the prudent course. Although she often reveled in rebelliousness, she didn't relish being considered odd, something entirely different.

She had married someone in many ways a stranger, a revelation to her, and though she firmly believed that she loved him, at close quarters, she often failed to recognize him as the person she loved. To her, love implied a perfect universe, the details of physical intimacy absent, details that then intruded into her everyday life with unforeseen consequences. She cast about to find and reproach the person who should have warned her. Reluctant to strike the most obvious target, knowing that caught in the dilemma of youth, confidence in total ignorance, she would have ignored any warning from her mother.

Often, Eduardo ate breakfast alone in the kitchen, no one but he and Gregoria yet up and moving about the cavernous house that slowly admitted through its large windows the light of the rising sun. Opening the external shutters on the lower floor was the first task of the day, and Gregoria went about the familiar routine listening to the calls of the morning birds that split the silence with reproachful shrieks announcing that all was not well within. For the old woman, Eduardo failed to disguise his dark look. After breakfast of buttered French bread, *asobado*, and strong black coffee, he went to the barn, saddled his horse, and rode off to inspect his domain, as if it needed supervision to receive the light of the sun. Listening to the receding sound of the hoof beats, Gregoria wondered whether they were headed to a definite destination. Surely, if Carmen Gutierez were within riding distance, he would have gone there, but she, having foreseen such an eventuality, removed herself to a place that required more than a day's ride. For that, Gregoria was thankful. Dealing with that alternative would have required more resourcefulness than she had.

At first, Gregoria believed Eduardo was merely unduly impatient with his bride. After all, what did he expect from so young a wife brought up to be a proper Catholic girl? If anything, a church dominated by men was responsible for the difficulty young people had in coming to terms with their sexuality, though clearly some like Carmen had no trouble at all. Some fortunate people, either by instinct or by fortuitous circumstances, took the teachings of the Church with a grain of salt and adapted them to fit the necessities of practical life. From all signs, Antonia should have been one of those, and that made coping with her aversion all the more difficult for her husband. Eventually, the degree of Antonia's reluctance to fulfill her conjugal duties became unexplainable to Gregoria, and Antonia's solution to the predicament, to grit her teeth and bear it, remained disconcerting.

Gregoria had early on hoped that Antonia would do better than that, and she was dismayed one morning, after Eduardo had ridden off in his newly customary bad mood, to come upon Antonia in tears and fetching water to fill the bathtub. At first Gregoria did not know what to make of the sight of the slight figure of the young woman, both hands on the handle of the bucket and stooped over by its weight, slowly moving down the corridor like an apparition of a penitent. Another childish prank was the first explanation that came to mind. The old lady half-expected to see Juanita at any moment also taking part in the escapade, for the two who shared the affection of the master of the house had chosen to act as pals, like two girls at a boarding school, rather than as a stepmother and daughter, which seemed to them an even more preposterous charade. As she got closer, uncertain whether she read panic or grief in Antonia's face, Gregoria concluded that the game she had stumbled on had gone sour.

"Ay, put down the bucket. I will call Manolo to carry the water," Gregoria said.

"I will do it myself," Antonia insisted. Being imperative for her was a natural stance, an attitude that had worked well in the past, but in the semi-darkened house, with the sun only emerging over the horizon, and with no other witness around but this old woman who had done nothing but smooth her way since she had arrived to be mistress of the house, Antonia longed for some other solution, if only she knew how to produce it. She put down the bucket hoping that Gregoria would do or say something to put a different hue on a day so badly begun. Gregoria, not yet having ascribed meaning to what she saw and reluctant to ask, merely looked at the bucket of water then at Antonia's face.

"I must cleanse myself," Antonia said. By some almost imperceptible gesture she communicated to Gregoria what had occurred.

"Oh, my dear, my dear," Gregoria said.

And Antonia clung to her as fervently as she would have clung to her mother.

"I did not imagine it would be like this," Antonia said.

"It won't always be," Gregoria said, hoping for that to be the truth and Antonia not one of those women who would never be comfortable with the carnal aspects of marriage—an unfortunate possibility.

"I don't know what to do," Antonia said.

"You will get used to it," Gregoria answered.

"You don't understand," the young woman lamented.

"Ah," Gregoria said, "how can I?" She well understood that believing one's experience to be new and totally incomprehensible to anyone else, especially to an older person, was one of the dilemmas of being young. She commiserated with the young wife, knowing that the old often forgot their younger years and failed to provide any clue that they had experienced the very same difficulties and doubts.

"Eduardo must hate me," Antonia said.

"That's very unlikely," Gregoria assured her. "He's somewhere out there hating himself."

"That's not any better, is it?" Antonia said, surprising her companion with that insight and giving her hope that all was not lost.

Clearly, the child could not be left to fend for herself, but clarity failed to take Gregoria any further. All the advice in the world would be useless in this case. The necessary change required something more drastic. Only one side of the problem being open to her made the matter more difficult, since she would never presume to say a word to Eduardo concerning the matter, even if he had nowhere else to turn for help. Ironically, Carmen Gutierez would have been able to advise him had she still been close by, but that would have stirred other problems, and Gregoria was thankful for the absence of that complication.

"I have a suggestion," Gregoria said.

Antonia, who had been contemplating her own feet, as if her toes were some divining instrument through which miraculous answers might be obtained, looked up to meet the old lady's gaze, a more likely source of relief.

"What if we take a little journey to visit Doña Echevaria?"

"Oh, I couldn't do that," Antonia exclaimed. "I am a Catholic."

"And am I not one also?" Gregoria asked.

Antonia had certainly believed so until that moment, and she didn't know what to make of the suggestion. Doña Echevaria was a Spiritist. Antonia had heard of such people, but she had never had actual contact with one, and she had only a vague notion of what they believed or practiced. She only knew that the Church inveighed against them, and she loathed adding another sin to the one she had already committed, whatever that was, whether refusing her husband's advances or succumbing to them or perhaps both.

EXPECTING HER THIRD child, the first two having been born at home, Antonia didn't see a need to change the routine. She felt safe in her own room with familiar objects and people around her. Why would she want to be in a strange place with strangers watching her do something difficult and graceless? She would rather have Gregoria and Ana Santamaria, the midwife, who delivered her first two, looking after her the way they had in the past. She would rather have those women than even her mother, a person often hysterical at stressful moments.

"It would be better to have a doctor," Eduardo said.

"What does a man know about such things?" Gregoria asked.

"We've never had a doctor before," said Antonia. "I don't see why we must have one now."

"In case of an emergency, a doctor is best," Eduardo said. "It's always good to be prepared."

"There's nothing a doctor can do that the midwife can't do out here," Gregoria said.

"Yes, out here, that's my point; the hospital is the place," Eduardo said.

"The hospital is too far away," Antonia said. "I'd never get there in time, and the baby will pop out right in the middle of the road."

"Of course, you'll have to stay with your parents when the time gets close."

"That's out of the question," Antonia insisted. Spending weeks in her mother's house would be intolerable, especially in the final uncomfortable months of pregnancy. Her mother had not always been that way, but as time passed, she was becoming less reliable. What could Eduardo be thinking of?

The enmity between Doña Clara and Eduardo had ceased, but Antonia considered that a development of dubious value. Doña Clara began to soften after the birth of the first grandchild, and after the second, she began to append superlatives to Eduardo's name. Antonia preferred their being on less friendly terms. She dreaded the prospect of their ganging up on her. But that was another matter. Still, Gregoria was always on her side—something Antonia never expected. Juanita also was won over, perhaps both part of the same process; to win one included winning the other.

"These are modern times," Eduardo argued. "We must take advantage of the advances of science." That line of reasoning got him nowhere with this audience, resorting to it already the first step in admitting defeat. He should have known better than to meddle in the first place. Even though nominally the master of the household, his authority reigned absolute only outside the house. Within, thrived a realm of women to whose wishes he deferred in fact, if not in appearance. Childbirth a woman's travail, he should have refrained from interfering, but he only wanted to be helpful.

"And what about the little ones?" Antonia said. "I can't just transplant them to my mother's house."

"They'll stay here," Eduardo said.

"Without me? How can they be without me? They're too young to be without me for so long."

"They'll be alright with Gregoria and Juanita," Eduardo said. "Isn't that so?" he inquired of the other two women, whom he saw as the primary agents of childcare in the household. His tone sounded neutral yet made the women uneasy and hesitant to respond.

"They know who their mother is, Eduardo. My absence would certainly make a difference to them," Antonia defensively responded, taking Eduardo's words as a reproach.

"Yes of course," he said, "I only meant that their routines wouldn't be radically altered."

"I am their mother after all," Antonia reiterated.

"Yes, papa," Juanita said, "children miss their mother." Her words referred to the matter at hand, but as soon as they had left her lips, she realized that her father had a wider context in which to apply them, and she scoured his face for signs of what he had done with them. She feared bruising an old wound to her dismay ever ready to bleed and the patient reluctant to admit his condition. She would have preferred that he acknowledged the ailment so that together they might engage in the recovery, but he persisted in stoic silence, vainly believing his affliction invisible to others.

Indeed, sometimes Juanita wondered whether her father really suffered or whether her Romantic imagination created that semblance. On this occasion, he again failed to provide her with any sign of pain, but she knew him to be a master of dissemblance and her concern persisted.

"Yes, I'm sure they do," he said.

Gregoria for her part kept silent wishing not to exert herself unduly. Increasingly, she felt exhausted when the emotional underpinnings of the Rincon family surfaced. She was like a choreographer creating a family dance with the stipulation that all the principal dancers perform to a different score. The task wore her out. The last few years were more than she expected, but she could consider them a partial success. Eduardo and Antonia had a workable marriage though not perfect. But was there ever a perfect marriage? The children were a long time in coming but they came, and that went a long way to stabilize the relationship. At the beginning, Gregoria had her doubts. There was just so much one could expect from a man, and she had feared Eduardo would reach the limit of his patience.

Eventually, her task at the Rincon household would come to an end. That realization startled her; she knew all along the time would arrive, having already undergone the same process with her own children. Suddenly they are no longer children, and the parents have difficulty adjusting to the transformation that occurs in several stages. More than once, Gregoria had to step back and remind herself to look again and evaluate what she saw. Juanita no longer a child, the change in her physical appearance was the least of the alterations. Suddenly aware of the changes transpiring in the young woman, Gregoria provided for them. New articles of clothing were required and the style of outer garments changed.

Almost without thought, Gregoria had prepared the girl for the routines required when the monthly bleeding began.

The maturing of the young lady spurred Gregoria to more often call her Juana instead of Juanita, but getting into that habit took time and seemed at times erratic. Juanita's maturing might have seemed more momentous had other changes in the household not also occurred. The number of young ones increased at a steady rate, Antonia pregnant three years in a row. The first-born, a girl, inspired the fear that a male offspring would never grace the family. When the first boy arrived Eduardo was pleased, as well as Don Aurelio for whom the arrival of a grandson went a long way to nullify his grievance and to justify his faith in Eduardo. Having little ones about the house pleased everyone, but the gushing fertility after the inauspicious beginning of her marriage overwhelmed Antonia.

Looking somewhat peaked one day, she complained to Gregoria, "I can't be pregnant again this year. I will be all worn out prematurely."

"You must restrain yourself, then," the old woman said.

"And who's going to restrain my husband? You don't suppose I am the one who initiates these activities."

Gregoria expected Antonia by that time to have learned to manage her husband, something essential to the preservation of a good marriage—or any marriage at all. "Sometimes I think you're as innocent as Juanita," she said to the mistress of the house.

"And how innocent is she?" Antonia asked in good faith, having grown to depend on her stepdaughter for emotional as well as physical assistance in running the house, especially after the children came. Juanita, possessing mothering talent in inverse proportion to her stepmother, took to her new half-siblings with ease and enthusiasm. Antonia might have begrudged her that, but she had been grateful for the assistance, and since the role fit Juanita's character, Antonia gladly obliged, being sensible about help in adjusting to life in Comerio.

Antonia grew sensitive to the relationship between her husband and his daughter, which seemed troubled, although they desperately clung to each other. Antonia sometimes wondered whether her own appearance on the scene caused strain between father and daughter. As a compromise between attempting to help and doing nothing at all, Antonia tried to understand, but everyone avoided discussion. The reason why father and daughter failed to communicate with each other, when they both wanted to, evaded Antonia. Unexpectedly ineffectual in this case, Gregoria refused to divulge the nature of the problem.

"They will work it out eventually," the old lady once said, when Antonia had confronted her directly. "God willing," Gregoria added, the code, Antonia came to understand, for, "There's nothing more to be done."

Indeed, the old lady had her suspicions but nothing she could share with the young wife without running the risk of derailing the marriage or, at least, causing a disruption. Antonia's ignorance, no doubt, was caused by her desire not to know, having before her living proof that Eduardo might still have another life. The father/daughter problem would hover in the background without anyone getting too frazzled. Indeed, Gregoria and Antonia took the lead from the principals, who went long stretches without showing any signs of discomfort. Of course, when still a child, burdening Juana with the responsibility of finding a solution, or even articulating the problem, had been hardly fair, but as she grew up, letting the matter rest on her shoulders became convenient.

Antonia had more immediate concerns. "Perhaps Doña Echevaria can again do something for me," she suggested.

"Doña Echevaria's power has its limit," Gregoria said. "I think this you have to do for yourself."

Antonia screwed up her face to indicate some disappointment. The expression momentarily harked back to a more youthful look, one that lurked beneath the fatty tissue that accrued with each pregnancy and that refused to depart, like an unwelcome relative who comes for a visit but stays indefinitely. Her plumpness concealed her more emotional than physical weariness. Just then, as the two women discussed the alternative to invoking the spirit world, Evita, Antonia's elder child, walked into the room clutching a red blanket, a constant object in her arms. Her mother's primary concern was that the four-year-old girl could hardly speak, while her younger brother chattered like a magpie, a reversal of the usual. Nothing wrong with her vocal chords, the doctor in San Geronimo assured them. But just to be certain, the anxious parents, at the instigation of Doña Clara, sought a second opinion from a more renowned physician recommended by the bishop.

"Of course that's what comes from living in the country," Doña Clara stated, to her an incontrovertible fact rather than a hypothesis. "Children pick things up much faster when they live in town, no question about it." The fact that Evita's siblings had no such problem failed to lessen her conviction of the detrimental effect of country life.

If the matter had only been that simple, she would have welcomed her mother's attempt at optimism, a natural search for explanations of the unexplainable. The more obscure the cause, or fortuitous the event, the more earnest the search for reasons. Antonia searched for an explanation of her child's affliction, but none of physical origin came readily to mind. She was left in the realm of moral transgressions that manifest themselves through physical consequences—a bridge between the physical world and some other, where morality transforms into an agent of human destiny. The alchemy that effected this transformation never clearly spelled out, she suspected a vengeful God who kept track of infractions and dealt out corresponding punishment.

Psychological sins, the most apt to be invisible to the community at large, known usually only to the sinner and those close to him, trigger these events. Penance required that they be exposed, but sometimes that never happened, the dread of discovery becoming the punishment. Fear of retribution had not been part of Antonia's lot. She thought herself more a victim than a transgressor until confronted with the need to find a reason for the calamity; then, she turned upon herself. She noted her reluctance to be a mother, and brought herself to believe that Juanita was more of a mother to her siblings than she who gave birth to them. She used that fact to scourge herself.

"I wish, Gregoria, that my children were not the ones to suffer for my sins."

The circumstances puzzled Gregoria, but she refrained from jumping to conclusions. "It would be a cruel God who would punish children for the sins of their parents," she said.

"Yes, but I can think of no other reason why this should happen to us."

"It's not for us to fathom the reasons," said the old woman. "Our lot is to bear our burdens with patience as our Lord did his cross. We should not take responsibility that's not ours. That's to take up someone else's cross or perhaps no one's, but it's pride to think we deserve it, if we don't."

"How are we to know?"

"Pray and you will have an answer."

"I have my answer," Antonia said, but she withheld the source of her certainty.

EDUARDO USUALLY STUCK to what he knew best, the management of his land. His holdings had grown considerably since he had first inherited a portion of his father's lot and he diversified his crops. He still grew tobacco, the best on the island, if he said so himself, and he acquired from John Walker the land across the stream. John Walker in 1918 had gone off to war and did not return, which Eduardo lamented, having grown close to him despite his oddness. Such a young man had no business getting killed in a war from which, win or lose, he had nothing to gain but the growth of his family's wealth. The profits from coffee and sugar went up during the war, but Eduardo considered a human life too high a price to pay for that benefit.

After the war, Eduardo began to plan a cockfighting arena on his land. It would be another source of income for the Rincon family but that played a minimal role in his motivation to build it. Conscious of his social obligations, he perceived responsible sponsorship of this activity a benefit to the community. The venture would be egalitarian in nature, since, unlike horse racing and breeding, it required little capital. The breeding of fighting cocks fell within the means of the *campesinos* and made the sport popular, but unregulated practice made it susceptible to unpleasant incidents. He had occasion to discuss the matter with his father-in-law at the *Club Nacional. Don* Aurelio favored the idea, but he warned Eduardo that not everyone would applaud his being involved in so plebeian an activity.

"That's my point precisely," said Eduardo. "The sport must be pulled out of the gutter."

"Wouldn't it rather pull you into it?"

"In the country it's impossible to make a living without stepping in manure," Eduardo said. "That's why boots were invented."

"Those of us who don't wear boots must be more careful, I

suppose," said Don Aurelio. "But I think you're right. Just because the sport is bloody doesn't mean it can't be respectable. In Spain the king and queen regularly attend the bullfight. But then again, bulls are much larger than cocks."

"You mean more expensive, don't you?"

"That too," Don Aurelio conceded.

"Blood sport for the rich is all right, but for the poor it's questionable."

"The poor attend the bullfights also," said Don Aurelio.

"Yes, but they don't own the bulls, which is more to the point," Eduardo said.

"Ah, so what you want is to further democracy."

"What I want is to create order out of chaos. If democracy is what it takes, I'm for it."

"The Americans are here but a few years and already you're becoming one."

"Whether we're American's is not up to us, is it? It has been decreed from Washington that we are."

"Americans understand democracy, but they would balk at cockfighting."

"Well, there you have it then. We can never be Americans."

"Cockfighting or no, we're not Americans until we say we are."

*

The *gallera* was not in operation long before Juanita's interest in it became apparent. At first she only made allusion to it in passing, which Gregoria tried to ignore.

"Lots of excitement by the *gallera*," Juanita said every Sunday on the way home from church, the *gallera* visible from the road.

"*Galleros* go to an early mass," Gregoria answered.

"As soon as the cock crows," Juanita responded.

Gregoria, unsure whether the girl was being facetious, decided to remain unruffled. "I suppose they pray for luck."

"No doubt," Juanita said.

Like a calm before the storm, a few weeks went by without any mention of the *gallera.*

"Well then, when shall we go to see the cockfights?" Juanita asked Gregoria as they both sat in the kitchen shelling pigeon peas that Manolo brought in from the field. Manolo's wife Inez was hired to help about the house after the children arrived, removing any need for Juanita to do anything in the kitchen. Indeed, Gregoria had nothing to do but to look after Juanita, who at that point needed no looking after. Still, Gregoria would not yield her place in the kitchen, and Juanita would not abandon her place by Gregoria. The same tasks she had performed when as a little girl she played at being grown-up, she at the moment performed as a grown-up playing at being a child.

"I know that you're trying to get my goat," Gregoria said, "so I will stay calm." She looked away from Juanita when she spoke, as if looking at the young woman would be a hindrance to maintaining composure.

"No, really, I'm not kidding," Juanita said. "I do want to go."

"And what makes you think that I would take you there."

"I thought you might prefer to go with me rather than I go with someone else."

"I am too old for such shenanigans," Gregoria said. "What would your father say if he found out, which he would, because nothing happens around here that he doesn't know about?"

"He would say nothing. He would only frown a little and walk away confused."

"He will blame me for letting you go."

"You took me to the horse races for the first time when I was a child."

"Horse races are different," Gregoria said.

"How so?"

"They just are," she said.

"Pedro will take me then, if you don't want to go."

"He talks to you now, does he?"

"No, but I will make him."

"You are so powerful?

"I will go to his house and ask him. He cannot refuse."

"You will do nothing of the kind," Gregoria said alarmed by this threat. Going to Pedro's house was nothing unusual for Juanita, having been going there since childhood. He, in turn, approached the door of her house, and once or twice, at Gregoria's insistence, entered through the kitchen, but he was never comfortable there and left as soon as he could make a polite escape.

"I guess he doesn't like it here," Juanita had said back then.

"He does what he's told," Gregoria said.

"No one asked him to leave."

"His parents taught him that he doesn't belong in the big house."

"Why?"

"Because it's true," Gregoria said.

On the other hand, he was always at ease at Gregoria's, and he was willing to have Juanita as a companion out in the open where he treated her the same as he treated the other children, but he knew she was not the same.

Juanita felt affronted when he began to avoid her. She could think of no reason why he should insult her after they had been friends since childhood when they played together in the *batey.* She often went to his house, sat at his parents' table, on a bench like the ones in Gregoria's house. They always were glad to have her, a hospitality that she would have been more than glad to reciprocate, but that was never accepted, not even by Pedro, who came to the door but rarely ventured to set foot over the threshold, as if to do so would result in some calamity that Juanita could only imagine. He seldom wore shoes, and she supposed that a connection existed between his unshod condition and his refusal to enter the house even when she assured him that the floor had no resemblance to glowing coals.

"That Pedro Soto is the strangest fellow," Juanita said to Gregoria one day as she helped the old woman set the table for dinner. "He treats me as if I were a leper, and I don't know what I have done to offend him. If he told me, then I would know what to avoid doing, but whenever I see him, he walks the other way. Anyone would think I was trying to collect a debt from him."

"This time," Gregoria said, "you will not be able to apologize for what you have done nor stop doing it."

"And what pray is my sin?"

"You have grown up."

"Well, he has grown up, too."

"Precisely," said Gregoria.

"You mean we cannot be friends?"

"You must now be careful who you befriend."

Juanita failed to see any reason for extra precaution in this case. What was there to be careful about? She didn't have to wait long for Gregoria to tell her.

"It was all right when you were a child to run about with whomever you pleased, and it was tolerant of your father to allow it. He never gave the matter much thought, otherwise things might be different, but now that you're a young lady, things have changed."

"I'm still the same person."

"No, you're not. You'll never be the same person again."

"I feel the same."

"Pedro knows you're not the same."

"He's just a fool. I will straighten him out."

"If you care for him at all, you'll let him be. He's not for you."

"What are you talking about, Gregoria? We're just friends."

"You're no longer friends, Juanita. Now you're acquaintances. He will always be a worker on this hacienda or on some other, and you will always be the daughter of the *patron*. Nothing can change that. You will do him a favor to let him be."

That truth remained irrelevant to Juanita, and Gregoria continually failed to convince the young woman.

"Juana, you must let Pedro choose his own path."

"Let him abandon me without protest?"

"You cannot make him think that there are prospects where there are none."

"Prospects of what?"

"You cannot make him fall in love with you. That can never be."

"Fall in love? I only want to go to the cockfights."

"You can forget that, too," Gregoria said. "You can't let it get about that you are reckless. You will ruin your chances for a good marriage."

"And what is a good marriage? Antonia made a good marriage, and she doesn't look all too happy about it."

Antonia too would sometimes spend time in the kitchen with them, but apt to get bored or break a nail or cut herself with a knife, she would be off in search of Mercurochrome and gauze and fail to return, getting lost in some catalogue from which she made plans to order innumerable items either to wear or to embellish the house but never executing her plan. After all, when would she have occasion to wear fancy clothes, and the house looked fine the way it was. Anything delicate and pretty was at risk of being smashed by the children who increasingly resembled wild things, whom she had no heart to discipline and Eduardo never home to do it. What ever could he be doing riding around the fields all day long? Did not all these plants grow on their own without encouragement from him?

"You must learn to curb your tongue too, especially about things you know nothing about," Gregoria said, but she could not deny what Juanita had observed.

"I live in this house, too, and I have eyes to see and ears to hear. Should I cut out my tongue?"

"I dare say you would be better without it."

"You blow hot and cold. This is not a monastery with a rule of silence, oh mother superior."

"Your sassiness will be your undoing."

"And what was Antonia's undoing?"

"You can leave Antonia alone. Each of us has our own cross to bear."

"Ah, just so, Sister Sylvester would approve of you."

"She doesn't have to approve of me, but you, my dear, must toe the mark."

Juanita did not argue the point further, and Gregoria took that as a good sign. On this issue, the old woman had anticipated some resistance from her charge and remained doubtful that she could present a coherent argument that would open the matter to rational resolution. Abandoning a friendship needed a powerful motive. Juanita had enough reasons to be ambivalent about her allegiances, and Gregoria had her greatest challenge yet before her. She had to see Juanita married well to consider complete the task that Carmen Gutierez entrusted to her. Soon the time would come to call on Doña Clara to fulfill her end of the bargain and provide some aid to Gregoria in taking care of Juanita, just as Gregoria had done for Antonia.

As she grew older, Juanita found the scope of her life constricting rather than expanding. Even on her father's domain, she had to be more careful of what she did and said and where and with whom she associated. But the temptations to do whatever she pleased did not decrease. Even her father, who had always been permissive if not indifferent to her movements, began to show some desire that she rein in her impulsiveness. He had always left such matters to Gregoria, feeling that a woman knew best the subtleties of raising a girl, but seeing his daughter suddenly a woman, much resembling the mother whose allure still haunted him, forced him to be more concerned.

Sometimes, on those occasions when he had a quiet moment—or when suddenly walking through a field or riding through some wild patch of uncultivated land he came upon some unexpected sight, a flower blooming in solitary splendor where least expected—the image of Carmen Gutierez under the waterfall overwhelmed him. That association worried him enough, though certain that Juanita had no need to use the waterfall as her mother had done. Still, he knew well enough that even without the waterfall, Juanita would have the same effect on some young man that Carmen had had on him.

As much as her father's newfound paternal concern annoyed Juanita, it gratified Gregoria—though she was disturbed by his failure to understand her objection to his plan for a cockfighting arena on the hacienda. Meddling in business issues, of course, was not her function, but over the years, as a partner with Eduardo in the raising of his daughter, a bond grew between them that transcended their formal relationship of employer and employee, so that the master of the house found himself at times asking the housekeeper's opinion on matters on which he thought she might have a useful or unique point of view. He recognized that the appearance of the world depended on the vantage point of the observer. Astride his horse, he saw something other than what he saw when standing on the ground. She objected to the cockfighting arena because it would, like any gaming establishment, attract a number of people of questionable character, in this case young men bent on squandering money that would be missed at home. More importantly, exposing Juanita to a greater number of unsuitable young men made Gregoria uncomfortable. Eduardo, however, considered a higher degree of vigilance a sufficient safeguard.

"It's not as if she will be in attendance there," he said to Gregoria when she brought up the matter.

"Do you know her so little? How will you keep her away? All her life she's been free to come and go as she pleases."

"She's a sensible girl," he said.

"She is that, when she wants to be," Gregoria said, indulging her ambivalence.

H AVING DEVELOPED A conspiratorial relationship that both relished, Doña Clara needed but a slight hint from Gregoria to launch the planning of a strategic move. As zealous as any two members of a political cell, they believed themselves instrumental in the progression of history, except that they aimed at preserving society rather than transforming it, to them the same thing, since to slacken their effort would lead to catastrophic consequences. If we consider history the sum of individual efforts, then this view is correct, and the two ladies cannot be faulted. The aggregate effect of individual actions is staggering. Tolstoy proposed the question: *What if every sergeant in Napoleon's army refused to follow him in the invasion of Russia?* The answer is obvious. The dictator would have been powerless. We can transpose the question and ask instead: What if every mother and grandmother ceased to be an engineer of family relations? Doña Clara and Doña Gregoria believed that under those circumstances, chaos would ensue. Neither one verbalized this belief, but they acted on it just as if they were following the tenet of a political or religious creed.

Doña Clara seldom made the trek to the country to visit her grandchildren, preferring that the Rincon family make the trip to San Geronimo. Don Aurelio, on the contrary, welcomed the chance to get away from town and often urged excursions to the Rincon hacienda. Once there, Doña Clara always found time for a private moment with Gregoria in which the two renewed their odd friendship. In a sense, the Rincons and the Castillos were two provinces of the same empire, and just as the Romans developed a need for an emperor of the West and an emperor of the East, the two ladies had divided the world between them.

"There are many eligible young men in San Geronimo," said Doña Clara.

"But not in Comerio," said Gregoria.

"The remedy for that is simple," said Doña Clara. She supposed that the trip between San Geronimo and Comerio was only difficult for those who lived in San Geronimo and that it was no trouble at all for the inhabitants of Comerio. Doña Clara proposed that Juanita visit her for a few weeks during which time she would see that Juanita met appropriate young men.

The physical trip to San Geronimo the least of Gregoria's worries, she feared that the plan would lead to nothing, because Juanita might have already decided on a course of action from which reason would be insufficient to dissuade her. But only effort might be lost, and in that lady's opinion, losing something replaceable was inconsequential. However, the expected opposition to the trip from Juanita never materialized. The young lady readily assented to the proposal.

Surprised, and having acquired from years of experience the habit of suspecting unexpected results, Gregoria immediately began to harbor another set of worries, prompting her to inquire whether Pedro Soto planned to be away from Comerio at the same time as Juanita. Finding that he was not, she relaxed somewhat but not completely. She began to ascribe to them more cunning than past experience justified.

"You really do want to go to San Geronimo?" Gregoria inquired several times to give the young lady an opportunity to reveal any scheme that might be burdening her conscience.

"Yes, of course I want to go," Juanita said. "I need a change of scenery. It will do you good also to spend some time in town."

"Oh, I'm not going," Gregoria said. "You will be Doña Clara's responsibility."

"It'll do you good then to have a rest from me," Juanita said.

"I will have time to rest soon enough," the old woman said, "but not yet."

✳

Gregoria never knew whether Juanita had a genuine interest in Roberto Andaluvio or whether she pretended to be interested in him to assuage the fears of her elders. A young man in all points acceptable to parents and guardians of young ladies, he possessed conventional good looks, a quality that recommended him at first glance, and which he followed up with manners that fell only slightly short of obsequious. On first meeting, he usually charmed new acquaintances, but soon after, doubt of his sincerity arose with no concrete evidence for so uncharitable a judgment. His chiseled features and square chin implied only honesty and forthrightness. Though in some people his wavy hair evoked the image of a dandy, ascribing to him that description solely on account of a natural feature, acquired through no fault of his, was unfair. He dressed well but without the fastidiousness that would have justified derision. His eyes had a habit of suddenly losing their intensity without apparent reason. In conversation, his interest did not correspondingly flag, giving the impression that he had a secret source of discomfort. This feature of his eyes perhaps supported whatever doubts his manners failed to dispel.

Even in saints, skeptics will find faults, and though no one proposed sainthood for Roberto Andaluvio, neither was there any reason to disparage him. Doña Clara gave the young man her unqualified endorsement and except that all her daughters were by then married, in gratitude for which she had commissioned a Mass to be said once a week for a year, she would have deemed him suitable for a son-in-law, and she would have spared no effort to enlist him in that capacity. She had acquired, while her daughters were single, the habit of hunting for young men who might change that condition. She often complained about the task, calling it the bane of her existence, but once the need to perform it vanished, she felt bereft of purpose, and she found herself on occasion behaving as if she still had marriageable daughters, until she realized in astonishment the redundancy of her effort.

Gregoria took Juanita's infatuation with the young man at face value. Her arriving, sooner or later, at her senses seemed a reasonable expectation, and why not sooner? The fact that after Juanita's departure from Doña Clara's house Roberto had allowed only one week to elapse before riding out to Comerio, and that immediately on his arrival he begged an interview with Don Eduardo, no doubt to ask formal permission to address himself to Juanita as a suitor, indicated to Gregoria that Juanita had given him sufficient encouragement. Gregoria also received by special delivery post a note from Doña Clara confirming the young man's intended call.

During that first visit, Juanita proved to be the model of propriety and good breeding. Gregoria felt gratified that the effort and expense of Juanita's education had some practical application, a point about which she was once doubtful and about which she assumed the responsibility of being concerned, since Don Eduardo had abdicated the role. Gregoria observed that Juanita knew how to play the courtship game very well, being definitely cool toward the young man to inspire his devotion. Where she learned to be so artful, Gregoria could not tell, and she doubted that such skills were on the curriculum of Sister Sylvester's school of etiquette, although Gregoria herself had never observed what went on there, and Juanita had always been laconic in her accounts of the place, which Gregoria had interpreted as a lack of novelty in the course of study.

After a while Gregoria became concerned that Juanita's coolness bordered on cruelty—that she carried her games a little too far. Life had room enough for games but also bounds to be adhered to for the sake of civility— there was no reason to be nasty to someone who was pledging love. Juanita relished keeping the young man waiting after he made the trip from San Geronimo.

"Well, how was I to know that he was going to show up unannounced?" Juanita justified herself.

"He always visits on Sunday," Gregoria said.

"Well, always is bit much. He hasn't been around always."

"Nevertheless, one must be polite."

"I can't present myself looking a fright," the young woman argued. "I'll be down in a minute."

A minute stretched out to an hour. Don Eduardo, when home, took on the task of entertaining the young man until his daughter made herself presentable. That gave the men a chance to get acquainted. Inevitably, they ended up in the stable, Eduardo convinced of no better way to get the measure of man than to see how he behaved around horses. He also considered his horses the best in the country, and showing them off provided an opportunity to unequivocally state his identity.

"I saw horses like that only in Andalucia," Roberto said.

"Did you? I'm not surprised," Eduardo said. "This one here is an Andalucian. They are handsome horses, very much like the Arabians."

"Yes, very pretty, indeed," Roberto said.

A young man emerged from the stable and was about to turn, when Don Eduardo call out to him. "Is that you back there, Pedro?"

"Yes, sir, Don Eduardo. It's me. Just making the rounds for my father today. He's a bit under the weather."

The young man himself looked indisposed, but to Don Eduardo and his guest, concerned with other matters, the mood of the stable hand remained invisible. But even had Don Eduardo or Don Roberto noticed Pedro's discomfiture, they would have ignored it, the young man merely a laborer performing his tasks and, more importantly, men customarily ignored each other's emotional nuances. Don Eduardo sometimes made an exception, in business matters always taking advantage of the circumstances. In this case, Don Roberto and not Pedro the focus of attention, Eduardo saw no connection between the two. Only Pedro was aware of the conflicting stance among the three.

"Ah well, I hope he's all right."

"Nothing serious, Don Eduardo, a little indigestion."

"I know how that can be," Eduardo said. "Your father and I are the same age. We have to watch how we indulge. I'm showing Don Roberto here the horses. Maybe you can run these three out into the corral so that he can see how they move."

"There's no need to bother," Roberto said.

"It's no bother at all," Eduardo replied. "It does them good to move around. You don't mind do you, Pedro?"

"Not at all, sir. My pleasure."

"Don Roberto is here to visit Juanita, but he has to be content with the horses until she's ready."

"The horses are always a good show," Pedro said.

"But not as good as Juanita," Eduardo said.

"That's not for me to say," Pedro replied.

"I suppose not," said Eduardo, "and what do you say, Don Roberto?"

"They're fine horses," he said.

Having seen the horses, Don Roberto was escorted back to the house to sit in the parlor and fulfill the supposed purpose of his visit, conversing with Juanita, who, though politely attentive, exhibited no trace of emotion except a hint of boredom. Gregoria, while fussing in the kitchen went by the door more often than necessary. Glimpses of the couple made her wonder what the young lady intended. The roaming about the hacienda the young man endured while waiting for his audience with the lady was an indignity mitigated only by the fact that Don Eduardo or Doña Antonia often entertained him while he waited. Indeed, the young man got more genuine attention from Antonia than he did from any other Rincon, arousing some the suspicion that he continued his visits for her sake.

He was always rewarded by Juanita's eventual appearance looking radiant and well worth the wait, but her toying with the young man went further than keeping him waiting on his visits. On several occasions she reneged on pledges to be in San Geronimo for functions planned by Doña Clara to provide opportunities for the young couple to be seen together and establish a public awareness of the possible union. Any discouragement from such treatment the young man kept secret. He merely redoubled his efforts to prove the intensity of his feelings.

WITH A BASKET on her arm, Doña Echevaria walked slowly and methodically between the rows of herbs neatly planted in her garden. She bent down occasionally to pick leaves that she arranged in her basket according to a pattern of unknown significance to her companion who walked along a parallel row, no room for two abreast along one file. Doña Echevaria was older than Gregoria but did not seem so. Her roundness became all the more pronounced when viewed next to Gregoria's wiry frame.

"The cooler she was, the hotter he got," Gregoria said.

"That's the way men are," Doña Echevaria said.

"Yes, but there's a limit to it, don't you think?"

"Perhaps she bewitched him."

"She has done that," Gregoria said.

"I mean literally, by magic," *Doña* Echevaria said.

"You mean she has been to see you?"

"I mean nothing of the kind," Doña Echevaria retorted.

"If not you, then who?"

"It's not for me to say."

"But you suspect?"

"She has known Sister Sylvester for along time, hasn't she?"

"That can't be. Sister Sylvester is a nun. It would be a mortal sin for her. The Church forbids her."

"It forbids me also."

"Yes but you're not a nun."

"Heaven forbid," said Doña Echevaria crossing herself. "Gregoria, sometimes you completely surprise me. After so many years, you still don't understand. A nun is all the more prepared to deal with such things. The Church makes her close to very powerful magic. They carry on against the likes of me because they want to keep it all to themselves."

"Maybe the priests do, but nuns are different."

"Ah, you're a child."

"Juana would have told me about Sister Sylvester long ago if there were anything so unusual about her. Other people, too, would have talked, but I have never heard anything of the sort until this very moment."

"Perhaps you're right," Doña Echevaria said, "but there's no reason to look for supernatural causes for things that have rational explanations. Everyone expects Don Eduardo to be generous to a son-in-law. Everyone knows Don Aurelio was generous to him."

"That's a different matter," Gregoria said.

"It was not to be then," said Doña Echevaria.

"It is a strange case that he should take offense at so slight an incident. Don't you think?"

"Ah, slight, you say, but what's slight to one person is not necessarily slight to another."

"That's true, but the oddity is that there was no forewarning of so sensitive a disposition."

"Better to find out now rather than later. He would have been difficult to live with."

"Do you think so?"

"I have only what you tell me to go by."

"You have not heard from anyone else?"

"I'm always the last one to hear gossip," Doña Echevaria said.

Gregoria gave no credence to that remark; being well abreast of gossip was the key to Doña Echevaria's business, regardless of the efficacy of her potions and remedies, or the veracity of her communications with other dimensions, about which Gregoria willingly suspended judgment. Had Doña Echevaria been looking at Gregoria at that moment, she would have seen the skepticism produced by her disclaimer, for Gregoria made no effort to hide it, counting on Doña Echevaria's intensity in the ceremonial task of picking herbs.

"He seemed like such a nice young man at first," Gregoria said.

"At first, but subsequently?"

"There were signs; I suppose if one were looking for them, there was more there than met the eye, but I wasn't looking."

"Ah, well, you can't see what you're not looking for," Doña Echevaria agreed.

"Perhaps it was too good to be true that Juanita had made such a turnaround."

"Are you saying that his turnaround invalidates hers?"

"I wasn't saying that," Gregoria answered, "but it's a thought."

"It's simple enough to know whether she's distraught.

"Nothing is simple with Juana."

The statement contained more than Gregoria previously revealed, though she did not intend to hide anything from her friend. Concealment was not an option, since Doña Echevaria could read everything in the cards or commune with the spirits who, of course, were privy to those things. They transcended human limitations, but apparently they had limitations of their own.

The two women walked back to the house, where Doña Echevaria brewed a fresh pot of coffee.

"She must have known all along how it would turn out," said Doña Echevaria.

"No, I don't think so," Gregoria protested. "She seemed genuinely upset when he broke off the engagement."

"Ah," Doña Echevaria exclaimed over the cup of coffee she had brought to her lips. From where she sat at the kitchen table, she gazed through the open door into the yard where the chickens strutted about, occasionally pecking at the ground at something they considered edible but was invisible to her. No doubt she would be able to see it, if she were a chicken. The absurd thought made her involuntarily smile as she imagined herself going about the yard pecking at the ground.

"You're amused," Gregoria said, annoyed by the familiar but enigmatic smile she could never get used to on the face of her friend.

Doña Echevaria refused to condescend to an explanation. She sat quietly looking self-satisfied, at the moment very much like a hen sitting on her eggs.

"He certainly didn't think it was a laughing matter," Gregoria said, "and who can blame him? Imagine how it looked."

"Yes, but who would have known had he kept quiet?"

"No one, of course, but it was the last straw."

"Last straw? I thought everything was going well."

"Everything was, but men's egos are very fragile. Sometimes to be made a fool is more tolerable than to be called one."

"So that's how he interpreted it."

"What other interpretation is there of finding a *bobo* in your pocket? Someone was sending him a message."

"It might have been one of the children not realizing whose pocket it was."

"Why would a child put a pacifier in a grown-up's pocket?"

"Why would anyone?"

"To send a message, of course."

"So it was a friend, do you think?"

"Whose friend?"

"Don Roberto's, warning him not to make a fool of himself over Juana."

"He didn't think it was a warning or that it came from a friend. He took it as an insult, but not knowing who insulted him, he could not demand redress."

"Who sent the message is a mystery, then. Perhaps a friend of Juana's."

"Who can say?"

"Who indeed," Doña Echevaria remarked. "But then again, some objects have mysterious powers. It's such a little thing, a *bobo*."

"A little thing, yes that's another interpretation."

"I didn't mean that," said Doña Echevaria, contemplating the size of the *bobo* and laughing with a shaking in her belly that progressed up her torso until it reached her face.

"You're in a laughing mood today," Gregoria said.

"Laughter is the salvation of the world," Doña Echevaria said.

"That's a side of you most people don't know."

"There's a certain seriousness required to make a living."

"This matter of the *bobo* has serious consequences.'

"Everything may be for the best," said Doña Echevaria.

"What do you see?"

"Only the obvious."

"I am afraid for Juana."

"Juana cannot avoid her destiny."

"Then you do see something."

"No more than you."

"I would rather see something better," Gregoria said looking down at the floor for footprints that would console her by revealing a well-traveled path.

IF GREGORIA AND Doña Echevaria believed that the demise of the relationship between Juanita and Roberto Andaluvio had a positive side, Doña Clara had a totally different view. At minimum, she presumed the young man was gravely insulted in a manner he refused to reveal. The *bobo* story seemed too ridiculous to be taken seriously. Certainly, it needed deciphering, but she had yet to come up with a convincing translation. Having introduced them, she feared the young man's chagrin would come to rest at her doorstep, a more than annoying result, when she had previously imagined taking credit for a splendid wedding.

She hoped Roberto would come to see her so that she could express her regrets and clear herself of any blame. She looked forward to hearing his account, but the wait seemed hopeless. At the end of a week she concluded he had given up on her and had unceremoniously placed her in Juanita's camp, the logical place after all, since by all social mores she was related to Juanita and consequently committed, right or wrong, to support her.

"I must speak to him," she said to her husband. "I do want to know what happened, and how can he think I had anything to do with it if I don't even know what happened?"

"Of course, you know," said Don Aurelio. "The pacifier pacified him."

"Oh, don't be ridiculous," she said, annoyed that her husband believed such a story.

"Ridiculous? The message was clear," he insisted.

"Don't make fun of me. I can't bear it right now. I've been totally embarrassed—after I made such an effort to bring them together."

"You did your part. The outcome is not your responsibility," he assured her.

"I suppose you don't have any responsibility for Eduardo and Antonia being together?"

The subject never having come up before, his wife's inadvertent mention of something about which she had been silent for so many years momentarily flustered Don Aurelio. He instantly suspected a misinterpretation of what she said—more meaning often being ascribed to words than intended by the speaker. Indeed, Doña Clara did not intend to upset her husband, and she did not wish to divert attention from Roberto's courtship. She wanted to deal with having to face blame for the debacle, but Don Aurelio, at the moment wrapped in his own guilt for promoting a relationship that may have caused undue hardship to its participants, longed for immediate reassurance. Eduardo turned out as reliable as Aurelio had anticipated, and his daughter could not point to any concrete infidelity, but surely there had to be something else disturbing her.

Of course, one child turned out deficient, an act of God, or of nature, if there was any distinction between the two, but one had to bear with unavoidable anomalies. For his part, Eduardo seemed to take that in stride, but then again, as far as Don Aurelio could see, Eduardo took everything in stride. Don Aurelio tried to maintain that view of his son-in-law, but occasionally, he glimpsed some facet he had failed to predict. Sometimes, by chance stumbling on Eduardo, Don Aurelio noticed a strain on the younger man's face that quickly disappeared on his becoming aware of company. Aurelio began to suspect that whatever bothered his daughter also took a toll on Eduardo. Inevitably, his speculations prevented him from blamelessly looking away.

"Well, then, perhaps this time you've come out on top and you have only to be thankful," Don Aurelio said to his wife.

Doña Clara became increasingly annoyed with her husband's inability to see her predicament. "I feel like a fool," she declared, "and through no fault of my own."

"Isn't that, my dear, a contradiction?" Don Aurelio said, trying to point out the obvious lack of logic, although aware that living in the same physical world did not ensure the acceptance of the same set of rules. That conundrum that he sometimes tried to decipher exhausted his patience, as he found no acceptable explanation other than men and women are different in more ways than the physically obvious.

"And of course I have no idea what Doña Gregoria thinks about the matter," she declared giving her husband another point to consider.

"I'm sure she's not taking any blame," Don Aurelio said trying to console his wife. He suspected that Doña Gregoria was reacting just as strongly and perhaps feeling even more responsible for the demise of the love affair intended to favor her protégé.

"You seem to know everything about the event," Doña Clara said, "so tell me what exactly it is that requires blame, because that's what keeps me from sleeping every night."

Don Aurelio had failed to notice his wife's insomnia, but he refrained from admitting that he missed that part of her ordeal. He often fell asleep before she did, but she would wake him up whenever she had trouble, and not having been recently jostled in the middle of the night, he presumed her lack of sleep took place in her dreams that she often failed to distinguish from physical reality.

"There's nothing for you to worry about," he repeated. "Everything unfolds according to a master plan beyond our control."

She kept quiet for a minute as if examining the veracity of his words, and Don Aurelio considered the possibility of his wife applying reason to the subject under discussion. That hope quickly vanished when she turned to him with relief. She had an approach to her problem. "Roberto will listen to you," she said, "so please ask him to come and see me. It's the least he can do. After all, I did try to do him a favor. You must ask him."

"He'll show up when he's ready," said Don Aurelio. "Before then, you'll only risk hurting him more than necessary."

"On the contrary," Doña Clara insisted. "I must speak to him."

Don Aurelio was poised to continue his protestation at being asked to participate in the ongoing travesty, when the unexpected arrival of a visitor interrupted the conversation. The discussion was transpiring on the veranda facing their back garden when Clementina, the housekeeper, ushered in the caller. Seeing Roberto Andaluvio walk through the door momentarily surprised Don Aurelio and Doña Clara, both relieved at seeing the solution to their respective problems suddenly appear, eliminating the possibility of creating more complications by further scheming. At least, Don Aurelio drew the conclusion that life's problems had the potential of disappearing by chance, and his wife saw nothing unusual about getting a break she assumed she deserved.

"Ah, Don Roberto," she exclaimed as she restrained the impulse to extend both her arms to offer an embrace, realizing that after all, he was not her son. Whether the word *son* passed through her mind is another matter. More likely, she merely had an inkling of a conflict between her impulse and social custom, an unusual state of mind for a person who often assumed her desires to be the criteria for social acceptance. "We were just talking about you," she continued smiling at the young man and hoping that he would reciprocate. The fulfillment of that hope remained unlikely as his face plainly revealed emotions that prevented the smile she desired.

"No doubt everyone has been talking about me for some time, but finally I caught on to it," Roberto said slowly changing his attitude from defiance to self-pity.

Doña Clara reacted with relief. "Ah, better to be talked about than ignored," she said, immediately realizing that her words implied an acceptance of the negative talk about the young man, when in fact she longed to know what actually happened. "Only the rabble believe the silly things they hear," she added trying to make amends but suspecting that those words made him feel worse.

The young man looked to Don Aurelio for a sign of support, but receiving none, he turned again to Doña Clara for consolation. "I came to explain to you," he said, "that I had no choice but to do what I did."

"Indeed," Doña Clara agreed, but immediately realizing that she did not actually know what he had done, she added, "And what did you do?"

"Not what I actually wanted to," the young man declared looking chagrined.

"Yes, of course," Doña Clara said restraining her annoyance at having her ignorance extended longer than she wished, an unusual situation in which she thirsted for actual facts, as opposed to her more common stance of being content with imaginary ones.

"I had to do what I did," he continued, "after having been publicly insulted."

"Who insulted you?"

"Well, that's what complicated the matter and made it impossible for me to avoid the disaster," he said irritating Doña Clara further by delaying a direct answer to her question.

"Ah, so you had an altercation with Don Eduardo," she said, driven to guess what had happened.

"No, of course not," he responded at first surprised that anyone would think him such a fool but quickly realizing that her conclusion was reasonable enough.

"Who then?"

"No one in particular. That's the strangeness of it all."

"No one insulted you, and you insulted no one, and that created a problem between you and *Señorita* Juanita. I am totally confused and more so than before you arrived. If there's a reason why you don't want to tell me what happened, I can understand. So let's change the topic right now and talk about the weather. The rainy season is about to begin, and we'll have to spend a great deal of time indoors, which always gets boring with nothing to talk about. It'll be even worse this year. What do you suppose, Don Roberto?" She glanced at the young man and then turned her head to look across the garden and up at the sky where the white clouds showed no sign of wanting to discharge.

Roberto became more disturbed at inadvertently upsetting Doña Clara. In fact, he failed to pick up the reason for her anger as he tried to tell the story of what happened at the Rincon hacienda the week before. He had lost his temper at being insulted. Who insulted him became a mystery to which another was added when he roughly reacted to Juanita's response. He harbored no doubt that she was amused to see the *bobo*, but she suppressed her impulse to laugh, which he should have appreciated.

Instead, he prevented her from defusing the situation. She placed her hand over the *bobo* to keep anyone else from seeing it, but he rejected that course of action and held up the object demanding to know who had placed it in his pocket. He saw immediately that everyone in the room found the matter amusing, including Doña Rincon, which indeed surprised him since, in the Rincon household, she was his strongest supporter. Her amusement at the insult increased its enormity and eliminated any possibility of his staying calm.

With Doña Clara, Roberto was again on the verge of losing control of reason. He tried to recover and determine why she looked upset. "I'm sorry if I haven't been clear about what happened, but I've been telling you the truth: someone put a *bobo* in my pocket as an insult, except that the person was then too cowardly to step forward and look me straight in the face. What else can I say?"

"Then, the story of the *bobo* is true," Doña Clara said overwhelmed by the absurdity.

"Of course it's true," Roberto asserted, hoping that now, everything clear to Doña Clara, she would offer some consolation.

"But what has the *bobo* to do with Juanita? Do you suppose she was the one who put it in your pocket?"

"She was not the one," Roberto continued, "and I did not accuse her of doing so."

"Then I don't understand why your friendship with her has ended."

"I suspected that she knew who did it, but she wouldn't tell me, and at the moment I gave her an ultimatum that she did not accept. I put myself in a bind from which I cannot extricate myself."

"All you have to do is apologize and everything will be back to what it was before."

"I cannot apologize," he declared, his voice having difficulty remaining firm as if a fruit pit was caught in his throat and was choking him. The corner of his eyes seemed to gather moisture, which again caused Doña Clara to gaze out over the garden preferring to observe the roaming clouds.

Don Aurelio, who was silent until then, could no longer pretend that he did not understand the predicament the young man created for himself. The older man needed only to look back at his own youth to find examples of equal travesty that caused him pain and embarrassment. He survived them all, but the certainty that this young man would also survive did not mitigate the discomfort that prevailed at the moment. "Ah, yes, of course," Don Aurelio said, surprising his wife who expected him to maintain the negative attitude he expressed before the young man's arrival, or choosing to be polite, a silent indifference.

Don Aurelio would have been perplexed to know that his wife understood and recalled the comments he previously made about consistent logic. She then applied a similar criterion to his unexpected reaction to the young man's problem. "A reasonable apology is all that's necessary. Why is that a problem?" she asked couching her suggestion in a soothing tone.

"I cannot apologize," the young man reiterated. "That's too much humiliation after such an insult."

"But it wasn't Juanita who insulted you."

"But it's her duty to uphold my name, or at least it was if she was to become my wife. If she won't do it now, how do I know she'll do it then? I wasn't asking her to do a great deal. It's no great matter for a woman to apologize."

"You mean succumb to a man's demand," Doña Clara said.

"To protect my reputation," Roberto responded trying to clarify his stance.

"Do you love her?" Doña Clara demanded.

"Yes, of course I do," the young man automatically responded.

"Then you must not humiliate her."

His failure to make Doña Clara understand his point perplexed Roberto. He expected more sympathy from her. Again he turned to Don Aurelio searching for support. The older gentleman understood the predicament the young man created for himself, but having been married to Clara for so many years and having raised five daughters, he understood the absurdity of Roberto's stance.

"It all depends on what you'd rather have," Don Aurelio finally said, going along with the premise that a choice was possible, a matter seldom discussed. Actually, he vacillated on whether the young man had an option, but he acknowledged the appearance of choice, an assumption that made life simpler.

"I must do what I must," Roberto Andaluvio said.

"Yes, of course," Don Aurelio responded wondering whether the young man had explored the question. There was no sense asking him, since whether or not he acted consciously was irrelevant.

*

Naturally, more than Roberto Andaluvio's motivation to act foolishly had to be considered, and Doña Clara having satisfied her need to see the young man, began to wonder about Gregoria's reaction. Fretful as well as curious to see Juanita's emotional state at the moment, she refrained from expressing all her concerns. Don Aurelio certainly had an interest in finding out what Eduardo's reaction was or rather what he still felt. Eduardo would take personally an affront to his daughter, and the culprit surely would pay a steep penalty. So Clara's interest in making one of her unusual visits to the country, coincided with Don Aurelio's eagerness to observe his son-in-law's reaction to the event. He had fallen out of the habit of proposing trips to the Rincon hacienda, further away from San Geronimo than their own land to which Doña Clara made occasional visits, primarily to put a dent on the tedium of dealing with the same scenery and the same faces every day. Such a trip proved always a secondary option in coping with the boredom of everyday life. The first, keeping track of what the neighbors were up to, persisted.

Don Aurelio's learning from experience may seem too common to merit mention, but when there are too many exceptions to a rule, especially this one, it can't be taken for granted. He learned that urging Doña Clara to do something contrary to her habits or preferences seldom achieved the desired result, so he had stopped urging her to make the trip to the Rincon hacienda. She didn't keep him from going without her, but that created other problems. Unless he traveled under some business excuse, the difficulty of explaining Clara's absence lingered, although over time everyone pretended acceptance. Antonia understood her mother's town personality, and she knew quite well that the reluctance to make the trip did not indicate bad feelings toward her or Eduardo. Nevertheless, she longed for her mother to suppress her geographical preferences and perform her motherly duties in person.

On arriving at the Rincon's after the Andaluvio debacle, the cheerful mood of the place somewhat baffled the Castillos. They both expected to see a pervasive discomfort, at least in Juanita and her father, who from Don Aurelio's point of view were most affected by the recent turmoil. Doña Clara of course had a different view of the matter and expected Gregoria to exhibit emotional strain similar to hers before Roberto Andaluvio's visit. She subsequently felt relieved after the possibility of blame being cast in her direction diminished, and she proceeded to lower her estimation of him on hearing from his own lips the veracity of the silly story about the *bobo* that she still found difficult to believe and his reaction more difficult to understand. Even at her age, she had not completely accepted the oddity of some men's behavior.

Doña Clara ran into something other than what she expected, a condition that was becoming more frequent in her life. Everyone looked too cheerful, including Antonia whose satisfaction at seeing her mother was usually cloaked in discomfort. Antonia quite understood that the recent debacle of Juanita's relationship with Roberto was spurring her mother's visit rather than any need to see her, but that didn't seem to matter at the moment.

"My dear, how are you?" Doña Clara exclaimed having stepped down from the carriage that, even with the cushioned seats, caused great discomfort over the stony road. She greeted

Juanita, the first to emerge from the house on hearing the commotion out front.

"Oh, quite well," the young woman responded broadly displaying a genuine grin that Doña Clara interpreted as a heroic attempt to disguise regret, but she soon decided her interpretation deviated too far from reality, something that lately had become more difficult to accept.

Her daughter, with the grandchildren not far behind, glad to see her, pressed without reserve, causing some disorientation and forcing her to delay inquiring about her principal interest. Gregoria's absence from the immediate welcoming group provided some reassurance to Doña Clara that she hadn't completely miscalculated what she would find on arrival at the Rincon hacienda.

Doña Clara attributed her friend's absence to discomfort, and she imagined Gregoria trying to adjust her feelings before making an appearance. Until the last moment, Doña Clara hoped for the opportunity to employ the expressions of concern she took the trouble to prepare on the trip from town. She attempted to wait patiently for Gregoria to make her appearance, but either Juanita's guardian was too upset to make her entrance or there was something else going on about which Doña Clara assumed she had yet to be informed. The possibility of her patience being intentionally tested flickered through her mind but found no fertile spot, and before reaching the end of her patience, she attempted to exhibit casualness in making the inquiry about her friend.

"She's hard of hearing these days," Juanita offered. "She probably hasn't heard the commotion of your arrival."

Doña Clara took that to be a prearranged excuse, since surely even if Gregoria did not hear the noise in the parlor, the horse and carriage had by this time been taken to the stable and Gregoria would have heard them go by the back of the house and must have peeked through the window and recognized the carriage. Clara came to know Gregoria's habits that included surveillance of everything within sight of the kitchen.

"Then I'll have to go to the kitchen myself," said Doña Clara, making a gesture to stand up, while everyone was quite aware that she had yet to reach that point.

"Do sit down," Juanita urged. Having for some reason decided to be totally charming, she offered to find Gregoria and inform her of Doña Clara's presence.

Indeed, Gregoria, out of the house to fetch *recao* leaves from the vegetable garden behind the stable, had missed the visitors' arrival. As she walked in through the kitchen door, Juanita gave her the news of Doña Clara's eagerness to see her.

"No doubt she's unhappy about Roberto's behavior," Gregoria muttered. "We have to do everything to cheer her up, don't we?"

"She doesn't look at all distraught, only disappointed that no one here is," Juanita said.

"Um, that sounds quite likely," continued Gregoria, talking to herself, relieved that Doña Clara seemed to be managing to keep herself from becoming a problem.

"Come greet her before she gets into a mood," Juanita suggested more to see the expression on Gregoria's face than to really save Clara from apoplexy. The young woman followed the caretaker into the parlor where Doña Clara stood up to greet her friend. After hugging Gregoria, *Doña* Clara stood back to search for the discomfort she expected to find in Gregoria's countenance. Again she was disappointed, denied the opportunity to be of consolation to someone in distress. Either to avoid dealing with the consequences or to protect her from everyone's true emotions, they were all pretending nothing had happened. This last option she quickly discarded, knowing well enough that it was too improbable.

Doña Clara even considered her husband's mood unusual, since he, too, seemed to be pretending that nothing of importance had occurred, when she well knew he thought otherwise. *Don* Aurelio, however, had no emotional stake in finding matters to be what he imagined, or rather what he feared. Consequently, he quickly accepted a brighter side, since, like most people, he disliked prolonged discomfort. Nevertheless, curiosity compelled him to find out how the matter was resolved to make everyone, except of course Roberto, apparently content.

Don Aurelio suspected that, in this case, he would have no easier time assessing Eduardo's true feelings and that he would have to revert to his usual stance of accepting what he saw at face value, a habit he found useful enough even if it didn't ultimately hold up. The secret, or rather the method, for in reality it consisted of something so obvious it could hardly be considered a secret, entailed letting the subject make the first move. In this case, however, Don Aurelio suspected he would have to wait forever, since, in the past, he had found Eduardo to be rather circumspect about revealing personal feelings. True, the current situation might be somewhat different, since so much had already surfaced. Eduardo most certainly was aware of the talk in both Comerio and San Geronimo. But of course, Eduardo easily ignored all the talk in the world when he desired, a talent that Don Aurelio and many other people found impressive. More than once, Eduardo's attitude on a subject of public concern had a crucial effect, even when facts were involved, as if the definition of *fact* included the need of his support.

Don Aurelio waited for Eduardo to make the first move, or so he would have described his action were he asked, as he no doubt would be by his wife privately that evening. He certainly didn't expect her to wait until they got home. Very few people would have noticed any difference in Eduardo's behavior. At the moment, everyone else in the household dealing with personal feelings had found Eduardo's façade convenient, if indeed his attitude was only that. Possibly glad to be rid of Roberto, either because he found the young man inadequate for his daughter, or more disturbingly, because any relationship she had with another man he found vaguely threatening.

That disturbing explanation came to Don Aurelio suddenly without effort, as if his mind were merely a tree standing in a forest where that thought, like a bird, arbitrarily chose to land. In the natural surrounding, several sequences of events are possible: the bird might merely fly off to find a more convenient place to rest for the moment and only occasionally return; or it might find that part of the forest totally inadequate and fly on, never to revisit; or indeed, it might feel totally at home in that particular place and build a nest, lay eggs, and raise offspring, spending a complete season in that one tree. Of course, the tree has no choice in the matter, and only the bird determines the course of action. The question then becomes whether Aurelio's mind can be compared to such an object, for although it had the property of being able to provide a leafy home to a hovering thought, it also had the ability to transform itself at will into something totally uninhabitable by an intruder.

At the moment, Don Aurelio wished for a breeze strong enough to shake the branches and cause the bird to take flight. In search of that gust, he opened other compartments where he conveniently stored, to keep from disturbing anything else, memories of actions that affected the lives of his daughters. He could not hold himself totally responsible for the choices they made. Only in Antonia's case did he find himself in a labyrinth whose exit eluded him. There seemed to be no answer to the enigma confronting him, having stumbled on the possibility that he had followed a path with only the illusion of choice. The semblance of choice existed, but what proved the choice free of predetermination? He found himself troubled by the possibility of a world without choice, fated to a path that would lead him to a destination determined by a force other than his will. Didn't that also relieve him of responsibility for the consequences of his choices—choices being, after all, illusory? There was no way to know for sure. He had to live as if indeed he were responsible for the consequences of his decisions.

A more difficult question emerged. Holding oneself responsible was simple enough, but how fair was applying the same rule to others, if indeed their actions were beyond the power of the will? For instance, the question of the *bobo*: someone placed it where it would have an effect on the actions of others. Wasn't that person responsible for subsequent events related to the incident? Another option, that the *bobo* found its way to the controversial place accidentally, had to be considered. Could it have inadvertently fallen there by chance however unlikely that sounded? In that case, the results may be easily attributable to fate.

The fact that Eduardo seemed to be content with the outcome of the incident gave rise to another possibility that Don Aurelio found difficult to accept. The thought of Eduardo being behind the event made Don Aurelio question his own sanity. The unfamiliar paths presenting themselves, when previously he was well acquainted with the terrain, perplexed him, and the prospect of getting lost, as minute by minute the familiar landmarks disappeared, made some inner part of him momentarily shudder. He had not been to that place in a long time, but surely he had been there before, and if he found his way when he was younger and less knowledgeable, surely having acquired some experience, he would find his way more easily this time.

"Your cheerfulness has somewhat disappointed Clara, although yours she can handle well enough. Everyone else's, I'm sure, is getting to her," Aurelio confided to his son-in-law when they were alone in the study, the only room in the house still exclusively reserved for the men.

"Well, then I'll pretend to be sad over dinner," Eduardo offered. "There's no sense in disappointing her."

"Disappointment seems hard to come by in this house," Aurelio commented, purposely ignoring his sense that some waited to emerge.

The word "seems" reverberated in Eduardo's ears, and he wondered whether Don Aurelio was purposely revealing that he suspected matters to be different from what they appeared. He merely needed to inquire, but he refrained from doing so for the moment. He would rather find out for himself, before someone else discovered his confusion as to why he welcomed the *bobo's* appearance to drive Roberto Andaluvio away. Sooner or later, Juanita would attach herself to someone else and move out of the home she had shared with him since she was three years old, an event for him to look forward to, or at least be nonchalant about.

He need only look back at the appreciation he received from

Don Aurelio for the attention bestowed on Antonia. He received more than a welcome; he had been encouraged to proceed. Subsequently, he witnessed Aurelio's reaction to the departure of his other daughters, and even when the old man had minimal praise for the new son, he contentedly watched the daughter smile as she exited from her childhood home. Eduardo failed to foresee his own reaction to Roberto, having deceived himself and only examining his feelings after the suitor's exit. Sometimes simplicity obstructed a clear vision, and this time Eduardo was disturbed by his own conclusions.

Over the years, he had continued going to town to play cards with Father Rodrigo, and on those visits, they often talked about private matters not mentionable to anyone else. Perhaps at the next encounter with the priest he would vent on this subject, but it was Don Aurelio who stood before him at the moment. Though clearly not everything could be discussed with him in the same manner as with Father Rodrigo, with whom even views antithetical to religion remained within the scope of discussion, his father-in-law's willingness to listen kept Eduardo talking.

"Disappointment is a condition of life," Eduardo remarked.

"You seem to have avoided it this time," Aurelio responded.

"A postponement is hardly an avoidance," Eduardo continued.

"Some things are inevitable."

"I suppose so," Eduardo conceded. "The question is whether one's acceptance of the inevitable is always possible."

"It's always necessary," Aurelio said, "and always possible if we prepare for it."

"How do we prepare for the unknown?"

"We never know exactly when or from what direction a hurricane will arrive, but we prepare nevertheless."

"Sometimes we get an earthquake instead."

"We prepare for what they have in common."

"You mean we prepare for recovery."

"Sometimes that's all we can do."

Indeed, that was all, but the question remained whether recovery was always possible, the crux of the matter at the moment. The issue had yet to surface; whether it would come up at all was another question for which neither had an answer. Possibly, they had not yet formulated the question clearly enough to ask it but merely sensed something waiting to be asked. The uncertainty of whether either one of them wanted clarification persisted. Once the question was formulated, an answer would follow, and perhaps, they each suspected, an unacceptable one. Each vaguely alluded to the problem without an obvious solution or the impetus to examine it more closely.

*

On their way home a few days later, neither *Doña* Clara nor *Don* Aurelio felt at ease, both uncertain of what happened to deny them comfort, both glad to be leaving the place—a congruence seldom produced by departure from Eduardo's *hacienda*.

"Well, everyone is happy to be rid of Roberto," Doña Clara remarked on the way home. "So we'll never know who planted the *bobo*."

"Do we want to know?"

"Why it was done that way is the real question. All Juanita had to do was reject his courtship, and he would have gone away without feeling insulted."

"So you think Juanita planted the *bobo*?"

"I didn't say that. But she's not upset at the consequences. No one there is upset."

"Well, not about getting rid of Roberto."

"Nor about anything else as far as I can see."

Don Aurelio wondered how far that could be, but he kept the question to himself. Ignorance often a blessing, he wished to keep his wife from seeing more than was necessary.

THE NAUSEA CAME over him in waves. During each short respite, panic took over. It reminded him of the time he was seasick out on a boat with his uncle Tomas.

"You can make a good living from fishing," Tomas had said to Pedro, when the boy and his father, Manolo, went down to the coast.

"Mountain people make bad fishermen," Manolo said.

"You were not always from the mountains," Tomas said turning to his brother. "The boy might like to fish."

"The sea will be as difficult as the land and more dangerous," Manolo said. The sea for him a dark and inhospitable place, he liked the feel of the land under his feet. He liked the green forests and red clay of the hills.

"Let the boy decide," Tomas said, "Let him go out in the boat with me, and he will see if he likes it or not."

"Life is not like that," Manolo retorted. "Whether he likes it or not is of no consequence. I never thought to ask myself whether I like to plow a field or whether I like to be a farmer. If I want to eat, I must do it."

"But you made a choice to do that instead of something else. You chose to farm rather than to fish or to be a grocer or a blacksmith."

"I don't remember making a choice," Manolo said. "Life just happens. You do what you can in the time and place God puts you. Don Eduardo offered me a job to look after his horses, and I took it because it was convenient and possible."

"Well then, I'm offering Pedro a chance to go out on the boat. Maybe it's something that he can do."

The motion of the sea made Pedro sick, and he could not fish.

Again, he felt nausea like he had felt on the boat, but this time he had no discernible excuse. Maybe he was ill and would die.

That thought came to him, but it didn't make sense. If death were close, he would know, but he did not detect death anywhere near him, and there were no other symptoms but nausea—no fever, no chills, no sores, no ringing in his ears. Sometimes he had a mild dryness in his mouth. Death might be stalking him, staying in the shadows where it might not be seen. Death was not visible through one's eyes. One would see death differently, with another sense, not nameable, a sense reserved for non-physical things. Pedro did not sense death, only sickness that stretched out before him like the sea, making him unsteady, unable to get a bearing on any one point, causing him nausea.

He pretended to be well, hoping he would forget his sickness. No one else was aware of it. Perhaps it was not real. Perhaps his imagination was running amok, and he might safely ignore it. If he went about his business pretending to be alright, that would be the same as if he were. He needed to try to act normally. Carrying out the steps of every day activity methodically, one by one, might save him.

He followed the narrow path through the woods to old Federico's *bohio* hoping the old man would have words to make him feel better. Federico often put a different spin on matters. Older people sometimes failed to understand or made light of what young people felt, having forgotten the time when they went through similar stages or knowing that the outcome would be dwarfed by subsequent and necessary events. But Federico was not like that. The young man spoke to him, and Federico listened attentively until they got to the hut where a number of birds stood tethered, each to its own stake driven into the stony earth.

Federico trained fighting cocks. Potential champions were brought to his place out in the woods, where he took full charge of their care. The young ones wandered about freely on the rough terrain. The hard ground helped strengthen their legs and beaks. Later, when old enough to hurt each other, he tethered them inside the coop or out in the yard. Bred for ferocity, they had to be kept from each other until they got to the arena. So Federico had each bird on a long cord that allowed it enough terrain to exercise and fly to develop its wings.

Every morning at sunrise, he took them out of their coop and exercised them after dousing them with rum and water. To develop their alertness and intelligence and to keep them from growing complacent, he placed their feed in different locations each day. In the late mornings, he moved the birds back into the coop to protect them from the grueling midday sun. In the afternoons, he brought them out again for mock fights in order to detect any defect in their fighting style. Their spurs covered to prevent serious damage, he matched the young birds against each other by weight as he tried to correct any noticeable deficiency.

"That one there, he will be a champion," Don Federico said.

"He doesn't look any different from the others," Pedro remarked.

"Someday you will be able to see the difference," Federico assured him.

"For me, there may not be someday," Pedro answered.

Federico ignored the young man's comment and continued to talk about the bird. "I know his lineage. There are many champions in his bloodline."

"So it's fated," Pedro said, as if that were an answer to a puzzle.

"No," Don Federico continued, "sometimes the blood line is good, but the bird is a failure. There's no guarantee, only an increased probability. There can be bad training, or an unforeseen trait, or just bad luck."

"Luck is important," Pedro said.

"Yes, but we try to minimize the role of luck."

The bird scurried away when Don Federico approached. He bent down to pick it up. It fluttered trying to fly, but Federico grabbed the tether and pulled until the bird came within his grasp. It had not yet been tried in a bout and still possessed all of its natural adornment, crest and wattle, as well as plumage. In the not too distant future it would be trimmed for combat: its crest and wattle removed, its tail feathers cut within four fingers from its rump, its wings shortened and the feathers from its neck and breast removed to expose its bright red skin. It would in that guise appear an unmistakable warrior.

"His name is Aeneas. He is almost ready to make his debut as a fighter. You will see how well he does even against a veteran. Get Attila over there and boot his spurs," Federico said to Pedro, who walked over to a bird tethered at the far side of the yard.

The disturbance while feeding annoyed Attila, but he didn't put up as much resistance to being handled, as had the younger bird about to be his opponent. The spurs of both were fitted with padded leather casings. Some *galleros,* less elaborate with their equipment, improvised with paper or cloth. Federico used a boot over the beaks also to prevent them from blinding each other with a well-placed lunge. Many *galleros* didn't take that precaution, the spurs being the primary offensive weapons of the birds and the occasional beak prick considered a good way to arouse the fighting spirit. The two fighters lost no time in preliminaries, immediately engaging in a flurry of blows that would have caused serious damage had they not been booted.

"You see how Aeneas strikes at the head from the start. He knows that decisive action is necessary at the beginning. The fight can be won in the first few seconds."

The two roosters disengaged after the first flurry and walked around each other for a moment before initiating another outbreak of blows. After their third pass, Federico stepped in and scooped up Aeneas pinning his wings against his body. "He used to be distracted if his opponent flapped his wings, but now he knows to stay focused. That's the key to success in any enterprise," the old man said.

"That's easier said than done," Pedro answered.

"If a bird can learn it, so can a man."

"Their minds are simpler and have less distractions," Pedro said.

"Perhaps so," said the old man. He bent down to tie the rooster to its stake in the yard. Federico's fingers, rough and gnarled from a lifetime of work in the fields, were still dexterous and produced an elegant knot.

"They do what they do without qualm. They do it naturally, without agonizing about right and wrong. They have no conscience and no soul."

"That is perhaps true," the old man conceded.

"You have doubts?"

"It is useless to guess about such things," Federico answered, and after a pause he said, "You seem troubled lately."

"I'm sick," he simply responded.

"What does the doctor say?"

"It's not that kind of illness."

Federico refrained from asking for more detail. He already had an inkling of the boy's problem. He, too, had been young once, but that youth seemed to have been a dream, and though he had brilliant flashes of memory, he distrusted them. The difference between a dream and reality is sometimes difficult to distinguish. The memories of youth belong in that category. Life was ephemeral and its significance a problem beyond solution.

"Ah," said the old man, "perhaps you will talk to the priest."

"He will not help me," Pedro said.

"You never know," Federico continued.

"The priest and Don Eduardo are old friends."

"It's Don Eduardo then who makes you sick?"

"Perhaps," Pedro said.

"He has offended you?"

"Not yet," Pedro answered.

"You're contemplating the future then," Federico said.

"You make me sound foolish," said Pedro.

"I'm trying to understand," the old man said.

"Perhaps someone has cast a spell on me."

"Witchcraft?"

"Certainly."

"You suppose Don Eduardo goes in for that sort of thing?"

"Perhaps his daughter does," Pedro answered.

"She's only a child."

"She has grown up."

"That's sufficient magic," the old man said.

"You laugh at me," said Pedro.

"Not at all, but what makes you think witchcraft is involved?"

"I have but to see Juana for my illness to disappear."

"It seems you have stumbled upon the remedy."

"I must go away from here."

"That, too, might work," said the old man.

✳

Down in the pit, two roosters circled each other pretending to be deciding whether they really wanted to fight, the clash a foregone conclusion. Having brought them in, the handlers thrust them against each other head first, touching beaks, so that each bird perceived the challenge coming from the other, and each, still being held, tried to peck the opponent. Such close proximity, a natural insult, infuriated each bird. Nature endowed them with raiment worthy of royalty. One tended more toward a red hue, most of his feathers in that family of colors; the underlying brown accentuated by the more striking crimson and, here and there, a startling outburst of yellow. The other was a dark fellow, no less colorful but the palette underscored in black, just as majestic and aggressive as red, of which both displayed an abundant quantity.

The handlers withdrew from the pit and became spectators, like everyone else, imbued by the excitement of the contest. Each bird had its fans loudly urging it to be aggressive, but the combatants, intent on each other, seemed oblivious to the racket around them. There could be but one cock of the walk, and each took the pit as his territory to defend against an obvious intruder. Well-versed in the protocol of establishing hierarchy, they strutted in a regal and deliberate attempt to intimidate the opponent and make him realize the folly of standing against so splendid an adversary, the lift of the foot slow, but the planting of the claws swift and rhythmic, as if each arrived with a marching band inaudible to everyone else. Aware of his own looks, each appeared to prance in a show of majesty, examining every one of the opponent's feathers as if in a hall of mirrors. Each step taken by one was seen as an affront by the other.

Juanita and Pedro made their way to the top row of the wooden stand that surrounded the pit.

"I won't be able to see as well from back there," she said.

"Yes, you will," he responded. "You'll attract too much attention up front."

"No one will recognize me," she said.

With little hope that the subterfuge would be effective, he had insisted that she make an attempt to disguise herself. She dressed in clothes borrowed from his younger brother. She had first tried Pedro's clothes. "I look like a circus clown," she said once she put them on. "I'll attract more attention in these than if I go in my own." He agreed and fetched his brother's. Still, he doubted that she would be able to disguise her anatomy enough to pass unnoticed, but satisfied when he saw that she found a way, he could not for modesty ask her how she had done it.

From his gaze she guessed the question. "I tied them down with a rag," she said. Mystified that she would tell him such a thing, he kept quiet. They still had her face to consider. The light would have to be dim indeed. A hat of course would hide her hair, and if she kept the brim down sufficiently, no one would recognize her.

"We'll arrive late and quickly move to the back where no one will notice you. Try not to attract attention."

"If I'm too quiet it will seem odd, don't you think?"

"Just do what I do," he said.

The first part of the plan proceeded without a hitch, and ensconced on the top row of benches, Juanita tried to remain as inconspicuous as possible. Don Eduardo's appearance at the opposite side of the pit made Pedro jittery, but Juanita remained unfazed. If anyone, Don Eduardo could and had reason to recognize Juanita, and her blasé attitude about his unexpected arrival flustered Pedro. They had purposely planned the excursion for a day they expected Don Eduardo to be away. Pedro believed himself in the middle of committing some transgression, and he ascribed a more sinister aspect to Don Eduardo's arrival than mere coincidence. Several times, the young man was certain, Don Eduardo gazed directly in Juanita's direction. How could Don Eduardo fail to recognize his daughter behind such a flimsy disguise?

While her companion struggled with his apprehension, Juanita remained oblivious of her father. Her full attention was directed at the pit where the birds sized each other up in a macabre dance. The black bird attacked first, wings outstretched, making a leap at the head of the other. Both birds had metal spurs over their natural ones, devices calculated to make the damage they inflicted more deadly, in most cases fatal without interference from the handlers. The metallic spurs were burnished to a shine consistent with the seriousness of their purpose. The black bird's spurs flashed steel inlaid with gold, a touch of extravagance deemed justifiable by the bird's owner, mindful of the value of pageantry. Steel, a practical choice for an instrument of destruction, but the gold though unessential appropriately commemorated the presence of death.

The brown bird avoided a blow with a dexterous move of its head and a sudden display of speed that left him at the side of the pit, looking slightly ridiculous as his opponent strutted in the center. The supporters of the brown bird shouted louder, urging it to reengage, while the adherents of the black cock jeered derisively, attributing the momentary absence of the brown from the center of the pit to cowardice, though they all knew that the position of the brown bird was due to logistics and that it would return to the fray as soon as it recovered its bearing.

"The birds are so pretty," Juanita said to Pedro, who could not deny it, but at the moment he was more worried that the comment, inconsistent with the manly guise of the speaker, might have been overheard. Having let himself be talked into the escapade, he felt responsible for her.

"You mean magnificent," Pedro said between his teeth.

"Yes, magnificent," she repeated to keep him calm.

To salvage his pride, the brown bird, returning as if infuriated by having been made to look foolish, attacked, but with insufficient deliberateness to do any damage. Each made a pass at the other, and both sufficiently incensed, in a flurry of feathery blurs, picked up the pace of the combat. The brown bird also wore ornate spurs, less rich but no less showy, bronze inlaid with silver.

"Your father keeps looking this way," Pedro whispered to Juanita. That precaution was unnecessary since no one could hear him even if he shouted, everyone else in the arena intent on the birds.

"No, he's not," she said. "It's only your imagination. He sees only what he wants to see, and he doesn't want to see me here."

Her reasoning made no sense to Pedro, who never considered that Don Eduardo might have weaknesses just like any other man. Pedro was content to nurse the image of his *patron* as a man more perfect than others, otherwise the fact that he had more than others didn't make sense. He had to apply some order to the world to be at peace with it. Consistency an attribute of the human mind rather than of nature as a whole, achieving tranquility often required self-deception. Arriving at a consistent scheme, projected onto the world, his preconceived ideas determined what he saw.

"Oh, God!" Juanita exclaimed. "He lost his eye."

Blood spouted from the left eye of the bird, and keeping his opponent in sight became more difficult and his movements erratic. The black bird, sustaining less serious injuries, and sensing his opponent was losing heart, pressed the attack. Mercy absent from his repertoire of instincts, he used his spurs effectively. He had to ground his opponent to finish him quickly.

Juanita clutched Pedro's arm, which he interpreted as emotional distress on her part. "Do you want to leave now?" he asked, hoping that she'd had enough, and they could leave before a confrontation with Don Eduardo became inevitable. Perhaps Juanita was right, and Don Eduardo did not yet see her, but that still puzzled Pedro. His fear of discovery prevented him from enjoying the fight. He noticed that Don Eduardo more intently surveyed the crowd than the birds in the cockpit. Don Eduardo's lack of interest in what was happening in the pit added to Pedro's discomfort, but Juanita continued oblivious of her father.

"Oh, no, no, it's just getting good," she answered, dashing Pedro's hope of a quick getaway. She seemed to enjoy the risk that made him anxious. "Oh, poor bird!" she exclaimed.

The black bird rammed his opponent knocking him over. In a split second, he stepped on the brown's neck, and with his other spur, he cleaved the head of the prostrate combatant, that lay twitching in the sand. The color rose to Juanita's face, and though Pedro judged her concern for the dying bird to be genuine, on her face he read exultation.

"Now we must leave," Pedro said, "before your father discovers that you're here."

"He's leaving now," she answered. "See, he's moving toward the door."

Indeed, Don Eduardo having satisfied himself that everything was going well, saw no reason to linger. At the door, he exchanged a few words with the manager who ran the place for a share of the profit. Pedro thought that as the two men talked Don Eduardo gestured in his direction, but he perhaps he was letting his imagination overwhelm him, as Juanita claimed. Still, he thought leaving at the moment advisable, so Juanita would arrive home before Don Eduardo and quell any suspicion he might have seen her where she didn't belong.

"Now we can go," Pedro said, after the birds were removed from the pit, and the sand was swept smooth for the next contest.

"Why, is it over?" she asked.

"No, but it's all the same from here on in. You've seen what it's like."

"Nobody else is leaving."

"These guys are addicted to it," he said with some disdain.

"It?"

"The violence and the gambling too."

"Oh, we forgot to bet," she said.

"I wouldn't throw away my money like that," he said.

"We'll use my money," she countered. "I brought some." She pulled a wad of bills from her pocket and thrust it at him.

"I don't need your money," he said.

"It's not for you. It's for betting," she answered.

"Why do you want to bet?"

"Just for fun," she said.

"Is it fun to lose your money?"

"You don't always lose," she said.

"Are you lucky like your father?"

"No," she said, "not at all."

"You must look at the birds to decide which one you want to bet on," he said. "Unless you want to do it at random, which is just as good."

His anger took the excitement out of the betting, and she, defenseless, saw no way to convey her intention, that she merely wanted to have fun, not to offend him.

"If we inspect the birds now, you will be at greater risk of being discovered."

"What does it matter? My father is gone."

"He will be told," he said.

At the moment, she realized what he feared. But she believed her father did not have the temperament to harm Pedro. "Don't worry about my father. He doesn't care where I go," she assured him though uncertain whether that was still true.

"He cares," Pedro said.

She wondered what made him so sure. "We'll leave if you wish," she said.

Silently, they made their way home. They avoided the main road that led up to the big house, and instead followed the back trails they had frequented as children playing Indians and pirates or just hunters in a wild forest full of ferocious beasts. The forest tamed, all the beasts that had lurked in the shadows disappeared, moved somewhere else. But that place was closer than Juana and Pedro would have liked. They could no longer see the beasts, but they could feel them rampaging through their own bodies, with no way to hunt them down and kill them with their imaginary weapons the way they had done in years past. At that moment, they only had their wills to pit against the unseen enemy.

"I didn't want to make you angry," she said.

"I am not angry at you," he answered. He wanted that to be true, and by saying so, he believed he could point his anger, an arrow he could swing in any direction, away from her, but he saw no other target except himself. That would be preferable, he concluded. That would be simpler.

"There is no one to be angry at, not even yourself," she said. He was momentarily dismayed by his transparency, and he had to get over the discomfort of her scrutiny—something he could not escape. Her ability to guess his thoughts disturbed him, and her accuracy troubled him even more. He wondered whether she could actually read his mind, whether she could read anybody's or only his. Surely, it was not only his, or he would be compelled to acknowledge an inescapable bond between them. His lack of an equal power proved insignificant, since she never hesitated voluntarily to reveal her feelings.

"You need not be angry at my father, either," she said.

W HAT HE DID failed to bring him peace. He expected, if only fleetingly, tranquility, but looking back, he saw no reason to believe in such an outcome. Nothing ever to do with Juanita was without turmoil for him, even when they were children, before he was conscious of social differences, so long ago that he sometimes wondered whether that lack of knowledge had ever existed. He gave in to what she wanted, perhaps weakness on his part, surely he knew better. He tried to keep from making a mistake with Juanita, but the world persisted, oblivious of the fact that he only wanted to resolve confusion.

"I love you," she said, and what could he do then? Those words would have seemed inappropriate if they came from some other woman without any encouragement from him, but nothing from Juanita seemed inappropriate to Pedro. She only said what they both already knew, what they had known for a long time. He could not deny that he wanted her or that he loved her. For him, the two were the same. He could not deny nor assert. For a while, he was held back by the enormity of the possible consequences, not so much for him, a man who had nothing to lose, but for her, willing to sacrifice everything for him.

Shamed by her courage, he remained as unsure as always, each time surprised by her willingness to associate with ordinary folk. She waited for him to speak until she could wait no longer, and he assumed the burden of letting her take the first step. He feared seeming cowardly. How else might he label his hesitancy? He worried he lacked the strength to make the effort that would make him worthy of her and of her sacrifice. Recreating Don Eduardo's feat of rising in the world seemed to him impossible, and accepting Eduardo's largesse and becoming a hanger-on would be worse than failing in the attempt; then he would be giving up his pride, the only thing of value he possessed. Getting

Juanita in return seemed more than an even exchange, but doubt of being worthy of her became another burden.

"Meet me in the *cafetal*," she said. To a stranger the instruction would have seemed vague, but he knew exactly where she meant, an indentation in the ground on the side of the hill, a natural hiding place they discovered as children playing hide-and-go-seek with their companions, who for mysterious reasons never stumbled upon the spot where the two lay huddled together against the warmth of the earth that embraced them like a mother cuddling her children. They breathed hard in the excitement of the game, and they were frightened to hear what they did not expect and did not recognize at first: the earth's heartbeat pounding in unison with theirs. So close together, they felt each other's heartbeat, but the third one surprised and left them speechless as they clung to each other.

They didn't speak of it then or after. At first, they didn't know how to put so strange an experience into words; and later, when older, too late to speak, they feared sounding ridiculous, but they knew something had happened that made that spot their own. Nothing could change that, although the surroundings changed, as Don Eduardo cleared some of the larger trees to plant coffee on the side of the hill. The hiding place survived the change. The coffee planted all around obscured the spot even more. No one suspected that in the midst of the *cafetal* the heart of the earth might be heard.

In the dark, she walked to the *cafetal* after everyone else in the house retired for the night. Her heart beat loudly, and she wondered why no one emerged to inquire about the noise that permeated the evening. Only the moonlight illuminated the way to the appointed spot, but even that was unnecessary. Her feet knew the way without assistance from her eyes. The coffee trees in bloom, in the dark she could not see the small red flowers hanging in clusters from the branches of the low trees, but she knew they were there. When she got to the hiding place, Pedro was waiting for her.

He arrived at the spot against his will, or so he believed. He simply needed to stay away to save himself and her also. He said that to himself with every intention of walking to town and spending the night there. Surely, he could have a drink or two at the *cantina*. He would have no trouble finding a place to sleep that would be comfortable enough, but his feet refused to walk in the direction his reason urged them to take. Of the many mysteries of life, a man's inability to control his feet emerged as one of the most astounding. The struggle visible only to him, and he sincerely hoped also to God, if ever he had to give an account of his life as commonly supposed. He did not go willingly. That certainly would count in his favor if he had ever to answer for his action, which he knew to be wrong but which he could not prevent. This was perhaps what being possessed by the devil meant, a transparent event to the ordinary observer, a much less lurid occurrence than the one depicted in the imagination of the populace.

The matter would have been simple if it only entailed physical gratification—something from which they both could have walked away. But as he held her close to him, lying on the mossy hollow of the earth, he became aware of the irrevocable nature of the act, not always so, but on this occasion a pledge on which he could not renege, even though he had gone there against his will. Never having met the devil in person, Pedro only surmised the nature and character of that being, apart from the commonly held belief that he aimed to entrap humanity. To make love to Juanita was wrong, but to run from her would also be wrong. But what justifies persistence in an originally wrong condition? That had no answer, God's motivation was emerging as more complex. Creating man weak, He sent a supernatural being to plague him. If possessed, did Pedro act of his own free will? Did he have the power to prevail? If not, his choice of whether to walk to Comerio or to the *cafetal* was reduced to an illusion.

THE AFTERNOON HAD an aura of calmness manufactured by the two friends, an effect they had over the years wrought to perfection, so that the most turbulent occasions took on the guise of normalcy. Doña Echevaria served the ginger tea and sat down across from Gregoria.

"And what's to be done now?" Doña Echevaria rhetorically asked.

"What indeed," Gregoria countered adjusting to struggling against the current.

"And what of Don Eduardo?" This time Doña Echevaria's question was real. Like everyone else, she wondered about Don Eduardo's reaction to his daughter's seemingly inexplicable behavior.

"Poor man," said Gregoria, "I think he doesn't know what his reaction should be."

"You mean he hasn't said anything? That in itself is telling."

"I think he was completely surprised. He walks about the house as if someone hit him over the head with a club."

"That's not what one would have expected of Don Eduardo. Life never ceases to amaze," Doña Echevaria said, her placid face giving the lie to her words. She brought the cup of ginger tea to her lips and sipped it slowly, savoring the tangy liquid, to her a perfect metaphor of what life should be, more complexity in that taste than commonly supposed—the taste of that brew taken for granted, like the everyday details of living inadvertently lost, subsumed into generalities. She derived whatever powers she possessed from reversing that common habit, a secret she had no fear of revealing, simplicity placing it beyond the ken of most people. Anyone astute enough to understand its power didn't need enlightenment from her.

"You're surprised by his surprise, do you mean?"

"Well, that too," Doña Echevaria said.

"What else then?"

"Some people think that Pedro should fear for his life."

"What nonsense! Don Eduardo is a peaceful man."

"But such an affront!"

"What would he gain by making his daughter a widow?"

"He might save her from a hard life," Doña Echevaria said looking down into the cup where residues of ginger clung to the bottom. She gazed at them intently as if she were seeing the future in the Chinese manner of reading tea leaves, but that was not her way. She preferred the cards.

"There is no way to avoid that for any of us," Gregoria said. "This earth is a valley of tears. Our mother Eve made certain of that."

"To be sure," said Doña Echevaria, "the human heart is a strange instrument. Who would have thought that she would do this to her father after he worked all his life to prevent just such a thing from happening."

"He didn't work hard enough," Gregoria said.

"What more could the poor man have done? He couldn't very well keep her under lock and key."

"Perhaps it was inevitable given the circumstances."

"You mean the close proximity?"

"I mean growing up without her mother."

"She had you," Doña Echevaria said in a lapse of caution she immediately regretted.

"Obviously that wasn't enough," Gregoria said.

"Some things are written in the book of life. They cannot be changed by hook nor by crook," she said.

"What then of personal responsibility? How can God hold us responsible for our actions if they are predetermined?"

"That's a mystery. Perhaps he doesn't hold us responsible."

"You mean we can do whatever we want without sinning?"

"Would you behave any differently if that were true?"

"I will never know that, will I?"

"I suppose not," Doña Echevaria conceded, less interested in the metaphysical ramifications of Gregoria's musings than in the common gossip about Juanita's new life. "It will not be easy for her," Doña Echevaria said in an effort to bring Gregoria back to the practical. "It couldn't have been easy for her to move out of the big house."

"The alternative was unacceptable to Pedro, to move into his father-in-law's house."

"There's plenty of room there I suppose," Doña Echevaria said.

"You can never have two roosters in one hen house," Gregoria said.

"No, I suppose not. Still they haven't gone far."

"They have their own house on Don Eduardo's land, and Pedro still works for Don Eduardo. How long that will last, I don't know."

"It could last forever. If Pedro plays his cards right, he will make his fortune."

"That's what people say behind his back, and it rankles him."

"Gossip is little enough to put up with."

"You don't know this boy."

"Ah, is he still a boy?"

"Marriage doesn't make a man."

"Does it make a woman?"

"It doesn't do that either."

A S IF HER task were to distract the field hands, every day
Evita walked into the grapefruit orchard where Pedro su-
pervised the work. Some of the workers were glad enough to be
entertained, but the teasing annoyed others.

"Don Pedro," said Enrique Jimenez addressing his *capataz*,
"why do you allow her to interfere with the work? Some of the
men are upset."

"No doubt of that," said Pedro. "I am no different from the
rest of you."

"In this orchard, you're the boss."

"But in this hacienda I am no more than a *jibaro*, and she is
Don Eduardo's daughter."

"Are you not his son-in-law?"

"That I am," he said and walked away glancing at the sky,
where brilliant masses of white slowly floated across, changing
from one suggestive form to another.

Perhaps the transformation of the clouds held some meaning. His imagination continued to urge him to arrive at some
conclusion, but whether the clouds contained a truthful message
remained unanswered. Pedro lacked the power to interpret. He
brought his eyes back to earth as the image of evil slowly dissipated.

Again, he found himself in a predicament he didn't understand. Something beyond his control engulfed him without warning. The unpredictability of his life, of his actions, baffled him.
He moved as if he were merely a puppet compelled by invisible
strings. If he could only find the puppeteer and reason with him,
he might have a chance to save himself. Was it someone or something open to reason? That was a question without an answer.
Would questions continue to assail him forever? And would the
answers continue to elude him? He would be better off not thinking about such things. Surely, Don Eduardo was not plagued by

such mysteries. To him everything came easily, like the rising and the setting of the sun each day. Don Eduardo was born lucky. That was the only explanation.

And why was he, Pedro Soto, put on this piece of land that belonged to the lucky man? Why was he not born and raised on the other side of the mountain, or down by the sea where perhaps he would never have run into Don Eduardo or his daughters? He needed to deal with more than he expected, the matter turning out to be more difficult than he imagined. He didn't take his father's warning seriously, thinking that the old man was too ignorant to see that the world had changed, that it kept changing constantly, and that Juana Rincon knew exactly what she wanted, and that her father would not stand in the way.

He thought of the days when he was reluctant to enter the Rincon house even through the kitchen door. Now, he could enter through the front door just like any gentleman, but he still felt uncomfortable doing so. He felt Don Eduardo's eyes scrutinizing him the way he would a young colt when debating whether or not to buy it. This time, Don Eduardo had no choice. This time, the buyer was his daughter Juana, who always got what she wanted. She had Pedro Soto along with the land and everything on it.

In the past, Pedro's discomfort was brought on by his proximity to the Rincon house. It began to invade him before he reached the kitchen door, something that came on as soon as he set foot on the *batey*. But at least the dangerous area had its limit. Out of sight of the Rincon house, he was inarguably as much a man as anyone else. He had his connection to the other men of Comerio, and even down in San Geronimo no one could have disputed his manhood.

But something was added, something he could not exactly describe, but something he felt. He still went down to Comerio to hang out with the boys, but they no longer looked at him the same way. He was not one of them anymore. An invisible wall was erected. Slight gestures, invisible to outsiders but distinct to those who were raised in the mountains, conveyed the message. He wanted to shout at his companions that they were making a mistake, that he was still one of them, but he could not use words to express his discomfort. That, too, was forbidden. He downed another beer.

"Soon you'll be drinking like Don Eduardo," he heard Agapito Mundial say.

"And how is that?" Pedro inquired, annoyed to hear the name mentioned when he was trying to forget it.

"They say he can drink a whole barrel and still ride home unattended."

"I've never seen him drink more than a glass of anything."

"Maybe so, but his workers say he can out-drink any of them and still go home to satisfy his wife."

"You suppose she announces such things to them or talks to them at all?"

"Well, that's another matter altogether. She's a Castillo, town people. They're different down in San Geronimo."

"Ah, yes down in San Geronimo, but right now we're here in Comerio." Yes, he was a Comerian, and he didn't want his friends to forget that.

"Don Eduardo, too, was born in Comerio," Agapito said, as if he were trying to make some point that Pedro could not exactly label but that had a quality unquestionably annoying. "There was a time when he had nothing, before you were born. Back in those days, Don Eduardo plowed his own fields."

"Is that so? You remember those days?"

"I was just a boy back then, but I remember that Don Eduardo raced his horses, winning whatever race he entered."

"I don't suppose you remember the ones he lost."

"Did he lose any?"

"No, of course not, he never lost anything."

"Stay close to him and you'll learn a thing or two."

"And when I do, you'll still have a drink with me?"

"As long as you're buying," said Agapito Mundial.

But those were only words—what Agapito was supposed to say. Everyone had to say what was required, but the words had to be interpreted. They carried meaning absent from the official definitions, and Pedro could see, looking into Agapito's eyes, that his drinking companion would not in the future initiate anything with Don Eduardo's son-in-law. He was now in a world where he felt out of place and uncomfortable, and in that new setting, he had not yet picked up signs of acceptance. Besides, his old friends assumed that he went willingly, and they treated him with reservation.

On his way home, he took a detour to Don Federico's *bohio*. Pedro could still talk to the old man, who had an eye for the difference between one bird and another. He could foretell which *gallitos* would be champions, and he knew which should be retired before they started.

"Come to see the birds, have you?" The old man bantered, knowing that the birds were of little interest to Pedro.

"No, I've come to let them see me," Pedro said.

"Good," said Don Federico. "Maybe you can inspire them. They like to imitate a winner."

"Is that what I am?"

"I hear you're the cock of the walk."

"I suppose you heard that in town. At the *hacienda* it's a different story."

Don Federico perused Pedro's face, looking for signs of scars acquired in life's *gallera*, where the young man needed to defend himself against real and imaginary opponents. No doubt he could handle the physical ones. The imaginary ones were more dangerous. The imagination provided its fighting birds with larger talons and more ornate spurs. Don Federico looked for the wounds on the young man's spirit and he saw the bleeding. He wished he could take him out of the ring, but that was impossible. We were all placed into the arena by some supernatural power, and we each must execute our moves till the end. We could try to lend assistance, but it was only that and nothing more, futile, the outcome pre-determined and written in indelible ink.

"You must pull yourself together," Don Federico said.

"You see my problem?"

"I see that you struggle."

"I'm in a place where I don't belong. I have to find a way out."

"Why not accept what you have?"

"It's not that simple."

"Nothing in life is simple. Once in the pit, the bird does what it can. That's all that matters."

"Can I win?"

"Only you can answer that."

"No one can beat Don Eduardo."

"Is he your opponent?"

Pedro wondered why Don Federico was failing to see the obvious. Juana had taken the name Soto, but in everyone's eyes she was still a Rincon, and her husband was being asked to become one also. The current was being forced to flow uphill, for a Rincon a common enough occurrence but for a Soto an impossibility.

"I thought maybe you had an answer for me."

"You can leave Comerio without looking back."

"And Juana?"

"She'll follow."

"You're more certain than I."

Don Federico recognized the uselessness of his words. Everything was already decided, and to avoid frustration, humans merely needed to discover their predestined directions. That was the way to happiness. He might tell that to the young man, but that, too, would prove useless. Pedro had to discover the path on his own. Elders could point the way, but whether their advice was followed was a game of chance. Even intending to comply, young people behaved in ways unrecognizable to their mentors, whose advice was distorted by the prism of interpretation.

"I love Juana," the young man said, "but love can be as painful as the jaws of a vise."

The old man recognized that there was no way to keep the crank from turning, but he tried to point the way to an appreciation of the circumstances. "Don Eduardo provided the land, and you built your own house."

"He doesn't want to lose Juana."

"How far does she have to go to be considered lost?"

That indeed was a question. No doubt there was more to the story than commonly supposed. Gossipers claimed that Don Eduardo bought Juana from her mother with the stipulation that Carmen leave Comerio and have little to do with her daughter. But that was just talk; no one knew for sure. Time obscures the facts behind every story, as if there existed a number of templates in the collective memory and eventually all history is edited to fit into a variation of one of them.

"You must take Juana to a place of your own," Don Federico repeated.

Pedro saw the good sense in that advice, but transforming it into action was not simple. Distrust came between Pedro and his father-in-law whenever they found themselves in the same room. Most often at the dinner table, Pedro struggled to discover what he needed to do to convince Don Eduardo of his love for Juana. It became an impossible task; up a steep hill he rolled a giant stone that inevitably found its way back to the bottom.

✳

"Your father hates me," Pedro said to Juana.

"He doesn't," she retorted. "Stand up to him and he will respect you."

She did not reveal to him the encounter that she regretted, thinking she had gone too far and had been unkind to her father, when from her mother she had never heard a word against him.

"Why marry such man?" her father angrily asked.

"He loves me," Juana replied.

"He sees you as a means to rise in this world."

"No," she said, "the fear of that accusation is what kept him from me for so long. I have known him since I was a child, and always he kept a distance."

"And now he has found his strength?"

"No, I have found mine, and I have seduced him."

"He has let you believe that. What he wants is to use you."

"Were you thinking like that when you got rid of my mother?"

His daughter's words overwhelmed Eduardo. Never had she blamed him for the absence of her mother, and at the moment he regretted failing to make her aware of the tragedy of his life. He needed to deal with the moment, and suddenly the possibility of losing what he had left loomed before him. This time he intended to outwit fate. He had to predict its possible moves. Juana became the queen on the board. If he lost her, the game was over. He saw himself already at a disadvantage, failing to foresee Pedro's entrance. He could not deny that the boy was always there; it was he, Eduardo, who made all the wrong moves. But the game was not over, and this time he intended to stay alert.

He wondered what side of the board Father Rodrigo was on. He had married the young ones at their request without having consulted him or posting the banns in Comerio or in San Geronimo. Whether that was a move by the priest in his game momentarily flitted through Eduardo's mind. There was a more reasonable explanation: Juana resembled her parents more closely than her father was willing at the moment to admit. His reason urged him to let the boy in, but the backdrop against which he had staged his daughter was very different from everyday reality.

A BOUT TO RIDE away from the orchard, Pedro spied Evita approaching, and he guided his mount in her direction. "Come, I'll take you home," he said.

She raised her arms, and he reached down to swing her up behind him. He felt the undulation of her body against his as they rode toward the stable. Pedro about to dismount, Evita clung to him more tightly. "We're home," he said. Her face against his back, she refused to let go. He attempted to break her grip, but the feel of her body against his deterred him. The horse, sensing a change, stomped its right hoof calling for a clearer signal. Pedro tugged the strand of leather in his hand to one side, and the animal turned up a familiar path. Relaxing his hold on the rein, Pedro abdicated control of the animal but remained unaware of having made a decision.

When the horse stopped, Evita's arms relaxed, and she slipped to the ground. She gazed up at Pedro who at the moment vaguely sensed that he was being offered an opportunity to escape. He failed to recognize it, and only in retrospect did he identify the moment when more than the force of gravity was at work as he slipped from the saddle.

*

Evita's belly grew, to the family's consternation. "Who has done this to you?" her mother asked trying to remain calm.

Evita had no answer. Either she did not understand her mother's question, or she was determined to protect the man whom she sensed would be the target for retribution for the discomfort she saw around her.

"You must tell me who has done this to you," Antonia insisted.

"No one," Evita answered.

"You're going to have a child," her mother replied.

"It's a blessing," said the young woman.

Remembering her discomfort at the onset of motherhood, the ease she perceived in her daughter baffled Antonia. Eduardo, just as unable to get Evita to reveal the name of the culprit, kept his inquiry to a minimum, knowing that this development would little alter the social consequences of her disability. If she was happy, perhaps her pregnancy was a blessing. He refrained from voicing that opinion knowing that the rest of the family would not understand nor agree with him.

Moreover, discovering the identity of the culprit would force him to act with possibly unknown consequences. Antonia's demand that he extract the identity of the culprit seemed at best useless, and more likely, a mistake for everyone involved. He pretended to make an effort, but without regret, he accepted his daughter's resistance.

"I do not understand you," Antonia said turning the anger from herself to her husband.

"How can I force her to speak?" he asked. "She doesn't see things the way we do."

"Is that all you're interested in? What about us? What about me?" she inquired, his way of thinking this time, as often the case, beyond her understanding.

"I'm interested in her happiness and well-being," he said. "Why create a problem for her if one doesn't exist? Why burden her with guilt?"

"You mean she suffers for my sake?"

"Does she suffer at all?" he inquired, turning the matter in a direction Antonia had not considered.

"She was created for my own retribution, and that's why I must see that no one takes advantage of her."

"She is happy," her father said.

"She is socially ruined," Antonia retorted.

"Ah," Eduardo bitterly answered, "you have returned to a view I thought you had abandoned."

"Have you ever understood me? I have loved you to no avail."

Again caught in a dilemma, he tried to decipher a riddle the answer to which constantly eluded him. He had only one approach to the problem. He endeavored to be a good husband, although that had for him a vague definition and he considered fidelity something of dubious value. His attempts to understand his wife resulted only in frustration, and then with the usual reaction to his failure, she rubbed his emotional wounds with metaphorical lye.

"Why find her lover?" he inquired trying to be logical.

"To keep her from future disgrace."

"And also from future happiness?"

"For the first time, you consider ignorance an advantage," she snickered.

"She deserves some privacy," he answered, still struggling to make her understand the respite he was trying to preserve for the daughter unfairly burdened as retribution for family sins. "She will not reveal her lover, and I will not force her," Eduardo insisted closing the argument.

*

From the start, Juana's feelings were similar to her father's.

"Help me," Antonia begged her. "She'll tell you who the man is who has done this to her."

"If she hasn't told anyone else, why would she tell me?"

"You very well know she's been closer to you than to me," Antonia answered trying to suppress the resentment and acknowledge a shortcoming she would prefer to forget.

"Why insist?" Juana asked, hoping that Antonia would realize that there was no reason to delve.

"I have to know," Antonia said, "if only to keep my sanity. And she has to stop. How many more children can we allow her to have without a proper husband?"

Juana saw reason in that, but she refrained from promising to use her sister's trust to delve into her secret. She had a premonition that this time knowledge would be more painful than ignorance. Up to her last breath, the complexity of her reaction remained a mystery. She could not explain to herself why, of all the people involved in her life, her resentment focused on Antonia who did not participate in the betrayal.

"So you're going to have a baby," Juana said when her sister next dropped by to visit.

"I am," the young one said. "I'll be just like you."

"As long as you're happy," Juana said.

"Aren't you?"

"I am," Juana answered, "but it's hard work bringing up children."

"You'll help me," Evita said seriously. "You've helped me already."

"Have I?" Juana asked, beginning to suspect an unpleasant revelation.

"You helped me to get his baby," Evita said.

The statement disoriented Juana, and she searched for an image of what might have led her sister down the precarious path. The vagueness elicited fear. "Did I?" she asked, the sound barely emerging from her dry throat.

"Oh, yes," Evita answered. "Our children will have the same father."

Juana's first reaction was to shut down, as if a gust of wind had for a moment blown out the light of a candle, but the intensity of the heat in the wick caused it to burst again into flame. She quickly discarded the possibility of falsity in Evita's words, the young woman's face radiant with satisfaction at imitating her sister. Painfully aware of regaining consciousness, she regretted its return. The need to keep it submerged suggested, if only for an instant, a means of escape, but eternal blankness remained an unacceptable option. She chose to let personal control diminish and abandoned the semblance of power over her mind and body. Unintelligible sounds emerged from her throat as she fell to the floor.

The scene frightened Evita, not realizing that her words had caused the turmoil. Instinctively, she called for her father, who on his arrival was confounded by the scene of his daughter undergoing a seizure, another reminder of God's inclination to punish him without sparing his children. No foam emerged from her mouth, but lacking detailed knowledge, he overlooked that fact and attempted the usual procedure of placing a barrier between the upper and lower teeth of the victim. He had grabbed a wooden utensil from the kitchen for that purpose, but she resisted his efforts.

On seeing her father, guilt supplanted Juana's feelings of victimization. He had put one knee on the floor on descending to examine her. She reached up, and having his daughter's arms around him reminded Eduardo of another woman whose image both pained and comforted him. Submitting to the necessity of the moment, Juana held on to him tightly, something she had not done in a long time. Feeling more vulnerable than ever, she kept her eyes closed, unsuccessfully trying to restrain the tears, as she eased the hold on her father.

"What is the matter?" he begged.

The sound of his voice forced her back to reason. An enigmatic problem faced her. Confiding in him would trigger another chain of events with catastrophic results. To tell the truth would force her father into a fit of violence against a man who entered the family through her scheming. The two men whom she loved would be removed from her life—one dead and the other imprisoned. That outcome seemed inevitable. Even if she kept quiet, she could not guarantee Evita's silence. Evita saw no wrong. Her impairment prevented the recognition of evil in the world; intelligence, a condition necessary for evil's existence, made her lack, a blessing in disguise.

Juana searched for clarity. Her sister did not elicit resentment, nor was her innocence attributable to her handicap. Had she been normal, Juana would have just as readily forgiven her. The girl did not elicit pity but acceptance. Though obviously irrational, that view at the moment seemed normal, and Juana embraced it. She focused her energy on preventing another tragedy. Dealing with one greater than the one already oppressing her would be unbearable. Reason directed her along a path of appeasement, but emotion gave rise to images of violence, where she saw her husband's body dismembered without pity. Seeing him in pain briefly relieved her, but she still loved him, and contemplating his demise proved just as painful as his betrayal. Her father's voice came through the protective barrier she temporarily constructed but at the moment approaching its limitation. "Talk to me," he insisted. She kept her mouth shut, involuntarily shaking her head.

Evita, seeing her father completely absorbed by her sister on the floor, attempted to gain a share of attention. "I was telling her about my baby's father, and she fell to the ground," she said, expecting her father to appreciate her words.

A vast chasm immediately began to emerge for Eduardo, and nothing could prevent the catastrophe. His attention focused on his prostrated daughter, her pain regained for him a tragic semblance. Anticipating an undesirable answer, he still asked her: "What did she tell you?"

Her ability to make decisions paralyzed, Juana remained silent.

"I was telling her that Pedro is the father of my baby," Evita continued, trying to draw Eduardo's attention and succeeding with a greater result than she expected.

He had to accept the unfortunate but clear conclusions, the unpleasant task he imagined transformed into a tragic one. Only an unknown force could provide a positive outcome. Overwhelming anger made the negative results of action insignificant. He stood up resolved to perform the required action, but even the first step brought back memories of that previous event that had shattered his life. He kept his gun locked in a box since the day he realized he forever had lost Juana's mother. That gun destroyed the possibility of an ideal life, and he had sentenced it to life-long imprisonment, but at that moment it required parole.

Her father turned to leave, making Juana aware of his intentions and forcing her to accelerate recovery. Whether she wanted to save him, or Pedro, or both equally, at that moment unclear to her, she rose in haste and continued down an uncharted path. Placing her arms around his neck, she begged in a conciliatory tone, "Listen to me, please!"

For Eduardo, ignoring his daughter would have been another sin against the woman entwined in his psyche. Juana's arms around him reminded him of her mother, someone whose needs he was bound to honor.

"Listen to me. Please, listen to me," Juana continued, trying to maintain her voice clear in between the sobs impossible to repress.

Whether the circumstances affected her voice, or whether Eduardo's ears created the illusion, Eduardo heard Carmen, and the sound forced him to control the call to violence. For the moment, he had to pay attention to that voice.

"Consider what I need," Juana begged. "To lose the two of you at the same time would be unbearable."

Fate had placed his daughter in a more painful position than he had thought possible until that moment. Again, the need to perform an execution would further destroy what remained of his life. Even if he could not pinpoint where he went wrong, a sense of guilt overwhelmed him. Every action in one's life results from previous actions. Again he could only trace a problematic occurrence to the thoughtless act that had deprived him of the life he wanted—but that, too, was forced on him by chance. He had accidentally gazed upon the bare figure of a woman who subsequently became the mother of the daughter whose happiness he would be destroying. Either God or the devil had control of the world, and he at that moment needed to face the task of resisting either one of them.

"I can no longer bear to see him," he said.

Juana, her arms around him, felt the change in his body produced by his decision to turn against fate and attempt to preserve his sanity.

"I will take him away," she said. "You will never see him again."

"You're willing to sacrifice everything for him?"

"To sacrifice him would be worse," she answered.

As part of his punishment he had to let her go. He understood. He gazed into his daughter's eyes, trying to find the solution to his dilemma. "Will you ever see who I am?" he hopelessly asked.

The question was meant for her mother—a question without the possibility of an answer.

E DUARDO NEEDED ONLY to point his horse in the right direction and keep riding, and eventually he would arrive at his destination. Carmen had left Comerio, first to San Geronimo then further away, but how far could she go on an island only one hundred miles long? How would she receive him if he showed up at her door? She had a husband, a complication. He couldn't just show up. He would have to be circumspect. He rummaged through the details in his mind as if planning to go after her, but the vague plan ignored all the troublesome obstacles. No doubt she would rebuff him again, and his efforts would be useless, but just to catch a glimpse of her would make the journey worthwhile.

Going so far, would he be able to contain himself and be content to just look at her from afar? That would require superhuman power, and if he could not keep himself from riding there in the first place, how would he refrain from confronting her? Better to exert what strength he had while she roamed far away, and he had some chance of success. But caught in her strong pull, to think that the ocean could escape the force of the moon was an absurdity. The morning ride was habitual. The sun only partially above the horizon when he put his boot in the stirrup and swung himself up. If he rode toward the sun, he would get to his destination, and perhaps, as in a fairy tale, he would there find what he sought.

✳

"You shouldn't have come," she said.

He searched her face for a sign by which to interpret her words, the timbre of her voice running counter to their literal meaning.

"It was not my choice," he countered.

"Then you understand how that can be," she returned. "I have no choice either."

"One of us must," he insisted. He could not reasonably explain what swayed him to succumb other than to say that love possessed him. Supposedly that explained enough, love a naturally illogical phenomenon, but that opened the door to the irrationality of everything else, too great a step for him to take. In that direction, he saw no firm ground on which to tread, only a precipitous plunge into an abyss. Whether that implied a necessary disaster was another question to which he had no answer.

"Did you ever love me?" The words escaped his lips almost imperceptibly, involuntarily, as if merely expelling breath. Ashamed to ask, to put himself in that position, aware of something happening as in a dream, he saw himself simultaneously a protagonist and an observer having no control over what he observed.

"How can you ask that?"

"Because I do not know the answer."

"Would I have given you Juana if I didn't?"

"Is that all then?"

"She's the best of us both. See that she has a good life."

"And you?"

"I will fend for myself."

"And me?"

"You have everything," Carmen said.

"I would trade it all for you," he said.

"You deceive yourself," she countered.

He wondered whether she had knowledge he lacked or whether she only pretended. He searched her face for a clue, but she refused to provide one. He would have to find the answer somewhere else. Perhaps in a similar dilemma, she had questions and no answers. But she gave no indication of that either.

Perhaps women knew the answers to everything, and only men stumbled about the world confounded by enigmas. There might be a God who found that humorous, as good an explanation as any for the unpredictable nature of the world. A moody God might be reasonably attributed with laughter as well as anger, but Eduardo could recall no passage of Holy Scripture to support a laughing God. Plenty of evidence for an angry God, but if He were capable of anger, He must have laughed sometimes. Man a reasonably funny joke, God must have a sense of humor to have created a creature who is able to reason but is driven by compulsion.

The consequences, not immediately obvious, had unfolded gradually, like a flower blooming, one petal at a time, that when fully revealed turned out to be something other than what he had imagined. Rather, he had imagined nothing, so that what resulted had to be significantly different. He had at first perceived her turning from him as a necessity that simultaneously appeared to be a solution. Although distraught at losing her, his doubts became irrelevant, and he felt relieved of the responsibility of having to make a decision.

Perhaps the traumatic character of the circumstances initially occasioned only numbness, Father Rodrigo's assessment of the situation—he in a delicate position, being privy to a fact unknown to Eduardo but significant in the development of subsequent events.

"She doesn't want to see me anymore," Eduardo told the priest, "and I understand that. Perhaps it's for the best."

"Did she tell you everything?" Rodrigo inquired.

"Everything? She is grief stricken. What else can be relevant at the moment?"

"Of course," the priest responded. He had still to decide whether to say more. But beyond that, the question of timing persisted. When could Eduardo hear more? He, too, needed time to heal.

Eduardo had resolved to go on with his life as if the incident of the *tiznados* had not happened, but of course he would have to go on without Carmen, because she refused to forget it. His resolve seemed at first simple enough, but soon he realized that turning his back resulted in more than he anticipated. Weeks or months may have elapsed before he concluded that his stance was unsustainable, or he may have reached it right away, certainly before Carmen began to show.

He rode out to the fields every morning and looked, out of habit, for her face among the field hands and not finding it troubled him. Repeated disappointment did not diminish his expectation. Every morning brought new hope. The excitement began to build as he put his boot in the stirrup and pulled himself into the saddle to survey from that height the path he would follow. Initially unaware of the reason for the quickening of his pulse, he rode to where the workers gathered each morning to receive their instructions for the day. His eyes moved furtively from face to face looking for the one who would calm him, and not finding it filled him with heaviness. His heart granite, he could hardly sit straight in the saddle with that burden in his chest. Every morning, he repeated the routine, as he made an effort to pull himself together and carry on as if nothing had changed. Everything was all right he assured himself, except that time failed to lighten the burden as popular wisdom had led him to expect, but rather, the intensity of his anticipation grew each day until he could no longer deny that only Carmen's appearance would allay his anguish.

One morning, halfway to the appointed place, he forced himself to acknowledge reality. Why ride all the way to the field to discover what he already knew? He turned the horse away from the accustomed path, and the animal, surprised at the alteration of the routine, balked momentarily, but at the insistence of his master's knees he submitted to the change in direction. He rode to the Gutierez place.

Before Eduardo could dismount, Doña Andrea came out to greet him, surprised to see him at an unusual hour. Don Juaquin himself already out in the fields, she knew that Don Eduardo would normally have been overseeing the commencement of the workday on his *hacienda*. She heard the heavy hoof beats of the horse on the hard clay of the *batey* and she peered out to see who was approaching.

"By God," said Doña Andrea, "it's Don Eduardo coming up the path. What on earth could he want here?"

"Tell him I'm not home," Carmen said.

"Why would I tell him that?" Doña Andrea asked. "What have you done that he should come to seek you out so early in the morning?"

"Ask him rather what he has done."

A look of consternation momentarily flitted over Doña Andrea's features like the ephemeral shadow of a bird passing quickly overhead, or as if a memory imprisoned in the secret labyrinth of her mind was on the verge of finding its way to the exit—but it was only a threat, and the guardians of her sanity, ever vigilant, beat it back into the darkness.

"How could he do this?" Carmen said.

Doña Andrea looked at her daughter with an air of confounded helplessness. Of course, she considered Don Eduardo showing up at such an unexpected hour strange, but that could hardly account for the sudden onset of fatigue that began to overwhelm her as soon as she recognized his unmistakable figure sitting in the saddle.

"Well, one must be hospitable," Doña Andrea said to her daughter, her behavior also strange enough. One had to make do, and if Don Eduardo showed up for breakfast he had to be fed, though surely less sumptuously than he was used to. No matter, one had to offer. No great bother, really, so why did she suddenly feel weak? "I must go out and see what he wants," she said to Carmen only because she needed to utter the instruction to herself. She knew what she had to do, but her body remained inert. She hoped that the words would set her going.

"Tell him to go away," Carmen said.

"I'm sure he will do so soon enough," her mother replied. "He couldn't have come to stay." And with that, she walked through the door out to the *batey* where the horseman seemed just as unsure of what to do as Doña Andrea.

"Good day, Don Eduardo," Doña Andrea said. "Won't you come in and have a cup of coffee."

"Some other time," Eduardo said. "I was riding by and

thought to stop and inquire whether Carmen is all right. I haven't seen her for some time."

"She's all right, Don Eduardo," the lady answered. "She's gone to Hormiguero to see my sister who is ill and in need of some assistance."

"Ah, is that all?" he said. "I sincerely hope your sister gets well soon and Carmen returns."

"She'll be back by and by," Doña Andrea answered, marveling at how easily the lies rolled off her tongue. The sudden surprise at having such an ability made her heart race faster and her breathing shallower. She hoped those physiological alterations remained invisible to Don Eduardo, a reasonable expectation, since he was gazing beyond her at the house.

He caught a glimpse through a darkened window of someone moving within. He had but to accept the invitation to a cup of coffee to end the charade. But then what? The matter was better left in the realm of shadows where things might or might not be what they seemed. Perhaps the shadow was not Carmen. If it was she, why force a confrontation against her wishes?

*

Every act affects the future; usually that effect is so gradual and so expected as to be practically unnoticeable, to some the same as insignificant. A confluence of events may produce a nexus from which many strands of influence emanate like the point at which a pebble enters the water to create concentric ripples. Who threw the stone or whether the stone hit the water at the precise point intended by the thrower is largely irrelevant to whatever objects floating on the surface are affected by the waves. The throwing of the stone seems an altogether different class of event than the waves rippling through the water. One seems, on first consideration, to be governed by willful intelligence, while the other is totally within the sphere of mechanical necessity.

Once the stone leaves the hand, the consequences are subject only to the laws of physics, exact and inexorable. Will and intelligence can be removed from deliberation by supposing that the sequence of events is initiated by chance. Suppose, for instance, that a nut falls from a tree overhanging a body of water. The ripples then are caused without the intervention of an intelligent will. There is no difference between a wave originated by a thrown stone and one set in motion by a falling fruit.

When he recalled the event, the darkness of that night most struck Eduardo, a night without moonlight. The stars, though they managed the usual and impressive ornamentation of the sky only served to make the darkness below more burdensome. The lack of moonlight went unnoticed until after the fatal shot was fired, and he began to assess the consequences of its absence.

Moonlight had ceased to be necessary for what transpired between him and Carmen. Past that stage where the silvery sheen aided the romantic imagination, she met him at the *bohio* at night regardless of whether she had the aid of the moon. Whether she had the ability, like a cat, to see in the dark, or whether guided there by light invisible to others and beyond physical phenomena, or whether her body merely retained a memory of the path often traversed, may be endlessly discussed without resolution. She knew the way, and she followed it without regret.

She found it unnecessary to question her actions. She assumed a necessity. She saw her life flowing along a natural course, much like the water of a river following a necessary path determined by factors other than itself. The event altered that attitude, though a clear and logical reason for the change was impossible to pinpoint. Only she could see it, or rather perceive it, the method of apprehension vague, but the effect unmistakable. Her remorse persisted, as if being at that place, at that time, contributed to the tragedy; or even more, as if she, herself, pointed the gun and pulled the trigger. In a sense, she correctly thought her presence determined the scene; were she absent from that place and time, with no reason for Eduardo to be there, the gun also would have been absent.

He sought her that night, expecting, after his conversation with Father Rodrigo, to hear a revelation that would change the course of his life, a change, after all, necessary as a consequence of its antecedents. When she entered the hut, he saw her as if for the first time. Only a few days had elapsed since their previous meeting, but she looked rounder and softer than he remembered. He had the illusion of reaching across a long stretch of time and distance to recapture someone whom he had once known and who was dear to him, but whom he only vaguely remembered. Perhaps his expectations created the illusion of a difference yet to come, or perhaps she always looked that way in the scarcity of light that existed in the room. Perhaps he saw in the difference of her eyes only their efficient adaptation to gathering what they needed to fulfill their function, but which he perceived as attractive intelligence.

He appreciated at the moment the helplessness he saw in her. Her lips slightly parted, but realizing the futility of the act, she stifled the plea about to be uttered. He blamed himself for that and was at a loss to know what he might do to reassure her. Condemned forever to be in the wrong where Carmen was concerned, he bore a punishment that lacked correlation with a particular transgression; the puzzling generality made the offence difficult to justify but the retribution easier to bear.

He prepared to hear what she had to say, hoping for expiation. He was only vaguely aware of the sin to be removed; although, like original sin, a generic transgression inherited from one's forebears, the sense of possessing it, or rather being possessed by it, remained inescapable. He approached the matter as he approached other problems, with a positive belief that a solution would present itself, and his responsibility lay in recognizing and exploiting it. He stood before Carmen in complete expectation of being presented with just such an opportunity.

She was reluctant to speak first, and that also he took as a reproach, as a sign that he had failed to comfort her. Ashamed, he relegated the lapse to the unintentional.

"I spoke to Father Rodrigo," he said.

She understood what he meant, but she remained silent. "I saw him, too, at the church," she finally revealed.

His indirectness made him feel foolish. "You need not be afraid," he said, as he sensed her slipping away from him. The premonition instilled fear in him. His consciousness momentarily illuminated, the way a flash of lightning during the night reveals the hidden landscape for an instant, only to plunge back into darkness leaving the observer uncertain of what he saw.

She considered his words carefully, trying to discern why he spoke of fear when she had no sense of it. She, too, ought to have felt it, and its absence revealed a deficiency in some quality necessary for survival.

"Why should I be afraid?" she asked.

"We're all afraid a little," he said, "of the unknown."

"I know you," she said.

"But you doubt me."

"No, not you," she said.

"What then?"

"Fate," she answered.

"We make our own fate."

"What would Father Rodrigo say to that?"

"Do you think him a fatalist?"

"No, he's like you in many ways."

"What advice did he give you?"

"None," she answered. "I didn't seek advice from him."

"From whom then?"

"From the Virgin."

"What did she tell you?"

"That I should leave the matter in your hands."

Tantalized for an instant by the prospect of lucidity, like straining to recall something just beyond the threshold of memory, keenly aware of the possibility of knowledge but frustrated by the inability to grasp it firmly, he heard the muffled sound wrapped in a blanket of disbelief. Having forgotten its placement, the lid shut on a snare of his own devising. He sensed the danger instinctively, but he could not yet see himself caught, the way an animal, intent on the bait, delays acknowledging the reality of the cage.

Indeed, the enclosure extended so far that its existence might have been doubted even by the most suspicious. The ample room gave those who wished to do so a chance to live their whole lives without ever arriving at the edge of their confinement. Only those with a perverse sense of purpose actively sought to arrive at the periphery, some to hurl themselves in futile fury against the bars and others only to contemplate the possible meaning of existence. Reasonable persons, in general, turned away to wander about in a studied pretense of indifference to the limitation of their freedom. Others manage to define it within the boundaries of their captivity. All of this he perceived vaguely, like a man cutting a path through a dense jungle, aware only of the tangled mass of foliage immediately before him but giving little thought to the forest in general.

The physical world draws attention away from such thoughts, often in pressing and undesirable ways, and so it did at that moment when he verged on following the faint call of understanding. The door of the *bohio,* which through no necessity of being closed remained always open, suddenly framed a blaze, which, in the distance, relieved the otherwise stark darkness of the night. The initial curiosity quickly transformed into alarm on realizing that a violation of normalcy appeared in the distance. The blaze loomed, centered precisely at the complex of sheds where the recently picked crop waited to be carted down to the coast. He grabbed the revolver from the table where he always placed it when he was there with Carmen, and sticking it in his belt, he ran toward his vanishing wealth. The automatic act did not indicate any conclusion about the origin of the blaze. He was concerned only that the flames be prevented from reaching the stable where surely the horses had already panicked.

By the light of the roaring fire, he saw faces he did not recognize, but he did not immediately register the black stain on those faces. Only when he reached the stable and found two strangers drawing out the horses did he connect the blaze to a purposeful human act. His gun then in hand, he fired without taking the time to be deliberate. The wild shot alerted the raiders to the arrival of an active defense, and true to their style, they retreated. For an instant, Eduardo caught sight of Gaspar Cienfuegos silhouetted against a burning shed and shouting orders to withdraw. The image remained there only a moment but long enough to arouse in the *haciendero* rage against an evil incarnate, but before Eduardo could aim his pistol the bandit vanished. Eduardo turned back to the stable from where he saw emerging a lone and hapless figure on whose blackened face the *haciendero* would have seen, had he been looking with his eyes, only confusion and panic. This time Eduardo fired with a purpose, and the bullet hit its mark. The noise of the gunshot reverberated in his ears for what seemed a long time, but eventually he differentiated another no less rending sound, Carmen's wail calling for the prevention or the negation of the act. He did not know whether her scream began before or after he fired.

She had followed close behind him, intending only to prevent him from putting himself in danger, though she had no more reason than he to suppose the cause of the fire to be other than accidental. When they reached the scene of the commotion, she accurately assessed the situation but saw no means of getting Eduardo to withdraw, persuasion impossible once his hand reached the revolver. She resolved to watch over him as if the force of her will were sufficient to protect him from physical harm.

The bandits fleeing, for an instant the prospect of success extinguished her fear. Her mind clear, the sense of mission sustained her but did not prepare her for the sudden recognition of a person whom she thought to be far away. Neither the darkened face nor the lurid light from the burning building that disfigured the natural features prevented her instant recognition. But perhaps the face was not what she recognized, but the totality of the person. The shock of that recognition for an instant paralyzed her.

For Eduardo also, the horror grew from moment to moment. Hearing her scream, he could only suppose that she, too, was mortally wounded. His confusion continued, seeing her exert a burst of energy as she ran past him to the spasmodic figure upon whom she threw herself as if to prevent his embarking on the journey.

"No, Tito, no," she pleaded for her brother to stay, but that entreaty proved as useless as the one which had failed to prevent the discharge of the firearm.

For an instant, the three froze in a lurid tableau, as if a demonic photographer had posed them for a macabre portrait. The illusion of stillness was brief, but the image lingered in the minds of the three for as long as they lived—for Tito, but a few minutes. He died before Eduardo had recovered his wits sufficiently to know what he had done.